Praise for Na...
and *Beh...*

"Overall, I enjoyed thi... tale. The plot has tw... ...I never saw coming, and the interaction between Kennedy and Rogan had me rooting for this couple the whole way. If you enjoy an edge-of-your-seat romantic suspense story, then don't hesitate to get a copy of *Behind the Scenes* and allow yourself to get swept into this fantastic novel."
—Sunflower at *Long and Short Reviews*

"I liked the overall premise and the setting of the story. A female heading an exclusive security firm is a novel concept and the constant danger and action that is seamlessly integrated into the story makes for a compelling read. Though I felt that the romance aspect of the novel didn't get an equal amount of attention as the suspense part, *Behind the Scenes* still managed to keep me turning the pages."
—*Maldivian Book Reviewer's Realm of Romance*

"My hat, were I wearing one, would also be doffed for Damschroder for doing such a remarkably superb job creating and executing such an intensely complex security job. With seemingly effortless aplomb, she manipulated and wove together the myriad pieces of characters, setting, and suspense, and produced one of the most detail-oriented and believable scenarios of a realistic security detail that I've read in romantic suspense. Ever."
—*One Good Book Deserves Another*

Also available from Natalie J. Damschroder and Carina Press

Acceptable Risks
Fight or Flight

NATALIE J. DAMSCHRODER

BEHIND THE SCENES

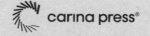

carina press®

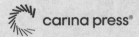

carina press®

ISBN-13: 978-0-373-00237-5

BEHIND THE SCENES

Recycling programs for this product may not exist in your area.

www.CarinaPress.com

Printed in U.S.A.

Dear Reader,

Long before DVDs and DVD extras, I loved behind-the-scenes documentaries that put you right on the set of a movie. I was fascinated by the process, the crew, the logistics and especially by the glimpse of the actors and actresses being real people doing a job. My "interest" became passion (okay, maybe obsession) after the *Lord of the Rings* movies came out, and I'll confess that Rogan St. James was inspired by Orlando Bloom (but shh, don't tell him!).

Many authors dream of hitting bestseller lists, getting huge advances or headlining conferences or reader events. But for me, the pinnacle of my success would be having a movie or TV show made out of my books so I could do a set visit and get to see it being made. I don't know if that dream will ever come true—it's certainly well out of my control—so writing this book was the next best thing. Of course, since I write romantic adventure, I had to have danger and intrigue behind the scenes while the main characters were falling in love. Should I ever get to hang out on a film set, that part I'd be okay with skipping.

I hope you enjoy Rogan and Kennedy's wild ride as much as I enjoyed writing it.

Thank you!

Natalie J. Damschroder

This book is dedicated to Jody Wallace
aka Ellie Marvel aka Meankitty's Typing Slave, for
all the support and friendship she gave me not just
for this book, but for all the years before and since.

Thank you to Jennifer Dunne of Bell Helicopter
for answering my questions so perfectly.
As promised, Jen, I didn't crash the helicopter.

Another huge thank you goes to Neringa Bryant for
reading an early draft and telling me all the places
I went wrong regarding independent film.
Any inaccuracies that remain are either my error,
or artistic license.

And finally, I'm so grateful for my editor, Liz Bass,
for loving my books for the same reasons I love
them, and for all her hard work making sure they
live up to their potential. A more brilliant partner
doesn't exist. Thanks, Liz.

BEHIND THE SCENES

ONE

THE SCREAM ECHOED against the cinderblock walls of the urban cavern, climbing higher and higher and ending in a gurgling gasp.

"That didn't sound good." Mark, Kennedy Smyth's assistant, handed her a headset and tapped a few keys on his laptop. "Team's in motion."

Kennedy adjusted the microphone in front of her lips, her gaze tracing over the landscape, calculating possible locations of the victim and her abductors.

"Wolf, you have a bead on that yell yet?"

"Working on it, Kennedy."

"You're too slow." She leaned forward over the low wall on the rooftop where she stood, eyeing a black-clad figure moving quickly and silently down the street. He paused, held up a hand, then motioned forward with his fingers. Two matching figures joined him, and they continued down the middle of the deserted road. Kennedy shook her head. Why did rookies always make the same mistakes, no matter how much training they had first?

Mark flicked a glance her way, then back to his laptop. "You going in yet?"

Kennedy shushed him irritably, her brain clicking through the beats. There was the report of a rifle. Splatter appeared on Wolf's sweater and he dropped to the ground. His weapon fell out of his hand, the clatter punctuating his groan in Kennedy's ear. The other two "stealthy" operatives followed suit within seconds. None of the shots looked like kill shots, but her operatives were fully disabled, nonetheless.

"Damn it." Kennedy ripped her headset off and flung it at Mark. She turned and stalked down the roofline, grabbing a pistol from the kit as she went. At the far edge of the roof she paused to pull her sleeves over her palms and stuck the gun in the holster on her hip. She swung over the edge of the roof, gripped the ladder tightly, and positioned her booted feet on either side. Sliding down two stories took her four seconds.

She landed in a crouch, gun in her hand, and spun as two figures came around either side of the building. Dropping to her back, she nailed one in the chest while the shot he'd fired hit his comrade.

"Shit!" The second attacker stared at his torso before slumping to the ground.

Kennedy rolled to her feet and ran past, pistol ready. She stopped at the corner, going low to check around it. Nothing. But she knew someone had to be there. She waited, listening and watching, but still nothing happened. Okay, he was waiting for her. She took a deep breath and whirled around the corner.

Her gun went flying. Then she did, as the heel of the guy's hand caught her in the chin, snapping her head back and sending her reeling.

She caught herself quickly, reversed direction, and ducked under his swing to clip him with her elbow. Then she grabbed his arm, twisted, and flung him over her shoulder.

The victim's scream sounded again. The echoes made it difficult—though not impossible—to pinpoint her location, but Kennedy could tell the target had been moved from her original position. She was too exposed here, so she ran through the nearest doorway, pounding around empty counters and down the back hall to the rear entrance. She kicked the safety bar, paused, then burst through the open door. No one.

Turning right, she continued running. A tall figure loomed up from behind a dumpster, laughing, but she was faster than he'd expected and she reached him before he fired. Before he knew it she'd wrenched his rifle from his hands, tapped him on the temple with the butt, and was past, cocking the weapon.

There was only one attacker left. Kennedy smiled, anticipation filling her limbs with energy. She continued down the street, running lightly now so her footsteps were barely audible. She was sure the victim was in the next building, probably upstairs, which meant the last person would be coming out the next door right about...

Now. She slammed on the brakes. A tiny figure flew out the door, but she'd expected Kennedy to be entering and her shots went wide as she crossed the alley, two-fisting the pistols á la Lara Croft. She even had a braid swinging behind her.

Too bad she was dead, Kennedy thought, firing a single shot that hit the girl in the forehead as she went down into a pile of leaves blown against the far wall.

Kennedy slowed, knowing everyone was accounted for. There remained only to rescue the victim and handle clean-up. But as she started up the stairs, a floorboard creaked over her head. It could just be the victim, but her instincts told her something was wrong. She waited, but heard nothing else. Still her skin prickled. She mentally called up the building's floor plan. Only one stairway up, and she was a sitting duck once she hit step five. The fire escape was out, too, they'd be covering that route. Her only chance was a diversion.

She silently backed down the stairs and glanced around until her eyes landed on a decent decoy. The throw pillow had a crossover back, creating a little pocket where she stuffed a heavy brass figurine. Creeping up to the third step, she heaved the pillow upward. It hit the wall, collecting two shots in midair.

Kennedy was up the rest of the stairs before it landed. She leaped the railing into the second floor hallway, her gun leveled at Mark. "Nice try, kid."

He grinned. "It's not over."

She fired. "It is now."

His grin turned into a scowl. "No fair."

She shoved him in the chest hard enough to knock him back. "You're dead. Lie down."

"It's still not over," he called, dropping to the polished hardwood.

"Thanks for the warning." Instead of gently approaching the victim, Kennedy shoved open the door and rushed in, grabbing her in a headlock before she could hit Kennedy with the lamp she held over her head.

"Assume nothing, right, Stacy?" she murmured in the woman's ear, tightening her hold when she struggled. Stacy sagged in her arms.

"Right. And you don't." She stumbled as Kennedy released her. "We never get you."

"I don't plan that you ever will. Mark, gather them in here, please," she said.

Her assistant relayed the order into his headset and leaned against the wall, still looking smug at his rare foray into the "field." He ran the electronics on their training ops, and the office the rest of the time. Luckily, he'd never pushed to be trained himself. He had the brains to be in the field, but not the physical skills.

Stacy, on the other hand, had both. The solid brunette usually handled logistics on their real ops, as well as working protection—bodyguard duty. She smirked at Mark's ribbing over their failed "surprise" and straddled the desk chair she should have been tied to during the exercise.

As Kennedy's heart rate slowed and the exhilaration of the chase seeped out of her, the rest of her paint-splattered team, and the three recruits they were training, straggled in.

Jefferson came first, the tall, lanky head of engineering who could be forgiven for losing his rifle, but only to Kennedy. When Rick, the shorter, top-fighter head of security came in behind him, she saluted him for managing to tag her. His people filed in next—Zip, the diminutive spitfire who'd flung herself through the door, and Jonathan, the calming influence on the team. The five bodyguards who'd handled background came in last and lined up against the back wall, nudging forward the three recruits who'd failed so predictably.

"Can someone please tell me what I did out there?"

"Um, I can." Wolf, the first recruit and the first one to be shot, tentatively raised his hand. "Surprise, relentless attack, and, ah, brainpower."

"We'll never be able to think like you," complained the second recruit, a twenty-one-year-old Navy SEAL Hell Week washout. He wiped his forehead with the sleeve of his shirt.

"That attitude will prevent it," Kennedy agreed. She pointed at Wolf. "You know the drills. You can recite back to me every single thing I've ever told you. But you have no confidence. And you," she turned on the washout, Hank. "You have an overabundance. You start out cocky, then drag up defensiveness when you fail. There isn't room on my team for either approach." She steeled her heart against Wolf's crestfallen expression and the mutinous anger in Hank's eyes. "I want you to go home and think about what happened today. If you really want to continue. Because it's only going to get harder from here."

"What about me?"

The third recruit stood behind Zip but held her chin high, determination sparkling in her eyes despite the patch of dried paint on her shoulder. Kennedy studied her, then looked at Wolf and SEAL-boy again.

"You have potential." Minimal, but she didn't say so. "But you have to be careful who you follow. This isn't the military." She tossed Jefferson his rifle and accepted her pistol from Rick, who had brought it with him. "You're all dismissed. Return the equipment, cleaned and primed, and hit the showers. Those on assignment tomorrow, go straight home. The rest of you, we'll meet back here at ten o'clock to start training again. Assuming there's anyone left to train," she added.

She pretended not to hear the grumbling, the murmured "stone cold bitch." If anyone ever dared say it to her face, she'd agree without hesitation. She couldn't be soft on these three—not now, and not in the field. If she had to guess, the only one who'd come back would be Wolf. His self-doubt probably stemmed from parents with overly high expectations who were too quick to lay on the disappointment. She could work around that, and he might make a decent operative.

The other two…she shrugged. They wouldn't be back.

Mark stopped her when she would have followed the group through the narrow doorway. "You have an appointment in your office." He took the pistol back from her. "I'll get this put away."

"I don't have appointments on training days," she reminded him, trying to get by.

"I scheduled this one specially. He's only in town for a day."

"A client?"

"Yes."

She shook her head, looking down at her dusty jeans and shirt. One sleeve was torn, the back of her left hand oozed blood through a scrape, and she could feel her hair falling all around its ponytail. Not to mention her bruised jaw and sore neck from Rick's punch.

"Ask him to reschedule."

"He can't. He's—just hold up, will you?" He grabbed her arm at the top of the stairs, ignoring her raised eyebrow. "You can't intimidate me anymore, Kennedy."

She sighed. "I know. I hate it." She leaned against the banister and folded her arms. "So talk."

"He's a movie producer with a big case for us. I know you don't do this kind of job," he rushed on, though she hadn't opened her mouth. "But he really pushed, insisting he had to see you personally, and wouldn't accept a no from anyone but you."

Well, that could only describe one person. "Fine. I'll see him. But I have to clean up first." She started down the stairs. "I'm not doing it," she warned over her shoulder. "So don't get your hopes up." She'd already turned down the job. She didn't do regular security, even for friends.

"I think you should reconsider." Mark matched her

long-legged stride across the blacktop only by running double-time. "It's a high-profile case that could really broaden our future."

She paused outside the building that housed the offices, wary of his persistence. "Which film is it?" Discussion hadn't gotten that far when she'd turned it down.

"Um, I can't remember. Something with guns." He reached past her and pulled open the door, motioning her in.

"Mark, don't bother with the chivalry. This isn't my kind of job."

Mark stopped to look at her with serious eyes. "Is it your place to decide who's more deserving of protection?"

A twinge of uneasiness had her avoiding his eyes when she walked past. He was right. She hadn't started this company to pass judgment on who was important and who wasn't.

Still, routine security for something as frivolous as a film shoot wasn't why she'd started the company, either. SmythShield was small, and focused exclusively on projects with a humanitarian goal. Projects like the one where her brother had been killed. Mark knew that. Suspicion overcame her uneasiness, and she flicked a glance back at her assistant. "This is that domestic terrorism picture."

"Ah, yes. Yes, it is, as a matter of fact."

"And they've cast Bailey Mutchinson."

"Oh, maybe." He moved behind his desk and sat, setting the pistol to one side and opening the appointment book.

"Then forget it," she joked. "I'm not basing my interest in a job on your interest in getting laid."

"I'm glad to hear that," boomed a voice from her office. "Since that's not what we're basing our decision to hire you on."

Mark lifted his head. "I guess he's early."

But Kennedy was already striding into the office. "Max!" Before she could say more she was enveloped in Italian silk via the bear hug of a gigantic man. She squeezed back, pushing away to examine her father's old friend. "Oh, my God, you've gone silver!" They'd talked on the phone, but she hadn't seen him in years.

He scowled, bushy metallic eyebrows squishing together over blue-gray eyes. "It was deliberate," he insisted, running a paw over the smoothed-back hair and giving the ponytail a shake. "Age equals wisdom, wisdom equals power."

"Perception of wisdom, anyway." She pulled away and circled her mahogany desk. Max's groan as he settled across from her drowned out the squeak of her leather chair. "Hollywood's portion of wisdom can barely fill a glass slipper."

"So cynical," he tutted, shaking his head. "Whatever turned you that way?"

"You and my father had a hand in it." She pulled a roll of peppermint LifeSavers from her drawer and popped one in her mouth, replacing the roll after Max refused one.

"So you're bankrolling this picture," she prompted, sucking the mint. Max Swanson had once been the most powerful person in Hollywood. At its peak, his studio had been connected with six of the year's Oscar contenders and five of the top ten grossers. Her father, now retired, had been one of the studio's attorneys. Kennedy grew up with Max's thunderous presence in her house.

He hadn't changed much, despite his studio's altered position. What went up must go down, and according to her father, they desperately needed a hit. When Max called her, she'd given a simple "no" without waiting for details, but had since heard through the grapevine—the news media and her father—about troubles the production was having.

"We've taken the bulk of the risk, yes," he admitted. "Which is why your involvement is so important now."

Kennedy tamped down the instinct to refuse again. She'd explained to Max when he first called her that working for him would take her and her team away from people doing more urgent work. People who saved lives, who gave jobs and health facilities to children and their poverty-stricken parents. He knew what had happened to her brother, and understood what drove her.

But behind Mark's words—*"Is it your place to decide who's more deserving of protection?"*—was an image of Justin, frowning. Max was family and deserved at least a hearing, a chance to tell her what had changed.

"Tell me more," she said reluctantly.

He sighed. "When word first leaked about the script, we got a couple of letters protesting it." He waved a hand in the air. "The usual stuff. People eloquently proclaiming why it was a mistake. We get them for every picture. But the more information leaked about the film, the worse it got."

Kennedy tried to remember what little she'd read about the story. "It's a pretty basic shoot-'em-up, isn't it?"

Max looked affronted. "It most certainly is not. There are guns, yes, but there is a deeper message. About the availability and danger of guns. About what drives people to peddle terror. Timely issues." He scowled. "If we can get it off the ground. Some of the protesting got more…passionate."

Kennedy found herself getting sucked in by Max's zeal and tried to pull back. "So why do you need me? Even passionate protest is still within the realm of your usual security firm."

"There's more." He tossed her an impatient look. "We've cast actors from all over the world. The Middle East. Britain. France. And Hollywood. When production started things got ugly. Uglier than the firm we hired wanted to handle."

"Like?"

He picked up his briefcase, propped it on his lap, and opened it. He tossed a stack of paper-clipped letters in front of Kennedy. "Threats against the director and some of the actors. And this." He dropped a large photograph on top of the letters. Kennedy lifted it and studied the image, though it was obvious what it was. A small box, half wrapped in torn brown paper, sprouted wires and contained an empty space in the center that would have held explosive. "Where was this?"

"Max Junior found it on his desk. He called the film's explosives people right away." He pointed to some grease stains on the paper wrapping. "He said there's a sign in the post office or somewhere, about grease on packages. The police can't—"

But Kennedy wasn't interested in the bomb anymore. "M.J. is directing this film?" She didn't remember him mentioning that before. But then, she hadn't given him a chance.

The laugh lines around Max's eyes and mouth tightened with worry, and he nodded.

"So it's not just a financial investment you're trying to protect."

"Of course not! It never was. My first concern is always the people. I hired the security company we've used before. But this—" he pointed a thick finger at the photograph, "—this is too big for them. I need the best. And you, my dear, are the best."

"What did the police say?"

He shrugged. "There's not much they can do. They certainly can't protect us. You can."

"And the explosives guys?"

Max pressed his lips together, as if not wanting to admit something. Kennedy waited. He shifted in his chair. Finally, he said, "It was a dud."

"The bomb was a dud."

"Well, not completely. It had plastique or whatever in it, but no detonator."

She handed the photo and letters back to him. "Doesn't sound like much."

"What *does* it sound like?"

Kennedy smiled at him. He was good. He knew better than to bluster at her or continue begging. Engaging her in logical assessment could hook her, make her start thinking about it, which would lead to taking the job.

"It sounds like someone's trying to scare you, or call attention to themselves with the publicity that usually goes along with these things. Would you shut down production? If it escalated?"

Max sighed. "I really don't want to. M.J.'s had a string of low-volume movies. The last one went right to DVD a year after it was in the can. This is really his last chance. Even I can't afford to back him again if this one fails."

That pretty much sealed the deal for her. "This isn't

what I do," she cautioned one more time. It didn't matter. She knew she was going to take the job.

Disappointment slid over his expression. "Are you turning me down? Turning M.J. down?"

"Not yet. I'm making sure you really want me. My company."

His face cleared. "Of course I do."

"My people are used to volatile situations. They're not average security guards."

"You think they'll be bored?" He spread his hands. "Hopefully, they will be!"

That wasn't really what Kennedy was afraid of. She had complete confidence in her team, whether facing new and innovative daily threats or unrelenting tedium. What she was afraid of...

"I want you in charge, on site."

That was it. "I have another job, Max. It's—"

Mark stuck his head in the door. "Hey, Ken. Just wanted you to know Franklin isn't going to Costa Rica. Deal fell through." He disappeared, along with her excuse.

"Kennedy, this is M.J.'s life," Max said with quiet force. "Read these letters. Then tell me this job is not worth your team."

She didn't move while he stood, blew her a kiss and departed. She stared at the stack of papers, reluctant to start reading. In truth, she didn't need to read them. She knew Max wouldn't have come to her if the situation wasn't serious. If his son—and cast, crew and investment—wasn't in danger. But somewhere in the back of her mind was the feeling that he had an ulterior motive she should be wary of.

She could hear the rumble of voices in the reception

area outside her office and knew Max was enlisting Mark to his cause. She sighed and picked up the letters, skimming them. They were full of vague and flowery language, implied threats more than specific ones. She really didn't think there was anything to worry about. The bomb was probably an attempt to generate publicity, either negative about the film or positive to the cause of this El Jahar, whoever they were. She'd never heard of them.

After a few minutes Mark entered the room and set a business card on her desk. "Max left this. He asked for your decision by tomorrow morning. He wants the team on the set as soon as possible. He gave me the details I need to get set up," he finished pointedly.

She shook her head. "I can't believe the studio isn't already secure."

"It's not Starshine's sound stage. They've moved to a smaller location to avoid the protestors and media. They were slowing them down, and you know, time is money. But that means looser security."

She stood and walked to the window, which looked out over the training ground. Originally an abandoned airfield, the property boasted three environments—the cityscape they'd trained on this afternoon, a jungle-like park, and a converted hangar that could be laid out like just about any building they had to penetrate or guard someone in. It was her pride and joy, evidence of the success of her company.

It had taken her ten years to bring SmythShield to this point. She'd accompanied company executives into some of the darkest corners of the planet. People who had brought jobs and health care to undeveloped countries, who had the funds to sponsor groups like Justin's.

She knew her clients' motives weren't all altruistic. But she'd taken care to accept jobs with companies who strove to make things better even while they increased their profits. The money SmythShield made from those jobs allowed her to provide services at reduced fees for relief organizations and groups for whom profit was something to laugh at. Enabled her to build this training ground so her operatives were the best, and her clients were safe.

"The last job we did was protecting a crew from rebel forces while a hospital was built to serve the employees of a shoe factory," she said quietly. "Not pretty-boy performers like Rogan St. James."

"Hmm."

She turned at a rustle of paper. Mark was flipping through the letters and not paying much attention to her. He absentmindedly clicked his ballpoint pen in his left hand, the noise grating on her nerves. "Is that gun still on your desk?" she asked, a bite in her voice.

"Taken care of." He didn't look up. "They don't save the world, Kennedy, but you never know what corner of it they'll brighten."

He was right. Just because she considered movies frivolous didn't mean the people who made them deserved to get hurt or scared. Their last job had required extra staff, a long-term commitment, and nonstop vigilance, even after she'd struck a deal with the rebel commander. They'd had only a month stateside, and some of the team had grumbled about having to go to Costa Rica so soon. She could give most of the team a break and take only a couple with her to the set. Hell, maybe an easy job would be good for her too.

"Okay, Mark. Call Max and tell him we'll do the job. And then send Rick and Jefferson in. We have work to do."

TWO

THE SWORD CAME down at Rogan with lightning speed, or so it seemed. He got his own sword high enough to block the blow above his head, then spun out from under. Using his momentum, he came around swinging at his enemy's exposed side, but the man was ready. The clang of metal reverberated up Rogan's arms and into his chest.

The two men stepped back, circled. Both were breathing heavily. His opponent thrust suddenly, and Rogan jumped to the side, grabbed the man's wrist and jerked him forward, slapping him on the ass with the flat of his weapon.

Charlie yanked off his headgear and glared at Rogan. "Nice. Slapstick. Just what I need."

Rogan apologized. "It wasn't intentional, man. I practiced that move a hundred times for my last film."

"I know." Charlie dropped onto a thick roll of mats against the wall, the tip of his weapon drooping to the floor. "It's just, she doesn't even want to try anymore, you know?"

Rogan turned away so his friend wouldn't see his eye roll, and retrieved two bottles of water from the mini-fridge on the far wall. Charlie and his wife Holly, both actors, were breaking up after six years of marriage. Charlie was miserable, but they hadn't spent more than three weeks at a time together in all those six years.

Both had successful careers and loved their work. More than each other.

Or at least Holly felt that way. Since they'd made the decision, Charlie had been blabbering on for hours every day about how much he didn't want this breakup. Rogan was tired of it.

"Up." He tossed the water bottle to Charlie, then grabbed two wooden staffs from the wall. "Work."

They renewed their pseudo-combating. Rogan didn't need the training anymore, not for *Coming of Day*, anyway, but it was the least boring way he'd found to keep in shape. When Charlie wasn't around to spar with, he brought in a trainer. Usually on a picture he didn't have the space or time to do this, but he had a few days before they finished moving the set. So he'd get his exercise and provide therapy for his friend.

Whack, whack, whack.

"So, they're sequestering you, huh?" Charlie asked between moves. "Trying to keep the paparazzi from blowing the 'secrets of the film'?"

"Nah, it's a security thing. Threats and stuff." *Thud.* Charlie doubled over. "Sorry."

"Good one." He wheezed for a moment before straightening. "Being in solitary with Bailey Mutchinson could be good." He waggled his eyebrows.

Rogan made a face. He and Bailey had worked on a picture together when they were very young. She was like an annoying sister. And he didn't get involved with actresses. He swung the staff low. Charlie jumped over it, aiming high with his own. Rogan ducked.

"Well how about that little actress from India, Miraya-what's-her-name?" Charlie paused to wipe sweat off his forehead. "She'd be a nice diversion."

"Quit projecting. I'm not getting involved with anyone on this film." He walked over to the fridge where he'd left his water bottle and took a swig. "You and Holly are a good deterrent."

Charlie's laugh turned into a moan. "You had to say that."

Rogan shrugged and drank again. "It's an excellent example. Getting involved with actresses is a mistake."

Charlie leaned his staff against the wall and grabbed a towel to swab his face and neck. "I don't get it, man. You're, like, the most celibate guy I know."

Hardly. He didn't need to be alone when he didn't want to be, and sometimes that's what he chose. But over the past few years he'd become very clear about what he didn't want.

"Sex is one thing. Complications are another."

"Sure." Charlie slumped onto the floor, his back against the roll of mats. "Not that I'm advocating marriage or anything, but at least an actress understands the business. Wasn't your last girlfriend a secretary or something?" He grimaced. "She couldn't handle you doing premieres in New York, never mind being on a shoot for six months."

"Yeah, and do you see her around?" He spread his arms, then capped his water bottle and sat next to his friend. "What do you care, anyway?"

"Misery loves company. Hey, what about Susanne Prescott?"

Rogan snorted. Susanne was the new It girl, starring in two well-received and top-grossing films this year, reportedly being inundated with offers.

"I talked to her for a few minutes at a benefit last week."

"I know. That's why I mentioned her."

"She's more driven than I am."

"And?"

"Driven people cause others to make sacrifices."

Charlie laughed. "It's called compromise."

Maybe for some people. But Rogan knew it wasn't that easy. His teacher father had compromised all the time for his family attorney mother. So had Rogan, because how could you argue that a second-grade school play was more important than getting a battered wife and kids to a shelter? She'd rarely been there for him, and though his father always had been, his own loneliness had been obvious. It had taken Rogan many years into adulthood to see that his mother's choices had cost her, too, but that couldn't make up for all the years of pain. Nor did he see any reason to follow in his father's footsteps.

"So no secretaries and no actresses. What's that leave?"

"Screenwriters."

Charlie raised an eyebrow.

"Sure. They can come on location and write for fifteen hours while I'm shooting for fifteen hours, then we can be together the rest of the time. It's perfect."

"If you say so." Sighing, he heaved himself to his feet. "I'd bet you the residuals from my next contract it's not gonna work out that way."

Rogan didn't bother to argue with him. Sometimes life didn't follow plans, but so far his had. No reason to doubt it would continue.

He walked Charlie out, then headed for the shower. His fax machine beeped as he was passing his office, so he stopped to see if it was new script pages from M.J.

The page started printing almost immediately, simple text on a plain background, and his blood chilled. He glanced around, looking for something to hold the paper with, then realized how ridiculous that was. It sat in the tray, waiting, and Rogan felt the tension in the room, heard the strains of distressed violins faintly in the back of his head.

"You need to reconnect with reality, mate." He snatched the page from the machine and scanned it. Rage reheated his blood. He started to crumple the paper, stopped, and reached for the phone, punching in M.J.'s number. He answered right away.

Rogan didn't bother with a greeting. "I got one at the house," he told his director, knowing he didn't need to say more. He listened while M.J. freaked, calmed, reassured him that security was being increased as they spoke, and told him he'd send a bodyguard over immediately.

"No, it's all right. It came on the fax. This building is secure." It better be, for the size of his monthly service fees. "I'm not scared, M.J., I'm pissed. This is getting ridiculous." He read him the note, a rambling, incoherent diatribe about the evils of Hollywood and the unspecified goals of El Jahar, a terrorist group who apparently found *Coming of Day* to be even more offensive than American troops in the Middle East. "Have you heard anything from Bailey? Call her. Call everyone, see how bad it is. And make sure your new security people know." He ignored M.J.'s additional assurances and hung up. Venting had calmed him, and he wondered if he'd blown this out of proportion. It wasn't any different from the letters that had been mailed or delivered to the studio. His fax number wasn't hard to get, as evidenced by the fan mail that started coming over it within months after he changed the number, which he had to do a few times a year.

But something told him things had just changed.

THE PHONE WAS ringing that night when Kennedy entered her house on the far side of the compound. She grabbed the living room extension just as her father's voice came over the answering machine speaker.

"Dad!"

"Hey, Sunshine."

She grimaced at the pet name that dated back to her carefree childhood. It had barely suited her then, and definitely didn't suit her now. She dropped her holster and laptop case on the coffee table and collapsed onto the sofa.

"What's up? I haven't heard from you in a few weeks."

They chatted about the classes he was teaching and the woman he was dating, about the landscaping he'd tried to do himself before hiring a professional to fix what he'd destroyed. Kennedy soaked in the laughter, aware it would be a while before she could be so relaxed again.

"So what's wrong, Sunshine? You sound distracted."

"I am." She thumped her booted feet onto the table next to the laptop. "Just got a new job today."

"Oh?"

She chuckled. "You never could play the innocent, Dad. I know you talked to Max."

"Of course I talk to Max. He's my best friend."

Kennedy rolled her eyes. Kenneth Smyth didn't do innocence well. "Well, you'll be happy to know I took the job."

"I was."

She knew it. "Before or after I took it?"

"Well, after, of course, but I knew you *would* take it."

"Whatever. I almost didn't. I thought it was frivolous," she admitted.

"The lives aren't frivolous." His tone had the solemnity that signaled a lesson to be learned. She cut him off.

"As Mark so eloquently pointed out to me, and why I took the job when I really didn't want to. Though you're both being melodramatic. The threat is hardly that intense."

"I'm glad you took it, anyway. And I know, deep down, you are too. You would hate yourself if anything happened to M.J."

She rolled her eyes to the ceiling, glad he couldn't see her. "I suppose."

Her flippancy didn't faze him. "I know that's all a façade, Sunshine. No one holds life more dear than you do, or you wouldn't have started SmythShield so young and worked so hard to make it a success."

Kennedy winced. She'd built SmythShield on skills she'd learned any way she could, as fast as she could, and on her brother's life insurance policy. That never made her feel noble.

Her father went on. "You'll do your usual best, save everyone, and get a credit on the movie. And maybe something more."

She frowned. "What do you mean, something more?"

"Well, you never know what might happen on one of these jobs." His innocent tone was even more exaggerated than before.

"What are you up to?" She heard the squeak of her father's desk chair and the chime of his grandfather clock.

The sounds brought back memories, all of them good, and warm contentment washed away the guilt. But it was tempered by unease. "Dad, you're not trying to match-make, are you?"

"Shoot, I lost track of time. I have an appointment. Love you, bye!"

She shook her head as she switched off the phone. It shouldn't surprise her. She and M.J. had often staged weddings and played house when they were little, and their parents had watched fondly. In fact, Kennedy remembered her father saying once that her mother had hoped they were practicing for the future. He might have decided to start trying to make her mother's wish come true.

She glanced at her memory wall, where she had photos of important moments as well as small ones, and scanned for pictures of M.J. He'd been family, nothing more, but she'd never be able to convince her father of that.

Her gaze bounced to her favorite picture of Justin, her brother. He'd just graduated from medical school and was taking a couple of weeks off before he started his internship. He had his arm slung over a woman's shoulders—Kennedy didn't remember her name, she hadn't lasted long—and was laughing at his sister, who was goofing around off camera. His face held the affection and contentment of a life happily lived, but she could never look at the picture without thinking of a life cut short.

Kennedy was driven by that knowledge, and the desire to prevent it from ever happening again.

THREE DAYS LATER, Kennedy and her small team arrived at the set just after dawn. She scanned the street around the building. There was almost no activity this early in the morning. She knew who owned all the surrounding property and what kind of crime they got down here—surprisingly little, for a semi-abandoned warehouse district. So far, everything had checked out, with no detectable links to known terrorist groups.

Once inside the warehouse-turned-soundstage, Kennedy quietly gave orders. "Rick, I want you and Wolf to check out the roof. They're shooting up there this afternoon." She'd decided this job would be perfect training for the new recruit. Wolf's classmates—SEAL-boy and the female recruit—had resigned. "Go through the building before going up. You should connect what you saw on the plans with the real-life 3D layout." She glanced around the cavernous interior, crowded with set pieces and equipment. "Prowl the premises until you memorize every inch. Stay off the set, don't get in anyone's way, but learn as much as you can. Report back to me at six-thirty."

They nodded and headed off, Rick bending toward the younger man, hands waving as he gave instructions. Kennedy pointed to Jefferson, who usually headed the engineering team. This time, he was it. "You have an appointment in five minutes with Paul Naihl, the production designer. He'll show you all the props and equipment and go over the daily schedule. I want you to know everything that could be sabotaged and how, and check it all before it's used, even if you checked it three hours ago."

"Got it." He loped off, scratching his beard as he craned his neck, taking in details.

That left the personal guardian team.

"The threat seems to be targeting the two leads and

M.J. specifically," she reminded them. "All three have gotten the letters at home, though the personal protection service they were using saw no evidence of anything more direct. But escalation can occur at any time. They're handing Rogan St. James, Bailey Mutchinson and M.J. Swanson over to us in a few minutes. I want you to scout around while I meet with M.J., then we'll make the switch." She watched them disperse, then crossed the warehouse to where M.J. stood with his current detail.

"Kennedy." He grabbed her in a big hug.

"M.J." She hugged him back, smiling. As lean as his father was massive, Max Swanson, Jr., hadn't changed much in the years since they'd lost touch. As kids, they'd spent hours by the pond at the Smyth house discussing their dreams of fame and stardom. Then they'd gone separate ways to find their personal versions of them.

"Thank you for taking this job." He held her by the shoulders. His smile displayed even white teeth that she'd cursed through her braces for years.

"Let's go somewhere we can talk." She followed him to a room that appeared to double as an office and production suite. A regular desk sat to the side, buried in paper. The entire left wall was pinned with sketches in varying stages of detail, and below them was a table strewn with masks, pieces of latex, models of buildings and CDs. The back of the room held a trio of computers with three different dazzling screensavers.

After taking quick inventory, she turned to M.J. "El Jahar is not a domestic terrorist group with ties to the Middle East."

"How do you know? The letters—"

"Are bunk. I read them. I researched what they said— gobbledygook meant to induce confusion and anxiety.

There's no terrorist group on anyone's radar that goes by El Jahar. The propaganda in the letters is straight out of the news." She shifted her weight and tried to keep from sounding accusatory. "They're not targeting *Coming of Day* because of its subject matter or a symbolic attack on the depravations of the American public," she said softly, aware there were probably ears pressed to the door. "The letters don't specify or even hint at their target. They just babble on about the reasons the movie is a threat to Islam and the Muslim community, reasons your overall casting is an insult and a symbol of American excess, blah blah blah. It's all ridiculous and illogical. This is either not a threat at all, or it's personal," she finished. "Why?"

M.J. fidgeted, patting his pockets and tugging his dark hair, then pulled a pack of cigarettes out of his pocket. She shook her head and he sighed, tucking them back.

"I don't know," he finally said, dropping into his chair. His eyes shimmered with tears. The cynic in Kennedy went *oh, please*, but the old friend patted his shoulder in sympathy.

"You don't know why someone would want you dead?" she half-joked. "Or why they'd say they do?"

M.J. shook his head. "I can't think of any reasons."

As Kennedy listed the obvious possibilities, his head kept shaking, the curls bouncing back and forth.

"Blackmail? Gambling debts? Bad investments with the wrong people? Drugs?"

His head came up with a jerk. "How can you ask me that?" The tears were gone, burned in the heat of anger. "After my mother and my sister, how can you possibly ask me that?"

"It hasn't stopped others," she reminded him. When he was ten, his mother, who had divorced his father and hooked up with a rising pop star, overdosed on heroin. His older sister, who lived with their mother, had been in and out of treatment centers for the past twenty years.

"I've never had anything to do with drugs," he insisted.

"Okay, what about your sister, then? Have you tried to help her out and gotten into something dangerous?"

"I haven't seen her in two years. Haven't talked to her since Christmas." His voice went shrill. "Why do you think it's me, anyway? Rogan and Bailey got those letters at home."

"That's not where they started. I'll be asking them similar questions, but the threats seem more centered on you. The letters to the actors could be decoys to mask El Jahar's real purpose."

He scowled. "Then that would be someone much more clever than my family or the losers they deal with."

"Okay, let's not worry about the who or why," she said, and M.J. immediately relaxed. "Let's concentrate on the how. I need constant updates on your schedule, and an overview for the entire shoot." He jotted notes while she told him what she expected on a daily and weekly basis. He nodded continuously until she pulled out a floor plan of the building and started showing him their vulnerabilities and how she wanted to reinforce the security.

"Kennedy, this is a low budget picture," M.J. protested when she mentioned the new alarm system she'd scheduled to be installed.

She snorted. "Starshine is bankrolling this film. It's not low budget, and if it is, it doesn't have to be."

"You don't understand. They'll only invest what they think they can recoup. My track record is a roller coaster. They won't give me more than they already have."

Kennedy rolled up the floor plan and folded her arms, thinking. Her normal response would be that either their lives and the film were important or the money was. But could she justify spending more money when she really didn't think the threat was that serious?

"Please," M.J. pleaded. "If we need to spend that much more money, they'll pull the plug. And I have to make this film."

She relented. "All right. We'll let it go for now. But if things escalate " which she doubted they would, " I reserve the right to change my mind."

"Thank you, Kennedy." M.J. stood and hugged her again. "I'm glad you're here."

"Me too," she managed, actually meaning it. It was good to see her old friend, if nothing else. "Come on. I'll introduce you to Shenk, your new bodyguard."

A few minutes later she rounded up Stacy and Clay, the other two protectors, and headed across the warehouse.

It was time to meet the stars of this thing.

ROGAN WATCHED THE group striding toward them and weathered a surge of adrenaline. The guy and two women wore nearly identical expressions of determination, and though he'd watched them come in and knew they were with the new security team, they didn't inspire warm fuzzies. More like fight or flight. The bodyguard who'd been assigned to him for weeks stiffened and stepped forward, putting himself in front of Rogan. He checked his instinctive move to the side to see better. Being protected wasn't coming easy to him, but he was learning.

The tall brunette in jeans and a leather jacket seemed to be in charge. She held out a hand to Rogan's bodyguard.

"Kennedy Smyth, SmythShield. This is my team." She gestured to the group that had fanned out around her. "Anything we need to know?" she asked the bodyguard, who shook his head.

"It's all in the briefing report."

"Okay, then. We'll take it from here. Thanks." She patted the man on his upper arm, closing in on Rogan and dismissing her predecessor.

Whether it was the patronization, the touching or the dismissal, Rogan wasn't sure, but the man's face darkened an instant before he grabbed Kennedy's arm, swinging her around. Her guy—about half the size of the one he was replacing—crushed Rogan back against the wall, shielding him. Somehow, in that second, his old bodyguard wound up on the floor, Kennedy's foot on his neck and his arm twisted between her hands. The other female SmythShield operative shielded Bailey, while Bailey's former bodyguard laughed.

"Nice work," the guy on the ground said, grudgingly. Kennedy let go and helped him up, and the guy on Rogan eased off so he could at least breathe.

"Just testing," his former guard said in a clearly insincere apology.

"SmythShield doesn't need to be tested."

He shrugged. "Reputation sometimes exceeds ability." He motioned to Rogan and Bailey. "They're all yours."

"Thank you."

Dismissing him for real this time, Kennedy turned to Rogan and his costar. "Let's try this again." She flashed a smile, and gone was the warrior she'd been a moment ago. Rogan was impressed despite himself. He wouldn't have guessed she had any charm in her, from the way she'd taken control.

"I'm Kennedy. We have a three-person personal detail on you two and M.J., where the threat has been focused. We'll be doing pretty much what your last personal security did, but we're probably more intense. Similar rules. You don't go anywhere without one of us. You don't enter a room, outside of this building, without one of us checking it first. If you see anything suspicious or of concern, signal us. We'll be watching. Don't worry about looking paranoid. You won't get laughed at. You *will* get scolded for not communicating with us. Got it?"

They nodded, Rogan suppressing an ill-advised grin. Kennedy focused on him.

"You have any problems being guarded by a woman?"

"No, ma'am."

Her eyes narrowed. "You have problems being guarded at all?"

"No. I understand the stakes." Not that he thought they were that high, but cooperation was the smart approach to take.

She nodded, seeming to believe him. "How about you?"

Bailey squeaked and shook her head. Kennedy nodded again, and introduced the people with her. They split up a moment later, the sturdy-looking Stacy following Bailey to makeup, Clay taking up position next to Rogan.

Rogan watched Kennedy stride toward the catwalk,

not realizing how focused his attention was until Clay touched his arm.

"You need to go to makeup?"

"No, I'm done."

"Okay." He stood at ease, waiting. Despite his smaller size, Rogan had a feeling Clay was better trained. Something about the loose-but-ready way he held his body, or the way he seemed to take in all the movement around them without getting distracted by it. Or maybe it was just that Rogan got the sense Kennedy Smyth wouldn't stand for less.

"She married?" he asked before he knew he was going to.

"Nope."

Rogan waited, but Clay didn't say more. His gaze went back to where Kennedy now stood talking to a tech and examining some piece of equipment.

She wasn't his type. But damned if he didn't find himself intrigued.

THREE

KENNEDY GATHERED HER team in the room the production used for meals while Bailey and Rogan were shooting under Clay's watchful eye. They sat in varying positions of comfort at the long tables, while Kennedy stood at the end of the room.

"Let's make this quick," she said, "and get back on the job, Rick."

He stood and shoved his dark bangs away from his frown. "The layout is exactly as we studied. The weaknesses we noted are as bad or worse than we thought. We can shore up most of them—doors, windows, ventilation—but we need that alarm system. A place this big, we should have two agents on the roof for vantage point, two patrolling the outside perimeter, two the inside." His tone made clear he thought she'd gone too light with the staffing. He had to feel strongly to let it show. "If we have to work with what's here, I'll do out, Wolf can do in, and I'll hit the roof periodically for a broader view."

"The alarm system's no go," Kennedy told him. Everyone groaned. "And you're right, we need more people, but they can't afford the expense, so we'll make do. I don't think the threat is broad enough to require full defense, so we'll focus on the assets instead of the property. Follow the patrol plan you just outlined, and rotate with Jefferson for breaks."

Rick didn't look happy, but he nodded and sat.

"Stacy. Personnel?"

The young woman consulted a clipboard. "The actors are usually in makeup by five-thirty. Both Bailey and Rogan are in almost every indoor scene, so they'll be here constantly." She didn't succeed in holding back a grin when she said the actors' names. "The rest of the cast is limited. We have a shifting roster of supporting actors, but not many extras—they'll be the riskiest. Not much advance notice. The second AD—assistant director—will give me a list each day and update it whenever they make changes so we can run background checks."

"Okay. Here's today's schedule." Kennedy handed the stack to Stacy to pass around. "We'll meet tonight after they wrap to adjust the plan, but this will be a seat-of-the-pants operation. What they're doing will change constantly. Since we'll be here for a month or more, I've rented rooms in a warehouse-turned-boardinghouse down the road. Here are your room assignments, so you can gripe at each other all day and get it out of your system." She passed out that list. "Any questions?"

Shenk, Kennedy's biggest but most laid-back protector, waved a hand. "We sticking with them twenty-four/seven?"

"The three principles all have secure home locations. We might be needed when they're out in public, but the threat has been to the production overall, so I think any real attack would take place here, for maximum impact."

They nodded and dispersed, moving purposefully out of the room to take up their positions or begin their tasks. Jefferson stopped Kennedy at the door, tapping an already half-filled legal pad against his palm. "They have a lot of props," he told her. "I think I'll be working longer hours than most, since I'll have to check everything out while the grips and electrics set up in the morning."

"That's fine. Just get a key from M.J. and make sure you get a code for the alarm system. Such as it is," she muttered. "And make sure there's a place to lock the stuff you've inspected," she reminded him, ignoring his false patience. "Let me know if you have trouble with that."

He nodded and walked off, flipping pages on his pad. Kennedy stood for a moment, surveying the scene. While they'd been meeting, more cast and crew had arrived on the set. A clang from the kitchen alerted her that the caterer had also arrived. The company had checked out, but she turned and went through the swinging doors.

Two young women looked up from where they were unwrapping trays of pastries. A just-as-young guy filled pitchers from a gigantic jug of juice. The kitchen looked standard, though a bit smaller than a restaurant kitchen. Kennedy pictured her team chasing some panicked bought-off crew member through here, then shook off the image. Being on set was screwing with her imagination.

"Where's your boss?" she asked the kids.

The guy pointed at the open back door. "She's at the truck."

"You have to keep that door shut and locked," she said, crossing to it.

"But—"

"Later." She exited into now-bright sunshine and walked over to the shapely rear end sticking out the back of the catering van.

"Excuse me."

"What!" was the ferocious reply. Kennedy backed up a step. She waited while the short, busty blonde emerged

from the back of the van and swept her hair out of her eyes. Her expression cleared as soon as she saw who it was. "Sorry. Everything…" She gestured behind her, then propped her hands on her hips. "What can I do for you?"

"You can increase your security consciousness."

"Huh?" She followed Kennedy's gaze to the open door. "Oh. You want us to keep the door closed?" She turned back. "You know how hard it is to get a tray of a hundred sandwiches through a closed door?"

"I understand there will be times you need to hold it open. We want you to ask a security agent to do it for you." Kennedy kept her voice low and her demeanor nonthreatening, and the woman, who had already apparently reached her limit for the day, relaxed.

"Sure. We can do that." She reached out and swung the van door shut behind her. "Anyone in particular?"

"Just ask. They'll find you one."

She went back inside and began her first sweep of the building. It was larger than she liked for the size team she'd brought, with more people and more movement. Maybe she'd bring another couple of agents out here, just to keep all the bases covered. M.J. would squawk at the expense again, and she hated to tie up people who weren't necessary, but there was no changing the configuration of the building or the level of chaos inside it. Even if she thought the threat was minimal, she didn't half-ass a job. She'd have Mark run the numbers. Maybe they could afford to give a family discount.

As she strolled through, she took the time to mentally identify members of the crew, staff and cast, all of whom had been generally briefed on the threat, informed of SmythShield's involvement and sworn to secrecy. Not that anyone expected that to last. Too many people to contain. No one had asked to leave the production, but maybe they all shared Kennedy's feeling that the threat was insubstantial.

Mark had conducted second-level background checks on everyone associated with the film. Everyone had checked out, though there were the usual few with financial or family-based vulnerabilities that made them possible targets for threat or bribery. If Mark had found them that easily, so could the enemy, if they wanted to.

The focus of the threat had narrowed to M.J. and the two stars, though she couldn't tell why. She'd already gone over areas where M.J. might be susceptible. Rogan St. James was more solid. His parents were doing fine financially, as was he. He had no siblings or significant others to be influenced by. He'd lived a typical mid-dle-class life that fame hadn't altered much—he kept a low social profile, didn't party, didn't gamble, didn't overindulge on anything. He had a reputation as a hard worker who took his career seriously. She couldn't see what would put him on El Jahar's radar, beyond his role in the film.

Bailey Mutchinson wasn't much different. She was high strung, and had gone the partying-starlet route for a while. Still, there hadn't been anything to tie her to a group like El Jahar. Assuming they were a group.

Kennedy strode through the wardrobe room, noting the number of places someone could hide between and within the racks of clothes. "Are you in here all day?" she asked one of the girls comparing items on a rack with a numbered list on a clipboard.

"Most of it." She snapped her gum and didn't look at

Kennedy. "No one's in here during lunch, but there are usually a couple of us while they're filming."

"Thanks." She moved on to makeup. Two actors she didn't recognize reclined in chairs with what looked like giant napkins tucked into their collars.

There were three sets in the giant building—one designed to look like an apartment, one like an office, and one with a blue screen and a variety of rigging. The only one in use right now was the apartment. Bailey and Rogan consulted on the couch. M.J. stood over them, waving his hands and making faces. Kennedy watched them all for a moment, but Rogan kept drawing her attention. She could see why he'd become so popular. On the page and screen he was gorgeous, but in real life you could feel his charisma, even from a distance. He had an energy that appealed to her, yet he concentrated on what M.J. was saying with a seriousness she wouldn't have expected. She didn't know why—at least not without uncovering prejudices Mark had accused her of and that she didn't want to have.

She glanced at her watch. It already felt like they'd done a full day of work, and it was barely seven. She looked up at the catwalk and dizzying array of lights and booms and whatever else was up there that she couldn't identify. She returned her gaze to floor level. Those catwalks were Jefferson's domain. But everything was going along smoothly down here, as far as she could tell, and she had ultimate responsibility for everyone in this building. So she headed for the metal staircase and the ceiling.

She paused at the top to study the layout and make sure she wouldn't disrupt anything. Jefferson spotted her from a platform about ten feet away and motioned to her. She walked over, looking down on the set where they were now running through the scene.

"Be pretty easy to sabotage something up here," Kennedy murmured to him.

"You're not kidding." He almost sounded gleeful at the challenge. "How do we feel about the crew?"

She shrugged. "About what you'd expect. Luckily, being a quote low-budget picture unquote, they have fewer people. A lot of them have worked together before. It's a small community. But you never know who could have been bribed."

"Nope."

"M.J. gave me a list of those he trusts completely and those he's unsure about." She shook her head. "Not much help, but it's a start."

"Quiet on the set!" came the call from below, and Kennedy fell silent. She watched the actors for a moment, then skimmed her gaze over the camera operators, production assistants, assistant directors and myriad others standing around watching. Then she looked straight at the people lurking in the shadows high above the crowd. They were all intently focused on their pieces of equipment or the scene below, except one man who darted gracefully and in complete silence from one spot to another.

"Now, there's someone I could use on the team," Kennedy muttered after the director had yelled "cut."

Jefferson grinned. "I know what you mean. I already knocked over a stack of filters and this place is so big, my footsteps echo no matter what I do." He held up a foot. "But he doesn't have these size fourteens, either."

Kennedy smiled. "Anything else to report?"

"Not yet."

The day went on like that, tedium alternating with teeming activity. At lunchtime the team kept watch over the crew shifting sets and equipment while everyone else met in the lunch room. When they'd finished, Kennedy relieved her team one by one for short breaks.

She was surprised, every so often, to find herself caught up in the shots being filmed. She'd dismissed the movie as a typical action thriller when she first read the synopsis. Bailey played the daughter of a Senator who dies trying to save staff and colleagues after the Capitol is bombed. She believes the government covers up the truth about the bombings, and Rogan is the reporter she goes to, who's on the same track. The closer they get to the truth, the closer the bad guys get to them.

But that was just the framework, the hook to get people into the theater. It was also about government culpability, the complexity and inevitability of damaged international relations, and a subtle but pointed question regarding how much those in charge really cared about the masses. It wasn't hard, watching Rogan and Bailey, to imagine their reasons for accepting these roles. Bailey would have wanted to be taken as a "serious" actress, while Rogan would want to do something important. She had to admit this was the kind of film that could give them both what they wanted.

Unless, of course, she failed to protect them.

THE ROOFTOP WAS utterly silent except for the rush of wind in microphones and the intense dialogue between Bailey and Rogan. The scene was one near the end of the movie, when their characters admitted their feelings for each other, just before the bad guys tried to crush them. The tension was palpable, but Kennedy didn't think it was because they were such good actors. It wasn't coming from them—it was coming from her team.

El Jahar had been noisy bluster so far. No one had been harmed, and with the exception of the dud bomb, the menace had been all talk. Even though Kennedy had been honest about her belief that the threat was minor, her people were well trained and didn't take anything for granted. There was no better time to escalate attacks than a new security service's first day on the job. She thought it likely that someone on the inside was involved or compromised, given the faxes to homes and mysterious delivery of the bomb to M.J.'s desk instead of through the clerk who handled the mail. So whoever was calling themselves El Jahar would know that things had changed and might expect them to be unprepared and unsettled.

"Cut!"

Action erupted around her, and Kennedy started to walk the perimeter of the roof. It was a good target, if someone had the right resources.

"Kennedy."

Rick's voice in her earpiece was low and cautious. He'd seen something. No, she realized, he'd heard something.

Helicopter blades.

She stopped next to the wall surrounding the rooftop and scanned the sky. The aircraft's approach was directly at them, which was unusual because they weren't in an area that saw a lot of air traffic, but not unheard of because there were freeways nearby. It didn't look like a medical or traffic craft, though. She skimmed the nearby buildings, wary of a diversion. At first, she didn't see anything and looked back at the helicopter. It was close enough that she could tell it was a 206B-3 JetRanger, a popular craft usually purchased for personal rather than commercial use. She had one at the compound, for training and for emergency transportation. There could be a hundred corporate owners in this city. But instinct told her this wasn't flying by just by chance.

"Get everyone off the roof!" She started herding people across the loose stone surface. Rogan, M.J., and Bailey were as far as possible from the door. Her team ushered people through it, and everyone was moving in an orderly manner, but they weren't all going to get inside before the chopper reached them.

Kennedy looked at the other buildings again, particularly the one across the street that was half a story taller than theirs and could hide a sniper. This time, she saw movement. "Get down!" she yelled at Stacy and Clay, who shoved the last of the crew and Bailey through the door. They immediately dropped, Clay pulling his weapon and aiming it at the sky.

M.J. and Rogan were partly exposed, partly hidden by an air conditioning unit. Kennedy jerked them behind it and shoved until they were on the ground, their backs to it, their feet under them.

"Don't move."

She braced her legs wide, her arms raised over their heads, and aimed her own weapon across the way, where she'd seen movement a moment earlier. The figure she'd spotted was out of range, though, and mostly concealed.

"Rick, Wolf. Get across the street and on the roof," she ordered into the open link. "I don't know how many there are or who's inside." She cursed silently. They didn't have enough personnel.

"On our way."

"Jefferson?"

"We're in, everyone's safe. No sign of anyone in the building."

"Good."

Kennedy kept one eye on the sky and one across the street. Both the chopper and the movement on the other roof could be innocent, but the hair on the back of her neck prickled, keeping her instincts on high alert.

The helicopter buzzed over, taking her attention as she tried to see identifying marks. A small thump had her spinning back just as a canister clattered over the wall, hissing. Yellow gas poured out as the can rolled toward them.

"Shit!" Kennedy ripped off her leather jacket and tossed it over the canister, then pulled M.J. and Rogan up and ran with them across the roof toward the exit, which happened to be in the opposite direction of the way the wind blew.

The chopper had turned and was making another, lower run overhead.

"Get inside!" she shouted, but as Stacy tugged at the door, horror swept over Kennedy. The door wasn't opening. She nudged M.J. toward Stacy, who pressed him against the wall under the slight overhang, and covered him with her body. Kennedy and Rogan couldn't get close enough. She tugged him to the ground and dropped over him, catching herself with her hands so she didn't crush him into the gravel. Her torso shielded his head while Clay made up the difference next to her, doing his part to protect their charge.

She braced for gunfire or another gas canister from the craft as it slowed to hover. Through her hair whipping around her head she saw a darkly dressed figure leaning out the side of the chopper and throwing something toward them. She heard a *chunk* several feet away. The whine and *thwap* of the helicopter's rotor changed as it lifted again. Kennedy raised her head an inch, and saw a knife embedded point-down in the soft tar under the stones, a sheet of plain white paper stuck to the blade.

She watched the aircraft disappear into the distance, then heard Rick give an all-clear signal from the other roof. Her alertness shifted from the large open space around them to the man lying still under her. Clay rose, freeing Kennedy's legs, and for a split second her imagination supplied a wholly different reason for lying on top of Rogan St. James.

She squashed the thought before she could process it, levered herself up, then pushed back onto her knees, cursing again.

"M.J.'s gonna kill me if I damage that pretty face." She stood while Rogan rolled over, then took his hand and helped him up. He had some red marks on his cheek, but no cuts or scrapes. "You okay?"

"Fine." He didn't let go of her hand right away, his gaze intense on hers, and she noticed his skin felt hard yet smooth. As if he worked with his hands, but pampered them too.

"Let's get inside." She handed Rogan off to Clay and Stacy. This time, when Stacy tried to open the door, she had no trouble. They ushered the actor and director inside as Kennedy crossed to the knife. She pulled a handkerchief from her pocket and bent. Grasping the knife just where the blade met the hilt, she yanked it out and grabbed the paper before it could flutter away. The message was much shorter than the previous letters had been. More suited to its method of delivery.

Coming of Day *will never see it.*
Final warning.

"Damn it," she muttered. "We are going to need more people."

ROGAN WAITED IN the secured cafeteria with the rest of the cast and crew after the rooftop incident. The Smyth-Shield operatives had herded everyone inside, and half stayed with them while the other half searched the building. Kennedy hadn't come inside yet.

He didn't realize he was pacing until M.J. stopped him with a hand on his arm.

"Chill, St. James. There isn't room in here for that."

Rogan glanced around. Several people were eyeing him warily. Though there were several feet of space around him, the cafeteria was cramped.

"Sorry."

"What did they do?" Bailey fretted, her arms tightly crossed and her face scrunched in a way he knew would make her scream if she saw the wrinkles. "After we came in. What did the bad guys do?"

"Nothing," Rogan told her. "They threw something down and took off."

"But M.J. said there was gas."

Rogan glared at the director, who shrugged apologetically. "It was a decoy," Rogan assured the actress. "Not harmful."

"But—"

"Bailey. Your turn to chill. Everything is fine."

But he didn't believe it. A few minutes later Kennedy came in. She told M.J. the building was clear, then debated with him at a volume too low for Rogan to hear, looking unhappy when M.J. clapped his hands and called everyone back to work. He bet she'd wanted them to wrap for the day, but M.J. wouldn't hear of it. They were close to behind schedule as it was, and any delays would be financially disastrous. Rogan was hustled back to makeup before he could speak to Kennedy. Three hours later, she was nowhere to be found, while Clay was ready to take him home.

He went, but stared out the side window from the backseat of their very solid, very ugly sedan. Clay drove deliberately and smoothly, just like he moved. Earlier, Rogan had studied the powerfully lean bodyguard's odd combination of relaxed readiness. He could use that for a role someday.

Now, though, Rogan barely paid attention to the route they drove. The helicopter bothered him. Why go to all that trouble, all that expense, and only drop a note? Why not strafe them with a machine gun or something?

He had to know what that note said.

"Take me back."

Clay looked in the rearview mirror. "What?"

"Take me back. I have to talk to Kennedy."

"She's not there. She'd have left by now."

"Then take me to her. I have to talk to her." Clay was shaking his head. "Fine. Then drop me at home, and I'll get my car and go look for her."

"Not a smart thing to do, putting yourself in danger over something so small," Clay said.

"Then take me to her," Rogan repeated, keeping his tone level to match Clay's rationality. "M.J. isn't going to let up on the pace, and I'm not going to get time tomorrow. I don't want to wait. I want to talk to her now."

Without another word, Clay turned around and headed back the way they'd come. A few minutes later, he walked Rogan into an old warehouse that had been partitioned into dorm-like rooms. The door closed behind them, blocking the throbbing beat of the nightclub two buildings away.

"She's not here," Stacy told them, frowning. "She's still back at the set. What are you doing here?"

"I need to talk to her," Rogan said.

Stacy's phone rang. "She should be here soon. Better wait instead of trying to chase her down." She moved away to answer her phone.

Clay stood with his back to the wall, between Rogan and the entrance. In one of the rooms across from them, the youngest SmythShield employee lifted weights. Down the hall, two others argued good-naturedly about baseball. No one paid any attention to Rogan, something he realized he wasn't used to. Not that he cared. But it made him think maybe he *had* gotten too immersed in the trappings of his career. Maybe the side effects weren't just hearing music and framing shots in his head.

"So, you work a lot of celebrity jobs?" he asked Clay.

For a second, sly humor moved through the bodyguard's expression, and Rogan expected him to make a joke about not working one now, but Clay controlled the impulse and only said, "This is the first."

"You could do stunt work," Rogan offered. "Maybe even double for Pitt."

Before Clay could answer, the door opened and Kennedy walked in.

Her posture shifted as soon as the door closed, as if she no longer had the energy to hold herself rigidly upright. Her ponytail drooped and her T-shirt bunched under her shoulder holster, but she made no move to smooth it. And still, as worn out as she seemed, she scanned the hallway and the visible rooms with an alertness and cunning Rogan had rarely seen. Her body was still perfectly balanced, ready to explode into action if necessary. He wondered if she ever got to relax.

He knew she had seen him immediately, but she paid him no mind as she checked in with her team, making sure everything was working okay and their room assignments were acceptable. The only acknowledgement he got was a hand signal to follow as she moved into the stairwell at the end of the hall.

Rogan and Clay followed her and witnessed the same routine upstairs. When she seemed satisfied, she opened a door at the end of the hall and stood back to let Rogan enter. The kitchenette sported a tiny table and two chairs, tucked next to a full-sized refrigerator and across from a counter with a microwave and hot pot. She gestured and he sat, feeling for a moment like a kid in the principal's office.

"You okay?" he asked.

She shrugged and dropped onto the chair opposite him. "Yeah, but I lost my favorite jacket."

Rogan didn't think she cared about the jacket. "I guess the gas ruined it."

"Very."

"And you don't like having your weapon exposed."

She frowned at him. "Who would?"

"You can take it off. I won't touch it."

That brought a flicker of a smile. "You wouldn't get to it, even if you tried. But thanks. I'm fine. What are you doing here? You're supposed to be safely at home."

"I wanted to talk to you about the helicopter. The note."

"There's nothing to talk about."

Rogan had to consciously relax his jaw. "As one of the apparent targets, I have a right to know what you think is happening." He sat still while she studied him, fingering a fork someone had left on the table.

"And if you're working with them, you'd love to know how much I've figured out."

His jaw dropped. But he couldn't argue with her logic, so he said, "Yeah, I guess I would. If I was working with them. Which I'm not."

"So why do you care what I'm thinking, as long as I'm doing my job and protecting you and the film?"

"I'm not the kind of person who just lets everything go on around me. I like to know." He tried a little takes-one-to-know-one strategy. "I'm sure you understand that."

"Sure. But the difference is that it's my job to know. Some things it could be dangerous for you to know."

He shook his head. "I don't buy it. Not at this stage. We're not in the military."

"I know feeling like you have no control is difficult. But you have to trust me. My team. We know how to do our jobs."

Rogan didn't detect any defensiveness or censure in her tone, and after her reaction to his former bodyguard's "test" and the helicopter thing, he did trust her. She knew what she was doing. But it wasn't enough.

"Can we meet halfway on this?" he asked.

Kennedy laughed. "How? By me telling you what you want to know?" He waited. Finally, she nodded. "You tell me why *you* think this group is after *Coming of Day*, and I'll tell you more about today's little show."

He was surprised. "You want my opinion?"

"I want to see if you've gleaned something from the letters that I can't, because you know things I don't."

Now he was more surprised. "You think this is personal." She didn't respond. "That never occurred to me. Personal to whom? Three of us got letters sent to our homes. Before that it was to the studio and the old security company. Doesn't seem very targeted to me."

Kennedy seemed to make a decision about something. "There is no El Jahar, Rogan. And their writings are too vague and chaotic, but in a deliberate way. Like someone was trying to sound random and crazy. But you can't make something random deliberately. Patterns emerge anyway. And none of the patterns here make sense. Not if El Jahar is a terrorist group with global pretensions."

Rogan thought about the letter that had come over his fax. He couldn't remember the exact content, because it was exactly as she described. "So you think it's about one of us."

"They may be targeting three of you to hide which of you is the true target."

"For what?" It made no sense. "There are a lot of ways to ruin or harm a person. Hiring a helicopter to drop a note doesn't seem very efficient."

"I agree." She sat back, lines of weariness in her face.

Rogan studied her, thinking. There was something she wasn't saying. What was the common element to all the events? He mentally listed them, and realized none had been designed to harm. "So what did the note say?"

"'*Coming of Day* will never see it. Final warning.'"

A slight surge of…something went through him. Not as minor as annoyance, not as strong as fear. "Final warning."

"Yep."

"And the movie won't see what? Day? That's like bad poetry."

Kennedy agreed. "It's psychological tactics. They want us to worry about what's coming next, and that it will be bigger. Of course," she added, "it could be that they expected more media coverage and got showier because they're not getting it. It might have nothing to do with any of you, except that something happening to you would be big news and couldn't be kept quiet."

All of which fed his earlier thought about the lack of harmful intent. He opened his mouth to ask. Closed it. Did he really want to know the answer?

Kennedy's watch beeped. She didn't glance at it, but stood. "You need to go home. My people need rest, and they won't get it if they spend all night ferrying you around."

He didn't move. He *did* want to know. "You're not taking this threat very seriously."

Anger and a flash of what might be guilt passed over Kennedy's face. "Do you have a problem with how I work?"

He shook his head. She was going on the offensive, which meant he'd hit a nerve. "You didn't bring very many agents, considering the size of the set and the number of people working it."

"We don't know the true nature of the threat."

Which wasn't an admission, he understood, but perhaps an acknowledgement. He rose slowly to his feet, noticing that Kennedy's T-shirt was now pulled tight across her abdomen, exposing a strip of skin above her jeans and accentuating her breasts. The woman was in incredible shape. His eyes traced the muscles in her arms, the tautness of her abs, even a cord in her neck when she shifted to adjust the holster. His gaze moved upward, and he thought he'd see anger when she caught him studying her. At least annoyance. After the tone of their conversation, the last thing he expected was interest. She quickly shuttered it, but it elevated a moment of attraction he would have dismissed to something more.

He looked away. What had he been about to say? Oh, yeah. "Did today change things?"

When he turned back she met his gaze head-on, not evading the implied criticism, and without a hint of chagrin on her face.

"I have more people coming tomorrow."

He grinned. "Probably a good idea."

"And the security system M.J. vetoed will be installed tomorrow night."

He nodded. "Thanks. For talking to me, and—you know." He waved a hand. She nodded and showed him out, walking at his side all the way down to the main entrance. He was hyperaware of her warm, spicy scent and the confident strength in her stride, despite her fatigue.

By the time he allowed Clay to accompany him home, confirm the security of his apartment and leave, there was a bubble of excitement in his chest he hadn't felt in a long time.

FOUR

KENNEDY DIDN'T GET to consider, in private, the look Rogan had given her and her unaccustomed reaction to it. Or the thoughts those few seconds had inspired. Not even to dismiss them as stupid, which they were. Having a fling with her protectee was *not* going to happen.

Rogan had asked some very good questions. The one she was grateful he *hadn't* asked was *why* her team had been ill-equipped to handle today's incident.

She didn't think anyone had noticed, since things could have been much worse. No one tried to get inside, and the gas canister had been full of nothing but colored smoke. The helicopter/knife trick was big, though. It showed their enemy had resources and intent, even though she couldn't tell what that intent was. Her belief that this was a nothing job had shifted drastically. She had to call in more of her team, and get that security system installed. Even if she didn't charge M.J. much for the additional staff, he would have to find the funds somehow, or consider shutting down.

She'd spent half an hour convincing the alarm company to reopen the order she canceled that morning. They'd be there tomorrow night, after shooting was done for the day. Not ideal. She didn't want to wait a whole day, but it was her own fault for letting M.J. convince her, and even more for coming into this job less than full force. She was grateful Rogan hadn't called her on it, though he'd obviously thought it.

She should never have taken this job.

Stop it. She *had* taken it, and screwed up. Her cavalier attitude, her superiority, hadn't ended badly. But it could have, and she had to face it.

The second day went smoothly, with everyone on high alert, including the cast and crew. M.J. crowed about the quality of the performances, proud of his actors for channeling their emotions from the day before. He crowed so much, Kennedy briefly wondered if he'd orchestrated the whole thing. But when five more team members arrived around noon, he greeted them with a soberness and relief she didn't think was faked. He, after all, wasn't an actor.

Steve, the electronic security firm's supervisor, met her after dinner with the specs for the alarm system. They argued about whether or not to wire the vents for gas and liquid infiltrants as well as physical ones. Kennedy won that argument. She wasn't leaving anything else to chance. She stayed and watched the installation, making sure no shortcuts were taken because of the lateness of the hour. She'd learned her lesson. By the time they were done that night and she left the studio, alarm armed and Andrew and Mick, her night team, on rounds, it was nearly one in the morning.

"So much for alertness tomorrow," she grumbled as she finally climbed into bed without the shower she'd craved.

The next day, just after she'd dismissed her team from their morning report, Rogan approached her.

"Aren't you due on the set?" she asked, starting her rounds. He kept pace with her.

"They're playing with the lights. I have something for you."

For a wild second, she thought he was going to give her flowers or something, but the idea was absurd.

He pulled a sheaf of papers from his back pocket. "It's a rundown of the cast and crew. I've worked with most of them before. I know you've done your own background checks," he said before she could. "But I thought some inside knowledge might help."

Kennedy stared at him. "It will. Thanks."

"You're welcome." Someone called his name, and he flashed that charming grin and backed away. "See ya later."

"Yeah. Later." She watched him pause to talk to a grip. She was close enough to hear him ask about the guy's fiancée's mother, who'd apparently been sick or something, before M.J. grabbed his arm and started chewing his ear. Rogan St. James had surprised her again. That was usually a bad thing. Doing her job right depended on assessing people, cataloging their strengths and weaknesses, and knowing how they'd act in any situation. Rogan's profile hadn't prepared her for him, but instead of making her tense and annoyed, the reality intrigued her.

And if she wanted to delve into her reaction to his possible interest…well, she'd have to admit he had a pretty nice ass. And long, powerful-looking legs.

Since she *didn't* want to delve into her reaction *or* his possible interest, she deliberately turned away and headed for the coffee table, for the third time already that morning.

Jefferson noticed. "Sleep poorly?" he asked when she joined him on the catwalk a moment later.

"How can you tell?" She covered her mouth while she yawned. Despite all the rough conditions she'd worked in, despite her intense training over the years, she had never overcome her need for a minimum of seven hours of sleep at night. It was her major weakness. She had stopped trying to hide it when she opened SmythShield, instead using it to teach her recruits about identifying their own strengths and weaknesses and using them to peak advantage or accommodating them as necessary.

"I'll catch up," she assured Jefferson. "I just hope we don't get attacked by a pack of Ninjas or something. My reflexes might be a little slow." She left him laughing and went to fax Rogan's crew notes to Mark.

She did catch up on her sleep over the next two nights, as the shoot continued amazingly on schedule. With only a week of indoor scenes left, M.J. and Kennedy met one night in his office to discuss the upcoming location shoot.

M.J. scrubbed at his scalp with his fingers, roughing up his already riotous curls. His attention focused on the list he'd had typed up for Kennedy. "Okay. The city part of the movie takes place in Denver, where the government bigwigs are having a secret summit."

"Denver?" she asked skeptically.

"Yeah, yeah. You know, Colorado's a core area for military installations and stuff. Besides that, they think no one would expect them to be there. It's not a political city like DC or New York."

He rattled on some more, but Kennedy wasn't concerned with the plot of the movie. "Relevance, M.J."

"Right. Okay, here's where we're all staying, and here's where we'll be filming." He began rocking back and forth, pointing with his pen at his list, then the same line on Kennedy's. She watched him bite his nails, change the order of two of the scenes on the shooting schedule, and snatch her paper to make the change there, as well. As if it wouldn't change again a dozen times before they got to that day.

She wondered what he was so nervous about. Mark had dug deeper and found no flags in M.J.'s recent history. Rogan's notes, too, had offered his opinion that the director had no enemies fierce enough to do what the so-called El Jahar was doing. Kennedy had Mark check out M.J.'s sister and even Max, and so far he'd still found nothing. But M.J.'s behavior was increasingly frantic and she didn't know why.

She outlined her general security measures for each location on the list. "I need to scout them ahead of time to plan properly. I'll leave for Denver a day ahead of the rest of you and start checking them out." She hadn't decided yet if she'd have the last four available members of her team meet them there. Jefferson could use his assistant for props and equipment, and with the locations spread out, a few more eyes and hands would be a good idea. Nothing had happened here since the helicopter, not even more letters, but deterrence was the main point of security. Public locations would be more vulnerable.

"I guess that's it," she said, and M.J. agreed. They gathered their papers and started out of the office, but M.J. held her back. "Uh, Kennedy."

She waited.

"I've got to tell you something."

Finally. "Go ahead."

His eyes shifted back and forth and he shuffled his feet. She waited some more.

Finally, he took a deep breath. "Have you talked to your father lately?"

"No." She realized she'd let more time than usual go by between calls. Her father tried not to bother her when she was on a job, so he hadn't called her, either. "Why?"

"Well, you know, I talk to mine about every day." He paused, grimacing.

"Yeah, so?"

"He keeps asking about you."

Light dawned. "About me, personally?"

"Yeah, and he's said some things. Like, about you and me, and how you had a crush on me as a kid…"

Kennedy burst out laughing. "M.J., we were friends, mainly due to proximity. I never had a crush on you."

He relaxed a fraction. "I didn't think so. But you know he doesn't let up when he thinks something is right."

"I think both our fathers have matchmaking aspirations." She told him about her last discussion with her father. "My mother always talked about it, and my dad goes through these periods of nostalgia. Maybe they're hoping to get something good out of this situation."

"Maybe it's more than that." He glanced at her from the corner of his eye. "I keep wondering if my father set this whole thing up."

Kennedy raised her eyebrows. "Whole thing? As in the threats? As an excuse to hire me?"

"Yeah. I mean, nothing too serious has happened. Just bad enough to get you here, you know?" He swallowed hard. "What do you think?"

"I think your father's too much of a skinflint to spend so much money on such a thing. And he wouldn't put either of us in danger."

He shrugged. "Like I said, the danger hasn't been real."

Kennedy held back her initial response. She wanted to say it was ridiculous. Her father wouldn't go that far. But Max, with his flair for drama and immersion in the world of make-believe, might. She watched M.J. continue to fidget.

"You're not still worried about my feelings, are you?"

"Not really." His brow gathered. "Should I be?"

"No." Shit, she really wasn't cut out for this touchy-feely stuff. "M.J., I know. I've known for years. Even if I *had* had a crush when we were kids, I'd be over it now." Then it hit her. If his father was trying to match-make…"But Max doesn't know, does he? Is *that* why you've been so twitchy?"

He sighed. "It doesn't matter. That has nothing to do with *Coming of Day*, or SmythShield. Don't worry about it."

Kennedy felt she should say more, but didn't know what. "All right. Stay here. I'm going to lock up."

She'd sent everyone back to the boardinghouse and was planning on driving M.J. home herself, because they hadn't known how late they were going to be. She did her usual nightly sweep, then armed the alarm, checked in with the night shift, and preceded M.J. out of the building.

Kennedy never entered or left a building without being aware of the possibility of an attacker standing next to the door. So when she caught movement in her peripheral vision, she instinctively sprang forward, using her momentum to get out of the way of the heavy object descending toward her head. She twisted, pulling her pistol out of its holster. Before she could bring it up the attacker barreled into her, knocking her to the ground. Her breath left her in a *whoosh* and she almost lost her grip on the gun.

The guy on top of her was massive and solid, and positioned so his most vulnerable body parts were out of her reach. She tensed, waiting for him to bang her head against the ground or wrap his hands around her throat, but he surprised her by rolling off and moving away.

She could still barely breathe, and her right arm tingled from her elbow's contact with the ground. But her assailant wasn't leaving. He was heading for M.J.

"Freeze!" she yelled as deeply as she could, pulling her gun around in front of her and holding it with two hands. The guy ignored her. Light from the security lamp above them reflected off his bald head. M.J. stood frozen in the doorway, his mouth half-open in shock. He didn't move as Baldy barreled toward him.

She couldn't shoot. M.J. was too close. Cursing, Kennedy rolled to her feet, raced after Baldy, and caught him with a kick behind the knees. He went down hard, bellowing in pain as his right knee cracked on the pavement. She stood over him, aiming the gun at the side of his head, trying to see if anyone else was around without taking her eyes off him.

It didn't work. M.J. managed a squeaky kind of warning just as she sensed movement behind her. She ducked, and in seconds the gun was off him, Baldy bounced to his feet and ran off, his curses and limping gait echoing in the darkness. Another set of footsteps retreated in the opposite direction. When she turned, she could see only vague movement in the shadows.

"Shit." Kennedy dropped her gun hand and put her free hand on her aching left side, where Baldy must have landed. On the ground near her foot she saw darker blackness against the gleaming pavement. She bent with a grunt and picked up Baldy's weapon. It was a metal paperweight inside a man's dress sock. Both were generic and would be impossible to trace. The paperweight could have fingerprints on it, but she doubted it would.

Sticking the weapon in her pocket, she lurched over to M.J. and leaned against the wall.

"Aren't you going after them?" he asked weakly, squinting into the darkness.

Kennedy stared at him. "I'd never catch them now. Did you call the police?" He flushed. "You didn't call the police?"

"I didn't even think about it." He looked fretful. "Do we have to call them?"

Kennedy pushed away from the wall. "You were almost killed. If you had gone out the door first, you might have been."

"But everything's fine. And it's late, and..." He swallowed, looking young and lost, and Kennedy thought she knew what was going on. Cops reminded him of the bad times with his mother, of his sister's problems.

Still, it was better to report the attack. "I'm calling them anyway. You don't have to deal with them if you don't want to." She reached for her cell phone.

"No!" M.J. cursed. "Please don't. If we call the cops, it will be all over the papers. The publicity will kill us."

"*That's* what this is about? The publicity? M.J., this was an attack! If it was El Jahar, it means they're escalating."

"If?" He jumped on the word. "You don't think it was?"

She tossed up her hands. "How should I know? It

could have been a random mugging and they cut their losses because I have a gun."

"Think about it, Kennedy. If it isn't El Jahar, the police won't be able to do anything. We can barely describe them, with the dark and how quick it happened. And if it is El Jahar, the papers would go berserk with the story."

Disgusted as she was with his attitude, she had to admit he was right. On the one hand, if El Jahar was seeking recognition they weren't getting, and still didn't get it from this, they could escalate things again. On the other hand, giving them what they wanted wasn't a better choice.

"Please, Kennedy. You don't understand." Tears thickened M.J.'s voice. "This is my last chance. If I can't make this movie, I'm done in Hollywood. Even my own father won't back me." He blinked hard, and she couldn't prevent the one tiny tender part of her heart from influencing her decision. M.J. was family. He was the reason she was here. She had no strength against his pleading.

"Fine. Let's go." Kennedy had walked down from the boardinghouse, as usual, so she drove M.J.'s car. He'd stopped being jittery and just sat, staring out the side window, until they got to his building. He started to direct Kennedy to the garage entrance, but stopped when he saw she knew where she was going.

She parked and they got out. M.J. hesitated. "How will you get back now?"

"I'll manage. I'm a big girl." She tossed him the keys and he caught them but otherwise didn't move. "What's wrong?"

"Nothing." He shook himself and walked toward her. "I was just remembering that mugger, or whatever he was. What was the point? I mean, if he was just a mugger, I guess the point is obvious. But if he wasn't, what did he want?"

"Who knows? If they incapacitated you or worse—and that weapon was heavy enough it could have caved your skull—it might have halted production."

"They'd get a new director," he protested.

"So they didn't know that. Or maybe *I* was the target. Maybe they've been watching and knew I'd come out first. They might have figured if they took me out the production would be more vulnerable."

M.J. frowned. "How could they be watching your movements without you being aware of it?"

"I'm not invincible, M.J." She grabbed his arm and led him to the elevator. "I can't see through walls or onto a rooftop a few blocks away." Now he looked worried, and she sighed. "Don't worry about it."

"Easy for you to say."

But it wasn't. She saw him safely into his apartment after scoping it out for intruders, made him set the alarm, and called him from the lobby once she got downstairs. Tonight had been a close call, closer than she liked.

She cursed, suddenly thinking of her team and the possibility that this had been a diversion, planned to get her attention focused elsewhere. It had worked, damn it, and she hadn't even thought about the risks.

She hit the speed dial for Stacy's phone and held her breath until she answered.

"Is everything okay there?"

"Yeah. It's quiet. Why?"

Kennedy lingered in the brightly lit, secured lobby of M.J.'s building while she quietly explained what had happened. "Do me a favor. Make sure all our people are accounted for, then coordinate calls to all the actors. I want to make sure they're all safe. Then signal me the all clear, or call if there are any problems."

"What about Andrew and Mick?"

"I'll call them myself."

"Gotcha."

She dialed Andrew's cell phone, glad she'd brought him and Mick in. They did the night shift because they were incapable of boredom, and had made a game out of noticing details. He answered on the first ring and assured her they were both fine and the building was secure.

"Stay alert," she told him. "Something feels off."

"Could that be because you were just, you know, *attacked*?"

"No. I'm fine. But the more I think about it, the more it feels wrong."

"Okay, whatever." His voice firmed, took on a more professional tone. "We'll stay alert and report every two hours."

She grinned. "Somebody's trained you right. I'll talk to you later." She hesitated, studying her phone, then pressed the buttons to call up Rogan's number from her phone book. Stacy was going to call him, and she was sure they'd checked things out thoroughly when they brought him home. But she felt compelled to check on him herself. Instinct? A hunch that he was the true target?

She hit the "send" button, then the "end" button. It might not be instinct. It might be that thing she refused to examine, and if that were the case, calling him would be a big mistake. It would send messages she had no business sending. But what if it *was* a hunch?

Shit. This was why she didn't get involved with people. Nothing fucked things up worse. She shoved the phone back in her pocket and the *thing* into a lead box in her mind, where it would stay. No more checking out Rogan St. James's ass, or being pleased at his "possible interest." Period.

When she finally exited the building onto a nearly deserted street, the doorman hailed a cab for her. She gave the driver an address several blocks from the boardinghouse. As they drove, she tried to pinpoint what was bothering her about the attack.

Baldy had tackled her, though he must have seen right away who she was. After they hit the ground, he hadn't tried to incapacitate her. And then he hadn't fought. Whatever his objective was, he hadn't worked very hard to meet it. First real resistance, he'd run.

And the second guy—person. She hadn't seen enough of the shadowy figure to determine gender. Why hadn't the two of them worked together to overpower her? If they wanted to hurt M.J., why hadn't he been the primary target? Why hadn't Shadow-Man struck her when she ducked, to give them more time?

No, something wasn't right. There were dozens of possibilities. They could have been trying to send another warning, however ambiguous, since there had been no message this time. Or they might have hired cowards who didn't like counterattack. They could have been after something, especially something she or M.J. would have been carrying. But what? A script was the only thing she could think of, and that was posted on six or seven websites already. So that wasn't it.

Another possibility was that the two had been unconnected. Two different raiders? A true mugger who had misread the situation? Competing factions of protesters?

Her head was beginning to hurt. She rested it on the seat and watched the lights flash by. Slowly, the possibility she'd subconsciously suppressed rose to the surface. Those guys had known she and M.J. were still there. How? Had someone on the inside tipped them off? Someone on the cast or crew?

Or worse. Someone on her team.

She dismissed the possibility as soon as she considered it. Everyone on this job had worked for SmythShield for years. None had any motive for starting something like this. She trusted every one of them with her life. With M.J.'s life.

Even Wolf? a voice asked. He was new, and didn't have the same loyalty that came from working back to back in steaming hellholes. But Mark's background research hadn't turned up any red flags.

Her phone beeped Stacy's all-clear signal. That mostly ruled out diversion. An obvious one, anyway.

She sat up suddenly, another thought hitting her hard. She pulled her phone out again and dialed M.J., who didn't answer.

"M.J., it's Kennedy," she barked to the answering machine. "Pick up the damned phone."

A click, then he came on the line. "Sorry. Sorry. Just a little on edge, that's all. Screening."

She frowned. "Are you taking something?"

He chuckled. "Besides Valium, you mean? No. I'm just on edge, like I said. What's up? Nothing else happened, did it?" Fear changed the tone of his voice.

"No, but I wanted to ask you…when I was occupied with Baldy and Shadow-Man, could anyone have gotten past you guys into the building?"

He snorted. "No. I had a death grip on both sides of

the doorjamb, with my fingers even wedged between the door and the frame. The light over the door is bright, and they would have had to knock me out of the way."

"Okay." She relaxed. Andrew and Mick would have called her by now too. There was no chance they'd overlook any potential hiding place. "You only saw the two attackers."

"Yeah, Baldy, like you said. He was big and his head was shiny, like he'd been bald forever."

"Not shaved."

"Right."

"What about the other guy?"

"Couldn't see much. He was tall, that's all I could tell."

She let out a breath. "Okay. If you remember anything else, write it down and tell me in the morning."

She hung up, climbed out of the cab and paid the driver. The night was silent, the club closed and everything else still. Uninhabited. Kennedy took a deep breath of fresh, clean air, unusual in this city any time of year. The winds and clouds and weather systems must be just right, she thought, checking left, right and behind as she strolled toward the boardinghouse. No one bothered her, though she saw a few dark shapes huddled in recessed doorways or behind dumpsters. Homeless or gangs, she couldn't tell, and they left her alone.

A few minutes later she was at the boardinghouse. Still uneasy about tonight's attack, she peeked into every room. Most of her team was already asleep.

Stacy was the only one still awake. Kennedy leaned against her empty doorway. The woman had spread a blizzard of paperwork around her on the floor. Rogan and Bailey's faces stared up from a dozen torn-out magazine articles. Printed lists alternated with hand-drawn diagrams and filled-up notebook paper.

"What's all this?" Kennedy asked her.

Stacy blushed and straightened her legs in front of her. "Just, you know, looking for patterns."

"What kind of patterns?" She crouched and picked up a crew list that had film titles written next to each name. Her eyebrows rose when Stacy snatched the paper away, her cheeks going even brighter.

"Nothing in particular. Hey, I talked to Mick and Andrew a few minutes ago."

Kennedy eyed her assistant and the photos on the floor. Stacy, to her credit, didn't grab at those, only raised her chin defiantly. Kennedy sighed. She'd hoped her staff would be strong enough not to crush on the celebrities. She wouldn't embarrass Stacy by pursuing it, but only as long as it didn't affect her work.

"What did they say?" she finally asked.

Stacy relaxed. "Site's secure, they still haven't spotted anything out of order."

"Okay, thanks." Kennedy pushed herself upright and headed for her own room. She should be reassured. Everything was the way it should be.

But that bothered her most of all.

FIVE

ROGAN SCANNED THE set between takes, looking for Kennedy. She'd been avoiding him all week. He'd been trying to find a moment when she wasn't working to talk to her, but she never took a break. He was always here early for makeup, but even at five-thirty, she'd beaten him to the warehouse. And she stayed long after he did, despite his own thirteen-hour days. He wasn't convinced she didn't sleep there.

Watching her during his down time had become automatic. Her focus was intense, her passion enticing. And no matter how many times he told himself he wanted to stay far away from intensity and passion—in other words, *drive*—he couldn't keep his eyes off her.

He could be attracted to a woman without acting on it. But he didn't like being in the dark. M.J. had told him about the attempted mugging, but he'd been working so hard to stay on schedule he wouldn't talk to Rogan about El Jahar anymore. He didn't know if there had been any more letters, or other attempted muggings, or anything else that Kennedy had kept quiet, which annoyed him. His position and the letter that made him a prime target gave him a few more rights than the average extra.

He finally caught her one day with a clipboard in the prep room, consulting with one of her team.

"It would be difficult to tamper with most of this stuff," the guy was saying to Kennedy, who didn't look convinced. He sighed. "Don't worry, I'm not taking anything for granted. I'm just saying."

"I know, but we still don't know what we're dealing with." Kennedy glanced at Rogan. He could see her split-second evaluation and dismissal, and frowned at the sharpness of his reaction. She hadn't seemed so dismissive before.

"That's it for now, Jefferson. Use Wolf if you need help with anything." She started writing on the clipboard. Jefferson moved across the room to a large cabinet. Rogan stood, ignored.

One thing an actor learned early was patience. He just waited. Kennedy checked her watch, turned and counted stuff on the counter behind her, turned back and leaned against the counter, making more notes. Eventually her writing slowed and she looked up.

"Am I in your way?"

Rogan stepped closer. She'd looked up, but not at him. She was still engrossed in her thoughts. Or pretending to be.

"You're never in anyone's way," he said. That earned him a shrug as she flipped pages on the clipboard.

"That's what I'm going for."

"Maybe some of us want you to get in our way." He cringed before he even finished saying it. What the hell was that? Candidate for the worst pickup line ever?

"I prefer not to," she said.

Rogan stifled a sigh. "Kennedy."

She finally stopped and let her clipboard drop to her side. "What is it?"

"What's going on? You've been avoiding me since the other night."

"I have not," she scoffed. "I'm always around you."

"Around me. Protecting me. Not including me."

She shook her head. "We both have our jobs here. You perform. I protect. That's the way it works."

He took a deep, subtle breath against his frustration. "I've been part of this. Part of the discussion and planning. Then suddenly you cut me off."

Kennedy set her clipboard down and gave him her full attention, but only for a second. She folded her arms and watched Jefferson walk out of the room. Rogan backed up to close the door. Kennedy's eyes narrowed. He had a feeling she didn't like that he'd separated her from her people. But then she relaxed them again, apparently deciding it would be easier to address him than dismiss him.

"My job can be easier if certain people have a basic understanding of the situation. You do. That's all you need."

"That's all?" Words flooded his mind, dialogue that he knew came from other people's pens. He didn't want to recite lines. But he didn't have any words of his own to use. He settled for, "How can it not help for you to tell me what's happening?"

"There is nothing happening!" Kennedy half-yelled. She pressed a hand to her forehead and laughed ruefully. "I don't know how you do that."

Rogan didn't say anything. He'd heard enough, seen enough, about Kennedy's legendary cool. He wasn't sure if he should be proud or ashamed that he'd shaken it.

"What have you learned about the muggers?" he tried.

"Nothing. There were no fingerprints on the paperweight, and neither of us can provide enough of a description to ID him." She shrugged and settled against the counter again, her arms crossed but not her ankles. She kept her feet planted, ready to move.

"So that's it. No more notes, no more attacks, no suspects or leads."

"Nope." She studied him a second. "Why are you so bothered by that? Do you *want* something to happen?"

Good lord, now she'd suspect him again. "No." He started to run his hand through his hair, but the hairdresser would kill him. He let it fall. "I just want to be more active, that's all. Not sit around waiting for someone to try to off me."

"Tell you what." Kennedy straightened, retrieved her clipboard, and crossed to the door. "Consider yourself deputized. You're in charge of Bailey. Keep her calm and responsive if anything happens. And trust me," she added, opening the door. "That's going to be a very important job."

Rogan followed her out, stifling a sigh. She wasn't wrong. But it wasn't quite what he was looking for.

THE DISASTER KENNEDY had felt hovering over the production and the security team didn't materialize. Nor did the personal disaster she sensed whenever Rogan tried to talk to her.

She was afraid her people would start to relax, and afraid their adversary was counting on that. She intensified her vigilance, double-checking everyone's work and roaming incessantly around the building until she'd annoyed or worried everyone in it. She tried to stay out of the way, but every movement showed her some other potential risk. Potential that never converted to reality.

At the same time, Rogan's hot gaze seemed to follow her around, and when he wasn't watching her, she caught herself watching him. Worse, when she first saw him in the morning, something in her chest felt lighter in a way she refused to name, refused to examine…but not refused to feel. For that, she cursed herself. All the watching was so *juvenile*. Ten times a day, she'd find herself thinking about him. The way he moved his hands when he talked, or how he made the whole crew laugh. She even caught herself imagining his opinion on some of her decisions, and that was just ridiculous. She rid herself of these thoughts a dozen times a day, but as soon as he appeared, they came back.

To her relief, the last day of indoor shooting finally arrived. She gave a pre-dawn pep talk to the team, cautioning them about letting their guard down. That was always when things went wrong.

Jefferson joined her at craft services between scenes. "You ready for Denver?"

"Is that a rhetorical question?" She added cream and sugar to her mug and turned to lean against the counter.

"You know, you're supposed to drink your coffee black and solid." He filled his mug halfway with regular coffee, the rest of the way with decaf.

She sighed, sipping the beverage and eyeing the set, where M.J. enthusiastically coached his actors. She pretended to be looking for problems, but was really trying not to look at Rogan's long legs. "And why is that the way I should like my coffee?"

He shrugged. "All the tough cops and PIs and stuff drink it that way."

"I may be tough, but I'm also sweet." She bared her teeth in the parody of a smile. "Are *you* ready for Denver?"

He grimaced and scratched his beard. "Yeah, close

enough. Rick's having a cow ten times a day about securing all the locations. He keeps telling M.J. he should cut some scenes. Even said it would improve the movie, anyway."

"Ouch. I bet M.J. didn't like that." Kennedy wondered why neither one had mentioned this to her. She looked around for Rick, but he was on outside patrol.

Jefferson opened his mouth to reply, but was interrupted by the blaring of a siren.

"It's the upper vent alarm!" Rick yelled in her earpiece. "Gas!"

A few screams followed. Someone yelled for them to get outside.

"No!" Kennedy shouted. That could be exactly what they wanted. She wasn't going to allow a mass attack. "Everyone get into the cafeteria and seal the door!" The people closest to her hurried to comply. She made sure Zip followed. As part of Rick's general security team, she knew how to seal the room. She heard coughing up on the catwalk and knew they didn't have much time. "Rick, you okay?"

"Yeah. I'm on the other side."

"Get on the roof. Take Wolf, and try to find out where this is coming from. Jonathan, get outside and secure the area. Be careful. I don't want you shot or captured."

"Got it." They had created outside access from an underground storage area so they could exit the building undetected.

Kennedy made sure Shenk, M.J.'s bodyguard, herded everyone in the right direction. She then ran back toward the wardrobe and makeup rooms. Rogan met her halfway up the hall.

"Where?"

"Vent near the roof. Get to the cafeteria." He ran the opposite way. "Rogan!" Before she could follow him, one of the assistants rushed out of the wardrobe room.

"What's happening?" She clutched Kennedy's shirt. "Is it an earthquake?"

Kennedy barely refrained from rolling her eyes. "No. Get to the cafeteria. Now." The wide-eyed girl bolted, followed quickly by the wardrobe staff. Kennedy hurried down the hall toward makeup.

"You can't take anything."

That was Rogan's voice. Kennedy moved faster, running but pausing to check the closets and changing rooms between wardrobe and makeup. They were empty, and she slammed to a stop at the door to the makeup room. The artist and her assistant were throwing things into bins and bags, even as Rogan snatched them out of their hands and tossed them on the counter.

"You need to get to the cafeteria immediately," Kennedy told them.

"I can't leave this stuff! Do you know how much it costs?"

Kennedy ignored the panic taking root in her own chest. Indulging fear that she would fail in her mission of keeping these people safe would cripple her.

"Just go. Now." She grabbed the assistant's arm and shoved her out the door. Rogan hustled the makeup artist behind her, and she finally responded, racing down the hallway. Rogan started to follow, but stopped when Kennedy turned right instead of left.

"What are you doing?"

"Checking the bathrooms."

"I'll help."

She didn't waste time arguing with him. They were

running out of time, and arguing would increase his danger. They found no one in there and started back down the hall.

"There's no one on the roof or outside," Rick reported over her earpiece.

"What about the gas?"

"I can't get close enough to tell. It's a knockout gas, we think. Wolf started to go over the side of the wall to check it and got woozy. Came back."

"Are you safe up there?"

"For now. The ladder is too close to the vent."

"Okay. Report if you see anything. We'll get you down."

"Roger."

"Kennedy, we need to seal this room off!" Zip yelled, sounding frantic. "Where's Rogan?"

"He's with me. Seal it. In eight minutes, go out the back door unless Jonathan or Rick say otherwise. Jonathan?"

"I'm almost out." In contrast to Zip, he could have been lazing on a beach. "Got slowed down by some heavy equipment."

"Make sure no one is around, then go to the back door. They'll be coming out in seven minutes."

"What about you?"

"I'm fine."

But she wasn't. She took shallow breaths, trying to avoid inhaling any gas that had reached ground level, and Rogan was going blurry on her. She tried to remember the layout of the building, but her brain rebelled. Rogan seemed to sway toward her.

"Get down. On the floor. Grab my foot," she ordered, hoping the gas was coming down from above and not through the full ventilation system. The alarm that had gone off was for the outtake, so she hoped the intake system was clean.

They both dropped to all fours. Rogan's hand closed around her ankle. He quickly got into rhythm with her movements and had no trouble keeping up with her. Her head seemed to clear as they crawled. They couldn't get into the cafeteria, because she'd ordered it sealed. They had to get to the front door, but she was afraid they wouldn't make it before passing out.

She hadn't stocked gas masks because she really hadn't expected gas to be a threat, despite her precautions with the security system, and she knew Starshine wouldn't want to pay for them. They were paying now, that was for sure.

She pulled her shirt over her nose and mouth, though it would have little-to-no effect, and glanced back. Rogan had done the same. He glanced up, his eyes sparkling with exhilaration. She narrowed her own eyes at him. Of course an action star would get a rush out of this. He probably took it no more seriously than he would shooting a scene.

Through her earpiece, she heard Jonathan give an all clear, then help Shenk and Zip get everyone out of the cafeteria into the fenced alley behind the building. Then Rick and Wolf reported from the roof, and Stacy asked where Kennedy was.

She couldn't answer, saving her breath. They'd emerged from the hall into the main room. The size meant the gas was more diffuse, and her breathing slowed, her head clearing. She risked standing. They had to move faster. Rogan slowly got to his feet behind her. Trying not to breathe, she motioned to the door and pantomimed running. He nodded and, without needing her signal, started ahead of her. She raced behind him, impressed with his speed and agility as he dodged cameras and leaped wires. Seconds later, they were outside, gulping in lungfuls of hopefully clean air.

Rogan leaned on her, laughing a little. "That was close."

She shrugged. It bothered her how close. She tapped into the coms to let the others know they were out, then couldn't help glaring at Rogan. "If you'd listened to me in the first place, it wouldn't have been a problem."

Rogan sobered immediately. "You needed help making sure everyone was out."

"That's my *job*, Rogan." Fear and relief had given way to anger. "I'm getting paid to protect you. All of you," she clarified hastily. "If protecting you means I get hurt, that's what I've agreed to do. And you violate that by ignoring my orders and putting *yourself* in harm's way."

He looked stricken, as though he hadn't thought about it that way before. "I don't want you to die for me, Kennedy."

His tone said a hell of a lot more than his words did, and her throat tightened. It was more than the knee-jerk reaction protectees often had when they realized their protectors would willingly put themselves in the line of fire for a stranger. She didn't know how to respond to that.

"Let's circle around to the others." She turned away from him and refocused on their surroundings. Goddammit, anyone could have approached while they were arguing. What was wrong with her?

She put her hand on her gun as they approached the corner of the building. The bright sun reflected off windows and random pieces of metal, nearly blinding eyes still adjusted to the dimness of the warehouse.

"We're not leaving it here, Kennedy."

She gritted her teeth and held up her hand. To his credit, he went silent. She peered around the corner. The side of the building was blank, the pavement empty. They walked down toward the back, where they could hear voices. Before they reached the group, Stacy came around the corner, slumping with relief when she saw them. Before anyone could speak, M.J. loomed behind her, panic evident in every line of his body.

"Oh, thank God!" He rushed up to Rogan and grabbed his shoulders. "You're all right!"

"A little woozy, but I guess that will clear."

"You must go to the hospital. I can drive you." He whirled to Kennedy. "You too. If he's woozy, so are you."

She shook her head. She was getting a headache, but now that they were out and away from the gas, they should all be fine. "Still think this was our fathers?" she asked him quietly, and his face paled.

"Definitely not. They might have been capitalizing on it, but they didn't plan it."

She agreed and led them to the rear of the building. Fierce little Zip, implacable Clay, and the other two bodyguards had gathered everyone into a group against the wall and stood in a semicircle around them, weapons ready.

Jonathan strode over to Kennedy, who asked, "Anyone else affected?"

"No. Just you two. Rick and Wolf are inspecting the grate now. The gas is gone from this side."

She followed him to the back and looked up, watching Rick hold on to Wolf, who had his legs wrapped around the ladder and his whole upper body parallel to the ground as he stretched sideways to the grate. A few minutes later, they climbed down to the group.

"We need to talk about this in private," Rick murmured to her.

She told M.J. to dismiss everyone for the day and stood by while he soothed fear and anger and one or two threats to leave the production. Then she drew M.J. and her team to the back alley again. She would have preferred to go to the boardinghouse, but couldn't leave the studio unsecured. There hadn't been time to arm the perimeter alarm. She turned, opened her mouth and glowered at Rogan, who stood next to M.J. She started to scold him for not going home as she'd ordered, but stopped, wearied by the effort before she started. He was determined to be part of this, fine, she'd let him be part of it.

"What did you find?" she asked Wolf.

"Looks like someone tampered with the entry alarm and attached a container to the exhaust fan. I couldn't get it out without tools. But the fan had been reversed to blow in rather than out. And obviously, they didn't know about the gas sensors. That foiled their whole plan."

"Probably." She was glad she'd pushed Steve to install them. If El Jahar—or whoever they were—had done this earlier, the old security team might not have detected it in time to get out.

"We're going to have to notify the police and get the fire department here to help us ventilate the building," she began, but M.J. shook his head vigorously enough to loosen his mop of curls. "What?"

"The red tape will delay us forever, Kennedy. We're

already going to be behind schedule. They won't find anything you can't find."

"You were willing to take Rogan to the hospital. That would have delayed things. And they'd notify the police."

"We would have said it was an accident on the set. They're common enough that no one would have questioned it."

"Oh, no? What kind of gas would you have said it was? And what would you report to the investigating officer when they came to see why you had such a gas?"

"Uh, Kennedy?"

"What?" She turned back to Wolf. He scratched his hand up and down the back of his head and lifted a shoulder, as if afraid of her reaction to what he was going to say:

"I don't think ventilation is necessary."

That took the edge off her intensity. "What? Why?"

"The gas was a high concentrate, low volume."

"What does that mean?" But she knew what it meant. High concentrate to trigger the alarm. Low volume so that when the fan blew it into the large spaces of the warehouse, it would dissipate to harmless levels.

What the *hell* was going on?

"But we have headaches," Rogan protested. "We were lightheaded in there."

He was right, but Kennedy knew why. She'd nearly hyperventilated trying not to inhale the gas, and no doubt he'd done the same.

M.J. was going to get his wish again. No police. If anyone had been hurt, she would call them without hesitation. But this act seemed completely dedicated to one of two things—showing them how vulnerable they still were, or pushing them to go public.

"I know a ventilation specialist," she said. "I'll see how quickly he can come over and test the building, confirm what Wolf found."

"What do you want us to do?" Stacy asked. Kennedy told her to assign some to take the cast home and a few to stay to secure the building when it was cleared. The rest could go back to the boardinghouse to rest. M.J. and Rogan refused to leave and huddled at the corner of the building, conferring about God knew what. Kennedy kept her eye on them while she started making phone calls.

Luck was with her. She reached her contact at the HVAC company and he'd just finished a similar job. He had the equipment to ventilate the building, should it be necessary, and would have one of his guys take a sample to the lab for immediate testing.

The rest of the afternoon was tedium. Bob and his men arrived, suited up, and started working. Hours later, she had confirmation of a clean building, and lab results.

"Fentanyl," Bob told her as he stripped off his contamination suit.

"The anesthetic?" she asked.

"Yep. Just like your guy said, high concentrate, low volume."

"So they weren't trying to kill anyone," she half stated, half asked, studying the lab report that had been faxed.

"Not likely. Someone with respiratory or other health problems could have been in danger, if they were close enough to the source. Not that anyone would be. The catwalks don't go close enough to that vent." He paused, and Kennedy looked up, knowing what was coming next. "What's going on here?"

"You know I can't tell you," she said mildly, walking toward his truck so he would have to follow. "Send me your bill. And make sure to charge for the rush job."

"Eh." He waved a hand at her. "If we hadn't come here, we'd have had a free afternoon. It's as much my benefit as yours. You be careful, Sunshine, you hear?"

"Yeah. Thanks." She smiled and waved as he pulled away.

"Sunshine?"

She sighed. She'd known Rogan was behind her, but had hoped he hadn't heard. She turned and walked back toward the building. "It's a long story. No one else calls me that," she lied, glaring at him. "Right?"

He laughed and held up his hands. "Right."

"Why are you still here?"

"M.J. Since we lost most of the day, he wants to work tonight so we can still wrap."

"Great. Too bad he didn't clear it with me, first." She strode over to the director and snatched the cell phone from the ear it had been plastered to all afternoon. "You can't go back in until tomorrow," she told him.

"But they said it's clean," he protested, grabbing for the phone. She held it out of his reach, ignoring the snickers of those around them.

"But it's not secure. You're not working tonight, so just go home and be glad this wasn't serious, or that would have *really* thrown things off."

He grumbled, but took the phone back and started making more calls. Kennedy gave instructions to secure the building, then started back around to the front door to do her own sweep. But Rogan followed.

"What do you *want*?" she barked, hoping to put him off and also trying to keep her mind on what she'd find inside, and off emotional truths clamoring to be recognized. Emotional truths she had no time for. She had stationed someone at each entrance while the building was checked by the HVAC guys, but she wouldn't rule out the possibility of someone slipping in. She did not need her attention split right now.

He didn't respond. She stopped in front of the door and faced him. "You need to go home now."

"I will. I just…" He huffed a laugh and ran his fingers through his hair. Kennedy had noticed he had to stop himself from doing that during the shoot, but since they were done for the day, he didn't bother. She wished he would. The rumpled look made him sexier.

He propped his hands on his hips, shook his head slightly and turned his gaze from the front of the building to meet her eyes, dead on. "It sounds ridiculous, but I want you to have dinner with me. Since we have an early night."

Those truths clamored louder. She shook her head.

"Why not?"

"I don't have time, Rogan." She started to turn away. He put his hand on her shoulder, and the warmth immediately seeped into her skin, all but shouting at her to accept how good it felt. She tried to look annoyed.

"You don't have time to eat?" he asked.

Kennedy blew out a breath. "I don't have time for dating games."

"Good, neither do I."

"Then what's this?"

He let go of her and lifted his shoulders, hands out. "Flirtation?"

Something intangible *popped*, and the tension faded. She smiled. "I expected you to say foreplay."

"Yeah, well, that would have been predictable." He smiled back and she hated it. It lit his whole face and contained more sincerity than most of Hollywood put together. His eyes crinkled at the corners and his mouth framed white, mostly even teeth with sensuous lips that Kennedy had to admit she was curious about.

No, not *had to*. Couldn't. Rogan was refusing to stay in his box, the one labeled "protectee." By chipping away at her definitions, he was exposing feelings she didn't want. He already meant more to her than her other protectees, and that set her up for a hundred new kinds of trouble.

So she shoved, harder than she wanted to. "If you want me to say I'm flattered, Rogan, I am. Thanks. But I'm not interested. Now go home."

He didn't flinch. Didn't even move. But his eyes changed. They turned knowing, just shy of smug, before he nodded.

"Okay." He tossed her a salute that somehow avoided being mocking, and headed off. Kennedy watched until he was safely in the car with M.J. and Clay, who was driving them home, then went into the building and found Rick.

"You're not going to like this," he warned, looking apprehensive, as if she would blame him for whatever he'd found. He led her to the makeup room. "I spotted it right away. It stood out, but I didn't touch it." He pointed. A bright pink piece of paper lay folded in the middle of a cleared counter. The counter Rogan had tossed makeup paraphernalia onto just before they got out of the building. Somehow, since then, the counter had been cleared so the paper would be seen quickly.

"Did you go closer?"

"No, this is about it. I saw your name on the paper and came to find you."

Kennedy looked at the floor around her, studied the chair in front of the counter, and looked up to the ceiling. She couldn't detect any trip wires or sensors. Unlike the wardrobe room, this room held only a few rolling, drawered carts. The items from the counter had been placed neatly on top of one. The walls to either side were clear and empty. No electronic eyes or laser beams ready to trigger a trap or weapon.

She motioned Rick back to the doorway. "Find the others and make sure no one left it there." People had re-signed in stranger ways, and though she had trained them better, it was possible one of her people had dropped it. But as soon as she picked up the paper, holding it by the corners, she knew that wasn't the case. The note had been printed in a common font and contained no salutation or closure. The contents gave her no indication of the author. But they did tell her one important thing.

The threat against *Coming of Day* was not about terrorism, gambling debts, drugs or getting in with "the wrong people." It definitely wasn't about matchmaking. It wasn't even about M.J. or the actors.

It was about her.

SIX

TERROR AND RAGE followed each other in waves. Somehow she was responsible for endangering all these people.

No.

Panic screamed at her to get them out, get them all out, but instinct and logic told her the danger was not imminent. She had her phone out and half of Max's number dialed before she flipped it shut. Knee-jerk reactions were almost always wrong. She had to figure this out before she talked to anyone.

It's all my fault. She couldn't wrap her mind around it, but the words were there in black and pink.

COMING OF DAY *means to portray the effects of domestic terrorism on regular people. But how can they know? No one connected to the picture has experienced that kind of loss.*

No one but you. Right, Kennedy Smyth? Your beloved brother Justin was killed trying to minister to such victims. His memory motivates you.

Yet still you've failed in your mission...over and over and over.

SHE *HAD* FAILED. She could admit that. The deaths of those under her protection or in her employ haunted her dreams, and their names were burned permanently into her brain.

But failure wasn't an ending, and it didn't cripple her. She could still do her job She opened her phone and speed-dialed the office. Mark answered on the first ring.

"I need research done on every person who's died while under SmythShield's protection or employ." She rattled off the names. "I need to know families, partners, anyone affected by their deaths. Status checks on all of them. Criminal records, forays into the big vices, failed jobs. Find out where they are and what they're doing now."

"What's going on, Kennedy?"

She told him about the gas, but not the contents of the note, though she knew he could put two and two together. "Send the data to me as you get it, at least today and tomorrow. I'll update you on our schedule. The gas put shooting behind." She hesitated, staring at the blank expanse of countertop where the note had been found. It stank of inside connection, and while that was still more likely to be a crew member…"Send the reports on Wolf too," she told Mark. The idea made her sick to her stomach, but she couldn't hide from the possibility anymore.

She hung up before Mark could question her further, then stood, unmoving, her fist tight around the phone. Facts and assumptions sped through her mind. It made sense now, that none of the incidents so far had been harmful. The first ones were designed to get her here. The last, to taunt. She'd been played, skillfully, and she'd allowed it to put everyone she cared about in danger. If this guy wanted her to pay, to suffer, there were all manner of targets around her. SmythShield's crew. *Coming of Day*'s cast. M.J.

Rogan St. James.

Not Rogan St. James. He was on the list, being under her protection, but if her enemy thought he meant more to her than the body she was guarding, he'd be moved to the top of it. That wasn't going to happen.

She forced him out of her mind and went out to do her job. She retrieved the canister that had emitted the gas and the remains of the detonation cap that had opened the nozzle. After Jefferson switched the fan's direction, she re-armed the alarm herself and tested the whole system to make sure nothing else had been tampered with. Then, and only then, did she walk back to the boarding-house and her room to think this problem out.

She locked her door and headed for the shower. She always thought well under the hot spray. She allowed herself a minute of blankness first. Time to isolate emotion, which she didn't have the luxury of indulging.

Her instinctive response to the letter's revelation was to run. Get away from the production. Her association was causing the danger, not protecting against it. But she knew it wasn't that simple. Whoever the culprit was, he or she had targeted the film before Max had hired her. That told her they were smart and operating coldly. They must have known her connection to M.J. and Max, and hoped Max would do the expected thing and hire her. That was a gamble, she thought, watching pearly sham-poo pool in her palm. What if Max had stuck with his usual security firm? El Jahar would have come up with something else, probably. It didn't matter, because Max *had* hired her, and she *had* taken the job, despite the fact that it wasn't her usual choice.

That was telling. They could have set something up out of country, or developed a fake relief group that needed protection. Maybe they didn't have the resources to do so. More likely, they thought a hit to her company at home, and to people she knew, would do more damage to her reputation and her psyche. It was probably seren-dipitous that M.J.'s career was in such trouble, though even that could have been planned. Some people plotted revenge for years before trying to get it.

Psychology played a big role here. They were playing threat games, trying to make her fear the loss of people she cared about. Most of her team was on this job now. An old family friend was on site and at risk.

Maximum threat. Maximum fear.

She shut off the water and squeezed her hair, then pushed the shower curtain aside and started toweling off.

What she wasn't sure of was how far the perpetrators were willing to go. Were they just trying to scare her? Or was everything they'd done leading up to something far more serious? Today was the turning point, for sure, but turning to what?

The implications shook her. The people who worked for her were loyal, hard workers who trusted her. She might be leading them right to their deaths.

And the movie people…Most had known there was some danger involved when they signed on. The ones committed before the threats escalated had been given a chance to opt out. And the ones most at risk, the high-profile actors and M.J.'s top staff, had been fully briefed. But none of that was any consolation to Kennedy. They may have known there was a risk, but she doubted any of them gave it much concern. They trusted SmythShield to protect them.

Which brought her right back to instinctive response. Her enemy had alerted her to the true target. They would know she'd want to withdraw from the production. Instead of removing the threat, it might heighten it. As soon as she pulled her people out, El Jahar would make their biggest attack, harming and maybe even killing the unprotected. That would serve their objective—her failure—just as well.

She finished pulling on flannel pajama bottoms and a snug cotton top and unrolled a yoga mat. She deliberately closed off her mind, focusing on the moves, on the stretch and release of muscle groups, on her breathing, deep and steady. She kept it slow, easy, going for soothing movement rather than working up a sweat. Tonight, she needed serenity. Tomorrow she would need strength.

Half an hour later, feeling loose and calm, she rolled up the mat and went to brush her teeth. She kept her mind blank while she did so, maintaining it while she did one final room check. Everyone was fine. For now.

Once she was back in her room, though, the click of the door acted like an on switch, starting a mental slide show experience told her she would be unable to halt. She crawled into bed and switched off the light so she could pretend to hide in the darkness.

The first SmythShield casualty had been Tobias Furchon, a veteran of several wars and former member of the Secret Service. He had been her mentor and helped her start the company, using some of his own contacts to get their first clients. He'd caught a ricochet in Africa and hadn't lived long enough to see home again.

Kennedy had told his family, what there was of it. His elderly mother, despite her grief, had been expecting such an end for thirty years and had offered more comfort than she'd accepted. His brother had never understood Toby's choices but supported his right to make them. A nephew who had worshipped his uncle his entire life had been devastated yet proud.

None of the other deaths had had the poignancy and deep-seated grief and guilt Toby's death generated. But Kennedy had felt them all, like spears, and internalized them as lessons for the future. Wyatt, well trained, had done everything right and fallen victim to the unpredictable. Thomas had been a model client, fully cooperative and protected from everything but the scorpion sharing his room. Nicholas, her tenth client's representative, had sacrificed himself to save a family caught between rebels and the shelter of the factory he was building. It didn't matter that Kennedy couldn't have prevented any of those deaths. They were still failures.

Others, like Marika and Owen, had been the opposite. Kennedy faulted herself for their training being incomplete or her judgment for considering them ready before they were. Their deaths had been senseless, preventable, and the hardest ones she'd had to confess to.

But not the hardest she'd faced. No, that honor went to Justin, her brother. Memories of anyone she lost always brought her back to him. From childhood, to manhood, to sainthood, her father would say. She had no blind spots where Justin was concerned. She knew her worship had been unfair. It set him on a pedestal no one could live on. He'd crashed, over and over, but never diminished in her eyes.

Kennedy rolled and tried to bury the images by burying her face in her pillow. Justin was her earliest memory—her devoted, fourteen-years-older brother, bending to show her a flower in the field behind their home. Unlike most of her childhood memories, this one was vivid. She could feel the glow of the sun and the reflected heat of the ground, scented with earth and grass and perfumed with flowers. The light gleamed off Justin's golden brown hair, sparkled in his dark green eyes. And when he'd kissed the top of her head, she'd looked up adoringly, clutching his hand and the flower, knowing life was perfect.

Counterpoint to her first memory of him was her last. The sunshine was just as bright, but instead of flowers and grass the air had reeked of sewage and trash. Instead of gleaming on his hair, the light had been absorbed by dark bloodstains on his lab coat. His eyes had no sparkle. They had no life.

Kennedy hadn't been there when he was killed, but over the years her mind had filled in the blanks with scenes from so many similar places.

Dreams took over memory at some point. Nothing that made sense. First, she was in the hellhole where Justin had died. Then she was sitting down to tea with her therapist. They talked about the shooting…no, the gas. About how Justin had died…about how she and Rogan were growing closer. Then she was on the roof, and a helicopter was pouring yellow smoke over her. The smoke didn't affect her, but she couldn't see, and suddenly knives rained down around her. She tried to dodge, like in a video game, but there were too many. The falling daggers turned into green computer code— the screensaver on her computer. She couldn't turn it off. Mark stood over her, telling her she always had been an idiot with technology.

That pissed her off. She shoved her chair back and stood, but it wasn't Mark laughing at her. It was someone she didn't know. He was pointing. "Failed," he said. "You failed. Over and over."

"Over and over."

She spun at the new voices, recognizing Toby's, Marika's, Nicholas's. None of the faces were familiar, but the voices were. "Over and over." They kept repeating the phrase. She felt her heart accelerate, felt her breathing start to labor. Fear was taking over. *Fight*, she told herself, and started to, but no one would come close enough to be kicked or hit. The room was full of yellow smoke again. Her head was getting fuzzy. Her vision was fading. She had to…had to…

"Wake up."

She jerked upright, instantly awake but disoriented. She was never disoriented when she woke. She looked to the right and saw Stacy in the doorway, holding a cup of coffee.

Kennedy relaxed, rubbing a hand over her face in an attempt to rid her brain of the dream images. Her legs were tangled in the covers. "What time is it?" she asked, extricating herself and accepting the coffee.

"Five-thirty. I thought you'd want to get a jump on everyone. Though M.J. probably has the actors in makeup already."

"Of course." She set the coffee down and stretched tense, sore muscles. Her night had eradicated the effects of the yoga. "Who's with them?"

"I sent Shenk and Clay to pick them all up half an hour ago."

Kennedy raised her eyebrows. Stacy had handled most of the transportation, because it gave her prolonged contact with the cast. "Why not you?"

The agent blushed. "Um, well…I didn't—"

As far as Kennedy had been able to tell, Stacy's celebrity crush had only made her more eager to guard bodies, and she hadn't cared which of the three she covered. But things had changed. Kennedy wasn't ready to share the full nature of that change yet, but she couldn't let it go.

"Things will be different on location," she told Stacy. "You'll need a more outward focus. Your surroundings will be more important than your principle."

Stacy scowled. "I know that."

"So why didn't you go pick them up like you usually do?"

The scowl held for about ten seconds before she sighed. "Because I'm afraid you think I'm going fangirl."

"If you have to worry about my perception—"

"Yeah, yeah, then it's probably right. I know. I'm loving working with movie stars a little too much." Her shoulders sagged. "Are you going to send me home?"

"Are you going to do your job?"

She brightened a little. "Of course."

"Then no, I need you." She stood and groaned, actually pressing a hand to the small of her back like an old woman.

"You okay?" Stacy looked concerned.

"Didn't sleep well. But I'm fine. Just need a shower."

"Okay. I'll meet you over at the studio, then." She hesitated, then said softly, "Thanks. And sorry."

Kennedy waved her off and after the door closed, dropped to the floor with another groan. On her back, she reached her arms overhead and lengthened her body, pointing her toes, then flexing her feet and stretching calves and hamstrings. Then she pulled up one leg at a time, clenching her teeth against the pain. Working through it was the only way to eliminate it.

She wondered, as she sped through her morning routine, what would happen when she revealed the letter.

Would M.J. fire her? Would Max? How many of her team would leave? None, she thought, knowing the level of loyalty she'd gained from them. Well, Wolf might resign, if he wasn't involved. Jefferson might suggest she step back and let someone else take over command of the job, especially since he'd be the top candidate. But they'd all stay and they'd all obey whatever orders she gave.

Even if it took them to their deaths.

No. She couldn't allow defeatist thoughts. There was no room for them here. She needed concrete plans, methods of defense. Of offense.

She needed help.

So the first thing she did when she arrived at the studio was corral M.J. in the maelstrom he called an office and put his father on speakerphone.

"We have a problem." She handed M.J. the letter. He glanced over it, looked up in shock, then looked back at the letter.

"What's going on?" Max barked.

"Sorry, Dad." M.J. read the letter to him. For a few seconds, no one moved.

Then M.J. set the letter on top of a computer keyboard balanced on a stack of books on Islamic terrorism. "How did they find out you were on the job?"

For a moment all Kennedy could do was look at him. Could that be it? That she wasn't the target at all but someone had learned of her involvement since she started? Was she really that egotistical, that blind?

She lifted the letter and reread it. No, she hadn't jumped six degrees of conclusions.

"M.J., I don't think it's as simple as that," Max finally said, his booming voice subdued. "Kennedy?"

"I wish it were." She sighed heavily. "My initial interpretation of this letter is that our so-called terrorist protestors are after me. That they lured me here to fail in retaliation for a past failure."

"What kind of failure?" M.J. scowled, looking frightened. "I didn't know you'd failed."

She had to laugh. "Thanks for the ego boost. Of course I've failed. I'm human. And my company works in very dangerous situations. It's impossible to never fail." She moved closer to the speakerphone.

"I already have my assistant checking out the families of everyone who has ever died while working for me or under my protection," she explained.

M.J. straightened. "Have there been a lot?"

Kennedy ignored him. "I hope to have a preliminary report tonight, and a better handle on who our suspect might be."

"I'm serious. How many people is it?" His voice was starting to sound shrill. "Do they want us dead? Really?" He lurched to his feet and tried to pace between piles of film canisters and boxes of samples. "I didn't think they really wanted to kill us. I thought it was scare tactics, trying to shut us down. That they might *hurt* someone to convince us they meant business, but to *kill* us?"

Kennedy stood and put herself in his way. "M.J."

He grabbed fistfuls of his hair and held his breath for a three-count before blowing it out hard. "Okay, I'm okay. Sorry. Unproductive." He sat on his chair.

Kennedy leaned against the counter, her arms folded. "What do you want to do about this?" she asked. They didn't respond right away.

"Dad, do you think we should—" M.J. broke off and glanced at her out the corner of his eye. "I mean, should Kennedy…"

"I don't think I should quit," she said. "Though that was my first reaction. Remove the target to eliminate collateral damage. But that could be exactly what they want. If I withdraw my team, they'll consider you vulnerable and attack. That would leave me humiliated, guilty and—" she motioned to the bright pink paper, "—a failure."

"But will it be more tempting to have you fail *on* the job?" Max asked.

"Maybe." She considered her next words carefully. "The safest thing might be to halt production."

Their reactions were predictable. M.J.'s shouted "No way!" blocked the first half of Max's thunderous roar, but didn't dilute what they did hear.

"…not spend millions of dollars of my own money to have everything go down the drain because of some bully. You bet your ass we're not halting production, and you're not pulling off this project. I don't care *who* suggests it!"

His panting was the only sound for a moment, as M.J. and Kennedy tried not to smile at each other. Kennedy didn't point out that Max himself had just suggested that the biggest risk might be for her to stay on the job.

"Then we need a plan," she said finally, when it was clear he had concluded his rant.

"Well, you're the planner, so plan. Text me when it's ready." A click signaled his disconnection.

"All right." M.J. slapped his hands onto his knees. "Where do we start?"

She pulled a chair up next to his and helped him clear some space on the table. "First, I suppose we need to know if everyone still wants to proceed. Anyone trying to leave the film?"

M.J. shook his head. "Bailey's the most freaked, but it's always hard to tell how much is real and how much is drama. A couple of the extras are gone, but we don't need them anyway. Two crew members left. Everyone else is determined to stick it out."

Kennedy nodded, impressed. M.J. apparently commanded his own loyalty. "What's the new production schedule?"

"We need two more days to complete here. Then we're off to Denver."

"I think we'll be safe enough en route," Kennedy mused, jotting notes on a legal pad propped on her knee, pausing to consult the schedule M.J. had pulled out. "We should separate the production and divide my team— I have four more people meeting us there—so there's protection for each group. El Jahar will want a concentrated target for maximum impact."

"Okay. That works fine. I'm going ahead with the cinematographer and art director, etcetera etcetera, to scout locations." He looked up. "Will you be with us?"

She shook her head slowly. "I'd rather be on the advance team, but I think it's risky to have me guard someone I share a past with. They might decide your death would hurt me most."

He paled, but nodded. "Yes, okay. You stay away from me."

She smiled. "I'll come when the cast does. Jonathan and Rick can come with you and scout security while you scout camera angles. You ship the equipment?"

"Some of it. We have to use local crew, so they'll have their own."

"Pay for extra security and insurance. Jefferson

will oversee the process. I'll divide the rest of the team among the personnel when the time comes."

"What about finding this guy—or woman?" M.J. asked, tapping his pen rapidly on the table. Kennedy stifled the desire to grab the pen from his hand.

"I'm working on it. Mark is already digging. We'll figure out who's most likely, and start searching." She smiled reassuringly. "If we're lucky, we'll find him and neutralize him before we go to Denver."

"Sounds great!" But he didn't look convinced. "Kennedy. Umm…" He glanced down. "I hate to sound… Well, this is none of my business, but it kind of is."

"Spit it out."

He shook his head. "You said I might be a target because of our relationship."

"Yeah. Maybe. Depends on who it is, and how much they know."

"And I'd be a bigger target if there was something more than childhood friendship between us?"

"M.J.—"

He held up his hands. "I'm not sayin'. I just wonder… if maybe you should focus the team on Rogan."

Shit. Kennedy stacked her papers and tapped them on the table's surface. If M.J. thought there was something there, anyone might. "Why? Bailey's just as—"

"Come on, Kennedy." He tossed his pen down. "Don't play verbal games with me. I know your thing is to avoid involvement, but if there's one thing I've learned about human nature, it's that we can't control how we feel about people. So just answer the question. Does Rogan need additional protection?"

She didn't hesitate. "No. Adding bodies would call more attention to him. Unwarranted attention," she added. She stood. "There's nothing between Rogan and me."

"If you say so." He looked unhappy. "Any other time, I'd push you two together. But now…"

"Exactly."

She left the office and the first person she laid eyes on was Rogan. She carefully smiled like she would at anyone on the set, hiding the leap of her heart she couldn't control, but not betraying herself by jerking her gaze away from him. He smiled carefully back, and she hoped she was the only one who saw the difference between his facial expression and his eyes.

Dammit.

She gathered her team for a very quick meeting in the cafeteria.

"The schedule has changed, of course, after yesterday's events," she started, and relayed the plan to her staff. There were a few questions about logistics and suggestions for matchups. Stacy volunteered to check out flight schedules and coordinate personnel.

"Good idea. Get a crew list from the AD. We'll need to have Mark do checks on the local people. Extras will be local, too, but it will be even shorter notice than we had here. Nothing we can do about that."

When it appeared they had all plans in place, the team stirred as if to leave the room. Kennedy stopped them.

"We have to get out there, I know," she said. She wasn't comfortable having just Rick and Jonathan on duty outside, listening on their earpieces. She was less comfortable telling them what she was about to tell. But it would be worse not to warn them, not to give them choices.

"I need your attention just a moment longer." She

waited until they were all looking at her. "Rick found a note in here after the HVAC crew ventilated the building. Besides the fact that someone on the other side accessed the building right under our noses, the note was very revealing."

She paused and sipped her coffee, then forced herself to make eye contact with as many agents as possible. "It turns out El Jahar's target is not M.J. or the production. It's not because of the script or the crass commercialism of the movie industry.

"It's because of me."

No one moved. There was no exclamation of shock or fear or even outrage. No uneasiness or accusation showed in anyone's posture or expression. But then, they were professionals. Not showing it didn't mean not feeling it.

Kennedy swallowed past a thickening in her throat. "We've decided it's safest to continue the job. But I refuse to make that decision for you as individuals. Any requests to be taken off this assignment will be granted, no questions asked, no harm done. You'll remain an employee of SmythShield if you wish, and be reassigned. Or you can resign with a strong recommendation."

Still, no one moved.

Anxiety sank its claws in Kennedy's chest. "You're all used to putting yourselves in the line of fire, but you've never been intended targets. Now, you might be." This time, Zip and Jonathan exchanged glances. His was almost a smirk, and when Zip turned back to face Kennedy, there was a light of anticipation in her eyes.

Finally, Jefferson folded his arms and firmed his stance. "I don't think anyone's going anywhere, Kennedy. We chose this profession because we love the challenge. We work for you because you care. So do we." His stern expression lightened into one of wicked glee. "Let them come."

Kennedy swallowed again, finding it harder and harder to do each time one of her team nodded at Jefferson's statement.

"The offer stands. No deadline." She had to clear the raspiness from her throat. "Thank you."

They filed from the room, offering arm punches and shoulder pats of encouragement and fealty. She accepted them stoically, but inside she was a roiling mass of emotion.

She'd always had a responsibility to these people. It had now increased a thousandfold.

SEVEN

"WHAT DO YOU mean, leave her alone?" Rogan glowered at M.J., who looked uncharacteristically firm. "I'm not stalking her, M.J."

"I know. I just think you're going to distract her, and we need her full attention on the job more than ever."

"That's crap. Relationships aren't interference." It pissed him off, the excuses people made not to get involved with each other. He looked up and scanned the warehouse, trying to spot Kennedy.

M.J. tugged him behind a monitor. "You've got to stop that." His voice was low, urgent.

"Stop what?"

"That." He actually grabbed Rogan's ear and jerked his head back around. "Stop looking for her all the time. Looking *at* her. It's…gonna get people talking."

Rogan snorted. "Since when has on-set gossip been an issue for you?"

"She won't like it. Leave her alone."

Something was off here. M.J. never cared what went on off screen. He didn't even ask his actors to be discreet if they were cheating on each other. All he cared about was his film. Rogan studied the director, wondering if he wanted Kennedy for himself. On paper, it was a good match. But the very idea made Rogan want to snarl.

"That's not for you to say, it's for her."

M.J. shrugged. "I'm just trying to spare you. She won't get involved with you. And I know how you get."

"How I—" He cut himself off. It wouldn't do any good to protest "how he got." M.J. had seen it in the way he researched a role, and had probably witnessed his few intense love affairs too. Arguing would do nothing but waste time, so he simply said, "Kennedy's a professional. She won't let her feelings affect her job. Neither will I."

"That's not the point." He looked miserable and pulled Rogan even closer. "It could be dangerous."

"To who?" Exasperated, he let his voice climb. "I'm not going—"

"Shh." M.J. winced and admitted, "To you."

"What do you mean?"

M.J. looked sorry he'd said it. "Well, you know. You got that letter and everything."

"What does that have to do with Kennedy?"

"You're a target." He scratched his head, propped his other hand on his hip. "She's got to watch out for you. If you distract her, you'll—"

"Enough." Rogan held up a hand. "You're talking in circles. And it doesn't matter." He eased his breath out to keep himself from sighing and looking even more lovesick than M.J. seemed to think he already was. "I'm not going to get involved with her."

"Why not?"

Since he asked with curiosity, not challenge, Rogan answered. "She's too much like my mother."

"Yes!" M.J. jabbed a finger at him. "You're right. She's *worse* than your mother. Definitely. You've got it. Just stay away." He swept his hand through the air. "Not what you're looking for. Not at all."

But as he walked away, whistling, Rogan finally

found Kennedy on the catwalk above them. And marveled that the more he told himself he didn't want her, the more he did.

KENNEDY TIRELESSLY PROWLED the building, consulting with all of her people, helping Jefferson check stunt cables and harnesses right before use, standing on the roof and surveying the skies and the ground, swinging over the side of the wall to double-check the vent. Most of her actions were redundant and unnecessary. El Jahar was creative. They were unlikely to attack in the same place more than once. But she was afraid they knew she knew that and would do the unexpected. So she double- triple- and quadruple-checked.

And everywhere she went, she found herself tagging Rogan.

If she went near the set, she made sure she knew he was in his chair, or on the sofa, or being harnessed to the wire. Mealtimes, she pulled craft services duty, guarding the rear door and positioning herself so she could see Rogan, at least out of the corner of her eye. Once she tagged him, she didn't need to watch him while she moved around the warehouse. He was like a pivot point around which she circled.

It was making her crazy.

Every time they made eye contact, she had to think about whether to hold it or look away. If they tried too hard not to look like there was something going on, everyone would think something was going on. Ditto if they allowed their gazes to linger. She wanted to look at him the way she looked at everyone else, but she couldn't *tell* how she looked at everyone else. Her tension grew so strong she knew everyone around her could feel it.

The tension and extra effort began taking its toll. She knew at two o'clock that if she didn't sit and eat she would collapse by the end of the day.

The cafeteria was nearly deserted. Kennedy nodded at a grip reading the newspaper and eating a piece of cake, then continued into the dimly lit kitchen. She prepared a plate of leftovers and stuck it in the microwave. She closed her eyes, dipping her head and rubbing neck muscles locked by tension.

"Let me," murmured a voice in the dimness, and firm hands touched the tendons between neck and shoulders. But that was as far as he got. Kennedy grabbed his left wrist, spun and wrenched his arm up behind him.

Rogan's yell echoed in the high-ceilinged room. Kennedy released him immediately. Her heart leapt. *We're alone!* it exulted. *Shut up*, her brain countered. She scowled.

"Sorry." She circled him and accepted his glare while he rubbed his shoulder. "You should know better than to sneak up on a security officer in the dark."

"Yeah, well, maybe you should have turned a light on. Then you'd have seen me."

He had to have been in the room when she entered because otherwise she'd have seen the flare of light when he opened the door behind her. And he was right—she should have realized he was there.

"What are you doing here in the dark?" she asked.

"Drinking water. What are you doing here in the dark?"

She motioned to the microwave.

Rogan shook out his arm and leaned against the butcher-block table in the middle of the room. "Right. So, shall we start over? You look tense." He motioned for her to turn. When she hesitated, he took her by the shoulders and spun her. "Don't worry, I'm not going to strangle you. I wouldn't dare try, now," he added.

"I am sorry," Kennedy said more sincerely, partly because she'd been inattentive and overreacted. Partly because his hands felt fantastic.

His thumb dug into a tight knot and a moan escaped her. Her eyes flew open and she tensed again, shocked by how easily he'd eliminated her guard. But she didn't move, reveling in the sensation of melting muscles as his long fingers stroked up her neck, then into her shoulders and down her spine.

She didn't want him to stop. She stood swaying with her eyes closed and imagined turning into his arms. Sliding her fingers into the hair at the nape of his neck. Pulling his mouth down to hers.

The microwave beeped and she eased away. His hands lingered, stroking across her shoulders and down her back as she moved out of reach. An ache followed, the knowledge that this couldn't be.

But then it was. Rogan caught her hand just before she got out of his reach, and tugged her slowly back toward him. His eyes met hers, and she realized just how good an actor he'd been for the last few days. Where before she saw mild interest, now she saw intensity. Need.

Purpose.

He put his hand on the back of her head and dipped down for the kiss she'd daydreamed. His mouth was hot, his lips firm under softness, moving gently on hers in introduction. He didn't push, didn't use his tongue, didn't pull her closer, and it made her crave.

He released her mouth but held her in place, his eyes questioning. He didn't give her a chance to say anything.

After glancing quickly at the unmoving door, he stepped toward her and put his other hand on her waist. Their bodies met now, and the kiss wasn't saying "hello, nice to meet you," anymore. Now it said, "wow, you taste good, I think I'll nibble on you all day." Desire took an interest in the hard chest touching hers, in the hips that angled away from her and the intriguing thigh that nudged between her legs.

It lasted long enough to convey intent and give her a hint of the pleasure in store, should she allow this to continue. Then he stepped back, looked at her without a smile—without any hint, in fact, that he'd enjoyed what had just happened   and left.

The microwave beeped a reminder behind her. She ignored it, staring at the slightly swinging door. What the hell? He couldn't kiss her like that and then walk away.

The microwave beeped again. Cursing under her breath, she hit the button, yanked her plate out, and slammed the microwave door closed with her elbow. Forks rattled when she snatched one from the tray on the counter, and she exited into the bright cafeteria, blinking rapidly.

The grip was gone. So was Rogan. Not that she'd expected him to be out there. She'd shoot off her little toe before admitting how much she'd wanted him to be.

Sighing, she sat at a table near the corner, facing both entrances. If he came near her again, she'd set him straight.

What had prompted him to kiss her? Maybe after all the soulful gazes they'd carefully not shared, a kiss was expected by normal people. She grimaced. This just wasn't her. She didn't moon over men. She didn't attract them, either. This was the worst possible time, and Rogan had to know that. So why? She licked her lips, tasting him.

M.J. swept into the cafeteria, eyed Kennedy sideways and gave her a tiny wave before zipping through the kitchen door. His air of avoidance answered all her questions. Angry, she jumped to her feet and caught M.J. coming out with a bottle of water in his hand. He jumped, looked over her shoulder and went for innocence.

"Hey, Kennedy. How's it going?"

"Did you talk to Rogan?"

"You mean, just now?" He pointed at the door with the hand holding the bottle. The other hand worried the light meter cord hanging from his hip. "Sure, I told him to go to wardrobe for the next scene. It's a new one, just written yesterday—"

"Not just now, M.J. Recently." She watched his eyes flick to his left. "You did. You told him not to get involved with me. Did you tell him why?"

She was glad he didn't try to deny it. He scratched the back of his head, looking sheepish.

"I kinda talked to him, yeah. I didn't tell him why he might be in danger, but I…I, well, told him to stay away from you. For a lot of reasons. He has no clue about the letter."

Kennedy bit back the urge to scream. "Do you know what you've done?"

His brows drew together. "I'm trying to save both your asses!"

"Yeah, well, you did the opposite. You made me forbidden fruit. Dammit." She turned away from him, spinning, trying to think of a way to salvage the situation. M.J. escaped, but she let him go. The idiot. Whatever he'd said, it had been Rogan-the-Bull's red cape. His mild interest in her had flared because he perceived her to be unattainable.

Kennedy sighed and retrieved her half-eaten meal, scraping it into the trash and cleaning her dishes. There was nothing else to do but keep her distance and hope Rogan got the message. If he didn't, she'd have to tell him the whole truth and hope he didn't freak out, putting the rest of the cast and crew into panic. That would hamstring her and probably lead to the termination of production, at least temporarily.

She really hoped he did.

The next day was half shooting, half preparing to move on to location. There were fewer cast and crew members on site than usual, which made SmythShield's job much easier. Kennedy spent much of her time approving plans for departure. She'd also taken some time to dig a little deeper in some of the areas of Wolf's background reports, and had found nothing.

Rogan didn't approach her during the few hours he was on site, which set her off balance yet again. Kennedy tried to keep her eye on him without anyone knowing she was doing it, a feat she didn't think she could manage to pull off. She hailed Stacy during a break between takes. She didn't want to tempt the "fangirl," but Stacy's extra role as Kennedy's assistant gave her more freedom than the other bodyguards.

"Stick extra close to him," she told her. "But don't be obvious about it." *Leave it at that*, she warned silently. She could see Stacy evaluating the request, remembering that Kennedy was the direct target, calculating Rogan's value as collateral and coming to the right conclusion.

She barely kept a grin off her face. Kennedy scowled, but Stacy just nodded and went back to her post.

M.J. and his senior staff flew out to Denver the following morning. Kennedy held her breath until Rick, part of the advance team, reported them securely in their hotel.

One group safe, two to go.

M.J.'s assistants texted Kennedy daily updates of his progress and scheduling changes, which she assimilated and incorporated into her own plans. Half of her people went to Denver with the crew and minor cast, again with no hiccups.

Which left the high-profile cast. Kennedy had decided she, Clay and Wolf would accompany the six most well-known cast members. Wolf had given her no reason to believe he was the inside guy, and she couldn't afford to take him off duty, so she was keeping him close. The remaining staff would accompany the other cast on a different commercial flight that landed around the same time. The exposure made her nervous, but M.J. had refused to consider asking for the money for a private jet, since they were already over budget. She made sure the airline listed them all with assumed names and arranged for a studio representative to meet them at the airport because those assumed names wouldn't survive airport security.

In the meantime, Kennedy spent hours poring over the reports Mark provided each day.

Toby Furchon's mother had died less than a year after Toby. Her mentor's brother was still firmly entrenched in his middle-America lifestyle, going to his accounting firm every day, taking his wife on annual vacations and blogging about his son, whose exploits on a search-

and-rescue team regularly made the local paper. Kennedy asked Mark to dig deeper on the nephew. He'd been the one most affected by his uncle's death, and chose a profession similar to Toby's. One that would give him information and access to the things he would need for revenge.

Thomas Helwig had been a workaholic CEO with no family, no significant other when he died, and no friends that they could tell, either outside of his company or in it. Wyatt Clark, one of her veteran agents, had been similar, though he had had parents who had since died and a sister who regularly attempted to climb Mount Everest. She had been on such an excursion for the last several weeks.

Mark sent her copies of letters from Nicholas Leghart's file. When he died saving his employee's family, Kennedy had gone to his wife's house to notify her. He'd had two children too young to remember him much now, but old enough to understand Daddy wasn't coming home. Kennedy still remembered the wide, pain-filled eyes that had inspired the last tears she'd ever cried. The letters she remembered well. Nick's wife had written them a month after his death, and on the first and second anniversaries. She'd expressed gratitude for Kennedy's compassion and kept her up to date on their progress. In the last letter, she'd announced her wedding. Mark had checked, and she was still married to the high school teacher and they had another child, now two years old.

The last two on the list were still incomplete when Kennedy left for Denver. Mark had managed to find some information on Marika Sudhoff's fiancé, but only enough to red-flag him. Kennedy remembered Vinnie Todesto as a swaggering, macho jerk. He'd hovered and complained about any assignment Marika was given. He'd also threatened SmythShield with legal action that never came to pass. Since then, he'd had one misdemeanor drug charge and made a lot of money before the stock market crash. He remained near the top of the list.

Then there was sweet Owen Houseal. He'd had great potential as an agent because of his ability to be dismissed as a wallflower. Kennedy blamed herself for moving him in too quickly. He'd spent less time than normal under supervision, and had gotten nervous when alone on a bodyguard assignment. The person he'd been guarding escaped without a scratch, but Owen had been shot. The non-fatal wound got infected, and he died two weeks later.

His family hadn't been very understanding.

And there were a lot of them. Mark had tracked down several of his eight siblings, most of whom had families and respectable lives. Two were currently in jail. But they couldn't be ruled out, because who knew what kind of network they had?

She sighed and filed the info with her notes, sent additional instructions to Mark, and completed her preparations for the trip to Denver.

EVERYTHING WENT SMOOTHLY through the airport and onto the plane. Kennedy did a walk-through of the plane, then took the last open seat in first class. On the aisle next to Rogan.

Of course.

She hesitated the barest instant before sitting. She'd been trying to keep distance between them, but if anyone was watching, it would become obvious. Especially if she started rearranging people. So she sat, suppressing a sigh.

Rogan grinned at her. "How lucky am I?"

"As lucky as can be, I guess." She watched the flight attendants and copilot greet boarding passengers and proceed with pre-flight preparations. Everything seemed normal, including the stares and whispers of a few passengers. Rogan and Bailey were both in grunge disguise, but fans recognized them under the ball caps and messy hair.

Rogan and Kennedy both requested Coke from the attendant, and Kennedy popped a piece of chewing gum into her mouth.

"Pressure bother you?"

"Not if I'm chewing gum."

Rogan didn't say anything else until they had taken off. Then he half turned in his seat and waited until she looked at him.

"Do you have a problem with me?" he asked, his expression serious.

"I don't have a problem with you, no." Her heart started to pound, and she wished he'd just accept that and be quiet. But of course, he didn't.

"Then why are you avoiding me?"

She swept a glance over the section. They were in the last row of first class. There was a galley between them and the coach section, and the attendants were making their way down the main aisle. The seats in front of them were empty.

Kennedy leaned closer to Rogan, ignoring the flare in his eyes. She kept her voice almost too low to hear. "What are you after, Rogan?"

He responded with his own low tones. "I'm not after anything, Kennedy. I like you."

Momentarily distracted from what she'd been about to say, she asked, "Why?" She wasn't used to being pursued this hard. Men usually saw her, hit on her, discovered she could outfight them, and moved on. Rogan had seen her abilities from the beginning but the more he saw, the more he seemed to like. She didn't get it.

"What happened to you to make you so suspicious?" he asked, his voice low.

"Nothing happened." He just watched her. "Nothing specific. I wasn't traumatized by a relationship or something." Still he watched her. "Just general experience. People have agendas, motivation. They don't do something without awareness of what's in it for them."

"I buy that, it's the nature of your job. You're more exposed to those kinds of people and less of the other kind."

"There is no other kind. Even good people still have to watch out for themselves."

"You don't think people ever do something for someone just to do it? Because it's the right thing? Because it's needed?"

His words brought Justin to mind. He'd been different. He and most of his colleagues. At least, that's how she remembered them. But she'd been a kid then. She did jobs with people like him now, and either the world had changed or she had. They wanted to help the people they were there to help, she didn't doubt that, but they also wanted credentials and experience and publicity because they wanted better, high-paying jobs or a unique line to use to get women. So, "No, I don't think most of them do."

Rogan's lips curled the slightest bit. "Most. You're not a total loss."

Kennedy snorted. Like she cared what he thought. She ignored the bit of her that raised its hand and said, "I do, I do!" Not only hadn't Rogan answered her question about why he wanted to get to know her, he'd successfully derailed her intent to end his pursuit. Before she could drag him back on track, he turned away, slipped his headphones over his head and picked up his script.

Shrugging, Kennedy pulled notes from her carry-on bag and started re-reading, adjusting the plans. After half an hour in the air, she got up and surveyed the cabin, glad to see her people were awake and alert and not too engrossed in magazines or music.

Then she moved back into coach to get the lay of the land. Things were calm here too. One bored child argued with his mother about wanting to go to the bathroom for the fifth time in half an hour. A baby fretted near the back, but not too loudly. No one seemed to have been drinking or have any problems with service. Kennedy returned to her seat and tried to relax.

But something was bothering her. She didn't claim to have any psychic ability, but she did have a strong subconscious that often picked up on anticipatory vibes. Something was going to happen, but she didn't know what.

Rogan put his script away twenty minutes before they were due to land and turned his attention back to Kennedy.

"So, what do you do when you're not protecting?" He rolled his head on the headrest to face her, his hands folded across his abdomen.

It was innocuous enough conversation, so she answered. "I don't have much down time. I read. Industry journals. International politics. That kind of stuff."

"You work out, of course."

"Of course." Someone in coach had just raised his voice. There were a couple of shouts. Kennedy couldn't see anything through the curtain. She looked at Clay and Wolf, who shook their heads. They couldn't see, either.

"What's wrong?" Rogan murmured, leaning toward her.

"Stay here," she told him. The first class flight attendant looked worried when Kennedy stood, and started toward her.

"It's okay," Kennedy said, and for some reason the attendant didn't disagree. She followed her to the curtain but stood there watching as Kennedy crossed back into coach.

The disturbance was in the far corner of the plane. One of the attendants seemed to be trying to do something to or for one of the passengers, who was shoving her hands away and periodically yelling something incomprehensible.

"What's going on?" Kennedy asked an attendant close to her, who fluttered ineffectually in the middle of the aisle. The woman immediately lost her agitation and tried to urge Kennedy back to her seat with firm, businesslike movements.

"I'm in security. I thought I could help." Her senses were on full alert. The man fighting the other attendant seemed injured or ill, not looking to start a fight, but he could be a diversion. She glanced over her shoulder. The first class attendant was still standing at the curtain, and Kennedy could see Wolf's back over the petite woman's shoulder.

The woman in front of her, young enough to be new at her job, relaxed a little. "He's just…acting oddly." The man in the seat was middle-aged, balding and portly. His eyes were rolling in his head but without the laxity that demonstrated lack of control. The gurgles in his throat were too rhythmic. He kept slapping at the attendant, who spoke in an urgent, faux-soothing voice, trying to determine what was wrong.

The ding signaling the fasten seatbelt sign sounded through the cabin. The staff started to direct people back to their seats. One hovered over Kennedy, who eased her aside and bent close to the man's ear, both to be heard over the captain's announcement and to avoid letting others hear. "You miscalculated, friend. We've still got at least fifteen minutes in the air, and you're losing your spontaneity. I suggest you have a miraculous recovery, because pretending to be sick is not getting you off this plane ahead of the crowd."

She eased back a little and raised her eyebrows at his suddenly focused eyes and still hands. He must have recognized the resolve in her expression, because he cleared his throat and nodded. "Um, thanks. Thanks, ah, for your help." He bent to retrieve his suit coat from the floor.

"Anytime." Kennedy straightened, picked out the supervising attendant and murmured what had happened. She savored the woman's fury for a moment before she returned to her seat.

"Nice job," Wolf murmured as she passed. There was no way he had heard her, but the coach section was noticeably calmer. She nodded and signaled him back to duty.

Not that he had left it. He'd improved a lot since his training. Kennedy tilted her head back, closed her eyes and took a deep breath. They were all working hard yet not crossing the fine line between tension and edginess. Except maybe for her. Her lid was close to popping off.

Warm, gentle fingers slid along the back of her neck and began working the tight muscles there. She allowed herself a half smile as the tension began to ebb. "You're making a habit of this."

"I just can't stand to see you in pain," he said softly, pressing the spots he'd identified in the kitchen as her trigger points.

She managed to stifle the moan this time and laughed instead. "I'm not in pain, Rogan."

"You're just so used to it you don't notice."

"Maybe."

The plane descended and began a slow bank. The chime sounded again, and the pilot made the brief landing announcement. Attendants bustled around helping passengers secure items and making sure seatbelts were fastened.

"So, what was going on back there?" Rogan asked.

"Some guy trying to pull a fast one. Get off the plane quicker by pretending he was sick."

"Slick."

"Failed."

"Have you seen anyone do that before?" he asked. "Or have *you* done it before?"

She didn't dignify his teasing with a response. She was back in complete protection mode, watching during landing for anything suspicious outside the windows or inside the plane. The odds of spotting anything outside were ridiculously low, of course, but they were impossible if she didn't bother to look.

"Okay, here's the deal," she said to Rogan. "I'm getting off the plane first. You guys will buddy up once you're in the jetway and let Wolf and Clay bracket you. Your baggage is being taken care of by a service. We'll head straight out to a rented van. My people will be along the travel route. If I give an order, you'll obey it without question and without hesitation."

He was shaking his head, but not negatively. "We went over it before we left."

She just looked at him.

"Yes, Mother. I've got it."

And he did. He and the others fell into place and followed Kennedy off the plane, stopping halfway down the jetway when she signaled, moving in unison after she'd scouted the waiting area. She spotted all her people exactly where they were supposed to be, and no one bothered them, not even fans. They got outside and into the van faster than she'd estimated, and Rick drove them toward the bed and breakfast where they would be staying.

Rogan had managed to get a seat next to Kennedy again. "Well." He grinned. "How does it feel to be irrelevant?"

"Terrifying."

An instant later, her fears were justified.

EIGHT

FOR MOST PEOPLE, everything would have happened extremely fast. But for Kennedy, there was no confusion. She knew the loud double bang was a tire blowing out and automatically braced for the swerving and Rick's curses as he struggled to control the van. She wished she had predicted the hard-sided carry-on that slid across the van's floor and smashed into her knee, though.

A moment later Rick had some control, though he still fought the pull of the blown tire. Kennedy looked behind them, but couldn't see any vehicles that appeared to be following them or surging close to attack.

The passengers were all conscious and no one seemed critically injured, so she unfastened her seatbelt and left Clay and Wolf to take care of them. She limped to the front and slid into the seat behind Rick.

"Sniper?" she asked, scanning the territory, though the likelihood of spotting any kind of hiding place was slim.

"Probably," he responded through gritted teeth. "What do you want me to do?"

Whoever had shot out their tire would be expecting the van to crash or stop close by. Then the second part of the plan, whatever it was, would kick in. But Rick was an exceptional driver and he'd managed to keep going for nearly a mile already. He wouldn't be able to keep it up much longer.

Luckily, traffic on the highway was sparse. There was an exit coming up, but El Jahar could have a backup plan. Or they could be smarter than she gave them credit for and expect her to keep going.

"Can you bypass the exit?" She noted the strain in Rick's forearms and the whiteness of his hands.

"A little way. Not too much farther."

"Okay. Hold out as long as you can."

She checked behind them again, but there were no cars nearby. The ones that had been close were now giving them a wide berth. She leaned to the side to look up through her window, then across the aisle to the far windows, making sure the helicopter wasn't heading for them. The skies were empty.

The next exit was coming up. She told Rick to get off and head for the nearest public facility. The ramp merged onto a commercial strip, and she pointed out a truck stop just ahead on the right. Rick aimed for it and barely managed to steer the vehicle into the big, open parking lot.

"Stay put and stay low," Kennedy told everyone, again making sure they hadn't been followed before she got out of the van.

She closed the sliding door behind her and looked around. Nothing. Not even ominous stillness signaling the coming of an attack.

Sometimes she wished her career came with a soundtrack.

With her hand on her weapon at the small of her back, she circled the van. None of the three people in the parking lot paid them any attention. A trucker was crossing from his truck to the diner. A scruffy-looking guy got into a rusty Volkswagen and drove toward the exit. A middle-aged woman spoke sharply to someone Kennedy couldn't see inside her minivan.

If this were the movies, her attention would be on the scruffy guy and they'd be strafed by machine-gun fire from the minivan as it suddenly appeared from off screen.

But this was real life, and Kennedy could plainly see the woman pull a child from the back seat and stalk toward the entrance with a neon sign proclaiming "clean restrooms."

She bent to examine the right front tire. It was shredded and the rim crumpled, but the starting point was at the front of the wheel and she could see the slice in the center of the tire. She pulled at it and found the bullet embedded in the metal rim.

She jumped up and yanked open the van door. "Where are the others?"

As she'd expected, Rick had called their backup. "They had trouble getting out of the airport. A minor accident. They're a few miles down the road. On their way."

"Let's get inside. I don't know where our sniper is." She kept an eye out while Rick circled around to open the side door and let everyone out.

"Kennedy."

Rick had frozen next to the open window of the passenger door. Kennedy followed his gaze to the driver's headrest. Her breath caught in her chest.

Double bang. She'd thought she heard the gunshot and the tire, but that hadn't been it. There'd been something else. Another bullet fired. A bullet that had ended up three inches from Rick's head.

"Let's move," she said quietly. She opened the back

of the van and told the others to grab their stuff and climb out. "Go inside," she instructed. "Find a spot away from windows and doors but don't trap yourselves." She charged Clay and Wolf with two of the actors each. "Bailey and Rogan, you're with me." She paused to check with Rick. "You okay?"

"Yeah." He was pale, a fine sheen of moisture on his forehead. He nodded, his shoulders squaring as he shook it off. "I'm fine."

"Okay."

They headed off, making Kennedy extremely nervous with their tempting line across the parking lot. But no one tried to run them down and she saw no signs of bullets.

The three groups split up once inside. Wolf took his two to the restaurant, Clay toward the lounge.

"How about the bathrooms?" Bailey pointed.

"Too dangerous. Only one exit." Kennedy turned and headed for the convenience store.

Rogan looked skeptical. "Lots of windows in here."

"We're not staying." She led them to the corner with the door to the back room and looked inside. Because the store served a truck stop, it had a slightly larger storeroom than the usual gas-station store. It was crowded with boxes, loose cleaning items, and grimy things she didn't want to look at too closely. But it had no windows and an unlocked rear exit.

"Stay here," she told them, pushing them back against the shelves so they were hidden by a stack of boxes. No one coming in either door would see them right away. "Don't come out."

She went back into the store. No one had noticed them going in, and no one noticed her now. Nice security.

Her phone had no signal, so she risked getting closer to the entrance of the store until she got two bars. She couldn't see her team yet, but there were now several cars moving around the lot, both coming and going, and she couldn't separate potential foe from innocent bystander. She called Wolf first.

"We're at a table in the back, near the kitchen. I scouted our escape route, but so far there's no one suspicious."

"Buzz me if that changes."

Clay had the same report from the laundry room.

Rick was outside watching the van. "No one's approached it," he told her, "not even the cop who circled the lot a minute ago."

"He apparently didn't notice how much it was listing," she said wryly.

"He didn't really come close enough. It was my unorthodox parking job I thought would attract him."

"Well, we're in a public place. El Jahar might have aborted."

"Maybe."

Kennedy didn't think they had, either. She couldn't assume so, anyway.

"Buzz me when the team arrives."

"You got it."

She retreated to the storeroom. Rogan and Bailey hadn't moved. "Good dogs," she almost said, amusing herself, but she didn't think they'd appreciate it. Especially not Bailey, who had the glazed look of someone scared too long.

"See anything?" Rogan asked quietly. He still didn't move. Not to look for himself, or in a misguided need to protect her. When she'd first headed down the path that led to SmythShield, the few men she'd gotten involved with had trouble trusting her to protect herself. They hadn't been able to battle their instincts, even if they respected her abilities. That Rogan did, even after their kiss and the way he'd pursued her, was impressive.

"There's no sign of anyone," she reassured them. Forcing herself to focus, to think of Rogan only as a client, she positioned herself near the back door and checked her cell signal. She had one bar of four, but it was enough to be buzzed.

"Someone shot out the tire?" Rogan asked after a moment.

"Appears that way." She cracked the back door and looked out on the empty space at the side of the building. The wall was empty, no dumpsters or anything to hide behind. She twisted her neck and looked out to the other side, where the truck pumps were visible. Two trucks were getting gas, and one more approached. She bent and absently rubbed her throbbing knee where the suitcase had gotten her.

The phone vibrated in her hand and she checked the display. Rick. She flipped open the phone and lifted it to her ear.

"Everyone's here. They're circling the lot. No one sees anything."

"Three cars?"

"Two sedans and a minivan."

"Okay. Have the van pull up to the restaurant for Wolf, then pick you up. One car can get Clay from the laundry room, but I don't know where that exit comes out. Have them call him. The third car can come around to the side to get us from the store."

A few minutes later a white Toyota Avalon pulled up.

She recognized her people, but waited to make sure no one followed them.

She didn't wait long enough. She had stepped outside and opened the rear car door for Rogan and Bailey when she heard squealing tires behind her.

She didn't waste time looking before she shoved the two in front of the Avalon and down to the pavement, falling over them and trying to shield both. Terror had a one-second hold on her breath and heart, then training made her go cold, alert.

Instead of gunfire, she heard a strange hissing. She shifted closer to the direction of the sound, putting her leather-covered back between the weapon and Rogan. There was a spattering sound, like water droplets, and the squeal of tires again. She raised her head a little and caught a glimpse of a red pickup truck as it careened around a tractor-trailer.

There was silence all around, now, except for Bailey's gasping, airy cries.

"It's okay," Kennedy told her, helping her up. "We're okay." A glance showed her she wasn't lying. No one appeared to be hurt, not even from her tackle.

"What *was* that?" Bailey screeched, staring at the car.

There had been someone in the back of the pickup. He'd been wearing a stocking mask and a black, long-sleeved shirt. Kennedy couldn't even tell his race, only that he was built like a man and squirting what looked like an exterminator's canister. Her nostrils flared against a pungent, unfamiliar odor. Bailey screeched, and pain flared in Kennedy's toe. She looked down and saw a hole in her shoe.

"Fuck!" She couldn't help the expletive as she quickly

toed off her boot and yanked off her sock, using the top of it to mop her toe. "Did it get you?"

"What?" Dave, their driver and part of Rick's general security staff, stood next to the car, staring wide-eyed. "What is it?"

"Holy shit," Rogan breathed. "Look at that." He pointed at the side of the car, where holes had appeared. Little ones, the size of water droplets.

Or acid droplets.

"Did it get anyone?" she demanded. They all exchanged looks, examined themselves, shook their heads. Moved away from the pockmarks in the pavement, the streaks on the car.

"Are you okay?" Rogan stepped toward her. She held up a hand and motioned him back with the others.

"I'm fine." Her toe stung, but it had barely touched her. Luckily. Frighteningly. The spray pattern indicated they hadn't used much, and most of the damage was to the car and the pavement. But if she hadn't pushed them around the car, if they'd been standing in the middle of the alley, would the damage have been worse?

It terrified her that this attack had come at Rogan. Had it been intentional?

She sensed Rogan's intensity behind her but didn't turn. She couldn't let him or anyone else see the fear in her eyes.

Jefferson was calming Bailey, who was inhaling deeply and waving her hands, but Dave sported a grin.

"Guess what I got?" he asked.

Kennedy hated games. She preferred agents who just told her what was going on, but they all seemed to enjoy dragging out their precious revelations. Now, though,

Dave's glee was just what she needed. She rolled her eyes when she said the expected, "What?"

He held out his camera phone, showing her the lit screen with the last photo he'd taken.

"The license number."

Forgiving him, she smiled back. "Nice work."

THE REST OF the group had been picked up without mishap and soon they were at Hart's Haven, the large B&B the production had rented. They'd chosen it not only for its size and central location, but for the state-of-the-art alarm system that included personal remote controls to allow individual, tracked access.

Kennedy made sure everyone was situated, the building's alarm system in place and armed, and then summoned Jefferson, Rick and Stacy to her room.

"How the hell did they know where we were?" she asked, pacing. "We could have been anywhere on the premises."

"Are you sure they wanted you personally?" Stacy asked. "I mean, they could have just driven around looking for some of us and happened on you."

Kennedy wished she was being egotistical, but it was too much of a coincidence. "What about the phones?" she asked Jefferson. "Could they have tapped the signal?"

He shook his head. "Our phones use top-level encryption. These are better than government issue. They're part of the reason you charge so much," he joked.

She again considered a leak. She'd made sure no one on the film knew any more of the plans than they needed to for their own transport. One of the cast that flew out today could have orchestrated the attack, but she'd already ruled out their involvement in the earlier incidents. None of them could have been involved in every single one. It was logistically impossible. Which brought her back to someone in SmythShield.

"I think Stacy's right." Rick absently shuffled a deck of playing cards with the B&B's logo. "I saw the truck circling the lot. I thought it was looking for a space. I lost sight of it before the rest of us got picked up. It was coincidence that they found you."

"I don't believe in coincidence." She sat on the couch and gave in. "I'm sending Wolf home."

"What?" came from Stacy and Jefferson, but Rick nodded and stacked the cards neatly on the coffee table.

"You think he has something to do with this?" Jefferson's shock turned pensive and he rubbed a hand across his mouth.

Kennedy lifted a shoulder. "He's the newest member of the team, and some things definitely point to inside help. We can't work properly if we're always looking over our shoulders. So it's a precaution."

"No, I guess it's smart," Jefferson acknowledged. "But once you suspect one of us, what's to stop you from suspecting all of us?"

Kennedy gave him a hard look. "You got reason for me to suspect anyone?"

He shook his head and cut Rick's cards before changing the subject. "What's the word on the cast? Anyone decide to leave?"

She let it go, because it was still unthinkable to her that any of the people she'd worked with for so many years could be doing any of this. "No, not even Bailey." Which had surprised Kennedy. The young woman had proceeded from panic to fluttery drama to anger, and swore no one was pushing her away from the role that was going to win her a fucking Oscar. Her words.

"We're going to be out in the open on this shoot," Kennedy said. "Crowd control will be impossible."

Rick picked up the cards again and riffled them. "That's going to have to be where we start, though. Unless you can convince M.J. to close down."

She shook her head. It would never happen. But she had to do something to get rid of the metallic burn of anxiety in the back of her throat, and the image of Rogan hitting the ground, skin melting under a spray of acid. Closing her eyes, she imagined throwing a giant blanket made of cotton batting high in the air, watching it float down over M.J., Rogan and the actors, the crew, her team, smirking in triumph as the top layer turned to Teflon and her enemy, on the other side of the blanket, was thwarted.

She opened her eyes and found everyone staring at her. She shrugged. "Whatever works, you do." She reached for the schedule M.J. had given her and studied it, glad they couldn't see into her fanciful mind.

"Okay, we take it one day at a time. Work in stages. Rick, you've seen the sites. You give me your preliminary plan for each site. I'll approve it and pass it to Jefferson, who will set up what we need while we plan for the next site. We'll maintain the same assignments whenever possible for consistency, but avoid being predictable. Bodyguards should make sure a different route is taken to the site each day. And it's even more vital that every piece of equipment is checked right before use."

"I'll need more help with that," Jefferson said quietly, knowing his request would put additional strain on them. "I've got Gina now, but I could use another pair of eyes."

"You'll get them." She didn't know how, but she would work it out.

They worked late into the night, trying to foresee the unforeseeable. She never would have anticipated an acid attack. There was no doubt in her mind that El Jahar would strive to be ever more creative, which meant SmythShield not only had to watch out for the expected dangers, they had to ferret out the ones that seemed ridiculous or impossible.

And she had to somehow accept the possibility of a traitor on her team, without letting it completely take over.

At two, she sent everyone to their rooms to sleep. She ignored her own order, though, and roamed the B&B, checking the alarm system, making sure the night shift was alert and wishing this was all over.

Feeling trapped, she disarmed the alarm at the side door and exited, then rearmed it using her remote and stepped out into the garden. The crisp, clear air immediately replenished her energy and took the edge off her tension. The sky sparkled with stars, visible even in the outskirts of the city.

This time, she knew Rogan was there. He lounged against the low brick wall in a corner of the garden, studying the sky. She moved toward him, too tired to be angry.

"You shouldn't be out here."

"Neither should you," he countered quietly, not looking at her.

Kennedy picked out the few constellations she knew. "How did you get out?"

He slid his hand into his pocket and pulled out a remote just like hers.

"Why did M.J. give you his remote?" She tried to keep her tone even.

Rogan's lips twitched. "I wanted to come outside."

"You shouldn't come out here alone. Especially when…"

"Kennedy." He finally straightened and turned to look at her. "Do you seriously think someone is going to attack us in the garden on this beautiful night only hours after spraying us with acid?"

She didn't know how he could joke about it, even mildly. His career—his life—could have been over. "I can't keep you safe if you won't follow safety precautions."

"But do you think they'll be attacking tonight?"

She felt her jaw tightening. "No," she finally admitted. "I think if they wanted to attack twice in one day, they'd have done it when our guard was down, when we first got here. It would be foolish to wait until our defenses are in place." She held up a finger before he could speak. "However. I don't pretend to be able to read minds. They could have a plant on the crew. They got into the warehouse. They could be watching right now, waiting for unexpected vulnerability."

He nodded. "They could. But they're not impulsive. Everything they've done so far has been well planned."

That was true, and why she hadn't hustled him inside. But his insight surprised her. "You don't think like a movie star," she said.

He laughed. "You mean because I *do* think?"

"Something like that."

"Actors are amateur psychologists. It's our job to understand people, so we can become someone else." The smile slid off his face. "Today was the hardest thing I've ever faced in my life."

Regret speared her. "I'm sorry. We weren't prepared—"

"Fuck that, Kennedy, I'm not scolding you."

She stared at him. He'd never used that word in front of her before. He turned fully toward her and gripped her shoulders with tense fingers. "Do you have any idea what it was like to lie on that ground with you on top of me and know that if someone wanted me dead, *you* would be?"

Her mouth tugged upward. "It wasn't the first time."

"No, but it sure as hell was different from the first time." He released her and dragged both hands through already-rumpled hair. "I barely know you. I kissed you once, and it was a helluva kiss, and I want more, but—" He shook his head. "I shouldn't be this afraid."

The more agitated he got, the calmer Kennedy felt. Every word he uttered gave her a stronger reason to terminate this thing. It wouldn't be hard to convince him an affair with her wasn't worth it.

And if she ached with disappointment? So what? He'd be safer, and her job would be easier to do.

"Have you considered leaving the production?" she asked, and his answer didn't surprise her.

"Not for an instant. M.J. needs this film, and I'm no coward, even if I am scared."

So he was a good friend, too, she thought, adding that to the pro side of the stupid list she couldn't help making. "What are you afraid of?"

He sighed, folded his arms over his chest and leaned back on the wall. "Everything. I'm afraid of getting hurt or killed." She must have looked stricken, because he added, "It's not that I think your team can't protect me."

"It's normal to be afraid, Rogan. You're in danger, even if we don't know how much. Being afraid is helpful. It keeps us from doing foolish things."

"I wasn't afraid before you came. I'm afraid of what getting hurt or killed would do to us." This time, he didn't let her speak at all. "I'm afraid that you'll get killed instead of me, and that's much worse. But what I'm really afraid of is why that frightens me."

Confused, Kennedy frowned. "Trust me, I try hard not to let myself *or* my clients get killed."

He growled a little, a sound of frustration. "That's not what I mean." He dropped his arms. "This is."

Kennedy could have stopped him. She knew a hundred ways to block an approach and put a man on the ground. She even had time to think of all the reasons why she *should* stop him. Instead, she let him touch her. Glide his hands down her back, align her to his body and catch her mouth with his.

Kennedy wrestled with herself. His mouth felt and tasted so good, and it had been so incredibly long since she'd touched a man this way. Been touched. Her body tingled under his hands, and desire sparked deep inside.

But what if someone saw them? What if they did have a leak on the crew or in the cast—or, yes, on her team— and they were looking out the window right now?

Steeling her resolve, she pressed her mouth hard against his, then pulled back sharply, like ripping off a bandage. He let her go, but the involuntary sound of protest in his throat nearly dragged her back.

"We can't, Rogan."

"Why not?" He huffed a breath. "Especially now,

when neither of us knows what's going to happen to-morrow."

A laugh snorted out of her. "Are you really giving me the 'have sex with me now, for tomorrow we may die' line?"

He smiled reluctantly. "Of course not. I just—" His cell phone rang. He slapped at it without looking.

"Why do you even want to?" She stuck her hands on her hips. "What is it about me?"

"Damned if I know." All the frustration seemed to drain out of him. "You're the opposite of the kind of woman I was looking for."

"Ah." She turned away and leaned next to him, not wanting him to see the effect his words had. She wasn't used to having hurt feelings, and she didn't like it.

"I've been watching you, and you're more confident and decisive than any woman I've ever known. There's no pretense to you. No concern that what you're doing is the wrong thing, or that you're not doing it right."

"And you don't like those traits in a woman?"

"I do. I didn't know that until I found them." He lifted one hand from where it was braced on the rough wall and gently twined his fingers through hers. "The problem is, they go along with other traits I don't like. You're driven. You have one purpose, and you're not going to let anything else fit into your life and derail that purpose, or alter it even an inch."

He had her pegged. She liked it, and hated it. It was all the reason he needed to stop pursuing her.

He lifted her hand to his lips. "Any chance that I'm wrong? Or that your future is more fluid than I can see?"

She shook her head slowly. "No, you've got it pretty much right."

"Why?"

Tugging her fingers from his, she moved away. "It doesn't matter why. It just is, and you're a smart man. You do your job, I'll do mine, and we'll have mutual respect between us." She glanced up at the sky one more time, amazed at the number of stars she could see this close to the city. She blinked when those stars blurred, and she cursed herself for becoming something different at the worst possible time.

NINE

"Wait."

Kennedy stopped halfway to the door and looked over her shoulder.

"Don't go in yet."

She sighed. "Rogan, don't you know what time it is? I really, really need my sleep."

"Sorry." He leaned forward and snagged her hand. "I'm just not ready to go in, and I know you won't let me stay out here alone."

Kennedy yawned, but allowed him to tug her back against the wall. "If someone dies tomorrow because I'm exhausted, it's all your fault."

"You won't sleep anyway, you're too wired. So relax a little, then just fall into bed."

"How do you do that? Just—state a fact about a person and be right." She raised a hand and closed her eyes. "I know, I know, you watch people."

He'd been doing more than watch her. He'd studied her. Absorbed her habits and how things affected her, even more than he'd realized.

They stood in silence for a minute, as if purging their conversation from the air. Rogan marveled at how still she could be and yet totally aware. There was no foot wiggling or finger tapping, and her head turned at a door closing inside the house or a bug chirping in the garden behind them. No wonder she was wired.

"Why do you do this?" he murmured. "I can't imagine a job more stressful."

She shrugged. "Someone's got to."

He didn't believe her. "Someone's got to remove garbage from the curb and unclog sewage pipes. You're not doing that."

One eye popped open and studied him, then the other. "People don't usually expect a real answer when they ask me that question. They want to hear greater good and using-my-skills kind of stuff. Patriotism and morality."

"I'm sure that's part of it."

"Nope." She cocked her head. "Actually, that's not part of it at all. I let the people I protect focus on that stuff. My job is just keeping them alive."

"But why? M.J. says your father is a lawyer and your mother was a stay-at-home mom before she died. What got you into this?"

"My brother."

Rogan froze. He couldn't believe she'd answered him. Anticipation rose, like when he was about to nail a scene, or watching a colleague about to nail theirs.

But when she continued, she spoke without emotion. She told him about her brother's altruism and his death, and her insane drive to become the best at what she did, to learn and excel. And about how, when she got frustrated at not being able to control who she worked for where, she started her own company with the money she'd gotten from her brother's insurance policy.

She didn't have to spell it out. Her story reinforced the list of traits he didn't like, and that she had no time or intention to make changes in her life. He pushed away his annoyance.

"You got successful pretty young."

"I was lucky. I had good people helping me. If Toby—my mentor—hadn't had contacts that helped get us our first few jobs, I'd have been dead in the water. And one hundred percent of my success is based on hiring good people."

Rogan didn't agree. She might hire good people, but her success was based on her determination and skill, on her ability to inspire others.

He couldn't help asking, "Where does Kennedy come in? Not the owner of SmythShield, but the woman?"

"I told you—"

"I know, you do nothing but work. That's pathetic."

"I'm not the only one in the world who does."

"They're all pathetic."

She laughed.

"What about getting married? Having a family?"

"My brother had no family."

He had a feeling that said it all. This went far beyond a driven woman needing balance. She was denying herself the things her brother had been denied, and that wasn't pathetic, that was sad.

"Why did you choose acting?" she asked, and he knew she was trying to keep it light.

"What's your guess?"

She didn't look at him. Her eyes had closed again. "Well, I don't think it's because you were trying to be anything but who you are."

"That's true. I had a good childhood, dedicated parents, lots of love. I was happy."

"So it wasn't escapism."

"Not for me. I just always loved watching TV and movies and then acting them out myself. Expanding on the stories. I had friends who *did* need the escape, and

I liked how the best actors could transport them away from their sad or painful worlds. But mostly, it was fun. Is fun."

Kennedy smiled. "That's the bottom line, isn't it? You got lucky and succeeded at a career that you enjoy."

He didn't like that. It was true, but made him sound shallow. "There's value in what I do." Damn it, now he sounded defensive.

"I know there is." She opened her eyes. "I wasn't criticizing. You told me to guess."

"Yeah, okay. My life has been pretty charmed. I haven't suffered much. And I picked a career I liked, instead of one that's selfless and sacrificing." He knew as he said it that he was letting his frustration and fatigue get the better of him.

"Like me." Her tone was flat, but not hurt. As if trying to show he didn't have the power to hurt her feelings. He kicked himself for saying something stupid, and yet her non-reaction made him angry, and that made him more stupid.

"I didn't say that. But yeah, like you, if you don't like what you do, if you only do it because of your brother."

"Okay, that's enough for tonight." Kennedy shoved away from the wall. "Let's go."

Rogan didn't argue. He'd made a right mess of the conversation, and by now there was no way to make it better. He followed Kennedy inside, said goodnight at his door, and felt her watching him as he locked himself inside.

His phone rang again, and he dug it out of his pocket to check the display. It had to be someone in California, and very few people he knew would call him so late. He didn't recognize the number, but had a feeling he knew who it was, so he answered it.

"Hey, Rogue-man."

"Hey, Charlie." He checked his watch. It was still late. "What's wrong?"

"I just wanted to give you my new cell number. Holly had the last one in her name and they canceled it on me."

"Okay, I got it. I'll store it when I hang up. Listen, it's going on three o'clock. I've got to go to bed."

"Shit, man, you're not filming tomorrow. You'd already be in bed if you were." Rogan heard him swallow. "I, uh, got the papers today."

Sighing, Rogan dropped onto his bed and prepared to listen—again—to Charlie's marital laments. Maybe signing the papers would give him closure or something.

But Charlie said, "Nope. Never mind."

"What?"

"I'm not gonna talk about me all night. You don't need to hear the same crap."

"Well, yeah, but I can't believe you're saying it."

"Yeah, fuck you too." But he was jovial about it. "So tell me who she is." Glee took over his voice now. "I told you being sequestered would be good for your love life."

"What are you talking about?"

"Come on. Why else would you be awake this late? Without being on your way to the set, I mean."

Rogan wanted to deny it, but he'd been hiding his interest for weeks. The need to talk about Kennedy burst out of him. "The last woman you'd expect."

Silence.

"What the fuck? You're really hooking up with someone?"

"Hell, no." The response was knee-jerk, protective, but the idea still sent a quiver of lust through him.

"Then what are you talking about?"

Rogan tried to put it into words. Kennedy's demanding job would always come first. But she wouldn't care if he was on location in Hungary for six months. He couldn't imagine her dressing in a designer gown and borrowed jewels for a movie premiere, but her ego wasn't dependent on fawning fans and spreads in glossy magazines. She had her own thing, her own passion. She was probably the strongest person he'd ever met.

And she needed him, the way his mother needed his father. It wasn't the kind of relationship he thought he was looking for, but his gut told him it was exactly right. He suddenly understood why his father had stayed with his mother for so long, had tried so hard to help her find balance in her life. Maybe she hadn't achieved it, but that didn't mean no one could. Did it?

He doubted anyone had treasured Kennedy Smyth, not in a long time. She inspired him to, and no one else had. Ever. He just hoped he hadn't done enough damage tonight to push her completely away.

All of that distilled itself into one sentence. "I found her, Charlie."

Charlie snorted, and when Rogan didn't say more, said, "Wait, I'm confused. Found who? Her? *The* her? The-woman-you've-always-wanted sappy crap? Really?"

"Yeah." If Charlie could see him, he would be all over the shit-eating grin that had spread across Rogan's face. "Really. *The* her. I think."

"Is she a screenwriter?"

"Not exactly. She's head of security for the production."

"Head of security."

"Yeah."

"Didn't you tell me this woman's some kind of Amazon or something? Does a lot of work in the jungle, protecting important people and doctors and shit?"

"Yeah."

"The exact opposite of what you thought you wanted?"

"Yeah." What he'd wanted before had crumbled away, leaving the truth of what Kennedy did to him. It was new, and there was a long way to go before it could be right, but that was the path he wanted to take.

Charlie laughed so hard he choked a sound suspiciously like a sob. "Oh, man," he sighed. "Look at us. Me falling apart, you getting it together. Circle of life, huh, buddy?"

Rogan hoped not.

THEY WEREN'T SHOOTING the next day, so Kennedy sent Rick and Jonathan with M.J. to the first location. She held a brief meeting with Wolf, who argued just enough against being sent home, giving in grudgingly when she told him he'd still get some pay. After Stacy left to drive Wolf to the airport, Kennedy spent the day in her room, reviewing Mark's most recent e-mails.

The truck's license plate hadn't panned out. The vehicle had been stolen in another suburb of Denver and abandoned not far from the truck stop. The vehicle was already back in its original owner's possession. She sighed and turned to the family reports.

Clive Furchon, Toby's nephew, bothered her the most. Mark couldn't find out where he was. He had tracked his employment record all over the country, but there were huge gaps between jobs. Most disturbing, he found a possible association with a survivalist group in Idaho. She told him to check gun records.

Vinnie Todesto's file had grown more interesting. The guy had made a play for Hollywood a few years ago. His biggest audition was for a movie underwritten by Starshine Pictures. Directed by M.J. Swanson. From what Mark could gather, he'd been turned down flat, his ego suffering more than just a prick.

She sent Mark a short text message. *Clive and Vinnie: Find them.*

The rest of Owen Houseal's family had six pages of their own, but none of it was helpful. They were living fairly decent lives, with nothing leaping out at her to red flag anyone.

She lingered over their records, her mind wandering in directions she'd been keeping it from all day. Family. Support. Love. Those were things she'd taken for granted growing up. But Rogan was right. She was a martyr, sacrificing all the other variations of family, and maybe even perverting the values of the one that drove her. But she couldn't conceive of anything different. Getting involved with a man put him in danger. Hell, even thinking about getting involved might be putting Rogan in danger. Children would never fit into her life. But so what? Having children wasn't the only noble endeavor in the world. Falling in love didn't make a person complete. Rogan couldn't heal her.

It was just as well he'd gotten annoyed with her last night and broken the connection they were weaving. He was safer, and so was she.

She spent the rest of the afternoon checking and re-checking their as-solid-as-it-could-get security. After dinner, she dragged Rick back to the intersection where they'd be filming the next day. The production would block off the streets, which should help keep non-film cars away, and local police would handle crowd control. They couldn't eliminate or investigate pedestrians and stargazers.

Kennedy studied the office buildings and shops surrounding them. Most of the buildings were modern, with windows that didn't open above the ground floor. The shops were typical storefronts. Kennedy entered them all and learned the back exits and alleys and which establishments had what kind of clientele and how many people at what time of day.

It was a wasted effort. Nothing happened except that M.J. was delighted with the quality of the takes. So she repeated the drill at the next location and the next, determined to be as prepared as possible for whatever El Jahar sent their way.

THREE NIGHTS LATER, the building alarm jerked Kennedy out of a dead sleep. Conditioned by training and experience, she leapt out of bed and ran out the door with her gun and alarm remote in her hands. Enough light filtered through the windows to tell her it was just after dawn.

She ran down the hall, studying the display on the remote. The alarm had been set off at the side door near the kitchen. She put on a burst of speed, dropped the remote into the pocket of her flannel pants and soared down the stairs.

"Freeze!" she shouted, and the skinny, shaggy-haired intruder froze with his back to her. He wore a faded T-shirt and baggy jeans and held a plastic grocery bag in one upraised hand.

Her pistol gripped in both hands, she closed the distance between them but didn't get near enough for him to reach her.

"Who are you?"

"Uh…I'm the…the…kitchen assistant." His voice shook, barely audible under the sound of the alarm. Kennedy held the gun in her right hand while she used her left to shut it off with the remote.

"Turn around. Slowly. Keep your hands where they are."

He did as she ordered, pivoting on one Birkenstock and almost losing his balance. "What…what's going on?" His pale face went whiter when he saw the weapon.

She didn't answer right away. The alarm had awakened everyone in the building and she felt them massed in the hall and dining room, peering around the agents, all of whom held their weapons ready, though not aimed directly at the young man. She knew Rogan was standing behind her, slightly to the right. It wasn't the best place for him to be, but she couldn't shift focus to move him.

"Kennedy," the proprietor, an older woman with a no-nonsense demeanor, said in a low voice. "Ozzie is one of my staff. He's okay."

She lowered her weapon halfway to the ground. It was enough to make him sag in relief.

"Rick," she called. He appeared at her side. "Split everyone up and search the house and grounds. Leave Zip."

"You got it." He melted away. Zip took his place.

"Get the cast into the parlor." It was one of the few rooms with no outside door and only one wall of windows. "Gather them on the far wall. Stay ready." She listened to the murmurs of questioning voices as Zip did as she'd been instructed. Brynn Hart, the proprietor, and Ozzie remained, the latter still too scared to go anywhere.

"Kennedy, what's wrong? I vouch for him." Brynn started to walk toward Ozzie but stopped when Kennedy moved her hand in a halt command. "What's wrong?" she repeated.

"Ozzie, where have you been for the last three days?" Kennedy asked, not looking anywhere but at him.

"I was on vacation," he said, much calmer but still shaking slightly. "Brynn said she'd make do without me. But I usually come in early and help the cook start breakfast. You know, baking bread and cleaning fruit and stuff."

"Brynn, why wasn't I told he'd be coming in this morning?" She had a staff schedule and Mark's report on each employee in her room upstairs. Ozzie wasn't on the list, probably because of his vacation.

"I didn't know," Brynn confirmed. "He was supposed to be off all week."

"It got cut short. Really!" He seemed to sense Kennedy's disbelief and rushed to convince her. "I was in a cabin, see, with my girlfriend and two other couples, right? Friends of ours, right? And, like, we had a fight. Me and my girlfriend. And the other girls took her side, and the guys took my side, and, like, what we were up there for wasn't happenin'. An' she had me buy her all this tourist junk, see, and I was broke. So I thought, crap, why not just go back to work? So here I am." He rocked back and forth, darting glances at both of them.

"Why didn't you call to say you were coming back?"

He shrugged. "I didn't think I had to. I been working here two years. I know Shaddy, the cook, she would just be happy to have help. And Brynn has us use time cards, so…" He trailed off and rubbed the back of his neck.

Kennedy looked at Brynn, who nodded. "It checks."

"All right." She finally disengaged her weapon and flicked the safety on. Ozzie exhaled in relief, then escaped through the swinging door to the kitchen.

"What branch were you in?" Kennedy asked the older woman, though she already knew from the background check. It was a rare pleasure to have a non-employee react so quickly to her signals.

"Army, of course."

"Of course." She eyed the inch-long white hair, the arms that had more definition than hers. Brynn looked better in her tank top and jammie bottoms than most eighteen-year-olds.

"So how does Army become bed and breakfast?" She moved toward the door and watched Wolf and Andrew crisscrossing the backyard.

"Retirement was boring. I needed people to order around." She moved up next to Kennedy and looked where she was looking. "You're thinking this isn't over."

"I'm thinking that if someone was watching us, this would be a good time to strike." They'd all been asleep, except for the night guard, so no one had communicators on them. She didn't know what was happening anywhere in the building, and the false alarm was a good distraction.

She drew in a slow, deep breath, and waited.

The scream came from the parlor. Bailey. Kennedy had heard that scream long and loud enough at the truck stop to have it imprinted on her brain.

But that was the only sound. No glass breaking or

booted feet. No gunfire or hissing gas. Kennedy had no idea what to expect when she pounded down the hall.

It certainly wasn't bees.

The parlor door was closed. Kennedy eased it open and moved inside. Brynn followed and promptly slammed the door shut.

Still screaming, Bailey flailed her arms through the air, fighting Rogan, who held her back. Everyone else stood stock-still or ducked the angrily buzzing insects that swarmed the room.

"Holy shit." Kennedy was at a loss. "Where did these come from?"

Zip pointed to the hall. "I didn't see anyone, but suddenly they filled the room. I shut the door so they didn't get into the rest of the place."

A good idea, but now no one could get out without letting the insects throughout the building.

Kennedy whirled at a yelp in the corner. Bailey had backed into it and was now clutching her hand to her chest.

"It stung me! I'm allergic! I'm going to die!"

Shit. Bailey reminded everyone of her bee allergy at each outdoor shoot. This wasn't her routine drama. Or at least, not all of it. Kennedy rushed over and pushed aside the cast members bending over their star. "Bailey, it's okay. We'll take care of you. Do you have an EpiPen?"

Sobbing and gasping, Bailey nodded. "In…in my bag."

"In your room?"

"Yes." Her gasps were heavier, but Kennedy couldn't tell how much was real and how much was drama.

"Okay. Try to calm down. Zip!"

But Brynn was already handing her the tool. "I had some at the front desk."

"Great. Hang on, Bailey." Kennedy gripped the pen and pulled off the safety cap at the back. "Hold still, hon." She swung the head of the pen against Bailey's leg and held it there. She looked up at Brynn. "Ambulance or drive?"

"Hospital's right around the corner."

"Okay. Rick!" she called.

"I've got her."

"Me too. I'll go with her." That was M.J.

Bailey's breathing had slowed. "Okay. I'm okay."

Kennedy removed the EpiPen and checked the window to be sure it had dispensed. Brynn took it from her to replace in its case, then handed it to M.J., murmuring to him about what to tell the doctor.

"All right?" Kennedy asked Bailey, who nodded and stood. "Anyone else allergic? Stung?" There were a couple of murmurs, but no one else looked like they were in trouble. The bees swirled over their heads, their buzzing a low hum in the room. Thank God they weren't hornets.

Now they had a new problem. Whoever had set the bees loose might still be in the building. She couldn't let any of them walk into an ambush, but Bailey needed to go to the hospital now.

"Out the window," Kennedy decided.

Bailey rushed over there, but Kennedy threw out an arm to stop her. "Let me check it first."

The window looked out on the side porch. Kennedy disarmed the sensor for this one window and raised it smoothly, silently thanking Brynn for her diligent maintenance. She crouched below the sill and to the side, trying to see the porch. There were blind spots, but she couldn't do anything about that.

"Damn, I'm going to look silly," she muttered, backing up. Then she dashed forward and dove through the window, rolling to cover the whole porch with the sweep of her weapon. It was empty, but David and Gina stood on the lawn, applauding. Kennedy ignored them and stuck her gun in her pocket, then reached to help Bailey through the window. Rick and M.J. hurried her to the van, Rick going ahead to make sure they were clear. Once Zip was through she took over helping the others out, and Kennedy vaulted the rail and advanced on the two jokers.

"Ha, ha, very funny, Kennedy looks foolish. But not half as foolish as the one responsible for letting the enemy into the building."

Their grins disappeared and they straightened. "What happened?" Gina asked.

"We didn't see anything," David added.

"Obviously. Someone got into the building and let a swarm of bees loose in the parlor, where everyone was gathered. You two were out here and saw nothing? No one came out the front door?"

"No."

"How did they get in?" Dave asked, frowning at the front yard.

"I think they timed it well. They moved in when the alarm was going off. I saw the initial breach, then stowed the remote and concentrated on that." She didn't have time now to check the system for more detail. "You two guard the front door. If you see anyone on the team, tell them to cover another entrance. He has to be inside."

Zip had gathered everyone on the porch. They huddled at the end, away from the window, where bees flew through a few at a time. Kennedy told her to stay with them and watch the window while she herself went back through, grunting when something sharp pierced her inner arm. She glanced down, saw the tiny puncture already swelling like a mosquito bite, and dismissed it.

Brynn was still on the phone, looking supremely pissed off. Kennedy passed her and eased open the parlor door to slip through, closing it without making a sound. The hall was empty. The foyer held no closets and she could see halfway up the stairs. There was a nice hidey-hole under the registration desk next to the stairs. She tiptoed toward it, her bare feet helping her move quietly. But when she rounded the desk, no one was there.

Shit. She was going to get this guy. He had to be a grunt, not El Jahar, but he could lead her to him. She knew it. Anticipation danced across her skin. He was close. She could hear his tension.

She waited, listening with her whole body. The sun had risen high enough to shine through the transom above the front door, reflecting off the yellow walls and bright white trim, illuminating the entire hallway and a lone insect flying a wavy pattern toward the rear of the building.

And the dancing dust particles in front of the antique sideboard. They drew her attention enough for her to spot finger marks above one of the cabinet doors.

Logic said a grown man couldn't fit into that unit, but Kennedy never dismissed instinct because of logic.

"Brynn!" she called.

The woman immediately came into the hall.

Kennedy motioned with her chin toward the sideboard. "What do you keep in there?" she asked quietly.

"Nothing." She looked bewildered when Kennedy moved toward it, but remained silent.

Kennedy readied her gun and jerked the door open. Logic had been right. A grown man couldn't fit inside.

But a six-year-old kid could.

TEN

"TIMMY HARRIS!" BRYNN grabbed the boy's arm and yanked him out of the cabinet. A plastic cage with a spout-like protrusion clattered out behind him, caught on the tail of his plaid shirt. "What the hell do you think you're doing?"

He was grinning as if he'd pulled a fast one. Brynn's fury didn't faze him, which told Kennedy he'd played tricks on the woman before.

"Who is he?" she asked.

Brynn straightened but didn't let go of Timmy's arm. "Neighbor's son. Regular Dennis the Menace. Thinks it's funny to switch sugar and salt in the dining room, short-sheet beds, put toothpaste on toilet seats, that kind of thing." She heaved a disgusted sigh and Kennedy spotted affection in her eyes when she looked at the boy. "Truth is, he's my step-grandson. I can't keep him away." Her face hardened. "But he's never pulled anything like this before, and believe me, his punishment will be…"

"Hold on." Kennedy took him from Brynn, cage and all, and sat him on the stairs so he was at eye level. "Timmy, who put you up to this?"

"Hey!" he cried, affronted. "I thought this up on my own!"

She looked at Brynn. "Anyone around here keep bees? Sell honey?" She wasn't sure they were that kind of bee, nor did she think a six-year-old troublemaker would be able to collect them or mastermind what had happened today, no matter how precocious. But she had to be sure.

"No," Brynn said. "It's against code, for one thing. And I know all my neighbors. There's nothing like that around here."

"So where did you get the bees, Timmy?"

He threw his arms over the top of the cage and pouted.

"Tell the truth, Timmy, and I'll convince your grandmother to go light on the punishment." She doubted that would matter to him. He hadn't even been frightened by finding a gun in his face. It would be a rare punishment that would crack his shield of indifference.

But he wasn't a good secret-keeper either, it turned out. He spilled the beans quite readily, after a few well-chosen, veiled compliments.

"A guy from the grocery store gave me the cage," he finally said.

"What kind of guy?"

"He bags our groceries. I talk to him while he works. He's kind of slow. But my mom says he does the best bagging ever. No wasted space." He emphasized that with a sweep of his arm. Kennedy looked at Brynn.

"He's probably talking about Al. He's mentally challenged," she murmured.

"Okay. Where were you when Al gave them to you?"

"Down the street, ridin' my bike. There's a bump on the curb, and I can pop a perfect wheelie."

"Great. What did he say to you?"

Timmy shrugged. "Just that it would be fun if I let them loose in the house."

"Did he tell you when or how or exactly where?"

"No. I saw all the people go into the parlor and

thought that would be cool. That lady screams loud."
He giggled into his hand.

She straightened. "One more question, Timmy. How did you get in?"

His mischievous grin reappeared. "Well, Grandma told me…"

Kennedy hid her amusement at Brynn's wince. She wondered what the tough old bird wanted him to call her, instead of Grandma.

"She told me I had to call before coming over, 'cause of the alarm system. But if I called, she'd've known I was comin', and then I couldn't get the bees out. So I was in the bushes thinkin', and the alarm went off. I figured it was a good time to sneak in, so I did."

"What were you doing outside so early?"

He shrugged again. "It's not early for me."

"And how did you get through the locked door?"

He dug his hand into his pocket and pulled out a key attached to a large rubber band.

Kennedy sighed and handed him over to his grandmother. Next stop: Al the Bagger.

IT TOOK A while to get everything situated enough that she could leave. Brynn finally got an exterminator to agree to an emergency visit to fumigate the parlor. M.J. called from the hospital where Bailey was being cleared to leave, no lingering effects. The doctor wasn't even sure there'd been a reaction. Her appearance at the hospital would probably generate a news report or two, but it would appear to be a simple sting, not an attack on the production.

The security breach wasn't a fault with the system, but with Kennedy. She hadn't looked thoroughly enough at the remote's display, a mistake she wouldn't repeat. Still, she tested each entry point and re-armed the system, and assigned one additional person to the night shift. Underneath the decisiveness and the planning was pure fear. El Jahar knew where they were. If they wanted to harm them, they could, no matter what Kennedy did. She doubted they had the resources to drop a bomb, though, or the manpower to swarm the set. So all she could do was hope her team continued to get lucky, and play defense.

She headed for the grocery store while the others all got ready for filming. She hated not being on the set, but since cloning and holograms were not an option, it left her to follow the lead while it was still hot.

When she arrived at the supermarket, an older, medium-sized chain store, she threw a few random items in a cart and headed for register seven.

Al was easy to spot. His huge, sloppy grin and empty eyes caused some of the patrons to smile back and offer a few words of true kindness or patronizing sweetness. Others avoided making eye contact or any other kind of contact, choosing longer lines or simply rushing through the checkout without responding to his attempts at conversation.

Kennedy stretched to grab the divider bar and began unloading the items from the cart. The older couple ahead of her moved on and she stepped forward, offering her own smile to Al.

"Hey, pretty lady!" he yelled. "Haven't seen you in here before!"

The cashier winced. "Keep it down, Al."

"Hi, Al," Kennedy said, pleased that the cashier had confirmed his name for her, since his nametag was hidden behind the floppy opening of his smock. "It's my first visit. Got any advice for me?"

He chuckled and started pulling her groceries toward him. "The paper bags are sturdier."

"Then paper it is." She swiped her credit card, then leaned on the edge of the chrome counter. "Beautiful day today, isn't it?"

"Yep." He methodically put the first two items into the bag.

"I bet you like to go out early, huh? Enjoy every minute of the day you can."

"Yeah, I like to. I come to work early most days. Not today, but most days."

"Oh? What was different about today?"

He lifted a shoulder and tucked the third item into the corner of the bag. "Had an errand to do for a friend."

"Over on Ridgemont? My buddy Timmy said he saw you."

Al's face lit up. "Timmy? Yeah, I saw him. Gave him a present." He snickered.

"He told me. Where'd you get the present, Al? They were beauties."

Before Al could answer, they were approached by a tall guy with gelled-back hair and a boring red-striped tie with his khakis and white dress shirt.

"What's going on here?" he asked, his voice low but hard.

"Just chatting," Kennedy said mildly. The cashier started tossing things into a plastic bag, clearly eager to keep her line moving. Al shook his head and reached for the bag, moaning a "no, no, no, no."

"It's okay, Al," Kennedy told him, putting her hand on his and taking the bag. "I can use this in my trash can."

"If you're sure." He sounded doubtful, but relinquished the bags.

The manager wasn't satisfied. He grabbed Kennedy's upper arm and spoke in her ear, a gesture that never failed to fire her engines. She kept her face impassive as he spoke through his teeth.

"Look, you seem to like Al. So leave him alone before he loses his job. This isn't the first incident—"

"What do you mean, 'incident'?" She pulled back to look at him but made sure her arm didn't slide from his grip. "I was just talking to the guy."

Al had started rocking and moaning. "Boss, I don't want no trouble, Boss. This nice lady is just a nice lady. Not like yesterday."

"What happened yesterday?" She kept her tone interested but not eager, though her heart raced in anticipation. She prayed Boss didn't shut him up before he gave her something useable.

"The bees. I got the bees yesterday. They make honey. The man, he told me to give them to Timmy. I liked them, but Timmy—"

"Okay, Al, that's enough." Boss let go of Kennedy and reached for Al. The store hadn't been very busy, but the few customers and all the staff were now watching the spectacle at register seven.

"It's all right," Kennedy told the manager. "Really. He's a sweet guy. You're upsetting him. Please."

He realized then that they were being watched and backed off. Kennedy waited until he was a few feet away before she patted Al on the shoulder. "Nice to meet you, Al. By the way. What was the bee guy's name? Do you remember?"

He looked indignant behind his thick glasses. "Of

course I remember. It was the same name as my butcher waaaayyyyy back when I was a kid. Same name. I remember it."

"What was it?" she urged, seeing the manager step toward them again.

"Vinnie."

She called Mark immediately.

"SmythShield." He sounded very chipper.

"Tell me you have more on Vinnie."

"Vinnnniiiiieee…let's see…" She heard papers shuffling. "Here he is. Well, not much more. After the audition fiasco, he hung around town bad-mouthing his agent and trying to get a new one. Nothing happened except no one wanted anything to do with him, so he moved to…"

Kennedy tapped her fingers on the steering wheel, impatient both with the red light and the delay.

"Florida," he finally said. "That's as far as I've gotten."

"How long ago was he in Florida?"

"Last year. But his forwarding order from that apartment expired."

She blew out a breath and hit her turn signal. "Okay. Focus on him. He's top of the list right now."

"Why?"

"Holy shit." She stomped on the brakes, halted by cars sitting bumper-to-bumper and fender-to-fender across the street. Three blocks away, at approximately the site of the filming, red and blue lights shone intermittently. Fear squeezed her heart. "I've gotta go."

She jumped out of the car and dodged vehicles to get to the sidewalk, unconcerned about leaving the car in the middle of traffic. No one was going anywhere.

When she got to the barricade, a stern-faced, uniformed cop stopped her. Kennedy pulled out her credentials. "I'm in charge of security on this shoot," she told him. He gave her a scornful look.

"Nice job." It wasn't a compliment.

The band of fear tightened around her chest. She had trouble breathing. "Are you going to let me by?"

"Wait till I get someone to vouch for you." He disappeared and another cop took his place. Kennedy could have gotten by him, but she didn't want to antagonize anyone. After a few minutes the first cop reappeared and pulled the barrier aside, motioning her past.

She ran through the crowd of officers, crew, and equipment toward the ambulance visible at the corner. *Don't let it be Rogan.*

M.J. caught her as she ran.

"Who's hurt?" she asked first, her voice as squeezed by fear as her heart.

M.J. looked solemn. "One of the stuntmen. He'll be okay. He broke his foot, but they think it's a clean break and it won't affect shooting. They're going to take him for an X-ray."

"How did it happen?" While he talked she surveyed the scene, cataloging details. The cops weren't there because of an attack, as she had feared, but were providing routine crowd control. Rogan and Bailey had drawn more and more people every day.

"We were working on a stunt. The awning." He motioned to a storefront that had a green-and-white striped awning over the door and window. It was torn on one side. "He hit off center, but the problem was when he came off onto the mat."

That was the giant pile of blue and white plastic

heaped under the awning. Jefferson and Gina bent over it, their heads together, looking grim.

"Did he hit wrong?" she asked.

M.J. shook his head and looked even more somber. "No, he hit fine, except feetfirst. That doesn't matter usually, but the mat blew."

She raised her eyebrows. "It blew?"

"Somehow. Peter went right down and hit his foot on the pavement. Felt it snap."

Kennedy winced. She knew that sickening feeling.

She went first to the ambulance and briefly spoke to Peter before they headed off. Then she walked over to Jefferson and Gina, who looked even grimmer when they saw her.

"Tell me this was an accident," she said, but she knew it wasn't even before Jefferson shook his head.

"Someone used a sander to weaken the side."

"A sander?"

"A small rotary sander, probably. There were six spots along the side." He pointed. "When he hit, the thinned material blew out, so it didn't cushion his fall."

She shook her head. "Wait a minute. I thought these things were designed to deflate on impact, like an airbag."

"They are," Gina agreed. She waved her over to the mat. "But the damage was done between vents. It blew out the whole side."

Kennedy hated to ask the next question. "Why wasn't it discovered?"

Jefferson didn't make excuses or evade responsibility. "We didn't look closely enough," he said. "We were looking for holes or sabotage to the pumps and vents, not subtle weakening. It was my fault."

"It was not!" Gina jumped to his rescue. "Jefferson was here at four this morning, testing it. He examined the whole thing. Look." She dragged Kennedy closer and pointed to the edge of the blowout. "You can barely see the abrasion."

Kennedy glanced at it. It was there, noticeable if you looked for it, not so noticeable if you were looking for something else. She looked back at Jefferson.

"It's our job to make sure these things don't happen," she said quietly. She kept her demeanor firm, not showing the sinking in her chest she always got when she had to reprimand someone she trusted. Gina's face turned red, but Kennedy ignored her.

"I know you're overworked. I know there are hundreds of things to check on the set. And I know you weren't being careless. I will back you up. But we can't let this happen again."

Jefferson nodded, and Kennedy started to walk away. Gina's strident defense of Jefferson reached her, and she paused.

"How can she blame you! That's not fair!"

"A broken foot isn't fair, either, Gina. She's right. It's our job. We didn't do it. And she's going to take the flack for it. Leave it alone, if you want to keep working for her."

Kennedy nodded to herself and kept walking. Jefferson knew how she operated. Nothing less than complete loyalty to her clients and from her employees. She supported him and knew he hadn't been slacking, but still had to answer to the ones paying them.

And to the guy who'd gotten hurt on her watch.

M.J. still looked solemn when Kennedy walked back to him. He was giving orders to technicians, getting ready to start shooting again, but with none of the shouting or flamboyant gestures he was prone to. He clearly understood that things were escalating. Luck was still on their side, for some reason. The bullets and acid had missed them. The bees were lazy rather than agitated, Bailey's allergy probably exaggerated.

Now someone had gotten hurt. Again, he could have been killed and wasn't, but Kennedy didn't think El Jahar cared either way. She really hated this job. Every other job she'd ever done, she knew who the enemy was and what they wanted, even if she didn't know where or when they'd come at her team or her protectees. Every other job, she was able to stay objective, distant. Not this one, and it just kept getting worse.

The ambulance had left, and the crowd was dispersing. Police routed cars through side alleys and traffic began to break up.

"I have to move my car," Kennedy told M.J. "I'll be right back, then we can talk."

"Save it for tonight." He barely looked at her. She couldn't tell if he was angry or not.

She angled between two sawhorses and started down the sidewalk. A tingle at the back of her neck told her someone had followed. She didn't need to look to know it was Rogan.

He strode along with her for half a block without speaking, hands in his pockets. People stared and murmured, and a few of the younger females squealed, but no one dared approach once they saw Kennedy's expression. Traffic was moving faster and she sped up. Rogan kept pace, annoying her. Not a good idea when she was already in a bad mood. She reached her car, pressing the button to disarm the vehicle and yanking open the door. He got in the passenger side before she could hit the power lock. At this point, it was easiest and safest just to drive him back to the set. If he was smart, he'd continue keeping his mouth closed.

She cranked the key and let the engine roar when it turned over. Slamming the gearshift into drive, she caught up with the cars in front of her, then edged into the right lane so she could park near the site. But before she got close enough, they heard the blare of a horn followed by the crunch of metal. Traffic ground to a halt again. Kennedy cursed and braced her head on the heel of her hand, her elbow on the edge of her door.

"I don't want to leave the car again," she told Rogan wearily. "And you'll be needed on the set."

"Not for three more shots."

She cursed again, more quietly. Weariness seeped into her muscles and dragged at her eyelids. She had constant responsibility for too many people. One of her best employees had screwed up, and she had to deal with the consequences of that, which included answering to the client, whom she'd failed. Now was not the time to be fending off advances by a Hollywood hunk who understood her too much and wanted more from her than she'd ever be able to give.

"I'm sorry, Kennedy, about the other night. What I said. It wasn't fair."

His soft sincerity and her emotional fatigue conspired to tear down all her remaining resistance. She glanced over. He was half leaning out the window to check the traffic, his hand braced on the top of the frame. His forearm was sinewy, his wrists and fingers graceful yet strong. He turned to catch her watching him, and his eyes crinkled in the corners, proof of the ready smile that lightly graced his mouth even now, though tinged with regret. He had a lean body with long legs making him two or three inches above her own five ten, and all of it combined into a package she increasingly wanted to open.

"Damn you, Rogan St. James," she murmured.

He pointed to the car in front of him. "He'll be able to move in a minute, and he's heading left. Then you can scoot by on the right."

Amused, she kept her eyes on him.

"There he goes. Go ahead." When she didn't move he turned to look at her, and the power of his sparkling brown eyes sent a shiver through her chest. He froze, awareness replacing the sparkle.

"Okay," Kennedy said. "I'll 'scoot' by." She put the car back in gear, then broke eye contact and turned the car the way he'd indicated. His gaze didn't leave her.

When she parked next to the barricade, one of the assistant directors ran up to the car, looking frantic. He opened Rogan's door and made sweeping motions with his arms. "Out, out! My goodness, where have you been! We've been waiting for you, and M.J. is *not* in the best mood. Oh, this is going to go horribly." He dragged Rogan out of the car, fretting when he leaned back in.

"Are we okay, then?"

Even knowing how wrong it was, Kennedy could only nod.

ELEVEN

M.J. LOOKED GRIM when Kennedy met him in his room before dinner.

"What happened?" he asked first thing. She told him, not leaving anything out or fudging her responsibility. She had spent hours that afternoon with Jefferson and Gina, examining every item to be used in every scene.

"So what can we do?" he asked, though she could tell what he wanted to do.

"You can fire SmythShield and hire another firm." She zeroed in on the most drastic action, the one she'd recommend in normal circumstances. "I can give you some names."

"Why is now any different than it was before?"

She had no confidence in her ability to second-guess this enemy. "It's not," she admitted. "It's logical that if my team isn't on this job, they'll leave you alone and try to get me some other way."

M.J. stood and started to pace. "Will you be able to take another job?"

She wasn't going to admit that quitting now would mean the end of SmythShield. Taking any other job would put the new clients in danger until she stopped El Jahar. She couldn't knowingly do that.

"My main concern is still that my withdrawal may not remove the threat to the production. I can refer you to some good companies, but…"

"But you're the best."

That was true, but she didn't repeat it. Part of her hesitation was a conviction that no one could do the job as well as she could, which some called a character flaw. It might be, but she didn't think most of her competitors had as much dedication as she did. Their training wasn't as rigorous, their screening and hiring not as tough. Their staff wasn't always as loyal. And she knew for sure they wouldn't care about these people as much as she did.

She didn't know if that was a positive or a negative.

"There's something else you have to consider," she told him. Fear flickered in his eyes when he looked at her.

"I know."

"Someone involved in the production sabotaged the mat."

"I know." He sat on the edge of the bed and put his head in his hands. "You did background checks."

"That was before we knew El Jahar was targeting me," she said. "We did regular criminal checks, but we didn't know El Jahar's motivation then. We weren't looking in the right places."

"And now?"

"Now, I have Mark researching connections to our main suspects."

He raised an eyebrow. "You have suspects?"

She only nodded. He didn't ask her to elaborate, his thought process already moving on.

"It might not be one of my people," he said, and a chill danced over Kennedy's skin.

"I can account for all of my agents' whereabouts."

She tried not to sound defensive. "And I trust them implicitly."

"What about the new guy?" He frowned, as if realizing he hadn't seen him.

"I sent him home as a precaution. You're right, I don't know him as well as I know the others."

Her willingness to consider the possibility seemed to appease M.J., but only on that one point. "So nothing's changed. You being here makes us vulnerable. But leaving could make us more vulnerable. My only option that might make us safe is to shut down production. And even then you're not sure."

Her face impassive, she nodded.

"I don't know what to do!"

For the first time since she opened SmythShield, Kennedy didn't know what to do, either.

AFTER LEAVING M.J., who said he would call Max and let her know what they decided, Kennedy went downstairs to get something to drink. Brynn stopped her on her way back upstairs with a glass of milk.

"This came today." She handed her an envelope, her expression understanding but aloof. Kennedy couldn't blame her. Their presence was endangering her and maybe even her family. She wasn't the kind of person to kick them out, and Kennedy doubted she was truly afraid for herself, but she also doubted she'd see Timmy around anymore. She'd also noticed Brynn cutting vegetables in the kitchen. She'd probably put some, if not all, of her staff on paid leave to get them out of harm's way.

Kennedy's burden grew heavier.

She thanked Brynn and continued up the stairs. Once in her room, she drank half the milk and studied the envelope. It was the plain white, security type that you could buy in any grocery or department store. Her name and the B&B's address were printed in perfect block letters. There was no return address, and the postmark was smudged.

She ran her fingers over it. It was too thin to hold anything but a single sheet of paper, with no bumps or wrinkles. She grabbed a letter opener and slit the envelope, then pulled out the piece of paper. The message was a few lines long, printed in block lettering on plain white copy paper. In the lower right corner someone had drawn a dagger dripping blood into a puddle beneath it.

SUCH A RESPONSIBILITY. *Stay, and they're in danger. Leave, and they're in danger. Quite a dilemma for someone used to making quick decisions with immediate consequences. And the uncertainty...when will they strike, and how? Most importantly, how hard? When will the game turn deadly?*

Stew over that.

AN HOUR LATER, she was still stewing. She lay on her back on the bed, one foot on the floor, her left hand playing with the letter opener. A knock sounded on the door. Still staring at the ceiling, she pulled her gun from beneath her right hip and thumbed off the safety.

"Who is it?" she called.

"Rogan."

Suddenly, what was happening between her and Rogan seemed much safer than what was happening around them. She wished she could indulge in easy flirtation, light conversation, even physical gratification to take her mind off her problems. It would work, but only for the time it took. Afterward, things would be worse.

Or better, her mind whispered. *Share the burden.*

It was the stupidest thought she'd ever had.

She couldn't find the strength to tell him to go away, so he opened the door and eased inside.

"You okay?"

"Hunky-dory." She put the gun back under her, after switching the safety back on.

"I sense sarcasm."

Kennedy shrugged. Rogan began to stroll around the edge of the room, glancing at the files stacked on her desk, touching her hairbrush and hair clip on top of the dresser. She didn't move but did stop staring at the ceiling to watch him prowl.

Get up. He's going to try to seduce you. She could read it in the way he moved, in the glances he sent her. But she was numb with indecision. She lacked the energy to move, never mind the quick-wittedness to parry advances.

"You ever kill anyone?" he asked out of the blue, surprising her.

"Why do you want to know that?"

"Insight. You're pretty closed up. I wondered why."

"Research for a role?"

"No."

She believed him. "Yes. I've killed when I've had to." She expected him to ask how many times or how it made her feel, but his attention had been caught by the paper on her desk.

"Don't." She launched herself up, but he'd already started reading. Her shoulders slumped, she watched his expression change from interest to comprehension to disgust.

Goodbye, seduction, she thought, accepting her disappointment. But he crossed the room and sat next to her on the bed.

"You've been under a lot more pressure than I realized," he said. "Who is this asshole?"

"If I knew that, I wouldn't need to be here."

Rogan lifted his hand and stroked her hair back off her face, resting his fingers on the back of her neck. Tingles followed their path and she fought a shiver.

"Why are you interested in me?" she murmured.

He stroked his other hand down her face, the side of her neck, her arm, to her waist. "You mean, besides this? Besides your incredible body and a face I could stare at all day?"

She smiled at his echo of her earlier thoughts about him. "Yeah, besides all that."

He leaned closer to her. The fact that he did so instead of pulling her to him was incredibly seductive.

"You know what you want, where you're going, and how to get there." His voice dropped and his lips brushed hers. Her own breath caught in anticipation.

"All that confidence is sexy as hell," he added, closing the distance and pressing his mouth onto hers.

Heat flowed through Kennedy. The numbness burned away, replaced by a growing hunger that made her forget why this was stupid. She wrapped her arms around his lean body and pressed close, her breasts beginning to throb, and accepted the distraction with unprecedented eagerness.

Rogan didn't take the kiss deep enough fast enough, so she tempted him with a stroke of her tongue across his lips. He immediately responded, plunging his tongue into her mouth with a groan. He wrapped his arm around her waist and tugged. She swung her leg up and over to straddle him. He was iron-hard against her, and desire flared so high she thought she'd incinerate. She pressed him back onto the bed, reveling in the strength of his hands on her, the heat of his body beneath her. The kisses went on and on, but they weren't even close to enough.

Rearing back, Kennedy stripped off her shirt, then started to lower herself again. Rogan stopped her.

"Jesus, Kennedy." He slid his hands from her shoulders to her breasts, tracing the edge of the black lace with his fingertips. She let her eyes close while he teased. Ripples of pleasure washed over her, tightening the ache between her legs. She rubbed against him to ease it, but it only worsened.

"You're way too slow," she growled, pressing his hands to her breasts and squeezing his fingers around them. He thrust upward and she arched, lost in the intensity of the pleasure. She savored the knowledge that in a moment he'd be inside her, driving her to a peak that would make everything else temporarily unimportant.

But instead of moving them along to that point, Rogan rolled so she landed on the bed next to him. His shirt hung open when he rose up on one elbow. She must have unbuttoned it, not really remembering or caring, and leaned forward to lick his nipple. His body jerked, but he pushed her back.

"What's the matter?" Kennedy asked, trying to control her breathing.

"I don't know." He looked a little puzzled as he studied her. "Something is, though."

Shit. She had a feeling this was the end of her pleasant mindlessness. She flopped back so she was flat on the bed, though they were lying across it so her legs hung off the side. "What are you talking about?" she asked, resigned.

"You're too out of control."

"And you're complaining?" she said incredulously. "Most guys—"

"I'm not most guys." He was starting to sound angry. "I don't have sex with whoever's willing, and I don't like being used."

She stared at him, unable to deny it, but also unable to assure him that wasn't all she wanted, all she felt. The reasons she shouldn't do this came roaring back.

Thank God no one had seen them.

Rogan glanced back at the table, where the letter lay open. "I think you desperately need a break from your problems."

"Rogan, I—"

"I know." The annoyance was gone. "Believe me, Kennedy, I know more than you think." He caressed her palm with his cheek, his stubble rasping against her skin. "Especially now that I've read that letter. But you're too important."

"For what?"

He shrugged. "For everything. Too important to this production to take the risks you think being with me would take. Too important to me." He kissed her hand and sat up, tugging her with him. "I don't want to make things worse for you. I want to make them better."

"You do," she murmured. "But you make them worse too."

He looked up from the buttons of his shirt and smiled gently, then bent and kissed her with such tenderness her eyes prickled. She closed them and held him in place when he would have ended the kiss, but didn't deepen it, even when her arousal surged again. She couldn't disrespect what he'd just said to her.

He released her lips but kept his face next to hers. "I want more than an interlude, Kennedy. So I'm willing to take all the time we need to get there." He hugged her, then let her go and handed her her shirt. "I'm guessing the reason M.J. keeps warning me off, and you keep pushing me away, is that letter." He paused, as if letting that realization soak in. "If this is personal, and they know I'm involved with you, I'm a bigger target."

"That's about the size of it."

"So why didn't you tell me that?"

Her tongue felt glued to the roof of her mouth.

Rogan nodded. "I'll stay away, then." He turned and left, clicking the door softly closed behind him.

"That's why," she whispered, hating herself.

ROGAN JUST WANTED to hide in his room and...think. So when Bailey called to him as he passed by her open door, he ignored her. But she called again, more imperiously, and he knew she'd follow him if he didn't stop. He backed up and poked just his head around the doorjamb. Bailey was shameless. If she noticed his current state, she'd offer to do something about it, and he really didn't want her to pursue him now that the stunt guy she'd been sleeping with was off the set.

"What's up?"

She sat on the floor, her back to the bed, and studied the toenails she was painting.

"I didn't get any hives." He just stared at her. She made a "duh!" face. "You know, from the bee?"

"Good to hear." He started to retreat.

"Rogan!"

He held his breath so he didn't yell. "What!"

"That's all? Just 'good'? Aren't you glad I didn't, like, swell up my whole face?" She shuddered and dipped her nail polish brush into the bottle, then blew at her feet. "That would suck."

"Of course I'm glad, Bailey. Suffocating to death would have sucked, too, I bet."

She smiled, and he blinked. It was a mischievous smile, and he thought he saw the woman she was below the fame hound.

"Yeah, probably. But guess what? *People* called my manager. He denied it, but they'll put it in 'Monitor' or something like that as a rumor. It's *perfect* timing, 'cause my agent's negotiating my next movie, and the buzz will make them want me more."

"That's great, Bailey. I'm happy for you." Rogan had half expected her to bail out of the production after the last few incidents, but her glee explained why she wasn't. She didn't care what was happening, was oblivious to anything but herself and her own benefit.

She scowled. "You don't care." The scowl turned into a speculative frown. "Why are you so pissy? You didn't get stung."

"No, I—"

"Ha!" She reared back and laughed. "I know! You went for Smyth and she blew you off!"

Alarmed, he pulled back before she could see it. "Goodnight, Bailey." If someone as self-centered as Bailey had noticed, everyone had. He hoped his retreat convinced her she was right. It would be all over the set, and if there was a mole, he or she would know. Then maybe Rogan wouldn't be a direct target, and some of Kennedy's burden would be eased.

The thought should have made him happy.

His bedroom was dark and quiet. He locked the door behind him and fell onto the bed. Need still clawed at him. God, Kennedy was hot. It had taken all he had to stop her, and he knew most of his friends would call him an idiot. But he wasn't stupid. Even if no one else ever knew it had happened, it would cause problems. As soon as she rebuilt her strength, she'd push him away so hard he could never get back.

He wondered why he wanted to. If they got involved, he could *always* be a target. That wouldn't be easy to live with. It wasn't like Kennedy would stop doing this job. It was very clear this was her calling. She'd protect the world until the day she died. Kids wouldn't be a good idea. He'd thought his life was disruptive, with a stable home and school and a mother who at least stayed in this part of the world. Their kids wouldn't even know their mother, never mind be nurtured by her.

But was that so bad? Having kids wasn't mandatory. It wasn't his major life goal. He'd always figured he'd have them, but didn't have a particularly strong need to. So wouldn't it be worth it to have Kennedy in his life?

He wondered what decision she would make. Leave, stay, end production. M.J. would never close down shooting, so it was stay and do her job, or leave and try to eliminate the risk to them.

He hoped she stayed, though he didn't want it to cause harm to anyone else. He wished he knew how to make it easier on her. Something besides sex. She'd been desperate, rushing him along. Pressing his hands on her breasts...

Lust surged again, and he groaned. She was right down the hall. He could change his mind. He doubted she would have changed hers. She'd take him. Or let him take her. He throbbed at the thought and almost took care of things himself. But he didn't want to do that, either.

He just wanted Kennedy.

EL JAHAR CONTINUED the psychological attack. Each day, Kennedy received a piece of mail identical to the first— plain envelope, no return address, smudged postmark, plain white paper with block lettering. The message in the second letter accused her of using people as currency, bargaining lives for money. The third said if she cared so little about people, maybe she should get a taste of what it was like for those who *did* care. The fact that the messages were so contradictory scared her. The author was in pain and irrational, and that could make him— or her—up the ante.

The final piece of mail didn't contain a letter at all, only a doctored photograph of her brother. The original was of him in his lab coat, smiling with his arm around a friend. The doctoring removed the friend and recreated his wounds with little accuracy but plenty of gore. Scrawled in red marker was one word: "Remember?"

By the time Mark called with information, Kennedy's frustration was at an all-time high.

"Gene Jabronski's your man," Mark told her gleefully. "He was part of a business scheme with Vinnie Todesto right before that guy's run on Hollywood."

"What kind of business scheme?" She paced by the barricade and kept an eye out for anyone who might approach and overhear. It was an overcast day, rain threatening, which was perfect for filming and kept the crowds away. M.J. had changed the shoot schedule to accommodate the weather—cheaper than manufacturing weather—and the last-minute change gave Kennedy a measure of relief.

"Something to do with dog racing, I think. They went to L.A. together, but Gene had smaller aspirations and apparently succeeded."

"You're sure about this?"

"No one else seems to have any connections. Not that I can find, anyway."

"All right. Thanks, Mark. Remind me to give you a bonus when this is all over."

"You bet." His laugh sounded odd, but she was already thinking ahead to confronting Gene, one of the prop assistants. She went to find Paul Naihl, the production designer, and Jefferson. She asked them to keep an eye on Gene until M.J. finished shooting. She didn't tell them why, but they knew. Jefferson's jaw tightened, and she knew she'd have to rein him in.

Shooting was almost done for the day, so when M.J. called the final cut, she motioned him over.

"We think we've got your inside guy." She led him and a local police officer to the prop trailer where Paul and Jefferson stood. She explained what Mark had found out. By the time they entered the trailer, she had never seen M.J. so angry.

He quietly asked the other assistants in the trailer to leave, then stopped Gene as he tried to follow. The scrawny redhead licked his lips and nodded vigorously.

"Sure, I can stay. No problem. What's up?" His eyes darted between them all, then to the door. "Am I in trouble, Paul? Didn't put something away right? Did something break?"

"Yes, something broke." Kennedy took the lead. "Peter's foot broke." His face went so white even his freckles paled, and she knew he would break easily, himself. "I think you know something about that, Gene."

He shook his head, like a dog shaking off water. "Nope. Nothing."

"If we look, will we find a small rotary sander among your possessions?"

His eyes darted faster and he licked his lips again. A bead of sweat began to trickle down the side of his face. She'd bet good money that he hadn't gotten rid of the sander. It wouldn't be conclusive evidence, but she doubted they would need it.

"Tell us the truth, Gene, and it will go easier for you," M.J. said. "Maybe you'll just get probation."

Gene slumped in his seat. "How'd you know it was me?"

"Vinnie Todesto." Kennedy watched him carefully. He frowned up at her, looking confused. His face cleared as it dawned on him, then darkened in anger.

"That bastard!" He stood and shook his fist. "He betrayed me! I'll kill him!"

Kennedy didn't enlighten him, but stepped back and let the officer take over, reading his rights. Once he had him secured, she stood in front of him and said, "I want you to tell me everything you were responsible for."

He didn't hesitate. His anger was palpable, but it wasn't directed at her or at anyone associated with *Coming of Day*.

"I set the gas canister in the vent and put the letter on the makeup table."

"What about the acid? The bees?"

"I had nothing to do with those."

"What's the point, Gene?" Some of Kennedy's frustration got through her outward calm. "What's his goal?"

He looked straight at her and she could have sworn he looked with pity.

"Loss. Pain. You'll see."

Fury filled her. She wanted to hold him, beat him, shoot him up with truth serum, but she knew it wouldn't do any good. She didn't think he really knew what Vinnie's plans were; he was just repeating something he'd heard.

"Is there anyone else on the production involved in this?" was her final question. He shook his head, of course, and of course she didn't believe him. They still couldn't relax—in fact, they had to be more vigilant than ever.

TWELVE

VIGILANCE CAME EASIER, for some reason, with Rogan's new agenda. Not that he'd told her he had one. After the encounter in her room, he changed. He treated her more professionally and coolly than he had since the first day. That made it easier for her to do the same, to lock up the attraction she'd let get out of hand.

But at the same time, he wouldn't leave her alone. Every night after dinner she reviewed the next day's plans with M.J. and her supervisors. Then she met Rogan in the kitchen or parlor and they talked. Mundane stuff that no one would ever see romance in.

Rogan had lived a "normal" life, an only child in a middle-class home with married parents, and even if his mother had spent more time and energy on her job, his father seemed to have made up for it. Rogan had gone to film school and done some stage work before attempting his first Screen Actors Guild-qualifying role, and his career had built steadily from there. He had barely had a break between pictures for six years.

Kennedy talked briefly about her parents: the mother who'd died in a car accident when Kennedy was eight, the father who'd introduced her to big things and encouraged her to dream bigger. She even talked a little about the brother she'd adored.

"So your father's retired, huh?" He sipped Brynn's

signature hot toddy and settled deeper into the fluffy cushions of the sofa.

"Yeah, he's playing gentleman of the manor on this big estate in Minnesota. Dabbles in gardening and ornithology. Spends hours in his library reading Darwin and Nietzsche."

Rogan grimaced. "Sounds interesting."

"It's boring as hell, and he insists on talking about his latest 'discovery' as if no one had ever read any of these books before. But he's happy." She drank half of her own toddy, made with only a splash of alcohol.

"I'd like to meet him," Rogan said, putting Kennedy on alert. Every so often, when no one else was around, he said something like this.

"I'm sorry it won't happen." She studied the pattern on the inside of her mug.

"Why won't it?" His leg slid closer to hers. She damned the hormones that surged just from that small movement.

"Because soon the shoot will be over, the production will disperse, and I'll be going back to my compound and trying to find out who and where El Jahar is."

He glanced toward the hall and lowered his voice. "So why can't I visit you at your compound?"

She gave a short laugh, regretting it when he looked hurt. "I don't tell anyone where my compound is. And I don't get visitors."

"You got Max."

She scowled. "My father told him where to find me."

"Thanks for the tip."

She rolled her eyes and shifted to stand, but before she could make a smart remark, he'd caught her fingers with the barest, most captivating touch. She froze, the contact both powerful and frustratingly weak.

The remote in her pocket beeped, alerting her that one of their people had disarmed the system and come in the front door. She pulled away, looking at Rogan sadly. God, he was gorgeous.

"I'm sorry," she told him. "I know I suck. You deserve better than my hot and cold. But whatever this is—it can't extend beyond the shoot."

He smiled. "I don't believe in absolutes. Why can't we just take it one step at a time?" He didn't let her answer, rising and leaving the parlor to carry their mugs to the kitchen.

One step at a time had already led them to this comfortable getting-to-know-you stage that just increased anticipation for whatever came next. And for Kennedy, that was going to make it much harder to stop.

THE SET ON the last day of shooting was unlike anything Rogan had ever worked through.

Instead of melancholy and giddiness, there was fearful relief. The few remaining cast members seemed rushed, as if they thought the longer they lingered, the more they pushed their luck. M.J. kept telling one young actress to stop looking worried when she was supposed to be beaming.

The crew muttered constantly to each other between takes. They worked more closely with Kennedy's team, and from what he heard, that team was still on high alert, which made the crew nervous. A few who'd been needed through the end had left, making everyone else's jobs a little harder.

Rogan paced around the set, fixing the shots M.J.

wanted in his head, not daring to move farther than a foot off the shooting area in case Kennedy tackled him for straying. He struggled to keep calm, shaking out his arms and legs and rotating his neck when they all tightened every five minutes. He'd be so glad when this was over.

He'd be so sorry too.

He'd only gotten a taste of Kennedy Smyth. Physically, yeah, he wanted more. Being near her every night had challenged his determination to hold out for more than tension relief. But he also wanted to deepen their intimacy, to talk about important things like her brother, or even the usual hopes and dreams. He had no trouble picturing her guarding hospital workers in the jungle or doctors in a desert refugee camp. But where was the depth in her life? He wanted to teach her how to relax, bring her out into the world a little. Give her something to look forward to at the end of a hard day.

M.J. signaled, and Rogan moved into position. He clicked the pause button on his thoughts, said his line, reacted to the nonexistent event after it, and unclicked pause when M.J. yelled "cut."

"All that pacing is making me dizzy."

Rogan stopped abruptly when Kennedy slid in front of him. She smiled, but he could see the tension around her mouth and in the way her eyes never stopped scanning the area. Her left hand spun the radio repeatedly, while her right kept touching the gun at her hip through her jacket.

"I was just thinking about how much I want to be with you even though we don't have sex."

Kennedy laughed and shook her head. "You could have had sex. You rejected me."

Rogan didn't bother looking to make sure no one was nearby. She wouldn't be talking like this if she wasn't absolutely certain they couldn't be heard.

"I want it. You know I do." He started to reach for her but pulled his hands back. "I'll wait, Kennedy. Even if I have to wait for you to capture El Jahar."

She shot him an irritated glance, then said a few words into the radio before giving him her attention again. "It's pointless to wait, Rogan. It's been enjoyable, but we're different, want different things…" She shook her head. "We're not having this conversation now."

"Okay." He knew it wasn't the best time. "When?"

Kennedy shrugged and strode away, and he felt dismissed. He just hoped she wasn't trying to dismiss him forever. It wouldn't work.

He wouldn't let it.

"WE'RE ALMOST THERE."

Kennedy winced at Jefferson's quiet comment as she rejoined him behind the cameras. Superstition would say he'd just jinxed them, but she didn't think a jinx was required. Something was going to happen today. She knew it. Vinnie had been trying to lure them into complacency, make them certain they were going to make the goal line. This was his last chance to make her pay, and she had no doubt he was going to use it.

Kennedy and M.J. had allowed the bulk of the cast and crew to go home unescorted, agreeing the bigger threat was here, where the high-visibility cast members were, where M.J. and his assistants were. Where Kennedy was.

Normally, she would be a machine. Emotion had a place in a job like hers—a touch of fear and anticipation boosted adrenaline, helped keep focus—but she knew how to keep it in check, to use it but not allow it any control.

Today was different. Being a personal target instead of a general one interfered. As did her relationship, such as it was, with Rogan. Her brain kept wanting her to think of what it would be like without him. Or was that her heart?

This last bit of filming was tedious, mostly reaction shots and pickups from scenes already filmed that M.J. had studied and found needing a little extra. Kennedy couldn't help being impressed with Rogan's ability to drop into the character for a few seconds, then right back into himself. He never flagged, never complained, even when he had to look shocked eighteen times in a row.

She wondered how someone got involved with a guy like that. How she knew he was sincere and not just dropping himself into another character.

Beside her, Jefferson beat out a jittery tattoo against his thigh.

"Why don't you take a break." She kept her voice even, her arms crossed and her feet braced in her usual ready posture, but he still bristled at the implication.

"I'm fine."

"You need a break."

He didn't raise his voice, but anger deepened it. "I don't need a break any more than you do. We got here at the same time this morning."

Practically last night, it had been so early. And she'd been up for hours before that, running through scenarios and jotting notes on how to handle them. They'd been unobtrusively drilling all week and were prepared for just about anything. Anything, of course, except what would end up coming at them.

"So go get me some coffee," she told Jefferson, flashing him a grin. "And while you're at it, sit in the break trailer for a few minutes."

He grumbled, but he went.

Kennedy continued to study their surroundings. Because it was very early on a Sunday, the crowds at the barriers were much smaller than they'd been for most of the shoot. They were in a business district, but the intersection was surrounded by tall buildings with private windows overlooking the street. Kennedy was attuned to everything: whether the people standing at the barrier milled about as usual, or moved with an odd tension. To the sound of the wind, in case it developed the rhythm of chopper blades. And mostly, to the windows that could open.

A few hours later, Rogan approached her while the crew reset the scene.

"Are you going home today?"

She shook her head. "We'll be here until the breakdown is complete."

His grin flashed in her peripheral vision. "I don't get an escort back to California?"

"Sure you do." She felt rather than saw the grin disappear.

"But not from you."

She ignored the pain in her chest. It was temporary. Their lifestyles weren't at all compatible, despite the attraction between them and the friendship they'd started, and once he was back in L.A. and she was home, she'd stop longing to step into his arms or ask him what he thought about something. She *knew* that, but it was so hard to believe when he was standing right here in front of her, smelling so good and understanding her so well.

Last night's nightmare flashed through her head. It was the one she usually had about Justin, only this time, it had been Rogan's blood, Rogan's staring eyes.

"Look," she said more sharply than she should have because of her blooming fear. "I'm working here. I have twenty people I'm trying to keep safe. Your ego will have to wait."

He backed up a step. She didn't look at him, but shame joined the cauldron inside her.

"Fine," he said quietly. "Sorry."

His next take was the most intense she'd seen. M.J. blasted him for being inconsistent and made him do it again.

Kennedy's muscles had stiffened from being in one position too long, so she began to walk the perimeter again, scanning the crowd and trying not to let part of her attention focus on Rogan.

She'd prioritized the areas of threat and split her focus among them all. Buildings, street, air, sewer, internal. She never ruled anything out, but since nothing had happened since M.J. fired Gene, they had almost decided they'd at least eliminated the inside threat.

They were wrong.

As she passed the camera, sparks flew out of it with a loud pop and sizzle. Kennedy ducked, and the cameraman cried out and jumped back, falling off the platform and stumbling to the ground. The sparks kept coming, but their intensity and limited range told her they were only a distraction.

"Everyone down!" she yelled, her mike open, and her team rushed to help the cast and crew comply. She crouched, her gun steady in her hands as she swept the area, seeing nothing.

"Report!" she barked, and one by one the operatives gave an all-clear. But she knew they weren't in the clear.

The cameraman had scrambled backward on his butt toward the nearest barrier. Kennedy scanned the area again, then checked on him. He was half under the barrier, turning as if to make his escape.

"Rick, suspect at your five o'clock. Cameraman. Help me with him. Jefferson, pay attention to the area near the sparking camera. I think he's planted something." While she gave those orders she kept moving slowly toward the cameraman, trying not to alert him of her intentions. He wasn't watching her, though—his eyes were fixed on something else. She looked back. Gina was disconnecting power to the camera while Jefferson carefully examined it. But something told Kennedy it wasn't the camera itself that was the threat.

Her heart sped up and her chest heaved. She knew if they didn't figure it out in the next thirty seconds, they could all be dead.

No, not all. El Jahar wanted her to suffer. What would they have planted? Where would they have planted it? Rick was only a foot from the cameraman now, and the guy had stopped moving away. Because he was out of range?

"Shit!" She needed to figure it out. What was out of place? She was tired, damn it, and her brain felt sluggish. She couldn't tell, couldn't see, couldn't think.

Taking a deep breath, she stopped moving and let her eyes and instincts do the work. Everyone was on the ground or crouching behind equipment except the SmythShield operatives, who prowled the set. Something was out of place, something that hadn't been there before. *What is it, what is it?*

Kennedy closed her eyes and visualized the scene she'd been studying for hours. Like a videotape, she fast-forwarded through the takes, through Rogan approaching her, then his last scene when he'd been too intense, handing Bailey a bouquet of snapdragons...

That was it! Her eyes flew open and she dashed toward the bouquet of roses on the prop table. She shouted for everyone to get back and get down and for Rick to secure the cameraman.

She slowed as she approached the flowers. She didn't know what to expect. A mechanical trap, venomous snakes—she wouldn't put anything past El Jahar.

She glanced around. Rick had both his gun and a knee on the cameraman. Everyone was under cover or a distance away, including Rogan, held back by M.J. and Bailey.

She focused her attention on the roses. There were three red ones and three white, stems cut short and wrapped with a wide white ribbon. No wires or metal were visible, and there wasn't room to hide much in between the blooms. She stepped closer, still not touching the bouquet, and sucked in a breath.

Plastique had been molded to each flower stem.

THE BOMB SQUAD made quick work of the bouquet.

"Simple setup," the squad leader told Kennedy. "Not a lot of product. It would have been a small blast."

"Large enough to kill the person holding them." Kennedy scowled. The guy shrugged.

"More likely blow his hand off, unless he was sniffing them." He looked curiously at her. "You're not regular security."

"No. There had been some threats." She didn't say more, just signed the form on the clipboard he handed her and smiled vaguely. "Thanks for the quick response."

He grinned back. "Slow day. You got a suspect for us?"

She motioned to where Rick and two police officers were standing over the cameraman. Kennedy had questioned him before the squad arrived. He claimed he was paid to put the flowers on the table. He said no one had told him there were explosives in the bouquet, but Kennedy wasn't fooled by the carefully worded statement. He knew, even if he hadn't been told. That was why he'd rigged the camera to spark, giving himself a chance to move away.

When asked why he'd do something so risky, he shrugged and said "Ten thousand dollars."

"Were you already paid?" Kennedy asked him.

"Half of it." He scowled. "I wanted to get my money before I did it in case I got caught."

He had little remorse for what he'd done, probably because it hadn't harmed anyone and he was taking the fall, thinking he was thousands of dollars richer. Kennedy doubted he'd been smart enough to protect the money. He wasn't going to profit from this crime.

Not that he believed them, and he wouldn't or couldn't give them any information on El Jahar.

Kennedy found a near-hysterical prop assistant inside a nearby coffee shop, where much of the cast and crew had gathered to be questioned.

"I already told the police what I know," she pouted, wiping tears off her cheeks. "It wasn't my fault."

Kennedy crouched in front of her. "Of course it wasn't. No one thinks it was. But I have to ask some more questions. I know you can handle it."

The assistant straightened her back. "Of course I can *handle* it."

"Were you always planning to use snapdragons for the bouquet?"

"No, it was going to be roses, but M.J. decided that was cliché."

"When did he change it?"

"This morning. I had to find a flower shop."

"Okay. Did you notice when the roses appeared on the table?"

She shook her head. "Rogan had the snapdragons the whole time. I didn't go near the table."

No one had noticed exactly when they appeared. It burned Kennedy that she hadn't either, almost as much as it burned her that M.J. hadn't notified Jefferson of the change in props. They might have spotted the bomb sooner if he had.

But that was irrelevant now. She straightened and thanked the girl. She had her answers.

If they had used roses as planned, Rogan would have been holding the rigged bouquet when the bomb was remote detonated, and he might have been killed. Even the small amount of damage the bomb squad leader described could have ruined his career or disabled him permanently.

Someone knew Kennedy had gotten close to him. Someone thought they had hit on the perfect revenge.

She shook open her phone and hit speed dial. "I'm through dicking around, Mark. Get me Vinnie, *now*."

THIRTEEN

WITHIN TWO DAYS, the remnants of the *Coming of Day* production were on their way back to L.A. Kennedy had wrapped up details, including reviewing the final report from the bomb squad, which contained nothing helpful. She gave her final verbal report to Max Swanson by phone the day the last of them flew out of Denver.

"Well, your bill is higher than I wanted," he began grumpily.

"Don't you dare try to talk me down. I bare-boned it for you already. *And* gave you a family discount."

"Hmph. It's your fault I needed you in the first place."

Kennedy closed her eyes against the guilt and curbed her defensive reaction. "It's not my fault someone targeted you to target me. And if you had let me turn down the job, none of this would have happened."

His laughter boomed over her cell phone. "All right, all right. I'm just glad everyone's safe and production is done. I'll set up an advance screening for you and your people when it's ready, probably early next year."

Kennedy couldn't care less, but the team would enjoy it so she thanked him and hung up.

She ended up flying to L.A. with Rogan and some of the crew members after all. He'd stayed behind when the rest of the first unit departed, and she hadn't argued because as long as she could see him, she wasn't wondering if he was okay. Her team accompanied the first unit home, then had a week off before reporting back to the SmythShield compound in Northern California.

She made sure they didn't sit together on the plane, but her finagling made her the target of his puppy dog eyes whenever she glanced up. She couldn't tell if he was playing or if they were real. That was the problem with getting involved with an actor. Or at least, that was what she told herself, as if she didn't already know him well enough to know he didn't put up a façade.

She followed him off the plane and made sure Clay was in position to take him home. He would remain on personal guard duty for a while, until they were certain he was no longer a target. Kennedy was catching a connecting flight and going straight back to the compound. She couldn't take care of Rogan herself, not when she needed to take the offensive against El Jahar. Rogan knew that, but he got in front of her after they disembarked and wouldn't let her by.

"I want to see you again," he said.

"I'm sorry, Rogan. I don't know when I'll be free to do that."

She avoided eye contact by searching for her gate and checking the cleanliness of her boots. But he grabbed her chin—firmly, no gentle nudging here—and forced her to look up at him. She couldn't get away without causing a scene. And her traitorous mind made her imagine what his kiss would feel like right now, with frustration pouring through him and lust burning in his eyes.

"I don't care when you're free, Kennedy. I *will* see you again." He did kiss her, hard but far too briefly. Then he nodded at Clay and walked off without looking back at her. She found herself watching him, hoping she was the only one doing so, and perversely glad that he wasn't allowing it to be over.

She buzzed Clay with her phone. He answered a second later.

"Be very careful," she told him. "Don't drop your guard for a second. He's still vulnerable."

"You got it."

The gate for her connecting flight was down the concourse. She had an hour so she slouched in a chair, her legs stretched out in front of her, and tried to catch a quick nap. But sleep eluded her. She missed the usual satisfaction of a successfully completed job. She couldn't put the case to rest. The cast and crew of *Coming of Day* might be safe, but there had been no definitive winner. She had thwarted El Jahar's intentions, but hadn't caught him. Just flunkies who knew nothing. And a six-year-old kid.

Her phone rang. Moving as little of her body as possible, she pulled it from her pack and looked at the display. Mark.

"I'm on my way," she told him, glancing over her shoulder to check the status of the flight. It was on schedule.

But that wasn't what he was calling about. The rapid clicking of his pen punctuated the excitement thrumming in his voice when he told her to get a flight back to Denver.

"Vinnie Todesto has a condo in Evergreen. I didn't come across it before because it's in his mother's name. But he's been there. He used a video rental card at the store down the street."

Kennedy sat up, all fatigue gone. "You're sure he's there."

"He is now. I called and he answered. He's not too bright. I pretended to be a telemarketer and he ordered *Playboy* from me."

Kennedy was already on her way to the ticket counter. "Get me an angle, Mark. I can't just waltz in there. Something that won't tie me up here in Colorado for ages, either."

"I got just the thing." Mark sounded smug and rightfully so, with the information he gave her. Kennedy wrote down the particulars, then rushed to change her ticket for the flight back to Colorado. She reminded herself to give Mark a hefty bonus when this was done.

Vinnic Todesto had an outstanding warrant for assault.

FROM THE INSTANT they pulled up to Rogan's apartment building, he was back in his world. He'd let himself wallow in the silence and seclusion of the car—Clay wasn't much of a talker—but when he stepped out, shielded by the bodyguard, he was instantly plunged into his usual normal. And marveled at how strange it was.

He doubted anyone had leaked that he was going home, but some days the fans seemed to hover outside, just in case. Clay tried to sweep him across the sidewalk and through the door Robby, the doorman, held open, but Rogan wouldn't let him. He never ignored his fans, and almost never waved without giving autographs. They'd been stymied by SmythShield for weeks, and he figured they deserved a little attention. He never forgot they were the only reason he still had a job.

"Rogan, you need to get under cover."

Clay's discreet muttering was almost lost in the tumult, but Rogan shook his head. He smiled at the tweener in front of him, and she flashed her braces and sank six inches closer to the ground, her eyes rolling in embarrassment.

"What's your name, sweetheart?"

"Kara."

"Kara, lovely name. How do you spell it?" He wrote as she stammered out the letters, then scrawled his signature across the magazine cover and handed it and her pen back to her, moving a few feet closer to the building, letting them pat his shoulders and rub his hair.

"You live around here?" he asked the young woman shyly hovering at the edge of a rowdy group of college-age kids. She shook her head, and her hair cascaded in front of her face.

"We're here on vacation," half-yelled another woman, tugging her blushing friend forward. "From San Diego State. Checkin' out where the celebs live, you know." She waved a star map in Rogan's face, and he tried not to cringe away. Instead he took it from her hand and signed it, then handed it to the shy woman with a smile and eye contact.

"I'm glad I got to see you. Enjoy your vacation."

"We will. Thank you." Her voice was soft but still audible under the noise.

Rogan scribbled a few more signatures before letting Clay drag him and his shoulder bag into the building. Robby had handled the rest of the luggage and had an elevator waiting.

"Thanks, man." Rogan slipped him a twenty and ducked into the elevator. "I appreciate it."

"Good to have you home, sir." Robby tipped his cap and the elevator door slid closed.

"Smooth," Clay remarked, shaking his head.

Rogan frowned. "What, tipping him?"

"No, the fans. You've fueled that girl's fantasies for the next six years."

He shrugged. "Part of the job, that's all. They go to my films, so I give them a little charm. It's no skin off my nose."

They rode upward in silence a moment.

"How do you think Kennedy would handle it?" he asked Clay.

"Probably wouldn't let you do it at all, but if it was a strictly routine body job, she'd have three guys on you, watching the crowd and your back." He bent and hefted a suitcase as they neared Rogan's floor. "She'd probably mark someone as a go-between for the stuff you sign."

"No, that's not what I meant." He lifted the other case and a backpack. "I meant as, like, my...girlfriend." He'd been about to say wife, but it hadn't been long enough for that, and was he *crazy*?

Clay had stuck the suitcase in front of the elevator door and, weapon out, was sweeping the hall. He froze, stared at Rogan, and then cracked up. "Your *girlfriend*? Oh, man, no way. Kennedy wouldn't stand it for thirty seconds. But that's even if she let you call her that." He laughed harder. "Rogan, man, you gotta think about that. Kennedy is—she's—well." He retrieved the case but didn't holster his gun, walking slightly in front of Rogan all the way down the hall.

Rogan stopped in front of his apartment and pulled out his keys to open it. Clay reached for them, dropping the bag he carried.

"There's an alarm," Rogan said. Clay nodded, but held him back with one hand while he checked the foyer and as much of the apartment as he could see. He nodded, and Rogan entered behind him, closing and bolting the door. Then he checked and disengaged the alarm. "It's cool."

"We assume nothing." Clay motioned for Rogan to stay put. Weapon up, he examined the alarm pad, then moved silently through the apartment room by room. Rogan caught glimpses of him in the hall, on the stairs, and moving across the railed hall on the second floor, checking everything. It took a while.

"Some place," he said several minutes later, jogging back down the stairs. "You're right, it's cool. I'm going to need the code to the alarm, and your schedule for the next several days. It would be better if you lie as low as possible." He lifted his cell phone. "I'm going to check in while you unpack."

"Hold up, Clay. What were you saying about Kennedy?"

"Oh, right." He slid the phone back onto his belt. "Are you serious? About, you know, getting serious?"

He didn't have to think about it. "Dead serious."

"Bad joke. All right, here's the thing. None of us have ever seen Kennedy do anything that wasn't work-related, except visiting her father twice a year. That's it. So you've got more to worry about than whether she can handle your fans. You've gotta think about whether you can handle what she's dealing with. Know what I mean?"

"Yeah, I do. Thanks." He left Clay to check in and do whatever he needed to do and went to unpack, whistling.

He knew what Clay meant. Kennedy wasn't unique. Lots of people lived for their work. When the right person came along, they managed to fit somehow. Life adjusted. Kennedy might take more time to adjust than most people, he had to admit. But more importantly, he had no competition, except her job.

He tossed a suitcase on the bed and started emptying it. What was she doing now? Probably holed up in her office, studying data and trying to figure out who El Jahar was. She'd be doing that until she stopped him. She'd probably put the staff on paid leave, at least the ones not still guarding him, Bailey and M.J. But that meant she had no help. No one to share her burden.

And Rogan already missed her. He couldn't picture her in that office, because he had no idea what it looked like, and that bothered him. She knew what his world was like, but he only knew her world in his context.

He looked at the empty suitcase on the bed, then at the pile of laundry on the floor. Kicking it aside, he crossed to the dresser and pulled open the top drawer, selecting neatly folded shirts and underwear and tossing them into the suitcase. He heard Clay moving around, probably checking the windows and door again. Rogan thought about asking the bodyguard for the information he needed, but he knew Clay would never give it.

He closed the suitcase and headed for his office, and his computer. There were other ways.

BY THE TIME Kennedy made it to Evergreen, she was famished and jet-lagged and more than ready to take Vinnie down and go home. Where she could sleep. And consider her priorities.

She rented a car at the airport and followed Mark's directions to the condo development where Vinnie supposedly was. On the other side of the city from Hart's Haven, the condo was only half an hour from where they'd been filming.

Mark said Vinnie had been in Evergreen for at least two weeks, going by his use of the video card. She hadn't asked how Mark had accessed that information. Her company had superior tracking abilities, but Mark had degrees in computer technology and connections she'd never been able to develop. She had no doubt she'd be bailing him out of jail some day. But in the meantime, his skills benefited SmythShield.

She stopped at a convenience store and bought a bagel and cream cheese, orange juice, coffee, a pack of gum, and an empty cup to pee in, if necessary. Stakeout-ready, she headed for Peaceful Villas, the development that housed Vinnie's condo.

She drove through the development first to determine the layout of the streets, mentally blocking out escape routes, shortcuts and dead ends. The buildings were designed for maximum privacy, unfortunately, so she would have a difficult time staking out from the car. Each unit had a garage and one marked parking space, half of which were full despite it being the middle of a workweek. Five-foot wooden fences surrounded the courtyards at each doorway, so even if she could go unnoticed in the parking lot she couldn't see anything.

She parked at the end of Vinnie's building and walked purposefully down the sidewalk. His garage was open, a chipped and rusty El Dorado parked inside. The only visible window on the ground floor was covered with a shade, and the upstairs windows reflected the sun so she couldn't see anything. A faint bark reached her ears as she passed. So Vinnie had a dog.

Pausing at the end of the parking lot, she studied the terrain. The woods climbed a slope higher than where she stood, and she could see traffic through the trees. Maybe she could find a better spot up there.

She made her way back to the car and around to the street on the other side of the ravine, parking in a small commuter lot near the woods. Armed with binoculars and a local bird field guide, she sauntered toward the woods and found a spot on a pile of dry leaves, high enough to have a clear view of the front of Vinnie's condo, over his privacy fence.

Four hours of tedium were rewarded when a pizza delivery guy came to his door. Vinnie came out to pay the driver without the canine welcoming committee.

Anger and triumph surged through Kennedy. The guy was most definitely the Vinnie she was looking for. He hadn't changed much in the few years since Marika's death. His T-shirt stretched across beefy shoulders and biceps and a less-than-flat stomach. His jeans were worn and dirty, though she knew he hadn't been working today.

Four hours with nothing to do had given her plenty of time to plan. Kennedy watched him go back in the house with the pizza, then pulled out her phone to call the police. She relayed the warrant info and the address where they could find Vinnie, and was assured someone would be there soon.

"How soon?"

"Twenty minutes. Can you remain in the area?" the nasally dispatcher asked.

"Oh, yeah." She had no intention of leaving until he was in custody on a charge unrelated to the attacks on *Coming of Day*. The assault charge gave her a way to neutralize him without the publicity M.J. was so afraid of, and as a bonus, she wouldn't be tied up in Colorado forever.

She drove back to the development and parked behind Vinnie's El Dorado. Leaving her weapon in the car, she pocketed her keys and went through the silent gate to the front door. As soon as Vinnie opened the inner door he'd see her and probably bolt, so after ringing the bell she turned her back. She doubted he'd recognize her ponytail. Maybe her ass, but by then it would be too late.

The instant she heard the soft *whump* of the seal being broken when he opened the door, she whirled and yanked open the glass storm door, moving inside before Vinnie even had a chance to react. She took grim pleasure in watching his startled expression become confused, then fearful.

"Kennedy." His throat bobbed as he swallowed.

"Vinnie." She advanced into the house, but not too far. She didn't want the police to be suspicious when they arrived. "Been pretty busy, have you?"

The dog she'd heard bark earlier growled at her. She glared and bared her teeth and the mutt backed down the hall, whining.

"I don't know what you mean." When she didn't approach him he relaxed a little, but edged toward the doorway to the living room. "What are you doing here?"

"El Jahar."

He frowned. "I thought it was al-Qaeda."

Kennedy rolled her eyes, but uncertainty sparked. "I'm talking about *Coming of Day*. Your attacks. Your vendetta against me."

"Huh? What vendetta?" His frown deepened, then cleared. "You mean 'cause of Marika? Oh, man, I'm over her. I don't blame you anymore." He rocked back on his heels and shook his head. "It was just a tragedy."

His words didn't jive with his activities. If they were his activities. Kennedy's doubt strengthened. He didn't seem to have the smarts for what had happened on the set.

"What do you know about El Jahar?" she asked more deliberately. He shook his head.

"Nothin'. I don't watch the news."

"You aren't trying to punish me for Marika?" she tried one last time, knowing what the answer would be.

Vinnic shook his head again, sadly. "She was my life, but she never would have stuck with me, anyway. She was way out of my league. I hated you when she died, but it wasn't your fault. It's the way life goes, ya know?"

A knock sounded at the door. The cops.

"Yeah," Kennedy said. "I know."

FOURTEEN

"What do you mean, it wasn't him?" Mark leapt up from behind his desk and followed Kennedy into her office. She felt an immeasurable level of security being back on the compound, and was more relaxed than she'd been since the *Coming of Day* job began. But she knew she wasn't immune to danger here, and neither were her people.

More frighteningly, Rogan still might not be safe, either.

"I talked to him yesterday. It can't be him. That's all." She sat to shuffle through the papers on her desk. Report requests from past clients, news reports, intelligence reports—the accumulation of several weeks' work. She was never going to be able to leave this office.

Mark was still hovering anxiously. "Did you have him arrested?"

"I reported his whereabouts and the warrant to the police. They took him away." And she would never forget the look of sad betrayal on his face. That the assault charge was solid and his own fault was the only thing that saved her from more guilt.

Mark collapsed into her guest chair. "So we're back to square one."

"Kind of. I need to re-review the reports on Clive and some of Owen's family. Clive was a concern and he's nowhere to be found. Owen's file had no red flags, but there might still be something there."

Mark's face darkened for a minute and Kennedy frowned at him, wondering what had made him so angry. "I read the reports, Mark," she said, thinking maybe he was insulted. "But I focused on Vinnie with the evidence you provided me and now I need to look into other possibilities."

His expression didn't change at first, but then he seemed to understand. "I'll pull the files."

"Give me a few hours to try to catch up here, first."

"You got it."

"Uh, Mark?" She paused. "Clay check in?"

"Yeah, two hours ago. They're on their way to a meeting at some studio."

"Thanks." She breathed a little more easily. Standard check-ins always went through Mark. She would prefer to take Clay's calls herself, since he was still guarding Rogan, but instinct told her not to change protocol.

She organized her desk and started with the phone calls. They had half a dozen requests for service, but she couldn't take any jobs until she solved the El Jahar problem. She had a bad feeling that his failure with *Coming of Day* would change things, especially after the flower bomb. El Jahar would be frustrated by his failure and that kind of emotion meant more escalation. She couldn't afford to split her attention again and put another client in harm's way.

That meant contacting all the potential clients and telling them she may not be able to take their jobs. Some had called with enough notice that she hoped she could still do them, but she couldn't commit. Next on the list was contacting her agents and putting them on sabbatical. She hated doing that. She had built a tightly knit team and risked losing some of them completely. But she couldn't afford to pay them full rate to do nothing, and she doubted most of them would go for long without working. She left messages for most of them and annoyed Stacy, who insisted she was coming in to work and no cowardly bully was going to stop her. Kennedy argued, but Stacy hung up on her.

Kennedy stared at the phone. "Well, that will get you fired anywhere else," she grumbled, then went back to her paperwork.

Finally, at six that night, she was able to turn her attention to the deceased employee files Mark had pulled. She pored over them for three hours, making lists of research she wanted Mark to do and calls she needed to make. She'd visit some of the relatives herself.

Only her growling stomach pulled her away from the office. She locked up, set the alarms and headed home, wondering if there was anything worth eating in there. She'd grabbed fast food on the way home from the airport last night and settled for coffee and a Danish from Mark's stash for breakfast. She hadn't eaten since.

The compound was quiet as she crossed the asphalt. Bird cries wafted to her from the jungle section and the near-dark soothed newly tightened nerves. She strode leisurely toward her house, something she didn't do nearly often enough. She needed to ignore her problems for one night. Tomorrow they'd still be there, bigger than ever, but tonight she was going to give her brain and her body a rest. Maybe she'd read something for pleasure instead of for work.

Her snort rattled the stillness. She didn't think she

was wired for that anymore. Besides, she realized when she entered the house, she didn't have anything to read.

She scrounged in the pantry and freezer and managed to make a passable pasta primavera. She took it with her to the computer, where she launched her Internet browser and watched the news-filled home page load.

Before the first image had come up, a familiar chime alerted her to an instant message. She cursed herself for not turning off the auto-launch and switched programs. To her surprise, the IM wasn't from a client or her father.

She smiled despite herself. She'd always admired persistence.

Glutton for punishment, are you? she typed below the greeting next to Rogan's screen name, *Rogan*S*J**. The reply came quickly.

You bring out the worst in me.

LOL. I've noticed. Everyone get home okay?

She already knew the answer to that, but it seemed polite to ask.

Nary a mishap. No snipers, no gas, and best of all, no bees.

She laughed again. Maybe it was good that he was so persistent. She was starting to relax.

What's up next for you?

After a minute, his reply came up. *I'm trying something new. Leaving tomorrow.*

New movie?

Not exactly.

She waited but he didn't elaborate. Shrugging, she flipped back to the news until the chime sounded again.

How about you? Work busy?

I wish. I'm not taking any new jobs until this El Jahar problem is solved.

His next line was marked with an angry emoticon.

I thought you found the guy. Clay told me you went back to Colorado to get him.

She hadn't relayed her failure to Clay, but the fact that he was still on the job should have been clue enough.

Is that how you got my screen name? she typed. *From Clay?*

A pause. *No.* The typing icon flashed, and a moment later, *Dammit, that would have been easier.*

She chuckled. *He's supposed to know better. Where'd you get it, then?*

I have my sources.

Kennedy had a feeling she knew who. *I'll yell at my father later*, she replied.

LOL.

They chatted for a while about silly, inconsequential things. Rogan mentioned a press junket for a movie coming out next month. She talked about the article she'd just read about the new spending bill in Congress and how nice it was to be home.

Tell me about home.

She hesitated, unsure how to start. People in her life either knew the compound or didn't care about it. But she found herself describing her satisfaction when she looked out over the urban section during a training op, or got down and dirty in the jungle. He asked where she lived, and she told him about her little house in a corner of the property, shaded by a large oak tree and wired to the max.

I'm a gadget junkie, she confessed.

Yeah, I can tell. Not me. I can barely operate my computer. In fact, I fried it yesterday. It won't even boot up.

Kennedy frowned. *Then where are you?*

A cybercafé. Don't worry, Clay's right next to me.

Fuck. That was totally stupid. She kicked herself for assuming he was on a private unit, and promised to kick Clay's ass later. She got up and retrieved her cell phone and earpiece from her bag, dialing Clay's number as she returned to the computer.

We can't do this anymore, she typed quickly, as if that made up for what had already been said. *It's not safe.*

Clay answered the phone, sounding wary.

"What the fuck are you doing in a cybercafé? Get him out of there now."

A frowning icon popped up in the IM window. She sighed. *Get a new computer, then. Go home now.*

"Kennedy, I can't sit on the guy."

"Take him home, Clay. And from now on, until I say otherwise, he goes nowhere he doesn't absolutely have to go." The gentle buzz of conversation in the background suddenly increased. There was a muffled roar. Clay cursed. Rogan shouted, the sound cut off by a thud and a clatter, as if Clay had dropped the phone. Kennedy listened, horrified, to shattering glass and a car engine, screams and sirens.

She didn't shout for Clay. He'd come back on the line as soon as he was able, but her heart pounded, her breath frozen, as she stared at the words in the IM window: *Rogan*S*J* is offline.*

It took forever. She heard crying, footsteps crunching on broken glass, indistinguishable voices. More sirens. Her phone beeped. She hadn't plugged it in when she'd walked in the door, something that was completely automatic. It figured, the one time she forgot was the one time she had to have it. She should go get the charger, plug it in, so she didn't lose the connection. But she couldn't move.

Then she heard a voice she recognized. Crunching closer to the speaker, then rustling.

"Kennedy?"

"Clay." The rush of relief was short-lived. "Rogan?"

"He's fine."

She almost slid off her chair, so abrupt was the release of tension. "Hang on, I need to plug in my phone." She ran to the kitchen, plugged the charger into the wall and shoved the connector into the base. "Okay, go ahead."

"Pretty basic. Asshole drove through the front of the building. It was a light crowd, so we've got some cuts and a broken wrist, but no serious injuries. Rogan and I were dead center." He hesitated, then admitted, "If you hadn't been yelling at me, we'd be dead. The driver had the lights off, and if I hadn't already stood up and dragged Rogan out of the chair to leave, we'd never have had time to move."

"Anyone ID the guy in the car?"

Clay blew out a breath. "There was no one in the car. He braced the gas and must have leaped out at the last second. But he left a note."

Shit.

"It was El Jahar."

"Something wrong?"

Kennedy didn't respond to Mark, who hovered in her doorway, watching her move maniacally around her office. She'd been up all night. After she ordered Clay to get Rogan to the compound, in one piece, she had to do something or go insane. She hadn't felt this vulnerable, this helpless, since Justin died.

She'd swept her house for bugs or cameras. Nothing. She'd forced herself to shower and change clothes, then did a perimeter sweep and found no breaches in the electrified, steel, barbed-wire-topped fence. The systems all checked out operational and untouched. A sweep of her office and the rest of the small main building yielded nothing.

So how had El Jahar known? The only remaining possibility was still too unthinkable. Every time she tried to force herself to consider it, she argued herself out of it. She'd worked with all of these people for years. If anyone had a vendetta against her, they'd had ample opportunity long before now.

Eventually, when it was clear she wasn't going to answer his question, Mark went back to his desk. Kennedy started making calls, trying to track down suspects while she waited for Clay and Rogan's flight, an overnighter.

The system beeped at Mark's desk, signaling the opening of the gate with an authorized key card, combination and voice print. Her heart jumped. Clay. And Rogan. But when the outer door opened a few minutes later, it wasn't Clay. Her heart sank as her entire team of operatives filed into her office and lined the walls.

Kennedy deliberately set her pen on the file on her desk and leaned back in her chair, forcing herself not to spin it back and forth and betray her emotions. "What's up?" she asked casually.

Stacy stepped forward. "We have to talk."

Kennedy dropped her façade of composure and rubbed her face with her hands. "Look, I understand it's hard to go without work, especially when I can't give you an end date. I'll give anyone a reference—"

"Shut up."

Kennedy raised her eyebrows at the woman's sharp interruption. "I beg your pardon?"

"We're not here to quit, you moron. We're here to work."

She sighed and shook her head. "I'm not taking any jobs until I figure out this El—"

Again, she was interrupted. "You're not taking any jobs until *we* figure out this El Jahar problem," the younger woman said, her stance combative. "Smyth-Shield may be your company, but it's ours too. We're not letting it go down the tubes when we can help."

Kennedy scanned the group. Every one of them looked resolute. "I don't know what you expect to do."

Zip rolled her eyes. "Come on, Kennedy. You trained us. We expect to track down leads. Do research. Analyze the *Coming of Day* data. You don't need to do it alone."

"We're not leaving you alone here, either," Wolf added, scowling. "You're probably the most competent person on the face of the earth, but you're human. We're gonna keep the compound safe." Next to him, Jefferson nodded. They all did. Their loyalty and support overwhelmed her, but along with the warmth spreading in her chest came suspicion. Every one of them felt this way? Not a single person was annoyed that she'd laid them off? Someone, maybe even more than one, could have different motives. They could want to be here because if they weren't, it would be harder to wreak havoc.

On the other hand, *keep your enemies closer.*

She shot to her feet, blinking against the prickle of moisture in her eyes. "Thanks, guys. I really appreciate it, and the help is welcome. But there's still a problem with pay. With no income for an indefinite period I can't pay you full salary."

Andrew shrugged. "So we'll work half shifts and you pay us half salary. No biggie. There are enough of us to do some good, still."

"You're all willing to do that?" A couple of people exchanged less-than-thrilled looks, but no one walked out.

"Thank you."

They crowded around her desk. Kennedy spent an hour parceling out tasks and assignments, and felt immeasurably better by the time Rogan walked in. Better enough that she didn't run to him, throw her arms around his waist and squeeze him to death.

But since she'd neglected to inform her team about the attack the night before, they weren't quite as sanguine in their reaction.

"What are you doing here?" barked Rick, crowding up to Rogan.

"How did you get in?" came from Zip.

"Where's Clay?" was punctuated by the release of the safety strap on Stacy's holster.

"I'm right here."

The bodyguard appeared behind the actor. Kennedy's mild amusement at the agents' reaction evaporated when she saw the tiny cuts all over his face and neck. Her eyes flew to Rogan, who looked exhausted but unharmed. Clay had done his job, then, but had suffered for it.

"You told me you were fine," she accused, turning the agent to check for more damage.

"I am," Clay said, dropping his backpack and slumping into a chair against the wall. He'd never been so unprofessional in front of her, and that worried her. "It's all superficial."

"Until they get infected. Clay, I didn't intend—"

"I know." He smiled wanly. "I cleaned them up at

Rogan's friend's place. We went there to book the flight and change. Our clothes got a little torn up."

Kennedy whirled on Rogan, who shook his head. "Not a scratch on me, honest. Your boy knows what he's doing. I ripped my shirt, that's all. He was a mess. Figured we shouldn't go back to my apartment, so we went to my friend Charlie's to doctor him up and get some clothes."

As soon as he stopped talking, the agents erupted with questions. Kennedy calmed them, and Clay gave his full report. It wasn't the way she usually did things, but there was nothing usual about this situation. When he was done, there was a loaded silence. All eyes were on her, and she knew what they wanted to know.

"Was Clay the target?" Stacy asked.

"No," he answered for Kennedy and handed her a plain white piece of paper. The same drawing glared up at her from the corner, the same unobtrusive printed letters in the center of the paper. The words were few, but powerful.

You're not as good at hiding your feelings as you think you are.

It was signed El Jahar.

She set the paper on her desk, and Stacy picked it up. She read it silently, then passed it on. It didn't take long for them all to read it. They looked at her, then swiveled their heads to look at Rogan, who kept his gaze on her like a dog on a steak. She expected solemnity, maybe a few looks of disgust, even letdown as they realized what she'd done. Instead, a signal seemed to sweep through them all. They relaxed. Smiles blossomed. Kennedy got three thumbs up and four winks as they filed out, Clay taking the rear.

Idiots, she thought fondly. She didn't speak until they were gone and Mark had closed her door behind them.

"I—"

She didn't get to say more because Rogan shoved himself out of the chair next to her desk and swept her into his arms. His mouth came down on hers like they were magnetized, and he kissed her with all the hunger he'd shown in his eyes.

Kennedy let herself get swept up in his passion. It felt good to let go, to forget what was going on. Intoxicating, in fact. When her head started to spin she loosened her grip on his shoulders and pulled back.

Rogan sighed and eased her against him in a hug. "Thanks," he murmured. "For not pushing me away."

Torn between doing just that or clutching him tighter, Kennedy kind of hung in the embrace. His grip tightened and he buried his face in her neck, inhaling her. "God, I missed you." His words were muffled, but they sent a shaft of something through her chest.

"I'm sorry," she said, breaking completely free and retreating behind her desk. Rogan started to follow her, changed his mind and sat in one of the chairs in front of it. "I really didn't want this to happen."

"You mean us, or the car through the window?"

She gazed at him helplessly. "Either. Both. They're connected."

He leaned forward. "If it hadn't put me in danger, would you have allowed us to go further? See where it could lead?"

"I don't know why you'd want it to," she sighed. "I know I'm not the kind of woman you want."

"You don't know that."

Her smile felt sad. "You think in all those conversations we had at the B&B, I wasn't listening? I'm like your mother times a hundred."

Rogan stared at her. "I never said—"

"You didn't have to. I have to observe and understand people in my job, too, Rogan. I can read between the lines. God, I'm sorry." She leaned her elbows on her desk, bracing her head in her hands. "You don't deserve all this. Not when we didn't even get to the fling stage."

Then he was there, next to her, his hand on her back as he crouched by her chair.

"Kennedy." He waited until she looked at him. "There's no place I'd rather be. Considering the circumstances, I think that says a lot about my feelings for you."

For once, she had no answers, no plan of action, no certainty about the decisions that had to be made.

He stood. "You're exhausted, and so am I. I'd try to talk you into coming with me to take a nap, but I have a feeling you'd refuse. So point me in the direction of a bed and I'll leave you alone while you work. Later, I'll make you dinner and we'll watch a movie—one of mine, of course—and snuggle."

The whole scenario was so foreign to her, to what was happening around them, she could only stand there, speechless.

Mark knocked, then poked his head in. "Kennedy, call on line two. About Clive."

"All right." She waved him in. "Mark, please make Rogan a key to my house and ask Stacy to take him over." She pulled her key off her ring and tossed it to him. Rogan was right. He needed sleep, and she had to work first. There was no place he'd be safer than in her house, on this secure compound. Even with the remote chance El Jahar was one of her own, he wouldn't try anything here and reveal himself.

To Rogan, she said, "You don't have to make dinner. I'll probably be late getting back. And this does not mean anything about us."

"Of course not." He grinned, then snatched a quick kiss before following Mark out the door. Kennedy watched him go, thinking how nicely he enhanced her office.

Despite everything, she was smiling when she answered the phone.

FIFTEEN

BY THE TIME she went home at seven, Kennedy had several solid leads and much better spirits than before. They'd confirmed a solid alibi for Clive Furchon, and if the other leads panned out, she'd leave in the next few days to follow up. She wasn't sure what to do with Rogan while she traveled. It wasn't safe for him to leave the compound, but she wasn't sure it was a good idea for him to stay here without her, either.

She was deep in thought when she opened the front door, so much so that she was jolted into awareness by the scents of roasted meat and garlic that assaulted her. Adrenaline rushed through her and she'd reached for her gun before she remembered Rogan was going to cook dinner.

"Shit." She relaxed her arm and closed the door behind her, then headed for the kitchen. She half expected to see Rogan wearing a frilly apron and humming as he pulled rolls out of the oven, and was surprised to find him sitting at the table reading a sports magazine. The kitchen was clean, no food or dirty dishes in sight.

Well, that demolished her vision. Of course, she didn't own a frilly apron and didn't have rolls to put in the oven. But still. She sat with him, absorbing the happiness of his smile when he looked up.

"How was your day?" He rose to lean over the small oak table and press a kiss to her mouth. Before she answered he got up and started pulling out plates and silverware.

"It was decent. Were you bored?"

He shook his head. "Hardly. You've got some pretty interesting things to discover in here."

She thought of the gadgets and weapons lying around and wondered if she'd made a mistake sending him here. "You didn't use anything, did you?" She laughed when he waggled his eyebrows. "So, what did you make me?"

In answer, he reached into the oven and set a platter of roast beef on the table next to a bowl of mashed potatoes and another of corn. She'd had the beef and corn in the freezer, but the potatoes she didn't remember.

"Did you go shopping?"

"No. The potatoes did have quite a bit of root growth on them," he admitted, sitting across from her. "But they're fine. You don't have milk for the potatoes, so I just cooked them in chicken broth and mashed them with butter and garlic."

She snitched a bite from the pile he served her and moaned her agreement. "You're a good cook."

"Had to be, in my family. My mother wasn't around to do it, so Dad taught me."

Kennedy sobered. She wouldn't be around to cook, just like his mother. History repeating itself would only leave them both hurt. She couldn't let them reach that point.

They ate in silence for a few minutes, and then Rogan said, "Tell me about your brother."

She concentrated on mixing her potatoes and corn together. "I have."

"Not really." He cut a piece of meat and ate it. "Your father said—"

She raised her eyebrows. "You talked to my father?"

"He gave me your screen name."

She'd thought that was all.

"I was coming here even before that car smashed through the window," he explained. "I didn't think Clay would bring me. It took me hours to convince Ken I was better for you than M.J."

"Ken, huh?" She sat back and set her fork on her plate. "How did you find him?"

"M.J. He has no doubt I'm better for you than he is."

She couldn't suppress a small smile.

"So. Can you tell me? About Justin?" His voice was soft, his intent unmistakable. He wanted to know her, the innermost her, the one she didn't show anyone.

Hell, why not? Maybe it would be the brick she needed to hold up the wall between them. The wall that crumbled with every moment they were together.

She took a deep breath, then looked at the remains of dinner on their plates and the leftovers to be put away. "Let me clean up, then we'll go in the other room and I'll tell you."

"*We'll* clean up."

Kennedy just nodded. They cleared the table, put the food away and stacked the dishes in the dishwasher. Rogan poured glasses of wine he'd brought with him and followed her into the living room.

Kennedy's living room told people—the few who'd ever been in her house—the most about her personality. The kitchen was functional, the bedroom sparse. Her workout room was like the kitchen, full of tools and nothing else.

But the living room was her haven, and she watched Rogan make himself at home in it, looking like he belonged there. The dark, plush and softly upholstered sofa and chair, with their high arms and supportive backs, seemed made for him. He ignored the large TV in the corner and her grandfather's roll-top desk that held her computer and all her secrets, well protected from him and anyone else, as he set the wine glasses on one of the many small tables.

The walls were bare with one exception. Her photo wall held framed shots of her family and friends with a few of her from preschool through last year. Of course, Rogan gravitated to that wall, even though he must have looked at it earlier. He studied the shots and occasionally smiled or frowned. Kennedy stood in the doorway and watched him leisurely examine every photo of her as if trying to read her developing personality. When she looked at the pictures herself, she admitted it wasn't hard to do. The ones she'd chosen represented things she felt and rarely revealed.

"It was here," Rogan guessed, pointing

A connection vibrated within Kennedy, but she asked anyway. "What was?"

"When you lost him."

"How do you know?"

"He's in most of your shots until this one." It was a photo with her dad when she'd graduated from one of her courses of training. Their smiles were contained, and they held their arms loosely around each other as if waiting for someone to insert himself between them. For a moment Kennedy felt as sad as she had then.

"You're right." She turned and walked to the chaise— really an elongated armchair—and sat, pulling her knees up in an obviously defensive posture. Rogan hesitated before settling across from her on the sofa, his spine curved comfortably as he balanced his wine on his flat stomach. He didn't say anything, just gave her time to say it her way.

"My brother was a god," she started, smiling when his mouth twitched. "It's okay, you can laugh. He was fourteen years older than I was. My father was still in law school when he was born, and my parents were very careful after that. They felt it was unfair to divide their resources and not be able to give enough of anything to multiple children."

"So he was an adored older child who could do no wrong?"

"Something like that." She drank some wine, picking out the cherry and oak flavors before swallowing. "He wasn't spoiled, but well loved and well adjusted. Or so I've been told. My parents decided eventually that they were happy with one child and scheduled my father's vasectomy. I was conceived the day before the surgery."

"You say it with such relish," he teased.

"Well, it was a definite hint about what I would be like."

He narrowed his eyes at her. "Thanks for the warning."

"You know it already." She waved a hand and swallowed more wine. "Anyway, he treated me like a princess, and I adored him. Idolized him his entire life. We fought, and I hated him sometimes, but he was perfect."

Rogan glanced at the wall of photos. "What kind of doctor was he?"

"A general surgeon. He joined a group like Doctors Without Borders, a smaller group that was privately funded. He spent half the year working in California, the other half traveling to countries that had no true medical system and making people better." She swallowed against the swelling in her throat. "Sometimes I think he was a saint. Other times, I know a lot of what drove him was ego. He wanted to help people, but he liked the nobility factor."

She looked at Rogan. He was watching her tenderly, and her heart melted.

"He was in one of those strife-riven African countries with no protection. He treated some serious wounds of members of one faction, and the other faction killed him for it."

"So in saving others, you're making up for not saving him."

"I suppose." She straightened her legs, downed the wine and set the glass on the table next to her. "I thought he should have had more protection, even though I wasn't even out of high school and had no clue what that entailed. The rest of my life was dedicated to providing others with security. I did the best I could."

"Why are you using the past tense?"

She raised her eyebrows. Had she? "Maybe it is in the past."

"Don't say that. You'll find El Jahar and remove the threat."

Tilting her head against the back of the chair, she murmured, "Maybe."

"Where did this defeatist attitude come from?" He sounded disturbed. She heard the tap of his glass on the table and the adjustment of the cushions when he stood. "I never met a woman with less self-doubt."

Her head was starting to hurt. Probably from the wine. And exhaustion. A moment after she thought it, Rogan's fingers were on her scalp, massaging in little circles. She couldn't believe how much tension she'd held there.

"I'm not a detective," she told him, keeping her voice low. "I don't solve mysteries. I don't usually find suspects. I just shoot them when they pop up."

"That's oversimplifying, and you know it." His fingers dug harder. "So you're willing to shut down Smyth-Shield to protect it from your enemy?"

"If need be." She winced at the pressure of his fingers.

"And what about me?" Definitely anger in his voice. "Are you willing to shut us down to protect me?"

Kennedy slid away from his hands and stood to face him. The floor lamp cast odd shadows so she could see the fire and pain in his eyes but not the lines of his mouth.

"I've been trying to tell you that all along."

His eyebrows dipped into the stripe of light across his eyes. "Isn't it too late?"

"Maybe. Probably." She stepped forward into the shadows with him and took his hand. "What do you want from us, Rogan?"

He shuddered with the force of his expelled breath and intertwined his fingers with hers. "I'm not sure." He brought their hands to his lips and rested them there, not kissing or licking or being seductive, just touching. "I think I want it all. I've barely kissed you, but I already know it won't be enough. Even sex won't be enough. You're deep in my system."

The last words sounded like a line, but in his husky tone they were more of a declaration. Kennedy nodded, her own decision made. As he'd said, it was too late. In a lot of ways.

"I don't know if I can give it all. Or take all you can

give. But I'm not running, either, Rogan." She stepped closer. "I don't run."

"But SmythShield—"

"Closing the company is not running. I won't put the other team members up against El Jahar."

"You put them in danger on every assignment," he protested.

"That's their choice. They're doing a job. They didn't choose to become specific targets, which is vastly different. But it's not just them," she added, forging ahead when he started to argue again. "I won't put clients at higher risk. If I don't take clients, there's no money to pay my operatives. No money to run SmythShield. So I may have to close it down for that reason."

He ceded her point. "Back to us. Am I making you *want* to run? Are you fighting your instincts?"

Kennedy moved to pick up their wine glasses and carry them back to the kitchen. "No. A lot of women might be frightened by what you make me feel. But I'm not most women." She set the glasses in the sink and turned with a purposeful look. "As you are about to find out."

Rogan followed her into the small bedroom. The only furniture was a king-size bed and a tall wardrobe with a nightstand and another floor lamp in the corner. Kennedy walked straight to the bed and knelt on the high mattress so she was eye to eye with Rogan.

He could tell she was still of two minds about this, or maybe four or five. She might have said she didn't run, but that didn't mean she'd accepted their relationship. Or the possibility of it. He wouldn't be surprised if she'd decided to work him out of her system. He'd done that on more than one occasion. He didn't think it would be so easy to do this time.

She looked up at him from under her lashes and lifted one side of her mouth in a teasing smile as she reached for the buttons on his shirt. The agent seductress. He caught her hands with his and held them against his chest. Crooking one finger under her chin, he lifted it so she met his gaze head-on.

"That's better." He tilted closer to kiss her, keeping his eyes open. She did the same, and for a moment it felt like they were challenging each other. Then Kennedy let hers drift closed and slid her hands up his chest and higher to feather through his hair. Her fingers on his scalp were like warm water, relaxing all his muscles.

"Mmm." She licked her lips, her tongue sliding over his, and he groaned and deepened the kiss. His arms encircled her and his fingers stroked her back, making her shiver. He felt her suppress it and pulled back.

"Let go," he whispered, brushing her hair away from her face. "Give yourself permission to relinquish control for one night."

Kennedy laughed a little. "Easy for you to say."

He smiled and continued to finger her hair, watching the light play on it when he stroked through it. "Easy for me to teach too." He buried his fingers deep, running them to the ends, then repeating the move, over and over.

When she swayed and went with the motion instead of tensing against it, he unbuttoned her shirt and jeans and slowly pulled her clothes off. Then he laid her back on the pillows and undressed before stretching out next to her.

He leaned on one elbow so he loomed over Kennedy, his other hand on her waist. "You're beautiful," he murmured, tracing the edge of her bra, then stroking his palm down over her abdomen. He'd never been with a woman so fit and yet so soft. Not an ounce of femininity was lost to her toughness.

"Rogan," she whispered, and he turned to face her, lowering to kiss her when she raised her mouth. The kiss became carnal quickly. He'd been wanting her so long, he couldn't hold back. He pushed his tongue deep into her mouth, drunk on the taste of her.

She rotated and tried to get above him, but he pushed her back, pressing down over her. She arched and thrust, gasping when he pulled her bra aside and closed his palm over her flesh. She writhed, pressing upward. She reached down inside his boxers and wrapped her fingers around his hardness. He froze, the pleasure too intense, too near.

"Oh, yes," she moaned. "Now. I want it now."

"Kennedy." He gasped when she stroked and squeezed him. "God, you don't exactly go for sweet and tender, do you?"

"No. I like it hot and hard. Driving." She bit his earlobe. "Powerful. *Now.*"

KENNEDY KNEW HER words sent him beyond the point of no return, and together they ripped off the rest of their clothes. Rogan climbed on top of her with a grace she had never seen in a man in bed before. Then he was there, pressing inside her, thrusting, and she was with him, opening and begging him to do it. He did. And something unprecedented happened.

Her mind went blank.

She didn't bother trying to get it back. It was blessed ecstasy to just feel. The burning pleasure in her breasts against his chest, her neck where his mouth pressed and gasped, her legs and arms, and mostly the center. She rocked upward, rubbing against him, and cried out at the sharpness of the orgasm that approached. She squeezed him internally and he shouted, bucking faster, pressing deeper, more roughly against her hot buttons. She clutched him, her vision gone, her world a mass of whirling gold and black, the only sounds their breath and the beating of their hearts.

They exploded together. She felt him pulse inside her, adding to the best orgasm she'd ever had. If she could have spoken, she might have told him she loved him.

She let him lie down next to her and pulled the blue quilt over them to keep the world at bay. They snuggled together, face to face, and Kennedy sighed. She'd never felt like this.

Rogan reached up and stroked her cheek. "You are so beautiful," he said again.

She smiled. "So are you." His eyes glowed with what she felt, and his face looked angelic. Pure contentment, as if nothing in life could ever be bad.

"That's never happened to me before," she mused. "You shut off my brain."

He quirked one brown eyebrow and she traced it with her forefinger. "I made you stop thinking. That's my claim to fame now?"

She laughed. "It's an amazing feat, believe me. Nothing makes my brain shut off."

Rogan settled his shoulders deeper into the pillows and tightened his arm around her. "Not even sleep?"

"It works harder then."

"How about…" He rolled his eyes up to the ceiling, as if thinking hard. "Watching mindless TV?"

Kennedy propped her chin on her fist on his chest and shook her head. "Makes it easier to think, actually. Not that I do it much."

"Taking a shower?"

"Ditto."

"Huh. I guess you are a hard case." He kissed her, but the relaxed amusement faded too soon. "Kennedy, we didn't use a condom." He cursed and looked over his shoulder. "I had one and didn't use it."

"I'm on the pill," she assured him, suppressing a spurt of irritation at his shift from lighthearted relaxation to harsh reality. "You were cleared medically for the film. Hopefully you haven't picked up anything since. And if you're worried about me, I'm clean."

"I don't sleep around."

"Okay." She sat up and looked for her underwear. So much for not thinking. Why couldn't he have let things stay unserious for a while? And then to claim he was the rare movie star who didn't take advantage of all the choices he had out there. Maybe he was, or maybe, unlike some of his fellow *Coming of Day* stars, he was just discreet.

But it didn't matter. He'd brought them back to reality before she was ready for it, and everything had come surging back. Worse, because not only did reality mean risk and separation, it now meant she'd know what she was missing. The relaxation, the moments of happiness she'd held so fleetingly, were completely gone, and the loss hurt far more than she'd imagined it would.

She pushed out of the bed, ignoring Rogan's entreaty to stay. Since she didn't own a robe, she snatched a giant T-shirt out of a drawer and pulled it on.

"I'm going to get a drink," she grumbled, but he managed to stop her before she'd gotten through the door.

"Kennedy, what did I say?" He stood behind her, one arm wrapped around her waist to hold her in place. He didn't seem to care that he was buck naked.

She shook her head. "It's not what you said, Rogan. It's a lot of things. Give me a minute."

He released her and stayed in the bedroom while she got them both glasses of cold water. When she returned, he was back in bed, leaning against the headboard with the sheet over his lap. She handed him the water and he grabbed her wrist.

"Sit and talk to me."

She rolled her eyes to the ceiling. She didn't do touchy-feely. Or at least, she didn't use to. It was never necessary before.

"You don't believe that I don't sleep around."

"Rogan, I don't *care* if you sleep around."

Liar. The little voice in her head didn't believe her, and she doubted Rogan did, either. But he didn't call her on it.

"Then what do you care about?"

"Uh-uh." She shook her head. "No more deep discussion tonight. That's the problem."

"Why?" He tossed up his hands. "Will you please sit down? You're putting a crick in my neck."

She circled the bed and sat on the corner opposite him, where he couldn't reach her.

"This was a retreat from reality. It worked. I know you don't understand how much it means that you shut off my brain, but it was amazing. I've never had this kind of luxury, and you got serious too soon."

She stood again, a strange anxiety building in her

chest that made it impossible to sit still. Heat burned behind her eyelids. Tears? Seriously? She crossed to the window and strained to see outside, folding her arms tightly as if to hold herself together. The bed creaked and she tensed, but when she stopped trying to look outside and looked instead at the reflection of the room, she saw Rogan had just rolled onto his side to watch her.

"I'm sorry," they said at the same time.

He didn't anything more, didn't approach, just waited. Kennedy sniffed and dashed her hand under her eye, appalled when it came away wet. What the hell was wrong with her? She was never this…this emotional. This vulnerable.

But you never talk about Justin the way you did tonight. That had opened a crack in her shield, and Rogan had slipped right through. She wasn't upset that her interlude had been interrupted, she was upset that it meant so much to her.

Her life was changing. Right now, right this moment, El Jahar and Rogan St. James were changing her life. Even if she eliminated the threat and sent Rogan away tomorrow, nothing was going to be the same.

SIXTEEN

ROGAN DIDN'T TRY to coax her back to bed. He just waited patiently until she'd pulled herself together, and the need to be back in his arms defeated her fears, however temporarily. All they did was sleep, but it was the best sleep she'd had in years.

Kennedy woke early despite the late night and left the house before Rogan opened his eyes. But first she indulged herself a little, drinking her coffee in the doorway and watching him. The early sun shone gold in the room, glistening on Rogan's skin. The muscles in his arms and legs stood out even relaxed, and she made an appreciative noise in her throat. His curls spilled over his forehead, and though his eyes were closed she felt like she could drown in them.

But she couldn't. At least, not this morning. She emptied her still-hot coffee into a travel mug and left, locking the door behind her.

Mark was already in the office, looking grim.

"What now?" She tossed her case onto a chair and slumped at the desk, feeling exhausted again.

"I thought you should know there's a problem with your plan."

"What plan?" She hadn't developed one yet.

"Your cancel-all-jobs-and-refuse-new-ones plan."

She sighed. "Mark, you've got to understand what's going on here. I was El Jahar's original target. Taking the *Coming of Day* job put everyone on that set in a very precarious position, and I'm not willing to do that again."

He scowled. "So you're willing to let the company go bankrupt?"

She widened her eyes. "Are we in that bad shape?"

He shifted. "You know we're not. Yet."

Of course she knew, but she'd been out of touch on the shoot. "You're right. We can't go very long without new income. I need to catch up on the books, anyway, so when you get a chance I'd like to see them."

His shoulders went stiff, and Kennedy braced herself for him to whine about not being trusted. He only stood and left the office, returning five minutes later with the checkbook register and a disk with the accounts on it. Kennedy thanked him, finished dealing with her phone messages, and turned her attention to tedium.

Four hours later she was still at it. Expenses were up, though income until now had been stable. Fuel costs accounted for part of the rise, but not all, and she spent far too much time poring over the tiny type on cell phone bills.

So now she had to protect her staff, save her company from El Jahar and avoid losing it to creditors in the process. They had a decent amount of cash, enough to pay the bills, but not to cover payroll for very long, even at half pay.

"Shit." She rubbed her eyes, shrugging her shoulders against the tension in them and trying to figure out her next step. Put Mark on expense reduction, or research? Where should she search next? Names and facts buzzed through her brain, too fast to snag anything, too noisy to hand over to her subconscious. Her temples started to pound.

"Lunch break?"

She lowered her hands and blinked at Rogan leaning against the doorjamb.

"I can't." She sighed and waved her hand at her paper-strewn desk. "I've got to get this junk out of the way so I can concentrate on El Jahar."

Jefferson turned sideways to slip past Rogan. He greeted the actor, then handed two files to Kennedy. "Surveillance logs from last night. Two cameras went down for fifteen minutes each."

Kennedy frowned at the printouts. "Malfunction?"

He shook his head. "Deliberate turnoff."

She handed the folder back, showing none of the fear the revelation brought. Her sanctuary was being threatened, if not completely violated. And that meant Rogan's safety was in question too. "Find out why."

"There's more." He nodded at the other folder. "I checked the logs from while we were gone. Two cameras went down almost simultaneously eight different times."

Someone had been here, on the compound, and was messing with them. It was a clear "see what I can do," another psychological ploy. Maybe even an attempt to make her think it was an inside job—or it actually was an inside job.

Suddenly, it was too much. Everything was closing in on her. Everything rode on solving these problems, and she didn't know how.

"Talk to Mark," she ordered, rising. "Find out if anything else odd happened while we were gone. I'm going out for lunch."

Jefferson raised his eyebrows, looked at Rogan, then back at her, then at Rogan again. When he turned back, his smile was wide and approving. "Good. I'll let you know what we find."

It wasn't good. It was foolish. They should stay here, where it was safer. But it didn't feel safe. She could only hope El Jahar wasn't watching at this exact moment.

Once outside Rogan led her to a new Mazda RX-8. "Snazzy," she observed.

"Clay let me borrow it."

"Where are we going?" She lowered herself into the passenger seat, pushing aside a twinge of anxiety at not being in control. "There's nothing nearby."

"I know. You're taking a long lunch today."

They drove through the sunny, breezy afternoon for a while, Kennedy watching the empty road ahead of them and behind, through the side-view mirror. After fifteen minutes without seeing a single vehicle or spotting anything suspicious, she relaxed.

As soon as she did Rogan said, "Okay, I need to know. Sunshine?"

Kennedy grimaced. He hadn't mentioned it for so long, she thought he'd forgotten. "Didn't my father explain it?"

"Nope. Refused. But he did refer to you that way a few times."

She sighed. "I hate that nickname."

"Explain why so I don't use it."

"You won't." She tossed him a glare. "If you value your Hollywood looks, you won't."

"You don't intimidate me, Sunshine."

She resisted for another minute or two, but finally decided there really was no reason to keep it a secret.

"When I was a kid, my dad brought me to a movie set. M.J. came with us, though he'd been to a lot of shoots before with Max. I was pretty awed by the whole thing and that day, M.J. and I decided we'd both go into the business."

"And?" Rogan prodded when she didn't go on.

"It's too embarrassing," she grumbled.

"Can't be. Come on," he coaxed, putting his hand on her knee and shaking it. "I'm dying of curiosity."

"All right!" She got it all out in a rush. "M.J. wanted to act or direct, but I wanted to be a lighting technician because when those lights went on it was like turning on the sun and they all started calling me Sunshine and the name stuck."

Rogan smiled the same "isn't she adorable" smile they'd all given her at the time. "So where does Bob the HVAC man fit in?"

Covering her eyes, she slumped down in the seat. "He was a friend of Justin's. When my brother went overseas, he asked certain people to keep an eye on me. They all call me Sunshine and sometimes they come in handy on the job." She peered out from under her hand. "Satisfied?"

"For now."

They fell back into companionable silence. Occasionally Rogan threw out a topic and Kennedy gave her opinion, sometimes sparking a fierce debate, sometimes agreement. The entire time, she split her attention, watching for threats that never materialized.

"How come you know so much about so many things?" he finally asked, pulling up to a roadside stand. They got out of the car and went to the window, where they ordered chilidogs and vinegar fries. They ate leaning against the car, looking across the road to the cliffs above the ocean. It was the view that had made Kennedy locate her HQ on the west coast, though she didn't have any view from her compound.

"So? How come?" he reiterated, feeding her a soaked fry.

"My job," she said around the potato. "The more I know, the better equipped I am."

"How do you get that knowledge?" He bit into his hot dog and leaned forward so the squeezed-out drippings landed on the gravel and not his well-worn jeans.

"Reading. Watching the news. Surfing the 'net." Kennedy had much less difficulty navigating her hot dog, and laughed when a large glop of Rogan's chili landed on the wet spot at his feet. He cursed, then tossed her a grin. The easy, real grin that made her heart leap.

She'd seen a lot of bad things in her lifetime. She'd hardened her heart as she'd hardened her body, and emotion wasn't something that ever sent her reeling.

Until Rogan. Somehow, the man made her feel normal. And she was beginning to think that was something worth holding on to.

"How about you?" she asked when he'd gotten his food under control.

"Pretty much the same thing." He swallowed. "Though I tailor it to my role, usually. I've played a lot of different roles."

"So I've heard."

He nudged her shoulder with his. "You haven't seen my movies?"

She gave him a look. "Yeah, I have time to go to the movies."

"Rent them."

"Maybe." But she knew she would. She finished her

hot dog and licked her fingers, then snatched up the last fry. "I'd better get back."

"Not so fast. I'm not done hookying you."

"Hookying?" She crumpled up her trash and followed him to the nearby can, then back to the car. "What does that mean?"

Rogan climbed in and started the car. "It means I'm forcing you to play hooky."

Kennedy snorted and fastened her seat belt. "Nobody forces me to do anything. If I wanted to get back, I'd drop you like a dead tree and take the car."

"Uh, I guess that means you *want* to play hooky?"

"I guess so."

"Good." He peeled out of the parking lot with a roar and rattle of gravel. "We're going to the beach."

ROGAN DIDN'T JUST go to the beach. He *did* the beach. He scoffed at Kennedy's suggestion that they bring a blanket down. Granted, her memories of lying in the sun with her parents, playing in the waves and eating cold fried chicken out of a cooler sounded nice. His mother had always been too busy for trips to the beach. So even though he lived near it now, he always made sure it was an experience.

He made Kennedy stop before stepping on the sand to remove her shoes and roll her pant legs, then stuck their shoes and socks behind a boulder. He picked up cool shells to examine and flat rocks to skip, but the waves were too high and breaking too hard, so he gave that up pretty quickly. He pretended not to notice Kennedy surveilling the area. She must have decided they were unlikely to be ambushed here, because she just walked behind him and laughed, even when he grabbed her around the waist and dashed into the waves.

He stopped near the rocks and showed her the creatures in a tidal pool, then pulled a flexible Frisbee from his back pocket. "Let's see how good you are."

She was very good, of course. The Frisbee had a long flight distance and soon they were half a football field apart, sending the red-and-black disk soaring. They'd caught it 126 times—Rogan counted—before a sudden gust of wind blew it sideways into the waves. Rogan would have raced out to get it, but Kennedy stopped him with a reminder of the car's leather upholstery.

"I could drive naked," he panted when he'd jogged up to her.

"Sorry, I don't want to be with you when you get arrested for that." She grinned and brushed sand off his face. "You're very exuberant today."

Rogan shrugged and looked out over the water. His mood was because of her, but after last night, he wasn't sure he should say so.

"I grew up in Ohio," he said. "I never even saw the ocean until I was twenty-two. I'm making up for lost time."

Kennedy's hand rested against his cheek, and when he turned back to look at her, she leaned up and kissed him gently. The sticky salt air aided the cling of their lips, and she held them there for a minute before pulling back. His chest ached at her tenderness.

"Hmm." He licked his lips. "What was that for?"

"You're beautiful."

He allowed himself a small smile. "So are you." He dipped his head and kissed her again, allowing her to feel the need climbing in him. Kennedy lifted against him, and soon they were wrapped tightly around each other. Rogan slid his hand up the back of her shirt, and hers caught in the rear waistband of his jeans.

"We'd better stop before someone shows up," Kennedy said, not letting go of him.

"Okay." His mouth descended once more, his brain losing focus. He backed her up to the rocks, angling them into a curve that hid them from the path descending from the parking area to the beach. Another large rock jutted over them, hiding them from above. "This better?" he asked against her lips.

"Mmm," was about all he got from her. Excitement filled him. Was she really going to let him do this? She was hot under his hands, responsive. He held her hips so he could rub against her, and God, she felt good.

He let Kennedy turn them so he was against the rocks. There was a flat spot at the perfect level, and he half-sat on it. She climbed on him, writhing against his hardness, sending all his consciousness up in flames.

He moved his hands around under the front of her shirt, unclasping the front hook of her bra and roughly stroking her breasts. She bit the side of his neck and licked the hollow of his throat, then tugged open a few buttons on his shirt and pinched his nipple. Minor pain pierced him with intense pleasure, and he sucked in his breath sharply.

"Kennedy, if we're not going all the way…" he managed to gasp out.

"You'd better believe we are." She backed up long enough to strip one leg out of her jeans while he opened his, then climbed back on and sank fully onto him.

"God, you're wet." He clutched her hips and helped her move, trying to go slow, to savor the slick heat gripping him. But she squeezed, and he gritted his teeth, unable to keep himself from thrusting harder and harder. She arched so she pressed against him, her hips twisting frantically, and he knew she was already close. When she cried out and tightened rhythmically around him he tried to hold back, watching her, seeing by the look on her face that she went to a second, higher peak. The pure abandon in her expression pierced through him, sharp satisfaction that *he'd* given her that. His own pleasure intensified and coalesced before he burst and lost sight of her in his blinding orgasm.

"Jesus Christ." Kennedy held on to his shoulders with both arms, her face in his neck. He hugged her to him, shifting her limp legs so she didn't slump to the sand.

"I wonder how long it will be this good?" she asked.

He rested his hand on the back of her neck, squeezing lightly, and kissed her temple. "Forever." He could feel her doubt, but he ignored it. He'd show her.

SEVENTEEN

DURING THE DAY Kennedy worked hard, though futilely, to find the Houseal relatives. At night, she worked hard at sex and conversation with Rogan. She began to get used to having someone to go home to, and had to admit it was having a positive effect.

Mark didn't seem to agree. One night when Kennedy was leaving at five, early for her, he gave her a dirty look as she locked her office.

"Off to play with the boy toy?"

She stared at him, surprised. "What are you talking about?"

"You know. Your little gigolo back at the house." He leaned back in his chair, lacing his hands behind his head. "He must be good if he's getting this much of your attention."

Annoyed, Kennedy pocketed her keys and walked over to drop files on his desk. "What business is it of yours?"

Her tone was sharper than usual, and he swung forward, dropping his arms. "I suppose it's no business of mine." He tried to laugh. "Just teasing you."

She studied him. He fiddled with the files, not meeting her gaze. If she didn't know better, she'd say he was jealous.

"Really, Mark, why does it bother you that I'm seeing someone?"

He shrugged. "It doesn't bother me. It's just odd that all these years you worked harder than anyone, and now when everything's going to hell, you're leaving early to play hide the salami."

His crude term and the implication that she didn't care about her team sent her blood pressure skyrocketing. She tried to rein in her temper, but leaned far over his desk and said through gritted teeth, "You'd better never repeat that opinion, if you want to keep your job. My private life, while nonexistent until recently, is still private. And you are still my employee."

She had to walk for half an hour to burn off her temper. When the initial surge faded, guilt and resentment replaced it. Mark's comments reminded her too much of what he'd said before she took the movie job in the first place. But how dare he call her out for being selfish? She wasn't entitled to some personal time, after all these years? *Bad timing.* Okay, yeah, it was vital that she solve the El Jahar issue. But it wasn't like she wasn't trying, for cripe's sake.

And it was only a week, anyway, before Rogan had to fly back to L.A. to record audio for *Coming of Day.* She couldn't go with him and take that much time away from the investigation. She debated sending Clay, but it might call attention to Rogan and make him a more attractive target. So he hired a service he'd used before, former Secret Service agents who had a good reputation.

Kennedy was surprised at how empty everything felt, even places Rogan hadn't been. She paused at odd times to prod at the unusual sensation, then spent just as long berating herself for the distraction.

"Got a sec?" Jefferson carried a large envelope into her office on the third day after Rogan left.

"If you've got an answer about the cameras, I do."
They hadn't been able to come up with how someone had
been shutting off the cameras. Or why. It had continued
to happen, and they had staked out the zones at night,
but no one had been caught. It was increasingly likely
that someone on the inside was involved, but Kennedy
couldn't pick and choose who was trustworthy enough
to help her determine who it could be.

Jefferson sighed and pulled a chair up next to her.
"No. Nothing yet. But look at this." He handed her a
large aerial photograph. "What do you see?"

Kennedy studied the glossy photo, orienting herself.
The ocean to the left. Mountains. She traced her finger
over them. They were east of the compound, so…

She raised her eyebrows. "How the hell did you get a
satellite shot of the compound?" The shot was centered
over it, so it wasn't happenstance that it had been taken.
He didn't answer. Squelching her curiosity, she leaned
back in her chair and held the photo up. Mark apparently
wasn't the only one with connections.

"Okay, this is, what, ten-thirty on Monday night."
Jefferson, Zip, David and Frank had been on duty that
night. She and Rogan had been in bed by then, she remembered. Well, actually, next to the bed. On the floor.
With toys.

She cleared her throat and looked harder. The compound had security lights strategically located to mini-
mize shadows, even in the jungle area. But the more her
eyes adjusted to the image and she could tell what she
was looking at, the more wrong it looked.

"Half the compound is dark," she finally said. "About
eight lights."

"Yeah. We don't have any sensors on the power system. I mean, we can detect a major outage, but not individual lights if they have power but someone turned them off."

They turned off individual lights for nighttime training, but Kennedy wasn't sure how someone outside could have done it. It wasn't like there was a switch on each pole.

"What made you get this?" she asked. "You were on that night. Did you see something?"

"I saw a light out. Went to get a bulb. Came back, and it was on. Zip mentioned that another light was out, but when I asked Andrew the next night, he said it was on."

"Could the solar sensors be off?" She knew they sometimes came on randomly during the day, but couldn't see why they'd go off at night.

Jefferson frowned at her. "Of course I checked that. They're fine. And last night every light was on all night. I've stuck light meters to the poles."

"So what's your take?" She handed the photo back.

"I think someone is messing with us," he said. "Coming in here, flipping off cameras and lights to psych us out. The cameras aren't that hard to shut off if they know what they're doing. And the light posts have foot rungs to climb for easy changing of the bulbs. All they'd have to do is loosen them."

That triggered something in Kennedy's mind. She dug through the piles on her desk until she found the Houseal file, then read rapidly. *There.*

"Owen's youngest brother Karl is an electrical contractor. He wires new homes for the rich and famous." She scanned further. "Specializes in full-house control. You know, where you use a remote to open drapes and turn on lights and stuff."

"Sounds promising. Where is he?"

"Supposed to be in Michigan." She lifted the phone handset and dialed the number of his employer.

"Grand Rapids Remote Electrical." The voice was guttural and nasal at the same time.

"Karl Houseal, please."

The initial response was a *snork* sound followed by a hack and spit. Ew.

"He ain't here."

"Will he be in later?"

A huge sniff, then, "Not this week. He's on vacation."

A buzz started in the back of Kennedy's head. She grabbed a pen. "How long has he been on vacation?"

She could almost hear the guy's eyes narrow. "Why you wanna know?"

She injected some testiness into her tone. "Because I wanna know when he's comin' to finish the job, that's why I wanna know. I left messages for the past two weeks! Jerk doesn't answer my calls. If he's…"

"Hold on, hold on!" Luckily, the guy wasn't too swift, because her hastily built cover was flimsier than cheap drywall. "He's been out of town for a month. I expect him back next week, but that's why he hasn't returned your calls." He hesitated. "What's your name? I didn't know he left any jobs unfinished."

"I'll call next week, then, thanks." She hung up quickly and made notations in the file and on her calendar. "Could be him."

"It's a lead, anyway." Jefferson sighed, sliding his hands into his salt-and-pepper hair and leaning back in the chair. "More than we've had since we got back."

Kennedy tapped her pen on the desktop. "I think I'll go up there Monday. See if I can bump into the guy. If

I call, he might get scared and run. And if his snorky boss tells him about the call first, he could still run."

"You got his address?"

"Yeah." She tapped the pen harder. "In fact, I might go up there now. Intercept him before he goes to work."

"Sounds like a plan."

"It's something, anyway."

But not much. After Jefferson left her office, Kennedy doodled on her planning pad. Going to Michigan would take a lot of time, and there was a high chance Karl wasn't there, wouldn't tell her anything, or wasn't involved. But at least it was a lead, and a solid enough reason to take action.

Too bad Michigan wasn't closer to L.A.

IT WAS RAINING in Grand Rapids.

Stakeouts in the rain always sucked. Not that they were ever pleasant, especially alone, but alone and raining were the worst.

Kennedy sat in her rented Chevy Impala outside Karl Houseal's home. Home was a bit of an overstatement, since it was a room over a garage in a neighborhood that stank of garbage, but that could be blamed on the heat they'd had the week before. Wearing a short-sleeved blue shirt and horrid blue shorts that made her look like a parcel delivery person, she'd gotten soaked taking a package to the house. A house-coated middle-aged-looking woman who was probably about thirty-six squinted at her through a cloud of smoke generated by the cigarette hanging from her mouth.

"He ain't home. I'll hold it for 'im." She reached for the package. Kennedy held it away.

"Sorry, I have to give it to the addressee. Any idea when he'll be home?"

"Prolly three, if he don't go to the bar," the woman muttered, already closing the door.

So Kennedy was sitting in the Impala outside with no air conditioning, no coffee, and an ETA of "prolly" three o'clock. Four hours away.

Luckily, the woman wasn't far off. At one-thirty, a rusted pickup pulled to the curb in front of the house. The guy who emerged carried a tool belt and wore a uniform shirt, though Kennedy couldn't see the logo on it. He shoved the door of the truck shut, then reached through the window and pulled out a six-pack of beer. Kennedy watched him go up the driveway and around the garage. He reappeared at the top of the exterior stairway on the side of the dingy building and opened the apparently unlocked door.

Not wanting him to get too comfortable, Kennedy climbed out of the car and crossed the steamy sidewalk, package in hand. It couldn't have been more than forty-five seconds from the time he closed the door behind him to when he opened it again to her knock, but he'd already popped the top on one of the beers. *Fast worker.* The logo on his shirt bore the initials GRRE, and a sewn-on patch on the other side said "Karl."

"Help ya?" His eyes went to the package in her hand, then the clipboard she held out.

"Package delivery."

He didn't question it, just took the clipboard to sign. Kennedy moved into the room and shut the door.

"Hey, what—!" Karl backed up, his eyes finally going to her face. They widened. "You!"

"Surprised to see me?"

"Hell, yeah!" Surprise darkened to anger. He threw the clipboard at her and she snatched it like a Frisbee. The play with Rogan had turned out to be practice, she thought, grinning.

Karl backed away. "What are you doing here?"

"I want to know what you've been up to." She kept on the offensive, moving toward him as he scrambled through the living area to a short strip of linoleum with a small refrigerator, sink, and stovetop. He only stopped when his back was against the avocado-green fridge.

"I been on vacation." Cornered, he resorted to belligerence, lifting his chin and baring his bottom teeth. "What of it?"

"On vacation where?"

"None a your business!" He flipped her the bird, and Kennedy lost her patience. She was on him instantly, a hand on his throat, and she smiled smugly when she towered over him. Or maybe he cowered below her.

"It's my business if you're trying to harm my people," she said through gritted teeth. "I want answers."

Karl whimpered. "Why would I want to harm your people? I don't know your people."

She rolled her eyes. How could she have had so many good operatives related to weasels?

"Thirst for revenge is hard to set aside."

"Revenge?" His voice squeaked. She let up a little. "Revenge for what?"

In answer Kennedy flicked a glance at a photo on the door behind him, one of the whole group of siblings, from the looks of it. Owen was part of the group, as was Karl. He twisted as far as he could, then pushed his eyes to the corners to try to see what she was looking at.

"Owen? You mean revenge for Owen?" He relaxed in

her grip. "Naw, man, I'm not that stupid. I mean, you're *trained* to take care of guys like me."

Not exactly, but she didn't correct him. She did let go of his throat, remaining close so he couldn't try to make a run for it.

"It was a while ago. You had plenty of time to plan it."

He shook his head, but resentment burned in his eyes. "Owen was the only one smart enough to do that," he said, hunched over as if still trying to catch his breath. "Don't get me wrong, the whole family hates you." He straightened. "But not enough to die tryin' to make you pay."

"Give me proof." It wasn't hard to tell when someone like him was lying, and he wasn't. But she never accepted instinct alone when proof was available.

"Proof? What kind of proof?" He paced sideways like a nervous panther, then realized he had a can of beer in his hand. His torn sneakers tracked the spilled half around the kitchen, but he gulped what remained. "How can I prove I don't want revenge?"

Kennedy folded her arms and tried to look like she was ready to hang there, despite the lack of anything to lean against. "You don't need to prove what you want or don't want, Karl. I just want you to prove where you've been for the last month."

His eyes widened again. "I know! I got it!" He held one hand toward her, palm out, and the other with one finger up. "Just hang on. Stay here." He rushed the few feet to an alcove that held a bed and dresser. On top of the dresser was a pile of small, crumpled papers. He grabbed a handful.

Receipts. Kennedy took them as he thrust them at her, checking the dates and addresses. Most of them were for booze or bars in Miami, but there was a substantial hotel bill and a couple of corner grocery receipts for cigarettes and potato chips. The dates were all during the Denver shoot, though the hotel bill reflected a stay dating back to the day before she'd arrived at the warehouse studio.

"You're missing some days," she commented, putting them in order. "You could have flown out to L.A. and back."

"Wait! Wait!" He ran back into the alcove and grabbed more scraps of paper. "I was there! I was there!"

Kennedy frowned at him. "What are you so afraid of, Karl? You think I'm going to shoot you or something?"

He looked at her holsterless hip and licked his lips. "Ah, no, not really. You don't want to go to jail any more than I do."

Jail, huh? The receipts, his antsiness, and how he lived began to add up.

"You're off the hook." She handed back the receipts. "But I'm curious. How could you afford all that? And a whole month off work?" She waved a hand at the wad of paper he now clutched against his abdomen.

He shrugged, sending loose paper drifting to the floor. "I saved. And I got a big bonus for the last job I finished."

Yeah, sure. "Why are you keeping the receipts?"

"I'm not." He looked sullen. "I had to do laundry."

She got it. He'd shoved the slips of paper in his pockets during his trip, and emptied them when he got home.

Kennedy felt a little bad for making him seem like a slacker to his boss. "Okay. Before I go, Karl. Anyone in your family talk about payback? For Owen?"

He frowned. "We hardly talk about him. He didn't fit in our family, ya know? He was the only smart one. Only one went to college, until Amy." Now that the danger had passed, he suddenly got very chatty. "My mom was devastated, but she got over it before she died. There were so many of us kids, but he was the one with promise."

"Your brothers and sisters seem to have made out all right, for the most part. Where are they all?"

He rattled off names and places. Some of the names Mark hadn't been able to track down turned out to be married sisters who, according to Karl, couldn't care less about how Owen died. Kennedy would double-check the file she'd left in the car, but she was sure those loose ends, once followed up, would eliminate the Houseal family as suspects.

Kennedy thanked him and left, feeling she'd been down this road before. Unlike Vinnie, Karl wasn't being taken away in handcuffs. Yet.

Oh, well, when he finally was, at least it wouldn't be her doing. She didn't buy his vacation excuse. She'd seen cutting tools by the sink, plastic wrappers in the trash—and he had six boxes of zipper sandwich bags stacked on the counter between the sink and the stove. She'd be willing to bet SmythShield that he'd been in Miami for drugs. If he was dealing, though, it hadn't been for long. Nothing in his apartment was worth more than fifteen dollars.

She made some notes in the file and was about to head for the rental agency and the airport when she decided to make the trip more worthwhile. The college sister Karl had mentioned, Amy, lived about two hours away. It wouldn't hurt to visit her, she decided, and turn another stone. Men didn't have a monopoly on revenge.

She stopped at a truck stop to change clothes and call Mark. He confirmed that what was in the file was all he'd been able to find on Owen's oldest sister. She'd stayed at home until all the kids had grown up, and had been proudest of Owen when he'd started working for SmythShield. Kennedy remembered her at the funeral, stout and tough looking, as she guessed one would have to be to keep seven younger siblings in line. She'd also tried to be stoic, but Kennedy could easily read the devastation in her eyes as she watched the casket being lowered into the ground.

Amy lived in a suburban neighborhood where the houses were close together, the lawns struggled to display any green, and people who lived there made desperate attempts to spruce up their homes. Kennedy counted eighteen of those shiny balls-on-a-cone things in three blocks.

She parked outside Amy's house and studied it. White aluminum siding, neatly trimmed bushes, an old but well-kept Camry in the driveway. No signs of kids, like bikes or balls or other toys, lay around. No fence in the backyard, though nowadays with electronic fencing that didn't really indicate whether there was a dog in residence. An American flag hung limply from a holder next to the front door. It was clean, and Kennedy would bet they took it down and folded it properly every night.

The streetlight overhead popped on, and the flickering bluish glow in the front window indicated a television being watched. She got out of the car, checked her gun, and strode slowly up to the carport door.

Amy only took a moment to answer. She looked much different than she had at the funeral. She was leaner, more muscular, yet appeared less tough. Her hair was longer and framed her face with gold streaks in the dark brown. Her makeup was nicely done, and she still wore the blouse and suit skirt she'd probably worn to work.

"Ms. Smyth," Amy greeted her, opening the door and motioning her in.

"Thank you." Kennedy moved into the spotless kitchen, then waited. Amy offered her tea and, slightly bewildered, she accepted. This wasn't the welcome she would have expected.

"Karl called you," she guessed, sitting at the kitchen table.

"Of course. He warned me you might come by. I'm surprised it took you so long." Her voice was deep and melodious and made Kennedy think of honey.

"What do you mean?"

She shrugged. "Someone's playing a revenge game, right? So your prime suspects would be us. Families of those who died in your employ. Maybe families of those who died under your protection."

Kennedy accepted the mug and tea bag and waited as Amy sat. The kettle she'd placed on the stove made a warming-up noise. They each unwrapped a tea bag and set them in their mugs.

"You're very insightful," Kennedy said. "What do you do?"

"You probably know I'm an attorney."

Kennedy nodded. "Makes sense. I didn't know, though. We couldn't track you past the waitressing job."

Amy smiled a little proudly. "Well, I was a bit lost after Owen died. I drifted. I wasn't deliberately trying to hide, though no doubt that's what you thought."

"It occurred to us." It also occurred to Kennedy now that Amy was awfully contained and rigidly pleasant. She sharpened her bullshit detector and watched the woman more closely. People that contained often had something to hide.

"I never blamed you for Owen's death." Amy rose and removed the kettle from the burner just as it began to scream. She brought it to the table and poured water into both mugs. "Some of my brothers and sisters did. Most got over it." She stopped speaking and returned the kettle to a trivet next to the stove.

"What are you implying? Do you think one of your siblings could be trying to get revenge?"

Amy pursed her lips as she dipped her tea bag, silent while she poured half-and-half and added sugar, removed the bag and set it on a dish, and stirred the concoction. Kennedy absentmindedly followed suit, waiting.

"I can't speak *for* my siblings, as I haven't spoken *to* some of them in several years," she finally said. "But I am a personal injury attorney, Ms. Smyth, and I will tell you one thing about human nature.

"Death is much more acceptable than injury. It's final. There's no more trial, none of the tribulations of life. No pain, physical or emotional. No loose ends." She tapped a finger on the table. "It's the ones who survive who have loss. The ones who have had to give up something vital, who have to go on fighting, day after day after day." Shrugging, she sipped her tea. "Some people want to sue someone when a loved one dies, as if punishment and blame can make up for the end. But they usually get over it, grief running its course well before we get as far as a trial. No, death is not the ultimate loss."

"I'm not sure I agree." Kennedy thought of Justin and how she felt after he died.

"Of course you don't. You haven't seen what I've seen. But consider something, Ms. Smyth. What would you do if you lost an arm? A leg? Your sight? Something that prevented you from doing what you've dedicated your life to doing."

Suddenly, Kennedy understood. "So you think I should expand my suspect list."

"No one feels more wronged or fights more powerfully than someone who has had their life taken from them, but continued to live."

EIGHTEEN

KENNEDY LEFT SHORTLY after, tea untouched. Amy had given her a list of her siblings' addresses, more complete information than Karl had provided. But she'd been adamant that they'd all moved on.

Her insight about loss without death had struck hard. Kennedy pulled out her cell phone before she'd turned out of Amy's street. Mark wasn't in the office, of course—it was too late. But she left a voice mail. "Mark, pull the files on all former agents injured in the line of duty. Not simple injuries," she added, "but disabling ones." She didn't need files to remember the details, but he would need the information to start tracking them down. She rattled off the names, said she'd be flying back tonight and would see him later in the morning, and hung up.

She'd just glanced down to set her phone on the console between the seats when someone hit the car from the passenger side, crashing into the rear quarter panel and shoving the Impala into a telephone pole.

Stunned, Kennedy sat frozen for a moment, unable for once to assimilate what had happened. Then she heard the roar of an engine and turned to watch a black sedan back away. She couldn't open her door because she was up against the pole. Bracing for another impact, she reached for her seat belt, but the sedan spun in a quarter circle and sped off up the street.

Pissed, Kennedy started the stalled car and gunned the engine, shoving it into gear and grunting in satisfaction when the vehicle responded. The rest of the left side scraped against the pole and the rear right tire sounded like it rubbed bent metal, but the car moved.

And boy, did it move. The Taurus had a long lead but stupidly didn't expect her to come after it. They were probably trying not to call further attention to themselves by driving recklessly, but that meant she caught up to them in seconds.

There was only one person in the car ahead of her, a dark shape with short hair and a wide neck. Probably a man. He hadn't noticed her and traffic was nonexistent, so she pulled up next to the driver's side and looked over.

She caught a glimpse of a dark-skinned, bearded face sporting a look of horror before he jerked the wheel right, riding up over the sidewalk and settling into the side street they'd nearly passed. Kennedy spun the wheel to do a tight one-eighty and followed.

But she didn't know these streets, giving her smasher a slight advantage. He jerked through a series of twists and turns and almost lost her twice before the Impala gave out, choking and cutting her speed. She made one last effort, slamming the pedal to the floor, hoping to overtake the car and force it to stop before she lost him.

It was no good. The Impala had enough juice to get past the Taurus, enough to jam it sideways against a warehouse wall, but Kennedy skidded too far around, leaving his driver door clear. By the time she'd gotten out and circled around to his car, he'd disappeared into one of half a dozen apartment buildings and alleys surrounding them.

"Shit!"

She kicked the crumpled front bumper on the Taurus, only momentarily satisfied when it fell off. Sirens approached. She holstered her weapon and pulled out her ID, prepared for the same old rigmarole. She was wasting a lot of time with cops lately, she fumed. The Taurus was probably stolen and would yield nothing.

"Who chased who?" the cop asked a bit later, chuckling as he observed the two cars. "Not your average hit-and-run, huh?" He licked the tip of his pencil and started scribbling. "Any idea who hit you?"

"No. I never saw him before."

Someone had gone to some trouble to make her think she knew, though. The proximity to Amy's house and the timing meant they wanted her to blame the Houseals. It seemed obvious that Karl had tipped off Amy in plenty of time for her to set up the hit. But Kennedy trusted obvious even less than she trusted coincidence. Someone thought she was stupid.

That someone was wrong.

SHE GOT HOME in the middle of the night, and as she drove onto the compound she could see that some of the lights were out again. Cursing, she parked by the office and sat, struggling to make herself get out and patrol the compound. Christ, she was tired. She shook her head and shoulders and struggled to remember what Jefferson had showed her about the outages. But the seven hours of sleep she needed at night had been far out of reach lately, and it had caught up to her. The thought of staying awake any longer was intolerable, so she left the patrol to whomever was on duty tonight and headed the car to her house.

There was only one thing she needed to do before she

collapsed into bed. As soon as she locked the door behind her, she pulled out her phone and thumbed Rogan's speed dial. She tried to let him check in with her because his schedule was so erratic, but tonight she caved to the need to hear his voice.

His line barely rang once. "Hey, babe," he answered, and she scowled.

"This is a secure phone. You can't tell it's me."

"I have ways."

"Rogannnn," she warned.

"You're the only one who calls this number whose ID is blocked. What happened?"

"What didn't?" She rubbed her forehead. "I'm exhausted. I'll tell you tomorrow. I just needed to make sure you were okay."

"I'm fine. I'm in bed, with a guy outside my door, another in the living room, and one outside my window. You okay?"

"Yeah, just wiped. I miss you."

Rogan chuckled, but somehow the sound was affectionate. "You must be tired, if you're admitting that."

"Savor it." She told him good-night and plugged in the phone, then fell into bed and was unconscious before she landed.

THE NEXT MORNING she went straight to her office to start poring over the files Mark had pulled, but her desk was empty, and so was Mark's chair. Thinking he might be getting coffee, she checked the break room. He wasn't there, either.

"Zip!" She spotted the woman at the end of the hall and called out to her. "Where's Mark?"

"I think he went to a dentist appointment," she called

back, disappearing around the corner to the basement stairs, which led to a workout center and sparring room.

Kennedy returned to her office, muttering. She'd bet he hadn't even checked voice mail. She pressed the speaker button on the phone and punched the codes to retrieve messages, but the mailbox was empty.

"Odd." She checked her personal messages. Three from Rogan at various times while she was gone. He said he didn't want to interrupt anything important by calling her cell phone but to call him soon, please, because he missed her dreadfully.

He actually used the word dreadfully.

Laughing, she erased his last message and listened to one from Mark reminding her about his dentist appointment. Kennedy frowned. She knew he hadn't mentioned it before, so why was he acting as if he had?

He'd left nothing for her on her desk, so she went to the file room and pulled the files she wanted.

Dante Bernard. He'd had his legs mutilated in Iraq when a child gave up her "toy," one of the explosives from the American smart bombs that hadn't done its job until far too late. Kennedy called his last known phone number. Disconnected. *Track Dante*, she wrote on a pad, and moved on to the next file.

George Shifondo. He'd been on bodyguard duty at the Capitol when someone attempted to kill his protectee by throwing rocks. One hit George in the head just right, causing brain damage. She called his sister's house, the last place they'd known him to be. The voice that answered was unmistakably his.

"George, hi! This is Kennedy Smyth."

"Kennedy!" He sounded delighted. "I was hoping you would call today!"

"You were?"

"Yeah! When can I come back to work?"

"Oh. What does the doctor say?" Guilt made it hard to concentrate on his answer. She hadn't kept in very good touch with any of these people. She'd been so busy focusing on who she was protecting *now* and who was next, and forgot about the past. Unforgivable.

"Doctor? Ach." He made a dismissive sound. "He says no guns. But we could be the cops and they could be the robbers, right, Kennedy?"

She moved the phone away from her mouth so he wouldn't hear her sigh. It was always sad when someone was changed like this. But as guilty and sympathetic as she felt, she still had to focus on *now* or there wouldn't be a future in which to address the past.

"Actually, George, if they told you no guns, I'm afraid you can't come back to work."

She braced herself for his response, but he was silent for a minute, then said, as happily as he'd greeted her, "Okay! Wanna talk to my sister?"

"If she's there."

"Hold on."

There was a bunch of scuffling noise, then the muffled pounding of feet going down stairs. Then George yelled, "Frances! Phone!" and she could picture him leaning over the banister like a teenager, shouting at the top of his lungs. She thought she heard "It's Kennedy!" before Frances picked up.

"Kennedy!" Fran's voice was warm. "So nice to hear from you!"

Kennedy's guilt deepened. "I'm sorry to bother you, Frances," she began.

"No bother."

"You may not say that when you hear why I'm calling," she admitted. "I'm sorry I haven't been in touch."

"Oh, my dear, we haven't expected you to be. George is well taken care of, and time has no meaning for him. He doesn't know how long it's been since he spoke to you. And you have more important things to attend to."

"No," she denied sincerely. "Not more important. More urgent, or so I thought. But not more important."

Frances waited patiently, and Kennedy swallowed. George as a suspect was ridiculous. "Has George left home at all over the last month or two?"

"No, dear," Fran said sadly. "I've taken him to the movies, of course, and shopping, but that's all."

It sounded like they both could use something to do. Kennedy jotted a note to look into brain injury programs in their area. She made an excuse to Frances and hung up, wondering if she was on the right track.

Diana Carson was the only one left. Kennedy couldn't help a bittersweet smile as she reviewed her chart. She and Diana had been two of a kind. They met before Kennedy started SmythShield. They trained together and were close friends, even after Kennedy became her boss.

But then there was the accident. The wounds she'd suffered had been severe. She'd wanted to come back anyway, but wouldn't have been able to fire a gun with her usual skill and her mobility would have been limited. Kennedy wouldn't have felt safe putting her in dangerous situations. The rebel gunfire had also caused internal injuries that led to a hysterectomy. She'd been struggling through rehab the last time Kennedy had seen her.

Because Diana had screamed at her to get out of her life and never come back, and Kennedy had done it. For the first time, the loss echoed inside her. Just like everything else, she'd closed herself off to it, left it on the outside of her ever-narrowing focus. No, that wasn't completely honest. She'd started cutting Diana out long before the accident. She hadn't even gone to her wedding.

"Hey, babe."

She jerked her head up, shocked that she'd been so immersed she hadn't heard anyone come in. Rogan leaned against the doorjamb, looking fresh and delicious in jeans and a dark green shirt, sleeves rolled to bare his forearms.

"Play hooky today." The heat in his eyes belied his casual stance. "I missed you."

The thought of playing coy never crossed her mind. She leaned back in her chair and lifted her hair off her neck. "I missed you too. I could have used some diversions."

His gentle smile became wicked. "I have plenty." He held out a hand and motioned with his head for her to follow him. "Come on. I've got the ultimate diversion."

She looked wearily at the files on her desk, and at the list of things she needed to do, and compared confronting her demons versus escaping with Rogan. And chose escape.

Some people would have been shocked out of their holsters.

Instead of going back to her house for sex, Rogan led her to his car—a Jeep Wrangler this time—and drove out of the compound. He wouldn't tell her where they were going, just chatted about how funny his recording sessions had been. Kennedy deliberately relaxed and laughed with him. It didn't take long before he turned the Jeep into the entrance of a state park and followed the winding roads to the base of a mountain. Kennedy helped him pull gear from the back of the Jeep.

"Rock climbing?" She looked down at her jeans and sneakers. "I'm not dressed for it."

Rogan nodded at a bag in the corner. "Clothes and climbing shoes in there." She checked, and sure enough, her own things were inside. He must have gone to the house before picking her up.

She looked up at where the cliffs rose above the tree line. The sky was a perfect blue, the light clear and crisp without being blinding. The clean air smelled of the unspoiled outdoors. She was going to be moving, challenging her body, giving her mind a rest. The prospect cheered her.

But it also frightened her. This wasn't like the beach, where they could see someone coming and get under cover. They'd be vulnerable on the wall, with no maneuverability.

"We shouldn't do this."

He didn't look up from the rope he was examining. "Were we followed?"

"No."

"You tell anyone where you were going?"

She hadn't known where they were going. "Obviously not."

"You bugged?"

Since she'd been running scans on a daily basis, she probably wasn't. "Only if you did it."

"So we're good." He smiled, ruggedly sexy and challenging at the same time. He was probably right, and she was tired of being afraid all the time.

"Thanks, Rogan." She pulled the clothes out of the bag. "I needed this."

"I figured." He hadn't stopped checking and packing the gear. "You've been cooped up too long. That's not the kind of woman you are."

"No." She smiled at the back of his head, pleased that he knew it. "Give me a minute to change."

She did that in the Jeep, then accepted her share of their gear and supplies and followed Rogan up the trail. She signed below him on the sign-in sheet under Plexiglas at the trailhead, and inhaled deeply as they started through the shaded woods. Energy pumped through her as if fed by the fresh air. Her muscles tightened and released in rhythm; her blood practically sang through her veins. It had been way too long since she'd done something like this for the pleasure of it instead of for training or on the job.

They were silent for the half-hour hike through the woods. They paused at the base of the cliffs to drink water and check their gear again. Kennedy had more experience, so she led. They climbed steadily until she reached a wide ledge, where they sat and enjoyed the view while they pulled out their lunch.

"What do you think, about halfway up?" Rogan asked, squinting toward the top of the wall.

"About." Kennedy took a bite of her sandwich, holding it in one hand while she flexed her fingers and stretched her arms. "I'm out of shape."

Rogan snorted. "You went up that wall faster than anyone I've ever seen. If you noticed, I didn't come close to keeping up with you."

"So my out of shape is better than most. Still." She switched hands and repeated the stretches.

"Get any closer to El Jahar?" he asked a moment later.

Kennedy sighed. "Only if you count eliminating suspects as getting closer." She told him about Karl and Amy and the latter's suggestion that maybe it wasn't a dead agent they should be searching for, but a disabled one. "I have no idea what would make her think of that, except things she's seen in her job. But it makes sense. It's not panning out yet, but it makes sense."

"Have you found the disabled agents?" He frowned at her. "How dangerous is it to work for you, anyway?"

"Pretty dangerous."

He held out his hand, smudged with chalk, and she laid hers on top of it. "I suspect it's even more dangerous to be you."

Before Kennedy could answer, her ears picked up a distant *whump-whump-whump* that sent icy panic through her veins. She didn't bother to think about it, just followed instinct. "Rogan, go. Descend. Now."

"What?"

But the helicopter was in sight already. Evidently remembering the chopper at the studio months ago, Rogan didn't ask any more questions. He rushed to stuff their trash into his hip pack while she checked the topmost belay. Then he swung over the ledge, the rope gripped in his hands. Kennedy braced against his weight. She watched him for a minute, rechecked the belay to make sure it was holding, and looked back at the chopper.

At first she thought it was the same one. The color and shape were similar. But as it grew closer, she saw differences. She didn't relax, though. What was it doing here—where she was—if it wasn't El Jahar? But how had he found them?

She checked Rogan, who was halfway down. When she looked back up, the helicopter was heading straight for her.

Turning, she found a crack in the wall and set a nut, hooking herself directly to the rock.

The chopper turned sideways and tilted. Wind from the rotors buffeted her and she clung to the rock, finding, to her relief, a bucket hold with her left hand. She prayed Rogan was far enough down. She didn't feel any unusual movement on the rope, but being blown around herself, it was hard to tell.

The wind changed and she looked back. The chopper had righted, and she glimpsed two figures inside. Though it wasn't far away, it was slightly above her and she couldn't see who they were.

Frustration spurred her to action. She gauged the distance to the chopper and unhooked from the wall. A quick glance showed her Rogan was nearly to the ground. She took a deep breath and before the helicopter could move, leaped.

She almost didn't make it. If the cliff hadn't sloped much more gradually above their ledge, allowing the helicopter closer, and if the fool pilot hadn't been far too close anyway, she would have fallen. Her left arm hooked over the near skid, her right hand slapping it and nearly sliding off as the bird jerked under her weight. She repositioned her hand and swung her right leg up and over the skid.

The pilot swerved away from the cliff. Kennedy tightened her grip when she felt the rope sliding through her harness, still attached to the belays. Tugs told her those belays were being pulled from the wall.

The chopper fishtailed, moved up and down, and shifted back and forth, as if they were trying to shake her off. Then it suddenly stopped, hovering. Kennedy didn't waste time. She pulled herself onto the top of the skid and reached for the cabin door, the numbers above it burning themselves into her brain. A scream of denial echoed in her head even as a quiet voice said, *I told you so.*

The helicopter dove suddenly, the door above her sliding open. She lost her balance and flipped back under the skid, her grip tenuous on the slick metal. She looked up, but at this angle couldn't see his face, only dark fabric and the muzzle of a semiautomatic pistol. A pistol not pointed at her, but straight down at the ground.

She kicked out but was too far from the shooter, who ignored her. He fired four quick shots, saluted her, and pushed backward into the cabin. Panic flooded her. She didn't waste time looking down or around to see what the helicopter was doing. Letting go with one hand, she grabbed a spare rope from her belt and flung it over the skid, then looped it through the carabiner at her waist and over the skid again. With a quick glance down to see how far—and how clear—the ground was, she let go of the skid, grabbing both sides of the rope and lowering herself as fast as she dared. The chopper hovered until she was only a few feet from the ground and nearly out of rope. When the helicopter suddenly shot forward, Kennedy let go and dropped. The short end zipped out of the carabiner, freeing her from the bird, and she free-fell for a couple of seconds before landing flat on her back, moss and pine needles barely cushioning the impact.

She fought to draw in a breath. The helicopter disappeared in the bright sky, one of several specks of black in her vision that began to clear when air finally filled her lungs. She was okay. They didn't want *her* dead, or they wouldn't have waited while she descended the rope. But the gunfire…

She rolled to her right, desperately scanning the ground for Rogan. He lay a few feet away and she scrambled to her feet, ran over and dropped to her knees next to him. He was conscious but gasping, holding his biceps with one hand and pressing his other to his hip.

"Let me see." Kennedy gently pulled the hand away from his right hip and parted the torn cloth, wincing at the sight of his blood. The crease in his skin oozed, but was relatively minor. The arm wound bled more profusely. Her heart pounded while she inspected the injury. The bullet had passed through the muscle, but didn't look like it had hit bone. She quickly fashioned a tourniquet and sling, then applied a bandage to the hip gash from the first aid kit they carried.

Rogan said nothing during this, just bit back moans as she manipulated him, but his color was a bit better by the time she finished. She drew her first full breath and closed her eyes briefly in gratitude that it hadn't been worse.

"We'll leave the gear here," she told him, stripping them both of anything detachable except the cell phone. She called for an ambulance, then helped him stand. "What do you think?" she asked after waiting for his senses to stabilize.

"I think the beach was a more successful date," he managed through gritted teeth, hopping to test his weight on the injured leg.

Kennedy chuckled and bit back the urge to apologize for letting this happen to him. "Just let me know when you're ready."

Rogan took a deep breath and nodded. "Let's go."

She supported him on his left side as he started to walk. He limped, breath hissing with every step. Kennedy could tell that he was trying not to put weight on her, though, and threatened to kick his good leg out from under him and carry him out if he didn't lean on her.

"You know I can take it, skinny man," she said, and he chuckled. They moved more efficiently after he complied.

"Talk to me," Rogan said after they'd gone a few yards. "If I'm going to make it out to that stretcher, I need to be distracted. Tell me what the point of that attack was."

"I'm not sure." She tried to keep her tone neutral, but anger vibrated under it. "But I was blind and stupid."

"Why?" He groaned when they had to step wide over a protruding root.

"I recognized the helicopter."

"Kennedy, stop being so damned evasive. I can hear your brain on fire. Whose helicopter was it?"

She glanced up through the trees at the empty sky. "It was mine."

NINETEEN

"SHUT UP."

"I won't." Rogan grabbed Kennedy's hand so the paramedics loading him into the ambulance had to stop. "Go. This is killing you. I don't need you with me."

He wasn't sure that was completely true, but he knew he needed her less than she needed to get to work. He couldn't imagine what she had to be feeling, knowing someone inside her camp, the team she trusted with her life and everyone else's, had betrayed her.

"This is more important, Rogan."

Warmth filled him. He hoped she meant it. Being shot had shocked him, sent him stumbling to the ground even as he watched Kennedy fall. It was cliché, but that instant had clarified everything. That day on the beach, he'd thought forever was possible. Now he wouldn't settle for anything less.

But Kennedy wasn't going to be ready for forever until she got rid of El Jahar. So he tried again to convince her to let him go to the hospital alone. She wouldn't listen. As soon as he was loaded, she headed for the Jeep. He watched her climb in just before the doors to the ambulance closed.

He wasn't critical, so the ambulance didn't speed through red lights, and Kennedy followed them almost immediately into the emergency room. She ignored him when he told her again to go, but they wouldn't let her come back with him because she wasn't a relative.

He'd never been so lonely in his life.

He understood, now, why his father had stuck by his mother despite her priorities being elsewhere. She wasn't just driven, she was passionate, and so was Kennedy. He'd rather share a woman with her passion than have someone completely available to him who didn't care so deeply.

Finally, after hours of treatment and shots and stitching and medication, followed by an interview by the police, who didn't seem to believe his version of events, Kennedy appeared in his doorway.

"You look like hell," he said, before she had a chance to. A smile flitted over her face. She looked worse than he probably did, despite his fatigue, the dulling effect of the drugs, and the dirt in his hair. She had the dirt and fatigue, plus his blood all over her. He held out his left hand, and she stepped closer to take it. Her touch was ginger, so he said, "That's my good side," eliciting another smile.

"I'm sorry, Rogan."

"Don't."

"It's my people, my fault. You were almost killed because of me."

The heaviness of her tone shot panic through him, driving away the lassitude of the drugs. "Don't," he said again, more sharply. "It's not your fault."

Sadness made her whole face seem to droop. "What I do is dangerous. If I made an enemy once, I can make one again. I can't put you in danger like that."

"You're the one in danger," he started, but she shook her head.

"That's just as bad. I don't ever want to make you feel like I did when he fired that gun."

"Isn't that my decision?" He cursed himself for making it a question instead of a statement, but he didn't think it would have mattered.

"I'm sorry, Rogan," she said again, squeezed his fingers, and left.

Despair was followed by anger, but neither survived very long as the pain meds pulled him under. He'd heal, then he'd get her back.

No matter what he had to do to convince her.

KENNEDY DROVE THE rental Jeep back to the compound, stopped at her house to change clothes, and went back to the main building. Completely numb the whole time.

Jefferson met her outside, looking grim, and accompanied her to her office. He shut the door behind them and locked it. Kennedy didn't react to his actions, just circled her desk and sat down. Suddenly, she was exhausted and sore and for the first time since Justin was killed, she wanted to crawl under the covers and never come out.

"I have bad news, Kennedy."

"I know."

He crossed the room and sat in the chair across from her, then leaned his arms on the desk. His expression was serious. She wanted to tell him not to bother.

"I got hold of a few more satellite photos and cross-referenced the times with the patrols at the gate and the perimeter, as well as who was where when those lights were off."

"I know." She stacked the files she had been studying on the corner of her desk to be returned to the file room.

He frowned. "Okay, well, the conclusions I can reach aren't good."

"I know." She flipped through message slips Mark left while she was gone, dropping them one by one into the trash can.

"Dammit, Kennedy, what's wrong with you? Aren't you listening to me?"

She looked up, unable to generate any emotional response to his anger. "It's an inside job."

He blew out a breath. "Yeah. That's what I think too. How did you know?"

"Because one of you just tried to kill Rogan." She stood. "Dismiss everyone from the compound. Make sure they're all off site before you lock down and leave. Don't tell anyone what you've found or why I'm shutting down. I'll be in touch with them in a few days. And Jefferson." She leaned forward menacingly. "If I find out it was you, I won't stop."

He had the gall to smile, though there was no humor in it. "I wouldn't dare, Kennedy. Don't worry. I've got it covered. Where are you going?"

The gentle understanding in his eyes put the first crack in her wall of protection, but she didn't acknowledge it. "Nowhere."

He looked like he wanted to say more but didn't. Kennedy waited for him to leave, then locked and armed her office, something she'd never done before. She'd never found it necessary to use the separate alarm and deterrent system she installed when the compound was first built.

She swept the building after Jefferson, making sure no one was left behind. She checked every place someone could hide. When she was out, she changed the alarm codes and set the system, arming the secret backup unit.

Then she left without looking back.

Just like she'd left Rogan.

"KENNEDY." HER FATHER knocked softly on her door and called to her in a gentle voice. "Are you going to keep moping all day?"

"I'm not moping." But if he looked in, he'd argue that point. She sat on the twin bed covered in one of her mother's quilts, hugging a throw pillow behind upraised knees. She wasn't moping, but trying to make plans around a bleeding heart probably looked a lot like it.

She tossed the pillow aside and rose to open the door. Her father gave her a relieved smile.

"Come on. I made cookies. You can bounce things off me."

He sat her down at the small oak table in the tiled kitchen and insisted on serving her milk with the gingersnaps he'd baked.

"Now," he said, settling across from her. "Tell me what's wrong. I guess I should apologize," he went on before she could, "for sending him down there in the first place."

Kennedy frowned at him. "Sending who down where?"

"The St. James fella. To the compound." He looked remorseful. "I wanted you to be happy, but I guess I was just meddling. I should have learned my lesson when our attempt to get you and M.J. together failed so dismally."

She realized what he was talking about and laughed. "You thought I was here because of Rogan?" The laughter spilled out again, tinged with a hint of suppressed hysteria. "No guy is going to make me run crying to my Daddy. I can't believe you'd think that!"

He grumbled under his breath while lifting his mug to his mouth. "What the hell sent you up here, then? What else could be that bad?"

Mirth gone, unable to sit still, she shoved her chair back and started to pace. The windows over the sink were open, and the cool Minnesota breeze pushed her hair back. It reminded her of the woods where she'd recognized the betrayal. And it made her think of Rogan.

"It's worse, Dad, much worse. But hold on, I have to make a call." She automatically pulled her cell phone from the clip at her waist, then hesitated with her thumb on the power button. SmythShield had all the phones' GPS data, which was probably how the traitor had tracked Clay and Rogan at the café, and her and Rogan to the cliff. She'd kept the phone off since she left the compound. Using it now might bring attention to her father.

She reclipped the phone and reached for her dad's landline. A moment later the hospital answered, and she asked to be transferred to Rogan's room. They were keeping him because of the blood loss, and she'd taken the excuse to leave him. But now she found herself unable to let go, and not just because she felt guilty.

"Yello," he answered.

"You sound good."

"Kennedy." It was a sigh of relief. "Where are you?"

"My dad's. You safe?" She'd wanted desperately to assign someone to guard his room, but she couldn't trust anyone. Any of her agents could be against her, and outside contacts were even less reliable. She'd done the best she could with the police and hospital security.

She heard the rustle of pages. "I'm fine. I'm getting

really sick of celebrity magazines, though. Why doesn't anybody bring me anything else? They all think I want to lie around reading about myself?"

She stiffened. "All who? Who brought you stuff?"

"Relax. My agent's here, and Charlie. *Somebody* called them." He waited, but she didn't admit she'd called M.J. and asked him to get someone out there. "Kennedy."

She caved. "I just didn't want you to be alone. I couldn't…"

"I know," he said quietly. "Any idea who it is yet?"

"No. Not at all." She pinched the bridge of her nose, eyes closed. "I keep thinking about each one of them, trying to find red flags in behavior, and nothing clicks. I'm too close to it. I trusted them all with my life. With your life," she added in a near whisper.

"I'm fine," Rogan assured her again. "My agent is freaking out—thanks a lot for sending him here—but the girls will go wild over the scars."

Her head came up. "Shit. Is the media hounding you?"

"Nah, not yet. The nurses are having a great time playing the heavy, keeping me all to themselves. Wait until I'm released. Then the paparazzi will go nuts. I'll need a new hat and shades."

Kennedy smiled, but caught her father watching her avidly, no doubt divining all kinds of things, both true and not, from her conversation.

"When will you be released?"

"Not sure. My agent is pushing them to keep me a few extra days as protection against the media. As long as they have the room and I'm paying for it, they will."

"Good." She eyed her father again. "I've got to go. The Hawk is watching me. Take—take care of yourself."

"Don't you dare." His voice hardened. "You tried to blow me off before. I'm not going to let you, Kennedy."

"It's no good, Rogan. I'm sorry. Goodbye."

She clicked off before he could respond.

Her father's eyebrows had disappeared under his shaggy gray hair when she hung up and sat back at the table. "El Jahar? Rogan? Is he in the hospital?"

Sparing any emotion—fear for Rogan and her people, betrayal and anger at El Jahar, stupidity for not seeing that someone from her *own operation* was gunning for her—she told her father what had happened.

"And now I have to figure out who's trying to make me pay, what they're making me pay for and how to stop them. And I have no clue."

The investigative mind that had made her father such a good lawyer took over, and the absent-minded scientist persona disappeared. His features firmed, his body drew up taller and his voice deepened. Kennedy missed the first things he said, she was too busy smiling fondly at the person who'd always been her rock.

She bent and kissed him on the cheek, making him splutter. "That's not the way to treat one of the finest minds in the entertainment business." He stopped, considered, and grinned. "Well, yeah, it is. But anyway." He cleared his throat. "You've got the order wrong. You need to figure out why they want revenge. Then you'll know who to stop and how."

"Yeah, that's easy." She gulped her milk. "I've only been working on that for two months."

"What's different now?"

"El Jahar was frustrated enough to blow their secrecy to try to get us. They're out in the open now, and they know I know. So they could make a move any minute."

She avoided looking at her father. "Especially if someone on my team—" She stopped. Sighed. "*Because* someone on my team is involved, it endangers all my people."

"And Rogan."

"He's safe enough at the moment." But she couldn't be sure of that, short of guarding him herself, and that would just keep him in El Jahar's sights. The urgency to get this over, *now*, just kept building.

And here she was, doing the typical thing and running home, to family and emotional safety. "I can't stay here tonight," she said. "I don't want to make you vulnerable. I have to move, and let them know where I am so they can target me, not my family."

He shrugged. "I can take care of myself. And I can put the local law enforcement on alert. Dan knows what you do. He'll protect me." He squinted thoughtfully. "I think the lawyer was on the right track. Every time I think about what she said about loss and pain, I get that *zing* of truth. You need to follow up on that."

She shook her head, frustrated. "George and Bruce couldn't be involved. They're not—"

"No. Not them. You need to go to someone who can understand loss and pain. So she can help you see why El Jahar is after you. Help you ferret out who El Jahar is."

Kennedy knew who he was talking about. "I abandoned her, Dad. I don't think—"

"No thinking, Kennedy. For once, feel."

She blew out a breath, annoyed that he kept interrupting her. She felt, when she was free to. But feeling was dangerous. It made you vulnerable at the worst moments—

He put his hand on hers, stilling her thoughts. He was right. She no longer had the luxury of systematically eliminating possibilities. She'd go to Diana and see if there was any chance she could help. If she *would* help.

If she wasn't the enemy in the first place.

KENNEDY LEFT HER father's the following morning without much of a plan. Fatigue dragged at her, slowing her thinking and making her feel like she would always be a step behind.

Instead of planning the immediate future, her mind became mired in the past. Kennedy relived the day she met Diana, the training they'd gone through together, their first secret mission once they were in the private sector.

The day they had declared SmythShield officially open, things had changed. For the first time, Kennedy was the boss and Diana the employee. Diana had deferred to her on everything, never overstepping or questioning. She'd been an ideal operative. But that had also meant Kennedy lost her confidante. And that, she realized, had been the beginning of her path to her current isolated, lonely life.

A path that had reached its destination the day Diana had been in the accident.

Kennedy remembered it as clearly as she remembered her brother's death. They had been guarding a construction site in Africa against two warring factions who were receptive to bribery, so Kennedy supplied them with medicine and food. All had been fine until one side ran out of the supplies and raided the other. Diana had gone to intervene before both groups decided to come back to the construction site and take out their frustrations on SmythShield and the workers they protected.

Diana had sped back in the Jeep, temporarily successful in calming the faction's leaders. But the second-in-command, who'd expected his leader to be killed in the altercation Diana averted, followed her and shot out a tire. The Jeep flipped, landing on her.

Kennedy swallowed the bile that rose at the memory. If the accident had happened in the U.S., they would have gotten her to a hospital and she would have had a long but full recovery. Instead, she'd lost her left arm just below the elbow and her right leg below the knee.

Goodbye, career.

And goodbye, friendship. The remnants shredded under the strain of the trauma. Internal injuries led to a hysterectomy, and Diana hadn't taken the loss well. Kennedy had visited her bitter, angry, combative friend less and less, until Diana shouted at her to stop reminding her of every damn thing and just go away. She had, and had never gone back.

It occurred to Kennedy that she had done a very good job of eliminating her past from her present. Justin's death had been the defining moment, and everything related back to it. What happened between then and now disappeared, unconsidered until forced.

Maybe El Jahar had a point.

But however valid that point might be, threatening the safety of people from her past, of people in her present and future, was not the way to point it out to her.

She strengthened her resolve. She'd examine her reality after this was over. In the meantime, she had to put a stop to the violence.

She had taken Rogan's rental Jeep back to the agency at the airport when she went to her father's, so she rented another one after her plane landed. She obtained a map at the counter and spent a few minutes memorizing the route to Diana's. She lived in a secluded, wooded area far from the nearest main road, so approaching without alerting her would be impossible. Kennedy was sure she had security all the way in.

She discarded the idea of calling ahead. What the hell would she say? "Someone's trying to maim people close to me and I think you might be involved." Yeah, that would get her in.

It took nearly two hours for her to reach the turnoff into the woods. She pulled over and studied the narrow gravel road and the trees encroaching on it, one sporting a dusty sign that read Private. After a minute, her eyes started picking things out. She sighed and backed the Jeep off the road. It wouldn't make it a foot inside the perimeter.

She climbed out of the Jeep and cautiously approached the turnoff. She paused with her feet on the edge of the pavement, smiling despite herself. Diana hadn't changed a bit.

The dusty spikes embedded in the gravel were obviously pressure-activated. They were the kind used to keep people from going the wrong way into a pay parking lot and would have punctured her tires like a needle through flesh.

She didn't need to go any further. Beyond the spikes would be pits, and snags, and possibly dismembering booby traps. Nothing deadly, but time-consuming, and if she missed something she could wind up hanging suspended in a net or at the bottom of a nine-foot pit for hours. Or days, though she was sure by now Diana knew she was here. She'd be expecting her to test her masterpiece.

Part of her longed to do it. It would take her back to

the old days, when they'd done this stuff for fun and profit. But that was also the part that wanted to hide her head under her pillow until the mess went away.

That part had never taken the lead.

So she returned to the Jeep, pulled out her laptop and cell phone, connected to Google Earth, and found the image of this area. She studied the roads and scars in the terrain. There was no obvious house, but it was likely hidden from above by vegetation. Maybe most of it was underground. This couldn't be the only way in, or Diana would never get out.

There. She spotted a thin, pale line that could be a road, and traced it back to where she sat. Then she spun the Jeep around and started following the road back. It took her another half an hour to translate the satellite image properly into the roads she traveled, but finally, she found what she was looking for.

The house squatted low, as she'd suspected, hidden under the trees. Only half a story stood exposed over ground level. She pulled the Jeep to one side of the welcoming landscaped driveway that circled in front of the house. Five cameras were visible, so she figured there were at least that many more hidden. The ground looked smooth, and she couldn't spot any signs of booby traps. She knew all Diana's old tricks, but she would have developed more, so she climbed out of the vehicle with not a little trepidation.

As soon as her foot touched soil the front door opened, and Diana stood in the doorway, her weapon aimed at Kennedy's heart.

TWENTY

"Hello, Kennedy. It's good to see you."

"Are you sure about that?" Her hand twitched toward her own weapon automatically. Diana disengaged hers and shook her head.

"I'm not gonna hurt you, Ned."

Kennedy relaxed at the nickname and withdrew her hand. "That's a relief." She stepped forward, studying the other woman. Diana stood solidly in the doorway, her pants hiding her prosthetic leg. Her prosthetic hand rested on the door frame, looking natural, and she seemed completely healthy. In fact, with a light tan and sun-streaked brown hair pulled back in a ponytail, she looked better than Kennedy had ever seen her.

But she didn't invite her in. She stood motionless in the doorway. "Well?"

Kennedy rolled her eyes. "Me, neither. Unless, of course, you're El Jahar and have been trying to punish me."

Diana's eyebrows went up. "Sounds interesting. Come tell me all about it." She turned and marched down a set of stairs into a very traditional kitchen. The hardwood floor was devoid of throw rugs, Kennedy noticed, and the cupboard handles were oddly shaped, but otherwise the room looked normal. The pine cabinets and table gleamed, the marble counter beckoned for food preparation, and the stainless steel stove sparkled. Everything looked new. Somehow, Diana was doing all right for herself.

"Iced tea?"

"No, thanks." She removed her jacket and sat, watching Diana moving smoothly around the room. She looked like Kennedy remembered, except for being older. Not at all like a woman whose life had been mostly destroyed. "I'm sorry," she said abruptly.

Diana glanced over her shoulder. "For what?"

Kennedy blew out a breath. "God. Where to start? I guess for leaving you, at least."

"Oh, please," Diana scoffed. "I sent you away. Pretty desperately, if I remember."

"A real friend wouldn't have gone," she said, watching closely for any hint of awkwardness or difficulty as Diana sat at the table. There was none.

"A real friend wouldn't have pushed." She sighed and shook her head. "Let's get this in the open and dealt with now. I was facing death, Kennedy."

"I know, and it's my fault."

"Shut up and listen. If you've been wearing a hair shirt over this all these years, you're an idiot." She pointed a finger at Kennedy. "I took that job. I knew the risks. And the accident was *my* fault. Even if you want to take a small portion of blame for what happened, you've more than made up for it." She curled and flexed her fingers. "I've got state-of-the-art prosthetics and the best medical care in the world. Your medical plan provides that.

"Now, back to the emotional crap. I wasn't facing death because of the accident, not physically, I mean. I was facing death because of depression. I felt like my identity was gone. And you were there, trying to help, and making me feel worse." She held up a hand when Kennedy reacted to the well of guilt and tried to apologize again. "*It wasn't your fault.* Will you accept that? I had attached my identity to you, to SmythShield. And I had to push you away so I could break that attachment and find myself again." She sighed and gulped some iced tea. "I won't say it was easy. But I'm so happy with myself now, I have to believe that the whole thing was the best thing that ever happened to me."

Kennedy stared at her, awed. "You're amazing."

Diana waved a hand. "Yeah, well, so are you. End of mutual admiration."

But Kennedy couldn't leave it at that. She'd never been gushy, but neither had she seen such determination, such passion about life. "Sorry, but I'm not done. You took tragedy and rebuilt yourself. I took tragedy and wallowed in it. I could learn a lot from you."

Diana frowned at her. "You mean Justin? But his death led you to SmythShield. I pay attention, Kennedy, I could probably tell you exactly how many lives you and your team have saved."

"Six hundred forty-one," Kennedy joked. "But I've never moved past it. Every single thing I do is still atonement or revenge or in honor of that one event in my life. It's stupid, it's stagnating, and I only realized it recently. Things have to change."

A sly grin spread across Diana's face. "Who's the guy?"

Kennedy shook her head. "That's irrelevant, though there is, of course, a guy, and his role in my life is part of what opened my eyes. But the whole El Jahar thing is what really changed my perspective." Her mouth suddenly dry, she stood. "I think I'll have some tea, after all.

I'll get it." She unerringly retrieved a glass and filled it from the pitcher in the refrigerator, adding a squeeze of lemon and a half teaspoon of sugar to cut the bitterness.

"Finally," Diana said when she sat down again. "What's El Jahar?"

"As far as I can tell, a grudge-holder." She told her about the letters to *Coming of Day* that led to the production's hiring her, about the incidents on the set and afterward, about the trails she'd followed that led to her.

"This person doesn't seem to want to kill anyone. Or at least," she corrected, thinking of the range of injuries, from Bailey's bee sting and Peter's broken foot to Rogan's gunshot wounds, "he's squeamish about it." She told her about Amy's words, about loss and pain. "That made me think of you, even though I put you last on the list because you were the most likely suspect and the one I least wanted it to be," she admitted, a crushing pain building in her chest. "I can't believe how much I've missed you."

Diana squeezed her hand briefly. "I never blamed you, and I never wanted revenge. Not even on the pack of rabid dogs that chased me. But I have an idea of who El Jahar might be." She was quiet a moment. "You're sure it's an inside job?"

"Yeah. They used my helicopter to gun down my boyfriend." She explained the rock-climbing incident and that she couldn't see who was in the chopper. "It was more than one guy, but he might have just hired someone to shoot while he flew or vice versa. He paid others to do his dirty work on the set, and probably used the phone GPS to track us. Jefferson's got other data backing up the theory too."

Diana nodded. "Okay. We've got to go back to the

compound. I'll figure out who it is, and we'll flush him out." She stood. "It will only take me a minute to gear up."

"Wait." Kennedy stood too. "Can't you just tell me?"

Diana shook her head. "I know who he *was*, but not who he is now. And I don't have any more pictures of him. I threw them away a long time ago. Besides, you know me." She flashed a grin and disappeared into the hall.

Yeah, she knew her. Drama queen. Kennedy pulled out her phone and powered it up while she waited. They weren't going to stay here long, so she wasn't worried about the GPS. She didn't keep photos of her team on her phone, but she could connect to the company server...if she hadn't shut it down when she closed up the office. Disgusted, she shut the phone off and shoved it back in her pocket.

Diana had said "he." Kennedy mentally paged through her team roster. She'd prefer it to be Wolf, knowing him the least amount of time, but that also made him the least likely. He never had access to the systems that had been interfered with.

Jefferson and Rick did, and it made Kennedy sick to her stomach to think she could have worked with them for so many years, only to have it come to this. No, it couldn't be her chief engineer or head of general security. The personal protection staff wouldn't have access, either. Which left...

Diana walked back into the kitchen, wearing a jacket similar to Kennedy's with a shoulder holster, an ankle clutch piece, and a knife strapped to her hip. Kennedy smiled. It was *good* to have her friend back, drama or no drama.

"So what are we doing?" Kennedy followed Diana down a short tunnel off the kitchen. "You want to see employee files?"

"We'll start there, and if I can't pick him out from that, we'll gather the team." There was way too much relish in her voice as she said it. Kennedy held her tongue, but even needing Diana's help, she was still running the show. And cornering El Jahar didn't seem the smartest option.

The tunnel ended at a brightly lit, white-painted garage. She whistled at the cars lined up in front of her. She had never mastered model years, but the Mustang closest to her was definitely vintage, as was the tiny Mercedes convertible next to it. The SUV on the far side was brand new and appeared fully decked out. A wide ramp rose to corrugated metal doors to the left. Daylight glimmered through narrow windows stretching their length.

She watched Diana arm a complicated alarm system. "What's with the obstacle course?" she asked as they slid into the little white Mercedes. She'd come back for the Jeep later. "Are you hiding from something?"

"Obviously not very well, if you found me." She hit a button that caused the door behind them to rise, then gunned the engine and backed up the ramp without looking. "It's what I do now. I design extreme security systems for recluses and people who want to keep the riffraff at bay." She spun the wheel as soon as they were outside, doing a perfect one-eighty on the gravel. "The course keeps me in shape too. I change most of it on a monthly basis. You'll have to try it next time you're here."

She shot out of the drive onto the road, flying past

the forest with a fearlessness Kennedy hadn't seen in her before. So, changes did happen.

"It's your ex, isn't it?" Kennedy said a while later. It couldn't be anyone else.

"That's my guess." Diana glanced through her blind spot to merge onto the highway. "He took my accident badly, especially the hysterectomy. I divorced him and he never got over me. I haven't heard from him in five years, and I thought he'd moved on. But I suspect he found another outlet for his...pain."

Kennedy didn't ask any more. She'd thrown herself so intently into building SmythShield that she never socialized. Diana had met her fiancé on a scouting trip for a new job. He lived in Chicago but traveled for work—Kennedy didn't remember doing what—and he rarely came to Northern California. He and Diana eloped shortly before the Africa job where Diana got hurt, and Kennedy had never met him. She was ashamed to realize she'd never even considered it. Their friendship had already deteriorated that far.

Thoughts of relationships made her think of Rogan, and the urge to talk to him grew until she pulled out her phone again to dial the hospital. The line rang several times, then clicked and a nurse answered, "Med-surg."

"I'm looking for Rogan St. James."

"I'm sorry, I don't—"

"It's okay, this is Kennedy Smyth." She gave the woman the code she'd set up through security, so they could let her calls through. The woman hesitated.

"Let me get my supervisor."

That shouldn't have been necessary. Her insides chilled as she waited for the woman to come on the line.

"Ms. Smyth, I'm sorry. I thought you knew."

Unease skittered across her back. "Knew what?"

"Mr. St. James was discharged. There was a large accident on the freeway, and we needed his space. He left several hours ago."

Fuck. Kennedy barely got out a thank you, then dialed Rogan's cell phone. It went directly to voice mail.

"Double fuck."

Diana glanced at her but didn't comment. Kennedy stared out the window, trying to think of another way to reach Rogan. Would he be flying home, or in a hotel room somewhere? She scrolled through her phone book until she found his agent's number, which Rogan had given her after the café attack. No answer.

That left Charlie. Rogan said he was in town too. Kennedy held her breath as she pressed send. He answered on the first ring.

"Charlie, it's Kennedy."

"Oh, hey." Silence. "Um, what can I do for you?"

"I can't reach Rogan."

Before she could elaborate, he said, "Oh, yeah, he turned his phone off because of the media calls. His manager's on vacation and someone leaked his cell number." There was a giggle in the background, and Charlie shushed her. "Try the nurse's station."

Fuck wasn't a strong enough word anymore. "I did. He was discharged. You didn't know."

"Obviously." Charlie sounded as concerned as Kennedy now. "You know where he'd go?"

"No, or I wouldn't be calling you." She took a deep breath. "Sorry. Just—tell him to call me if you hear from him."

"Will do."

She slapped the phone shut and tried not to urge Diana to drive faster. She wasn't exactly going slow.

"You okay?" Diana asked.

Kennedy snorted. "A few minutes ago I thought this might be all over by the end of the day. Now Rogan's missing."

"Rogan?"

"Rogan St. James."

Diana barked a laugh. "The actor? You fell for an *actor?* God, that's priceless. It's perfect." She laughed again. Kennedy just sighed and sank deep into her seat, thinking hard, trying to prepare for what was about to happen.

Knowing full well that was impossible.

THE COMPOUND WAS silent and empty when they finally reached it. Kennedy had kept trying, but still hadn't tracked down Rogan. He hadn't left any messages for her anywhere, and that clinched it. Something had happened, and the only way to find out what was to find El Jahar.

Kennedy led Diana into her office and booted up her computer. Diana pulled a visitor chair around next to her and sat.

"I don't know if I'll know him from one photo," Diana said. "I'd rather see him in person."

"Let's start with this." Kennedy leaned forward when the desktop appeared on the monitor. "The faster you ID him, the faster we can find him." She opened the directory that held employee dossiers. It was empty.

"What the hell?" The dread that had been heavy in her gut for the last two hours flared into full anxiety. She clicked a few other directories, then pounded the keyboard to call up the background files. "Fucking A!"

"What is it?"

Kennedy shoved to her feet and paced away from the desk, her hands buried against her skull as if to keep it from bursting. "It's wiped. The entire system. The shell is there, but all the data—"

"It's okay." Diana pulled the keyboard toward her. "Backup files? Paper? Don't you have pictures in a filing cabinet in a dusty storage room or something?" She tapped fruitlessly on the keys.

"It doesn't matter," Kennedy told her, suddenly weary. "There's only one person with the skills and knowledge to do this."

Diana stood. "Okay, then, let's go find him."

Kennedy shook her head. "That won't be necessary. He'll come to us."

THE MISSION ROOM was bigger than a conference room and held a massive oval table, overhead screen and projector, white boards and walls full of maps. There were two entrances, one from the main hall and one from Kennedy's office, where there was a small two-way mirror. She and Diana watched while the team gathered.

"That's everyone," Kennedy said when Zip closed the door. She didn't ask if Diana saw him. She could tell by her old friend's sudden tension when he walked into the room. "I guess it's showtime."

"I've got your back." Diana patted her shoulder as she went into the larger room.

She didn't bother thanking the group for coming on short notice. Betrayal was sour in the back of her mouth, and knowing who was responsible gave her no satisfaction. She'd never have thought it of him, so how did she know others weren't involved too? She got right to the point from the moment she took her position at the head of the mission table.

"One of you is a traitor."

Despite her bitterness, she couldn't help a small surge of pride when no one at the table moved. There were no shocked gasps, no murmurs or expressions of outrage. They looked at her with the blank expressions she expected them to use on the outside.

"El Jahar is an employee of SmythShield," she went on. Still, no one moved. Most of them had clear consciences. One was a master poker player. "I know this because of data Jefferson gathered. Because of psychological analysis and physical evidence. And because the idiot tried to kill me with my own helicopter."

"Do you know who it is?" Stacy asked quietly. She alone allowed her emotions to show in her eyes. They displayed anger and hurt, but mostly indignation.

"Yes." Kennedy swept her gaze evenly across all of them. "But—"

The door opened and she froze midsentence. Rogan walked in. Well, more like hobbled in, his right arm in a sling, his left gripping a cane. Kennedy fought to keep her body from sagging in relief.

"Sorry to interrupt."

The charming, easygoing actor had disappeared. His eyes burned, not only with fierce possession when they landed on Kennedy, but with something close to hatred as he skimmed the group. "Driving is kind of difficult for me right now, so I had to hire a car. Took a little more time than I wanted it to."

Confused, she said, "What are you doing here?"

"I was called."

"By whom?"

"El Jahar." His lips twisted in derision. "Which is too elegant a name for the cowardly bastard using it."

"When?" He'd left the hospital hours ago, long before she called the team here.

"Three hours ago." He stopped trying to bore into the brains of her team and looked at her. "Whoever it was told me to come here or he'd kill you."

Her jaw worked as she tried not to shout at him. "So you came?" *Are you an idiot?*

"No. I came because half an hour later, Jefferson called me and said you knew who it was and if El Jahar realized that, I'd be in danger again. He advised me to leave the hospital. El Jerkall called *again*, and said if I didn't come here, he'd blow up the hospital." He shrugged. "At least here, innocents aren't in the way."

Kennedy checked with Jefferson, who shook his head. "I never called him."

"So, who did?" Mark asked, his hand gripping his pen, thumb on the clicker but unmoving.

With effort, Kennedy pulled her attention back to the purpose of the meeting. She had to change her strategy, with Rogan directly in harm's way. She started to tell him to go into her office, but one glance at his face told her that was a losing proposition. He'd stayed in the background so far, but now that she'd been directly threatened with death she didn't think he'd be so accommodating.

Before Kennedy could answer Mark's question, the office door opened.

"Diana!" Jefferson, Rick and Stacy jumped up with delighted cries. Diana held them back with an upraised hand.

"Good to see you guys." She walked slowly around

the outside of the room. "I see lots of new faces, of course. And one that's not so new, though not exactly as I saw it last." She stopped behind Mark's chair and put her hands on his shoulders. He grit his teeth and white-knuckled the pen in his hand, but he didn't move.

"You think it's me," he said to Kennedy, his tone flat but a glint in his eye she'd never seen before.

She raised an eyebrow at Diana, who shrugged.

"You're Diana's ex-husband," Kennedy said. "You lost her because of me. Because of SmythShield. You've been trying to make me pay, after four years of working for me, learning everything you could use against me." The bitterness coated her throat again. He'd been a master at earning her trust over those years, offering his connections and skills to make her job easier, when all along his goal was to destroy her.

He stood slowly and moved out from between the chair and the table. Diana gave him a little room, but Kennedy doubted he'd do anything in here. Not with the entire team surrounding him.

"You're not wrong," he admitted, sounding completely reasonable and unfazed. "Diana's accident was the worst thing that ever happened to me, until she divorced me. I barely survived that. The only thing that kept me going was making the people responsible pay."

A glimmer of memory sparked in Kennedy's mind, news reports about an unusual attack in Africa four years ago. Nearly every soldier in two factions had suffered mostly non-fatal poisoning. A bogus aid group had brought in food laced with some chemical that made them all sick for weeks, until they figured out what it was. By then, the suppliers were gone.

"You didn't kill them, though," she said, aware that no one else knew what she was talking about.

Mark did. He shrugged. "Well, Diana didn't die, and they'd suffer more alive than dead. And so would you."

She thought of all the near misses. Bailey and the bees, M.J. with the muggers, Peter's broken foot. All the people who could have been seriously hurt, because of her. Because of him. And then Rogan, when Mark knew how much he meant to her. He had to have been thrilled when she started to fall for him.

She clamped down on her rage. "I don't get why it was so elaborate. Why didn't you just start picking off operatives or something?" Half the people at the table grimaced.

"Once I started working for you, I knew it couldn't be anything easy. You're too smart. Too talented. And—" He looked pained. "I liked you. I liked working for you. I didn't know if I could go through with it. But then your father told me about M.J. and Max, and I knew it was perfect. I could torment you with people you cared about. Until then, I hadn't thought you cared about anybody."

She shrugged, wincing internally as the knife struck home. "You're smart and talented, too, Mark. Very clever, feeding me misinformation while we were on the movie set. Must have been fun to send me running in circles."

Suddenly, fervor flared in his eyes. "You ain't seen nothing yet." Then he made his move.

Kennedy never expected him to do it. Not with a dozen agents in the room. But he had nothing to lose. So he rolled toward the door, coming up with a pistol in his hand, aimed at Diana. The cocking of a dozen weapons echoed in the room, but every agent hesitated, not wanting to provoke Mark into firing. They expected the threat to have the effect they wanted. But it didn't. He did fire. With deadly accuracy, right into Diana's prosthetic leg.

Then he sealed his fate. He grabbed Rogan and ducked out the door, his gun pointed at Rogan's head.

TWENTY-ONE

DIANA WENT DOWN, and everyone surged to help her. Only Rick and Stacy, closest to the door, began to pursue Mark.

Kennedy called them back. "He'll shoot Rogan. He's already done it once. And he'll shoot you." She checked her weapon and took a deep breath. "This is mine, guys. Diana's okay, but her leg will need fixing. See if you can help Jefferson and Gina rig it."

She went after Mark and Rogan alone.

Logic told her Mark would access the weapon room and try to shoot his way out. Instinct told her he'd already collected what he needed and was on his way out of the building by the time she reached the end of the hall.

She paused for a moment just inside the exit door, trying to think past the fear. Mark wasn't escaping. He was bringing the challenge into the open. He still wanted to make her suffer, and expected the entire team to come after him. He'd probably hide with the intent to harm each one, if he could. He was out of his depth, but maybe he didn't know that. He'd trained with them, but every agent individually was better than he was. *Dammit!* Why hadn't she recognized what he was? How could she have been so blind and stupid, especially once she knew she was the target? If only—

No. Too late for wishes and regrets. She had herself,

her team, and Rogan to protect now, and she was going to do her job. She'd deal with the emotional fallout later.

All of it.

She'd opened the lead-lined compartment she stuffed her feelings into, and it would no longer seal. Fear for Rogan made her throat tight, and cold sweat popped out on her skin. But she was still Kennedy Smyth, and she could still do her job.

So. Where would Mark go?

The urban training ground, she decided immediately. He'd always been most comfortable there, and if he'd done contingency planning, that was the place he would have picked.

She looked back when someone entered the hall. "Stay here," she ordered Rick. "I don't want anyone coming after us."

"Kennedy," he started to protest, coming toward her.

"You've always been an excellent operative, Rick. Don't stop now."

He stopped walking and shook his head. "He's going to—"

"And don't start questioning me, either," she interrupted, annoyed. "I know what he's going to do, and I have a plan."

He braced his hands on his hips and hung his head. "All right," he said after a second. "But take a communicator so we know what's going on and can rescue you if we have to." He winked, then pulled it out of his pocket, thumbed a switch and tossed it to her. "It's on. We'll listen in the mission room."

"Great. An audience." She stuck the communicator in her back pocket. "What if Mark has one?"

"He doesn't. I only have two of that model."

She nodded and checked the rest of her weapons. The backup revolver she'd strapped to her ankle before the meeting felt reassuringly heavy. She'd also hooked a sheathed knife to her belt. All of this was habit. She doubted she'd need any of them. Her intent wasn't to kill Mark, it was to counsel him.

Kind of.

ROGAN LET MARK drag him out of the mission room and down the hall. The further they got from the crowd, the better. The less urgent the threat to Mark, the less likely he'd be to panic and shoot someone.

Neither man spoke as they ran—or, Mark ran, Rogan stumbled, his teeth gritted against the pain in his hip—and soon they were outside the building and heading for the urbanscape. Rogan used the untidiness of their progression to remove his arm from the sling, hoping Mark didn't hear his hiss of pain as the hole in his biceps pulled.

Mark acted purposeful rather than desperate, so Rogan knew he had a plan. So did he. Of a sort. He hadn't had much time to form it, and it hinged on a few assumptions he wasn't sure were accurate. He didn't think Mark realized how much Rogan learned in his stunt training. Mark never worked in the field, so he probably didn't know any kind of fighting techniques. And hopefully, Mark wanted to keep him alive to torment Kennedy.

They stopped at the first alley, and Mark did something inside a barrel. He had to let go of Rogan so he could keep his pistol up, but his attention was off him for a few seconds. Rogan shifted his cane to his right hand and braced himself. When Mark turned away from the can he swung the cane up, hard, under Mark's gun hand. His arm went up, and Rogan thrust the bottom of the cane like a sword, hitting him in the gut. But his injury sapped his strength more than he'd expected, and Mark only stumbled back a step, his breath intact. He brought the gun around, looking furious. Rogan switched hands and backhanded the cane into Mark's wrist. This time, he lost his grip on the weapon, which went skidding across the macadam.

"Son of a bitch." Mark lunged for Rogan, dodging the cane and swinging his fist not at Rogan's face, but into his right arm.

Pain exploded through him, his vision going red. Mark kicked him in the hip and he went down.

So much for his macho fighting skills. He gasped for air, clutching at his arm and feeling wetness through his sleeve. He'd lost any advantage, and then some, so when Mark started to pull him up he changed tactics and stayed limp, using his pain and weight against him.

"Goddammit, St. James, get *up*." He struggled for a minute to pull Rogan to his feet, then dropped him. "Fine. I'll just shoot you a couple of times and let Kennedy freak out about that." He started for the gun, but the clang of a door from the main building stopped him.

"You luck out. But don't get complacent. I'm not done with you." He ran down the alley and around a corner. A moment later footsteps sounded from the other direction, slowing as they approached the alley.

Rogan struggled to get up, to warn Kennedy, but pain with each movement froze his breath so that he couldn't talk.

And then it was too late.

KENNEDY HOLSTERED HER gun to keep her hands free as she approached the first alley. Something moved to her right, but just as she focused on it an explosion of heat and light to her left flung her sideways. She slammed to a sudden stop against the wall of a building before crumpling to the ground. So much for thinking he didn't want to kill.

"Jesus Christ." Kennedy rolled to her hands and knees, squinting against the afterimage in her vision. It took her a minute to catch her breath and clear her vision. Her shoulder had taken the brunt of the impact, and pain radiated from that point. She hadn't hit her head. Her ribs were okay, and though her hip ached slightly and she'd have a hard time walking tomorrow, it wasn't debilitating now. She pushed to her feet and moved her shoulder gingerly. It circled with full range of motion, but screamed in protest the whole time.

Putting it out of her mind, she stood where she was, waiting. The explosion had occurred in a barrel at the corner of a building. The explosives in use in the compound were like those used in the movies—big noise and light effects, little damage. A few flames flickered above the rim of the barrel. Other than that, there was no movement, no sound.

Kennedy slowly pushed away from the wall, willing the fog in her ears and vision to clear. Mark had been smart, his attack well timed, leaving her disoriented and vulnerable. But he had squandered his advantage by not immediately following up with something else.

Something moved again on the ground a few feet away. She whipped out her pistol and crouched, but as the smoke dissipated and her vision cleared, she saw it wasn't Mark.

It was Rogan.

No.

Terror froze her in place, a world without Rogan looming in her future, unacceptable. Then, with a click, she switched into agent mode, her focus on their surroundings as she ran to Rogan's side. There was no other movement, no sign of another weapon.

"I'm okay," Rogan croaked as soon as she reached him. He coughed and rolled onto his back. His right arm was red with blood, and his pants had a small red stain on the hip, as well as a smear of dirt that looked a lot like a footprint.

"How bad?" she asked. "And where is he?"

"I'll be all right." She helped him sit up, and he pointed. "He went around that corner."

"Can you walk?" He nodded, wincing. "Go back to the main building. David and Gina are EMTs. They'll patch you up. I'll be back soon." She helped him stand and pointed him in the right direction, but he wouldn't start walking.

"Kennedy—"

A few months ago, she would have ordered him away and been done with it. But she'd changed. He'd helped her change.

"Rogan, I know you want to protect me. But you've got to trust me. I know what I'm doing. How to handle him. I'll be okay."

He cradled her face in one hand. "I do trust you. And I don't want to get in your way, or distract you. But letting you go, when I won't know what's happening…" His other hand tightened on her arm as he looked back.

Kennedy relaxed and reached into her back pocket. "You'll know. In fact, now everyone knows."

He grinned at the communicator. "Good. I want them to." The smile faded to intensity. "I know this is the wrong time and place, and I don't want a response. But you have to know, just in case."

A new kind of terror joined the one she'd just adjusted to. "Don't."

"I have to. Kennedy, I love you." He kissed her, hard at first, then softening into tenderness and sorrow. Then he let her go and limped toward the main building without looking back, and she knew he really did.

Dammit.

When he was halfway across the macadam and she was fairly sure Mark wasn't hiding with a sniper rifle, ready to take him out, she turned away. She had to get out of the open. She was too much a target here, standing between white buildings while wearing dark clothes. She ran past a few buildings and ducked into a doorway. She didn't need to assimilate her location. She knew this "city" better than if she had lived in it. And she'd had things built into it that none of her people knew about, not even Mark.

She dodged left, into the living room of the apartment. Mark might have expected her to come in here, because it was the closest shelter to where he'd blasted her. But he would have set a trap in the hall or kitchen, thinking she'd run out the back or up the stairs. Instead, she ducked into the empty fireplace and stood up, reaching high with her right hand to grasp a lever. When she pulled it, a piece of the outer wall opened. She wedged her left foot into a step carved into the brick and launched herself up and out, rolling forward and landing on her feet in a narrow gap between buildings that was too small to be called an alley.

She stood still, listening. Nothing behind her. Nothing to either side. But a couple of blocks over she heard the echo of feet scraping on pavement. Was he being careless or trying to lure her? Or both?

Judging the location of the footsteps and their direction, she moved on an intercept path. Just before she reached the street he was on, she stopped and began to climb the side of a wall. In the lower six feet, foot and handholds were barely discernable in the stucco façade, and it was a struggle to maintain her grip with the damaged shoulder and bruised hip. But once she got above eye level the dents became rung-like and she quickly scaled to the roof. When she peered over the edge, she saw nothing.

Generally, she liked roofs. She could see a lot without being seen, and the walls and angles offered some protection. The building she stood on now was the tallest in the compound, but not the one she usually used to observe training. It was narrow and full of surveillance equipment. If Mark had had time for advance planning, he'd probably disabled these units.

Sure enough, most of the cables had been detached and cut so they couldn't be reattached or spliced. He didn't want her tapping into any of the cameras on the site, or even the audio wiring the buildings to headquarters. If he'd had time to do this, he'd had time to set up any number of booby traps.

Kennedy crouched in one corner and pulled the communicator from her pocket again.

"Did Rogan make it back there?" There was no response. Her heart slipped up into her throat. Then Rick said, "I'll get him. Don't split focus."

Fuck. She looked toward the main building, but Rogan

wasn't outside it. "He's either inside, or the idiot is somewhere out here. If you don't find him in the building, Rick, stay there. I'm moving on." She stuck the communicator back in her pocket, knowing he wouldn't argue with her and risk Mark hearing. Though she wanted to go back and find Rogan, she had to trust that he wouldn't do anything stupid, that Rick would meet him in the hall and all would be fine.

She had to go forward.

One of her rules was to never go back on your own route. So instead of going down the outside of the building, she eased open the access door in the roof and dropped into an empty room. Though laid out in office suites, this building wasn't furnished and didn't have any secret passages or exits. Because of this, it was also the hardest to booby-trap. Again she waited. Silence.

"Where did you go?" she mouthed. The floor was carpeted and absorbed her footsteps. She checked the hallway, then, finding it empty, ran down it to the stairwell. When she eased the door open, it creaked loudly in the echoing vertical tunnel.

But there was another sound. Kennedy pulled her gun and thumbed off the safety, holding it in front of her as she started down the steps. It was a familiar sound, but odd. Out of place.

Toenail clicks began to accompany the panting, and she realized it was a dog. She tried to predict the breed as it came up the stairs. Medium size, solid, not growling or prowling, just panting and trotting along. She wanted to be down to the next floor before it got up to it, so she picked up her pace. That made her footsteps louder, and the panting stopped. She froze, doubting it made a difference. The dog knew she was there. Nothing to do but dash for it.

She ran hard, but heard the dog bounding up to the landing. He was going to beat her. She leapt from five steps up, aiming for the door's crash bar, hoping to be over the dog's head and able to shut the door behind her. But he jumped as she hit the metal bar, snarling and slobbering as he tried to get a grip on some part of her.

They tumbled through the doorway in a tangle. Kennedy struggled to push the pit bull away enough to get her foot between them. She flailed hard, determined not to let him get his mouth around her, though she felt the scrape of his teeth more than once. The taste of blood seemed to inflame him, making his movements and growls more frenzied.

"Where...the hell...did Mark...get...you?" she grunted, hitting him in the side of the head to no effect. Finally, she got her foot on his chest and heaved. His teeth tore her jacket as he flew away from her, his feet already scrabbling for purchase when he hit the ground.

Kennedy jumped to her feet and brought her gun up, pity and determination at war within her. She would not die by this dog's bloodlust, but she hated, really hated, to harm an animal.

To her amazement, the dog stopped as soon as the gun was aimed at him. He sat down, cocked his head at her and whined.

"Well, I'll be damned," she muttered, holding the pistol steady as she backed away. The dog didn't move. "Who trained you?" She doubted Mark knew about this little trick.

The dog stayed put until she reached the corner office at the other end of the hall. She shut the door and locked the handle, stupidly, she knew. But hand-to-jaw combat made you do stupid things sometimes.

The window in this corner opened to the outside, and a ledge took her to a ladder into another alley. She knew now that Mark was playing games, probably watching her somehow. If he'd wanted to finish her off he could have done it with one kick to the head while she'd wrestled the dog. And games were no fun if they couldn't be seen, so he had cameras somewhere. Perhaps, even though he'd cut cables on the roof equipment, he'd re-routed the master so he could watch all the hidden cameras she had in every building.

There was one building, however, that she had never wired. It was the one Stacy had hidden in, during that long-ago training session the day Max came to hire her. Mark knew it wasn't wired. That was why they'd ambushed her there, trying to best her. It was something all of them strove for, a personal challenge that she never discouraged. Only now did she see something more sinister in Mark's desire to get the drop on her.

He was destined for disappointment.

"You got lucky."

Kennedy froze as Mark's voice echoed around her. She had never installed a loudspeaker system. He'd had more time to play than she thought.

She didn't answer, both unsure he'd be able to hear her and unwilling to play his game to that extent. He waited while she stood, statue-still, waiting.

"Next time, I won't borrow a dog from a cop."

Kennedy stifled a laugh. He'd borrowed a cop's dog to commit murder? He was insane.

"Not really," he said.

She frowned, wondering what he was responding to.

"I know you think I've gone over the edge. But I haven't. I'm fully aware of the consequences of my actions should I fail. But I won't fail."

Delusional, too, she thought, and this time he didn't act as if he'd read her mind.

"I really wanted you to suffer like I did."

Kennedy wasn't going to stand around listening to his selfish monologue. She started walking, going deliberately in the wrong direction, away from the building he was probably in, as he talked.

"Diana was my angel. I know that sounds cliché, but she was so pure and we were so happy together."

Not the way Kennedy had heard it, but she wouldn't argue. Diana hadn't rhapsodized about their marriage, but she hadn't complained, either. Maybe she'd kept the two parts of her life completely separate.

"She went on and on about SmythShield, though."

Okay, maybe not.

"Like I was never enough for her. I was missing part of her the whole time we were married. I thought if we had a baby the balance would shift back to me. But SmythShield ruined that. It stole her from me. *You* stole her from me." His voice turned menacing. "I'll never forgive you for that, Kennedy."

She kept moving, unsure whether or not he was watching her but unwilling to lose the element of surprise. She moved away from where she thought he'd be until she reached a building that had been nearly demolished in training. She climbed through the rubble, clenching her teeth against the pain in her shoulder when she had to push some debris away from a trap door. This wasn't hidden, but she hoped Mark had forgotten about it. The underground passage led to several key intersections in the training ground, most importantly into the crawlspace below the building he was in.

She was getting tired. It was time to end the game.

Ironic, she thought a moment later, trudging through the dark passageway. She'd just begun to consider the value of a non-solitary life and here she was, playing Lara Croft, determined to win her battle alone.

For the first time, she wondered if this life was going to be right for her anymore. She'd known changes were afoot, but she thought them to be small ones. Reconnecting friendships. A relationship with Rogan. Allowing people into her heart and by her side as well as backing her up. But was her life compatible with any of those? Could she make those changes alone or would her entire existence have to change?

Put it out of your mind. The passageway ended a dozen feet away, and the most difficult part was ahead. She had to concentrate.

As she neared the crawlspace entry, she holstered her weapon. Her shoulder stopped throbbing. Her hip stopped aching. Her heartbeat slowed, and her brain went cold. This was a game no more.

She bent and crawled into the opening, pausing to pull her T-shirt over her nose and mouth and breathing shallowly so the dust her hands and knees kicked up wouldn't make her sneeze. She kept her movements fluid and silent through the small tunnel while she listened for a presence in the rooms above.

Nothing.

She could be wrong. Mark might be in another building. But she couldn't doubt herself. If she was wrong, she'd move on. Hesitating while she second-guessed herself would make her a nice target.

Her fingers bent into the corner where floor met wall an instant before her head would have bumped it. The crawlspace ended in a narrow opening between walls. Kennedy twisted onto her back and pushed herself through the opening, struggling upright and hissing as rough wallboard scraped across her abdomen.

Still there was silence on the other side.

She was inside the wall of the kitchen now, and she prayed her luck would hold and he wouldn't hear her climbing. There were no foot or handholds here. It was counterpressure up two floors, feet braced on opposite walls, hands and back pushing to hold her in place.

The smooth reinforcement had been a brainstorm when she was planning the training ground. She had wanted the ultimate escape route but had never had occasion to reveal it to SmythShield trainees.

Now she was glad she hadn't.

Several minutes later she was at the top. All she had to do was pull herself over the edge into the ceiling, find Mark and get the drop on him. Literally.

She was almost there, holding her breath, spider-crawling across the uninsulated attic beams. She heard a sound below her and paused. *Click-click. Click-click. Click-click.* Mark was down there, clicking his ballpoint pen. Waiting.

She smiled. Two more feet and then she had him.

But she'd misjudged. Her plan was to stand on a beam, then jump through the Sheetrock to the floor below, landing at least partly on Mark and disabling him. Before she could stand, though, he spoke.

"Nice try, Kennedy. I didn't know about the wall. But it doesn't matter."

Then something smashed upward through the ceiling,

throwing her off balance. She fell sideways and landed with one knee and one hand on the busted Sheetrock, which gave way. She crashed to the floor below, with nothing—definitely not Mark—breaking her fall.

The impact slammed through her, vibrating up her arms and legs, whooshing the air out of her lungs and sending blackness into her head.

TWENTY-TWO

KENNEDY WASN'T OUT long. The dust hadn't settled when awareness came back, along with pain and coughing and blurred vision. Mark stood over her with an M-16. She didn't have M-16s on the premises, so she had no idea where he'd gotten it.

Didn't matter. He had her.

She rolled onto her back and away from the debris. Coughs spasmed her entire body, and she let them come while she bought time and gauged Mark's frame of mind.

He just stood, watching her. Finally, she gave one last cough and fell back, her arms out to her sides, legs limp. She let defeat take over her posture and invade her expression when she looked back up at him.

"I don't get it, Mark," she rasped. "What did you hope to gain with all this? You wouldn't get Diana back."

He shrugged. "I tried six times to get her back and she never came. It doesn't matter anymore. All that matters is making you pay."

"Yeah, by harming those I care about. I get it. You don't have much nerve, though, do you, Mark? All you hurt was my pride." She writhed a little against the pain in her ribs and shoulder and…well, just about everywhere.

His implacable expression darkened. "That was a problem. I started working here so I could learn your vulnerabilities. You don't have any."

She laughed. "Yeah, that's me. Invincible."

Annoyed, he kicked her. Fortunately, the blow struck her good hip. She buckled even though the kick hadn't been that hard.

"I could have gone after your father, but I felt a kinship with him. He understood. Justin's death humbled him. But not you. You played with lives. Put more and more people in danger."

She looked up at the ceiling, part of her wanting to defend herself, to argue. But it wouldn't do any good. He was convinced, and nothing would change his mind. She was done with the talking.

But he was too far away for her to do much besides get shot. So she lifted one limp arm and rubbed her head. "How did you get all that help? The helicopter in California, the driver in Michigan. The cameraman. The car through the café. Where did you find them?"

"Ah." He grinned, and she knew she'd hit the start button. His arm relaxed and the tip of the gun dropped too low to fire at any part of her body. Now, if only he'd pace a little. Lose himself in his bragging and come closer.

"I've worked everywhere." He shifted his weight. "In just about every major industry. Including Hollywood and the Army. I have connections. People who owe me."

"Enough to commit crimes for you? That's impressive."

One foot shuffled, then the other. *Yes, that's it. Move. To your left. To your left.* He started talking about where and how he'd met certain people. Kennedy stopped paying attention to his words and concentrated fiercely on his position. He moved to his right. *No, no, to the left.*

His laugh caught her attention again. "Hank was a

kicker. The SEAL washout didn't mind going up against the bitch who thought he wasn't good enough. He came in handy several times."

Kennedy remembered the recruit's qualifications. "He flew my chopper?" She made her voice deliberately weak.

"Yeah, thought it was hilarious to take it out under your nose." He shrugged. "Course, he wasn't so keen on the shooting you part. I tried to get him to lift when you were descending that rope, but he held steady till you hit the ground. Haven't seen him since."

He waved his gun hand, the barrel arcing through the still-drifting dust cloud, and leaned left. Kennedy struck, scissoring her legs around his and wrenching them so that he fell backwards. The gun didn't go off, and he didn't lose his grip on it as he fell. She jumped to her feet, drawing her pistol and aiming at him with both hands, her legs straddling his waist.

"It's over, Mark," she said quietly. The M-16 rested on the ground, over his shoulder. He'd never get it pulled around before she shot him, and he knew it.

But she'd misjudged him. Or his desperation. He kicked up, striking her in the back. Not hard, but enough to shift her position and her attention. Then he slid downward between her legs, standing swiftly before she'd spun. He swung the M-16 against her left hand and her gun went flying, the shock of the impact sending electric pain from her wrist to her elbow. Then he brought the muzzle back around, aimed once again at her heart.

"Mark."

Diana's voice in the doorway was all Kennedy needed. She slammed her right fist into his jaw and he went down in a heap. She caught the M-16 in her left hand as he fell.

"I thought I told you to stay in the mission room," she said without turning around. Now her right hand hurt too. She shook it.

"We heard the crash." Diana's voice was strained. Kennedy looked back to see her standing on one leg, the prosthetic missing. Her face was white. Rogan, looking just as pale, with blood now seeping down his shirt sleeve, leaned against the doorjamb next to her.

"I locked the others in," Diana said. "Well, jammed them in, more like."

"With what?"

Her grin was small and quick. "My leg. What else? It wasn't working, anyway." She tilted her head toward Rogan. "Met him in the hall, resting. He's a wimp."

"Hey."

Kennedy swallowed against the lump in her throat. Diana had crossed the compound on one leg? And Rogan had come back for her, even with his injuries? She didn't deserve that kind of effort. "I—"

Diana waved a hand and shook her head. "Don't start. I grabbed a Jeep. I don't hop for anyone, not even you."

Rogan straightened, looking virtuous. "I would."

Kennedy stared at them, then did the only thing she could do.

She laughed.

"So, what are you going to do with him?" Diana asked her minutes later. They'd bound Mark before he came to, then Kennedy and Rogan dragged him down to the Jeep while Diana hopped behind them, complaining that she could help.

"How the hell did you get upstairs without us hearing you?" Kennedy asked, bracing to heave Mark into the back. She waved Rogan back. She was too tired and he was too hurt. Instead, she slapped Mark, twice, hard, and shoved him until he climbed into the back on his own.

"Practice," Diana said without arrogance.

Rogan drove one-handed, with Diana in the passenger seat while Kennedy kept her gun trained on Mark in the back. But he just sat unmoving, staring at the floor.

"What are you going to do with him?" Diana repeated.

"I don't know." Kennedy wasn't sure she wanted to go through the hell of prosecution, but letting him go wouldn't be very smart, either.

"Let me talk to him before you decide, okay?" Diana asked softly.

"Yeah, me too," Rogan growled.

Kennedy hesitated. She hadn't been friends with Diana for a long time, despite the rapport they'd re-established so fast today.

But that rapport was strong, and Diana gave Kennedy a quick glance. "I don't want to help him escape, you know. If I had, I would have said your name upstairs, not his."

Kennedy smiled. "Maybe you just didn't want me to really hurt him."

"Maybe."

There was enough seriousness in that one word to give Kennedy more pause.

"You can talk to him. In the cell. Locked."

"Fair enough."

They got back to the main building just as the operatives burst out the front door. Everyone had at least one weapon. Rick, leading the pack, stopped short as Rogan pulled up in front of them.

Kennedy had never seen Rick so angry. He lifted his gun and cocked it at Diana's head. She had been sliding out of the Jeep and froze, balanced on her one leg.

"Rick, it's okay." Kennedy circled the front of the vehicle and stood at his shoulder. "She came to help."

"Is that why she stripped wiring from her leg and strapped the door shut?"

"And jammed the foot through the handles?" Zip didn't take her eyes off Diana. Her gun was at the ready but aimed toward the ground.

"I didn't want any of you hurt in this," Diana said firmly. "Kennedy didn't want it. Mark did. And since I'm the reason he did, it seemed only fair for me to be the one to rescue her."

The breeze blew Diana's ponytail up behind her and tossed Kennedy's loose hair over her shoulder and into her face. A small piece of paper skipped over the ground between them, swirled up against Diana's shin, then was gone. Nothing else moved.

Then chuckles started, erupted into laughter, and the tension broke.

"Rescue Kennedy," Rick said, shaking his head. "Good one." He sobered and narrowed his eyes at Rogan. "You took this one with you, though."

Diana shrugged. "Call me a romantic."

Kennedy looked at Rogan and jumped to his side just as he lost his grip on the Jeep and started to slide. "David! Gina!" They ran around to grab Rogan's arms. "Get him to the infirmary. He might need to go back to the hospital."

"I don't." His protest was weak, but he went with

them. Kennedy strode back around and grabbed Mark by the scruff, dragging him out of the backseat and shoving him at Rick.

"Search him, and be thorough. I want to make sure there are no keys on him before I put him in the cell. The rest of you, set up a two-hour rotating watch. I'll be in my office."

She walked away, concentrating on a normal gait so they wouldn't know how beat up she was. After shutting herself in the office before anyone could catch up to her, she poured water into a glass from the thermal pitcher on a side table, took two ibuprofen, then just sat in her chair for a long time, eyes closed, mind blank, willing her minor injuries to heal quickly.

The phone rang. No one answered it outside, so on the sixth ring she lurched forward and snatched it up.

"What?"

"Well, Kennedy, that's quite rude," her father said mildly. "As SmythShield's reputation for service and cordiality are important to you, I can only surmise that you are in quite a state."

She supported her head on one hand. "You could say that."

"You found Diana?"

"Yeah."

"And was she responsible?"

"In a way." She drew in a long breath and explained, succinctly, what had happened.

"Mark? Incredible." She was glad he didn't say either "I can't believe it" or, worse, "I knew it."

"And how is Rogan?" he asked, and she closed her eyes. *Shit*.

"Bad. He's in the infirmary. I don't know how he's doing."

"Well, I'm sure he'll be okay."

She wished she could be as sure. She wanted desperately to be with him, but that same desperation kept her away too.

"I gotta go, Dad. I'll come up for a real visit when this is all over."

"All right, dear. Say hi to Rogan for me, then say yes."

She snorted at him but didn't argue, and was rewarded by his delighted laughter as she hung up the phone.

She held it on the hook for a minute, trying to decide what to do first. It didn't take long to prioritize.

Ready for action again, she unlocked her office door and went out into the deserted reception area. Mark's desk was clean except for a single sheet of paper. She stopped to glance at it. The list had two names next to every two-hour guard shift, along with phone numbers for each person. Stacy must have made it up and left a copy for her.

She looked at her watch, then at the corresponding line. Rick and Wolf were on duty. Judging by the quiet in the building, probably everyone else had gone home to rest until their shifts.

She was surprised, then, to find Jefferson repairing the conference room door Rick and the others had all but ripped down. A mangled prosthetic leg lay on the floor nearby.

Wolf was seated down the hall at the top of the stairs, a rifle across his lap and an old Game Boy in his hands.

Kennedy waited until he pressed Pause and looked up. "Do I owe you an apology?" she asked.

He frowned at her for a moment. "You still don't trust me. You think I helped Mark?"

Mark hadn't named Wolf or any other SmythShield employee when he was bragging about his connections, and Stacy wouldn't have put him on duty if there'd been any chance he was dirty.

"Did you?" she pressed, just to test his reaction. When he gave her a simple "no," she nodded, satisfied.

"Where's Rick?" she asked him.

"Downstairs, in front of the cell."

She went silently down the steps, by now every muscle in her body protesting. Rick stood leaning against the wall, arms folded, looking through the small barred window in the door.

"Hey," he said when he saw Kennedy. "I thought you'd be with Rogan." He kept his voice low.

"Can't yet." She couldn't ask the obvious question. As long as she didn't ask, the answer would be, "He's fine."

She peered through the window. Mark sat slumped on the suspended stone slab bench, to the left of the door. Kennedy had had the cell built so they could safely experience what it would be like to be captured. No one ever had been, but incarceration in another country was always a possibility.

"Mark," she said. He didn't move.

"He catatonic?" she asked Rick, who shrugged.

"I'm no shrink."

"Me neither." She thought about that for a minute, then held out her hand. "Give me the keys. Go up and tell Jefferson I want to meet in a few minutes, and get Stacy on the speakerphone in the mission room, please."

Rick frowned but didn't protest. "Wolf is coming down," he said, but she shook her head.

"Tell him to listen and keep alert but stay upstairs unless I need him." Rick nodded and went upstairs. She could hear the low murmur of his voice, then Wolf's louder questions.

"How will I know if she needs me?" he asked his superior, and Kennedy mouthed the words as Rick said them.

"You'll know."

Then his footsteps receded down the hall. The beeps of Wolf's game didn't resume, and Kennedy turned, satisfied.

She fit the three keys in succession into the locks and opened the door without taking her eyes off Mark. He still didn't move, but she saw his eyes flick around the room.

"All right, Mark, here's the deal." She shut the door behind her. One lock automatically engaged, the only one she had access to from inside the cell. She waited.

"I'm not interested in deals," he said sullenly.

"I think you'll be interested in this one." Taking a chance, she crossed the room and sat next to him. "I won't report your actions to the police, if you agree to be checked into a secure mental health hospital and give me your medical power of attorney."

He exploded off the bench. "Are you crazy? Put my life in your hands? I can't trust you!"

"Kind of ironic, isn't it." Leaning back against the scratchy wall, she folded her arms, the keys hidden in her right hand, sharp ends between her fingers. Just in case.

"Mark, think. You could go to jail for attempted murder, multiple counts. The gunshots Rogan took will certainly put you away for a long, long time."

"Yeah," he scoffed, "you've got a lot of proof."

"I have your confession," she reminded him. "Once someone sets foot on the urban training ground, recording starts. You know that. I can prove you knew that before you went in there, so you can't claim coercion. You couldn't disable the entire system. And I have Diana's testimony, not to mention all the people in the mission room who heard the whole thing over this." She held up the communicator, which was on. "Still recording, by the way."

"I cut the surveillance," he said weakly.

"You think I leave my most important communications tools that vulnerable?" She shook her head. "I thought you knew me so well."

He stood, fists clenched, and she let him think about it. "Where are you sending me?"

She held back her relief and named the facility she had in mind. It was a private hospital with a wing for involuntary treatment, maximum security. It wasn't as secure as jail, but she couldn't bring herself to go that route unless she had no choice.

He hung his head and murmured something she didn't hear.

"What did you say?"

"I said all right." His head came up. "Where's the paperwork?"

"I'll bring it down to you tomorrow. It will take a little while to make the arrangements, so you'll be in here a few days." She hoped. The holding cell wasn't real, wasn't meant to hold a true criminal. But she didn't let him see her doubts or lack of trust in her eyes. She stood. "Do you want us to bring you anything from your place?"

"No," he said quietly. "I don't need anything."

Kennedy went to the door and paused, watching him. "For what it's worth, Mark, I'm very sorry this happened. You were a good assistant and a friend."

His defeated expression became distorted by a sneer. "Friend? I wasn't your friend. You never had friends."

She left without responding. What was there to say? He was right.

TWENTY-THREE

SINCE SHE HAD already decided to rectify that, Kennedy started with Diana. She found her on the couch in her office. She looked up when Kennedy entered.

"This sucks," she complained.

"I know. We'll have the new leg in a few days."

"No, not that. I mean, that sucks, but it's not that I don't have a leg to walk on." She shoved herself up. "It sucks that it takes so much out of me to be without it. I need to alter my training regimen. I rely on the prosthetic too much."

Kennedy nodded, understanding. She sat in her desk chair. "You can stay with me at the house until your leg comes."

"Thanks." Diana studied her, her eyes sad. "What are you doing with Mark?" Kennedy explained. Diana shrugged. "It's better than he deserves, but I appreciate it nonetheless." She eyed her shrewdly. "How do you feel about it? This was a big betrayal."

"It is." She considered. "But I felt much worse knowing it was one of my own without knowing *who* than I do knowing it was Mark."

"Because he was newer? Not an agent?"

Would it have been more painful if it was Jefferson, or Stacy? Less painful if it was Wolf? She remembered the iciness that came over her when she realized it was

Mark, and the anger and determination when she went after him on the compound.

"No, because he wasn't the Mark I knew anymore," she realized. "Because the moment I knew he was an enemy, he ceased to be a friend. I didn't know him, so the pain dulled immediately." She'd always feel it, though—for having let him get close, for the fear and pain he'd caused her staff and her client, and most of all, for what he'd done to Rogan.

"I have to admit to being grateful for one thing. He woke me up to what a miserable excuse for living my life has become." She hesitated, not sure how Diana would react to her proposal. "I need to make some changes. I don't want to work like this anymore."

Diana glanced at her. "You mean, saving the world all by your lonesome?"

Kennedy rolled her eyes. "I have a team of sixteen, Diana. Hardly by my lonesome."

"I know what you're getting at, though." She reached for a bottle of water on the table next to her. "You're living the job. You don't want to do that anymore."

"Basically." Kennedy took a deep breath. "I want to change the structure of SmythShield. I want to run it from home—which is almost a necessity now that my assistant is unreliable," she added tongue-in-cheek. "My operatives are good enough to run the on-site themselves. I'll supervise them from here. But I want more than that."

"You want a partner."

Kennedy raised her eyebrows. "Am I that obvious?"

Diana dropped the bottle into her lap. "No, but you're beating around the bush so much I had plenty of time to figure it out. What do you want me to do?"

"Merge our companies. You can run the security division and I'll run the protection division. Both can expand with the contacts we each have. We'll cover more and achieve more." She let the business tone drop from her voice. "I didn't realize how much I missed you until you came back."

"Until you dragged me back."

"Yeah, that too. More than I want a partner, I want a friend. I don't know if—"

"Oh, please. Let's not get mushy here. We were good friends, best friends, and that doesn't disappear just because it goes on hiatus for a few years." She pushed herself to her foot and swayed a second. "You got me."

"Thanks." She stood to help Diana, who stopped her.

"I questioned your choice, at first."

Kennedy frowned. "What choice?"

"Rogan St. James. For someone who keeps behind the scenes at all times, you certainly picked a boyfriend in the limelight."

"I didn't pick him, he picked me. I didn't have room for him, but he insisted on making some."

"And?"

"And what?"

Diana blew out a breath. "I'm so glad you're finally opening up, Ned."

She couldn't help laughing. "And it wasn't so hard to make room. For him." She shifted, and they started toward the door. "He comes from someplace totally different than I do. He's the opposite of intense. He works incredibly hard, but loves it so much it seems like he's lazing around." She stopped herself before she started to gush.

"I'm happy for you." Bracing herself on the wall,

Diana stopped next to Jefferson. "Hey, babe. Wanna give me a ride up to the house? I think Kennedy has someplace more important to be."

Kennedy gave her new partner a key and went to the infirmary, where Gina sat outside writing notes in a chart. "How is he?"

Gina looked grave. "He's lost more blood and on top of what he lost before, he could probably use a transfusion. He popped several stitches. But he wouldn't let us take him to the hospital, so we fixed him up, hooked up an IV for hydration, and tucked him into bed, which he barely allowed." She heaved a deep sigh. "I'm glad you finally showed up. He was driving me nuts asking for you."

Kennedy thanked her and went inside. Rogan slept in the hospital bed on the far side of the room. She walked over, taking a hard chair from the foot of his bed and setting it noiselessly at his bedside. She sat, her eyes still on him.

He didn't move. Shadows under his lashes and deeper hollows in his cheeks hinted at his pain.

"Rogan," she whispered. He still didn't move. She slid her hand under his, sighing at the warmth and finally, finally, letting the worry ease away.

She leaned one elbow on the bed and stroked the hair away from his forehead. "I'm sorry this was such a battle, Rogan. I've fought so hard for so long not to feel, it was difficult to change."

But she had. Justin, and losses after him, were no longer her driving force. She'd found something more positive to drive her. Diana, who could laugh and be as tough as ever, despite her leg and arm. Her team, who'd always been loyal but had shown her in the past few weeks just what that loyalty meant.

"I have a lot to appreciate," she said. "A lot I didn't appreciate before. I took it for granted. And there's more."

She traced a finger across his eyelid, which twitched but didn't open. His lips were dry, but she leaned to kiss them anyway, backing up only inches afterward. "I haven't told anyone I loved them since Justin died. Not even my father. But I'm going to say it now, Rogan." She swallowed, though it wasn't hard to get the words out. In fact, it was harder to try to hold them in.

"I love you, Sunshine."

Kennedy reared back. Rogan's eyelids had flown open and he'd said the words she had been about to say. He looked at her with such clear eyes she knew he'd been awake nearly the entire time she was talking.

"It was my turn," she complained, letting him twist her hand so their fingers entwined. He tugged, pulling her down to his level.

"Say it now," he whispered, shifting so he was close enough to kiss. "Please."

"I love you, Rogan St. James." The words ignited a spark in his eyes, something she'd never seen before but that she knew was broadcast in her own. It was something she hadn't felt in a very, very long time. Happiness.

A smile broke across his face, and he lifted his left arm, IV and all, to cup the back of her head. The kiss was tender but passionate, giving Kennedy a glimpse of the future.

"There's a lot to talk about," she said when they broke for air.

"Yeah, but not tonight. Tonight, we revel in it. Tomorrow, we face M.J. and his fury that I messed up his post-production schedule."

She laughed and kissed him again.

"Come in here with me," he demanded, breathing hard.

"Rogan, we can't—"

"I know we can't." He patted the left side of the bed. "Just come over here on my good side and lie with me."

Kennedy circled the bed and carefully laid down next to him, her head on his shoulder. Her left knee slid of its own accord onto his thigh, and her hand rested in the center of his chest.

"Ah," he sighed, closing his eyes. "Right where you belong."

Her mouth opened to protest automatically, and she closed it, amused at herself. She belonged a lot of places. Between her clients and harm's way. In partnership with Diana. At her father's house, his daughter. As a friend, many places.

And now, yes, in Rogan's arms, holding him in hers, she was where she belonged.

ABOUT THE AUTHOR

NATALIE J. DAMSCHRODER became a writer the hard way—
by avoiding it. Though she wrote her first book at age six
(My Very Own Reading Book) and received accolades for
her academic writing, she hated doing it. Colonial food
and the habits of the European Starling just weren't her
thing. Shortly after graduating from college, however,
she found her niche—romantic fiction. So instead of
using her Ohio Wesleyan University degree in geogra-
phy and environmental studies, she became a novelist.
She has had seven novels and nearly two dozen short
stories and novellas published in ebook and print since
2000, to almost universally positive reviews. The first
book in her Brook Hollow trilogy, *Kira's Best Friend,*
placed second in the 2006 More Than Magic contest.

When not writing, Natalie works as a therapy chiro-
practic assistant and freelance editor, as well as mother
of two awesome daughters (the oldest has been dubbed
"the anti-teenager") and wife of the most patient husband
in the world. Her three cats remind her when it's time
to stop working and feed them—otherwise, she might
never leave the computer (until Supernatural comes on
TV). You can find her online at www.nataliedamschro-
der.com , www.gabwagon.com, or http://supernatural-
sisters.blogspot.com.

* * * * *